Helen in Exile

Also by Ian McLachlan:
The Seventh Hexagram

HELEN IN EXILE

A Novel by IAN McLACHLAN

The Dial Press New York

The very end of myths
is to immobilize the world.
—Roland Barthes, *Mythologies*.

Published by
The Dial Press
1 Dag Hammarskjold Plaza
New York, New York 10017

Manufactured in the United States of America

First printing

Design by Francesca Belanger

Library of Congress Cataloging in Publication Data

McLachlan, Ian, 1938–
Helen in exile.

I. Title.
PZ4.M1604He 1980 [PR6063.A2472] 823'.914
ISBN 0-8037-3561-8 80-15837

For Dominique

Paris was on his way home from Sparta with his stolen bride, when, somewhere in the Aegean Sea, he met foul weather which drove his ship all the way to Egypt. There, some of his servants, wishing to get him into trouble, told against him the whole story of his abduction of Helen and his wicked treatment of Menelaus. On hearing of this the Egyptian king Proteus passed the following judgement: I cannot punish a stranger with death but I will not allow you to take away your ill-gotten gains. I will keep this woman and the treasure, until the Greek to whom they belong chooses to come and fetch them. As for you and the companions of your voyage, I give you three days in which to leave my country—and to find an anchorage elsewhere. If you are not gone by then, I shall treat you as enemies.

Meanwhile, the Greeks had sent a strong force to Troy in support of Menelaus's cause. Their ambassadors were received within the walls of the city and demanded the restoration of Helen together with the treasure which Paris had stolen. The Trojans, however, gave them the answer which they always stuck to afterwards—sometimes even swearing to the truth of it: namely, that neither Helen nor the treasure was in their possession, but both were in Egypt. The Greeks, supposing this to be a merely frivolous answer, laid siege to the city and persisted until it fell; but no Helen was found, and they were still told the same story, until at last they believed it and sent Menelaus to visit Proteus in Egypt. He sailed up the river to Memphis, and when he had given a true account of what had happened, he was most hospitably entertained and Helen, none the worse for her adventures, was restored to him with all the rest of his property.

—Herodotus, *The Histories*

Part I

SEPTEMBER

Chapter One

Helen

Her first memory was of betrayal.

Not of having been betrayed. All children remember that, the sudden removal of love.

Helen's first memory was of betraying.

Try to survive that.

Actually, to be more exact, my first memory is of a monkey's bum.

We lived at that time, in 1944, in Saint Jeannet, a small village pressed into the side of the cliffs that rise up steeply ten miles inland from Cannes. If I had looked to the south I would have seen the Mediterranean shimmering far away in the evening light. But I don't remember ever noticing the sea.

The cliff—the Baou, it is called—juts out into my memory, and still its shape appears by accident in my paintings, flat-topped, though I cannot see the top, it rises up so high above my head. The Baou is not like a monkey's bum; it is a barren prow thrusting out into the fertile coastland. I am not allowed to try to climb the Baou, even its gentle lower slopes; it is dangerous, and men have died on it. But there is a large round rock just behind my mother's house, maybe forty feet high, that at some point long ago became detached from the cliff face and rolled all the way down here. In my dreams sometimes it starts to roll again. But during the daytime, if I am careful, I can play on it. It is soft, worn smooth, but in the centre a deep cleft has opened up, and I am allowed to pretend I'm a climber, my back braced on one side, my feet shuffling on the other. When I get stuck I have to be helped down and listen to people telling me that little girls should not be climbing rocks. But it is my rock, and in the evening sun its surface, which normally is ochre tending to orange, has become a bright pink—no, deeper, almost rose-coloured, with streaks, even, of purple. A monkey's bum.

I lived in Saint Jeannet for nearly a month two years ago and never once saw the rock approach anything like that colour again. But there it is in my memory, my first memory. I don't remember where I first saw a monkey—a zoo in Marseilles or Nice or perhaps on a visit to my grandparents (on my father's side) in Paris—I don't remember the actual animal, but I remember dancing when I saw it again in the rock. Standing in the open space in front of the house I dance for joy at the likeness. I think I am calling out—to no one; there is no one nearby—*"Regarde mon rocher, c'est comme les fesses d'un singe."*

I see myself in old snapshots, a little girl, plump and stocky in embroidered dresses and heavy leather boots. My arms are raised and I am smiling at whoever holds the camera. I am wearing a cardigan that my mother has knitted from wool unravelled out of her old sweaters.

I am alone. I see the rock, I hear the car.

Cars never come here, except occasionally at night when I am supposed to be asleep. We live beyond the village in an old farmhouse surrounded with orange and olive groves. You have to know where you're going to come here; cars must wind their way through the maze of alleys in the old walled village and then plunge down the steep curving hill that ends at our gate. And besides, nobody has any gas because of the rationing.

The car is a dirty black Citroen, not an army truck, but the man who gets out of it is wearing a uniform. I don't remember ever having seen my father, I dream that he might be dead, but at the same time, whenever I see a man in uniform I think he is my father. So I run forward; but the uniform is black and his black boots are covered in dust. He is very big.

I have seen this man a thousand times since then in third-rate war movies, so I don't know what he really looks like. Just that he is very big. But I remember what he says exactly.

He walks over to the edge of the *terrasse* and looks down into the valley.

I stand beside him, looking up.

He says something I don't understand, the accent guttural.

I beg his pardon.

He says it again more slowly: *"Que c'est beau."*

I look out over the tops of the olive and orange trees that fall away in terraces. The olives are twisted and ancient, a dark greyish boring green. Against them, the orange trees are in delicate blossom. The oranges themselves will be bitter and useless, except for preserves, but it's for the blossom that they are grown, for the perfume factories in Grasse. Nobody bothers to pick the flowers anymore. The factories have closed down because of the war.

And yes, it is beautiful. *"Oui, monsieur,"* I say obediently.

His fingers play with my black curls. "Where is your mother?" he asks.

"Mummy's in the cave." I point towards the path that disappears in the trees.

"Qu'est-ce qu'elle fait?" The *"elle"* is pronounced "ull."

"She's playing with the radio."

He turns and calls two men from the car. One of them is in uniform, the other not, they both carry guns. They run along the path, the guns rattling. I am afraid but I don't do anything. I hear two shots. I look at the rock but it has faded to a dull brown. Then they return, pushing my mother and the Canadian, whose shoulder is bleeding, in front of them. My mother's face is set and she doesn't seem to see me. The men kick her two or three times as they try to force her into the back of the car. As the door slams shut, I run over and look at her. She isn't crying, she never cries.

It is the expression of hatred for me on my mother's face that makes this my first memory.

Just before dawn Helen wakened with something glued to her thigh. She had been asleep for less than two hours and she didn't know where she was. She could feel the roughness of the old sofa against her ass and the heaviness of the man's body curled against her. It was many years since she had wakened with anyone's body in her arms. Still, she didn't know who it was. She shivered. There had been an old sleeping bag on top of them, but the man had pulled it around him, leaving her back uncovered. To be fair, she had been too hot, slippery with sweat, when she went to sleep. She looked down at her body, one breast squeezed under his head, his soft cock like a slug sticking on her thigh. She tried to pull away, a spring pressing into her back. He stretched with her, then peeled off like a piece of sunburnt skin.

Jean-Claude's head still weighed on her. She stroked his long brown hair; it was soft and clean, but she hadn't realized how bald he was going. She smiled. Jean-Claude would hate the thought of going bald, would hate even more the thought of somebody lying here like this, curling his fine hair with her fingers and thinking tenderly of his going bald.

She tried to roll over onto her back and couldn't. How uncomfortable it was, wedged in here against somebody you didn't even know. She examined the moulded plaster patterns on the ceiling; that took all of thirty seconds. Then she looked at Claire's paintings on the walls. Claire, whose apartment this seemed to be, whose absurd sofa was bent on crippling her, had only just begun to paint. Already, she talked of having discovered her true medium and asked about arrangements for grants and shows. They were very passionate paintings, filling the semi-darkness with hurricanes. Helen smiled again; she didn't like them at all.

She stroked Jean-Claude's chin, feeling the stubble with her fingertips, so rough for someone who seemed—at first, anyway, from a distance—so gentle. Last night, she remembered, she had realized how he lied about his age. Putting the dates together as they talked about their childhoods, she knew he must be nearly as old as she was, nearly thirty, though he would deny it angrily. Poor Jean-Claude, he would insist on being twenty-five forever.

She was surprised at how full of energy she felt, how superior to whatever might have happened, how full of tolerance and forgiveness. Of these others and of herself. Still, she wasn't going to think about that yet. She propped herself up on her elbow and squinted at the digital clock on the other side of the room; as she looked it flicked from 5.47 to 5.48. God, Jean-Claude was capable of sleeping till eight, at least. She couldn't stay here with this stupid spring in her kidneys for an eternity of one hundred and thirty-two quite separate minutes. She thought of how simple it would be to kill Jean-Claude; how easy to escape. Very tentatively, so as not to waken him, she stretched her right leg up and braced her calf on the back of the sofa, then her right hand. As she lifted her weight, she almost slipped back on top of him. What a way to die, Jean-Claude, squashed by a lady, an older lady at that, almost middle-aged, falling on you from a great height! The second time she made it, swung herself over, knocked a rubber plant on its side and ended up on all fours, naked in front of the window, the sun beginning to rise through the trees on the square.

Lightly, she rose and walked to the kitchen, put some water on to boil and looked around her. She ought still to be drunk, but instead she felt quite sober—no, better than sober. Automatically, she began to tidy up the mess of the party, half-eaten sandwiches, a large piece of Brie with a cigarette stubbed out in the middle of it, cups and glasses full of sour liquids. Claire's life was always in such disarray, so that what pleased Helen was how ordered and comforting the kitchen was. Even now, beneath all the garbage, stood neat rows of jars full of herbs and spices, flour and beans. She found a teapot and made herself some Earl Grey, not too strong because there was no milk left in the fridge, and went back to the living room.

Jean-Claude was sprawled across the whole of the sofa, so she sat on the floor with her back against it, her head resting on his ass. She balanced the mug on her pubic hair and felt its warmth in her thighs. So now, Helen, what has happened to you?

No, she didn't want to think about it yet.

In the corner near the fireplace somebody's foot had knocked over three glasses; one of them was broken. That was when Liz had said, "Why don't you men kiss each other the way women do? Are you scared of being called faggots? Look at Thérèse and me." The two of them had rolled over on top of each other.

Then Jean-Claude had had to prove he could do it, too.

They had made him kiss Akiyo, though neither of them liked the other or wanted to, with all the women sitting round applauding, lighting up a joint as a reward for the two men.

Later, much later, and so vaguely she could hardly be sure it had really happened, she had built a gigantic fire in the grate and sat in front of it with Jean-Claude talking about what it had been like to grow up at opposite ends of Montréal.

Only then did she let herself think about David, the man she had been married to for nearly thirteen years. She had known him when she was still just a child. Tonight, this almost past night, was the first time she had allowed herself to make love to somebody else. She rubbed her wrists. She mustn't say that to anyone, because they would only laugh, Liz most of all. But what did she feel about it? To her surprise, nothing. Nothing, that is, except contentment, the sense of having done what needed to be done, of having pleased herself. No guilt. A little self-mockery, but no guilt. She had been brought up with the presence of guilt in every shadowy corner of her life; it was the strength of the faith they had tried to fit round her head like a steel cap. And now she was astonished to find it had no power over her at all; she had pleased herself, and was delighted to have done so.

But how did that affect David?

She poured another cup of tea.

"Can I have some too?" Jean-Claude whispered.

She had forgotten him completely.

He smiled at her sleepily. "What time is it?"

"Nearly seven." She gave him the mug.

"Oh, God!" He reached out and put his hand on the back of her neck. Her body was taut, twisted towards him.

She looked for the selfishness she had remembered when she lay awake beside him, but could find no trace of it. He stroked her ears.

"What do you have to do today?" she asked as she crawled into the space he made for her again on the inside of the sofa.

"Teach," he groaned.

"What?"

"Do you really want to know?"

She didn't. But she nodded.

"Herodotus."

"My grandmother is Greek."

"Where from?"

"Smyrna. My mother was born there before the Turks burnt it down."

"And you?" he asked.

"What?"

"Do you always say 'what'? What do you have to do?"

She kissed him softly. She could feel him getting hard against her and then his fingers between her thighs. She was moist, but she put her hand on his. "No, Jean-Claude, just be still."

For a moment, he pulled away from her, offended, but then he was kissing her again. His teeth rubbed against her earlobe, nibbling her earring, and she remembered again what she had felt last night, a feeling that came not from him or what he did to her, but from herself. Her body invented his lips.

Noises came from the kitchen, voices, the sound of somebody running water into a glass, gargling, spitting loudly in the sink. She couldn't make out what they were saying, didn't know who they were until she saw Claire and Akiyo in the corridor. They had opened the front door and stood kissing in the bright sunlight, Claire naked and Akiyo dressed. As she watched them, Helen remembered them standing there like that a few hours ago, Akiyo still with his clothes on, Claire naked, lurid in the glow of the flames, watching her as she sat astride Jean-Claude. They had stayed there for a long time and she hadn't minded at all, though after she came she looked round and saw they were gone. And now they stood kissing in full view of the street, Claire bending down to Akiyo's mouth, enfolding him, her hair shining in the sun.

Akiyo pulled away and Claire held on to his hand for a

moment, then leaned against the door as he ran down the steep steps. She came back into the living room and slumped down in the armchair.

Jean-Claude turned his head and looked questioningly at her.

Her legs were stretched out; thick blonde curls. "He's really quite nice," she said.

"Who?" Jean-Claude asked.

"Akiyo." Claire flicked her head. "He seems like a bit of an asshole when you first meet him, but he's really quite gentle. Even if he can't get it up."

Helen stroked Jean-Claude's back.

"And then his body's really nice to look at when he's asleep. Very smooth and brown in all the nooks and crannies. I had this awful dream and I said, 'Wake up, Akiyo, I'm having this awful dream,' and he didn't mind at all."

"What was it about?" Jean-Claude asked.

"Tunnels." She laughed a deep gurgling laugh and they laughed with her.

"Why tunnels?" Helen asked.

"I don't know. I guess it's all the men I'm fucking."

Helen and Jean-Claude went on kissing.

After a while, Claire said: "Helen, I've just thought of something very profound. If you don't fuck you don't have to feel sorry when you say good-bye. Remind me of that, will you, Helen? I'm never going to fuck again."

They laughed kindly, mockingly.

"But it's true," she protested, laughing too. "Look, even when you're fucking someone you know is a mistake, and you wish they would go away, just disappear, even when you're fucking them, well, when they do go away, there's still that little" —she shrugged and made a hiccupping sound—"just that moment when you know you're on your own again. Maybe it's best to only go to bed with impotent men. Yes, Helen, I strongly advise it."

She got up and did her catwalk strut over to the sofa. She stood by Helen's feet, tickling them. "You two aren't going to fuck, are you?" she asked.

Helen shook her head without looking at Jean-Claude.

"Don't mind me then," said Claire and clambered in on top of them. She pulled most of the sleeping bag over herself. "That's better." She leaned her head on a cushion. "Waken me if I seem to be dreaming of tunnels."

Jean-Claude went on kissing Helen's neck absentmindedly; a lot of Claire's body was between them.

"I ought to go," he said, not moving.

"Why?" Claire asked.

"I've got a lecture to finish writing."

"What's it about?"

"Jesus, who cares! Herodotus."

"Fucking Greeks!" said Claire. "D'you know Giorgio?"

"My grandmother's Greek," said Helen.

"He's not Greek, he's Italian," said Jean-Claude.

"Well, he's a fucking Fascist, anyway. He spent all one night explaining to me that he didn't have time to fuck me. I mean, look, I know I'm indiscriminate, but I'm not that fucking indiscriminate. I'd sooner fuck a fly."

Helen spluttered with laughter.

"What's the matter? It wasn't very amusing, you know."

Helen stroked Claire's unshaven legs. "I love you, Claire," she said lightly.

They lay like that for a while, dozing, moving softly against each other. Then Claire heaved herself round—an earthquake. "Helen," she said urgently.

"What?"

"I really want to see your paintings."

"I don't know what you'll think of them—the new ones I'm doing. The last two shows, I was sure what I thought about them. They were safe and good and I didn't like them. I like these; it scares me how much I like them."

"I know, you told me last night. That's why I want to see them." Claire paused. "What do you think of mine?"

Helen drew away. "Well, they're full of . . . energy."

"Last night you said they were shit," Claire laughed. "Akiyo said exactly the same thing." She stretched down to find Helen's hand.

"I've never done this before," said Helen.

"What?"

"This."

"Well!" Jean-Claude looked at her in disbelief.

Claire's grip tightened.

"In that case," Jean-Claude said patronizingly, "you should do it more often." He kissed her on the forehead. "I ought to go," he said, still not moving.

"Good-bye, Jean-Claude," said Claire and turned her back on him.

"Do you want me to make some breakfast?" Helen asked.

He shook his head and stood up limply. They watched him hunting for his clothes, vulnerable now, his sex dangling, an afterthought.

"André has a bomb," Claire said yawning.

"A bomb?" Helen repeated.

"André is crazy," said Jean-Claude, his voice muffled by the sweater over his head.

"Not really a bomb," said Claire. "Not yet. Half a dozen sticks of dynamite. He's carrying them around in a bag." She laughed. "An Eaton's shopping bag. He asked if he could leave it here because the police are watching him. I said they were probably watching me, too."

"What's he going to do with it?" Helen asked.

"He hasn't made up his mind. He says there's no point in blowing up mailboxes anymore. Maybe a church." She put her finger on her chin in mock seriousness. "But then should it be a Protestant one or Catholic? Which has done the greater harm? I said a synagogue because he's Jewish."

"Brother André's heart," Helen whispered slowly, childhood horrors coming back to her.

They looked at each other, wide-eyed at the thought. Claire began to laugh uncontrollably.

"Claire," said Jean-Claude. They turned to him. He sat in the armchair zipping up his boots. He looked at Claire blearily. "The Greeks are not Fascists. They never have been."

"Giorgio is," she said and stuck her tongue out.

For a moment, he looked as though he would hit her. "You are such a goddamn bore," he said and got up.

Helen followed him to the door and stood with her arms around him as Claire had done with Akiyo. He was taller than she was and she reached up to him on her toes. His body was hard inside all the clothes, the leather coat. "Jean-Claude," she murmured, "don't go away. I don't mean now. I mean, don't disappear."

He held her tightly.

"Hey, you. Jean-Claude!" Claire called from the room.

"What?"

"Plato was a Fascist, too."

They ignored her.

"I think I like you," Helen said. She wasn't sure that she did, but she felt the rightness of saying it.

"Thank you," he said. He went to the top of the steps. The sunlight hurt his eyes.

Down below an old man limped by with a spaniel on a leash. He stopped by the railings but didn't look up and see her.

Jean-Claude hesitated, then came back and held her hand and kissed her again. Finally, he went carefully down the steps, saying *"Bonjour"* to the old man. She stood and watched him cross the Carré St. Louis and vanish on the Rue St. Denis.

Shivering, she closed the door and wandered back into the middle of the room. Suddenly, she felt drained. She should have driven Mark to school, David would have done it, what would he be thinking? She didn't know where she was, where her clothes were, what she was going to do. Her stomach was empty.

Claire came to her and, as their breasts touched, Helen thought, I mustn't keep on thinking I've never done this before. She sighed with the warmth. Then she realized there was something she had to try to say. "Claire," she said, beginning to cry, "your paintings . . ."

"Shh," said Claire, holding her. "They're shit. That's all there is to it."

Long before this I should have brought David into the story.

It's unfair to have waited so long, allowing him to become a shadowy stereotype, the deceived husband, the poor figure of fun in the background. For eighteen years, since I was still a child, he has been the most important presence in my life. David who listened to my dreams, who paid for my paints and my food, who was there when our children were born, who suffered my anger without understanding it. Oh, David, you are worth ten of Jean-Claude.

So why do I now deceive you?

I don't know. I don't know the answer to that question. It's something I will have to work out.

You were always much older than I was, David, always in control. (How will you control this? I wonder maliciously.) Only five years in fact—thirty-five now—but you've always been old, haven't you, always seemed so much older than the people round you?

When I was twelve I would stand for hours at my bedroom window, squinting up the street, trying to catch glimpses of you.

I stayed there for so long, my face against the glass and the frame. It's a wonder there isn't a permanent groove in the right-hand side of my head. I guess that would have been only during vacations because you were away at school in the States, but to me it seemed to go on all year, for many years. Mostly, all I saw was you getting in and out of cars, you standing leaning on cars talking to your friends, big cars with deep rear seats into which I tried to peer to see if there were girls sprawled inside. I should have thanked your parents for giving you an M.G. for your birthday, they made things so much easier for me. Now I could see the girls who were with you, laughing, blonde hair—were they always blonde?—blowing in the wind. I knew everything about those girls, sisters of your friends. I investigated their backgrounds, their potential, more thoroughly than any jealous mother. I didn't envy them, I became them, living out all that you did, all you didn't do together.

Even at that time, as I think back on it, there was a restraint in the way you behaved, opening doors, shaking hands, laughing, listening, as though you must always be sure to do the correct thing. I put it down to perfection.

I never tried to get close to you. I was too young and it would only be pathetic to be caught drooling. In all those years, from twelve to sixteen, I never allowed myself to walk past the gate of your house more than twice in any one day. I would have climbed trees and fences or hidden under thorn bushes to avoid letting it be seen that I was interested in you. Our parents were coldly disdainful of each other and I hardly knew your sister Rosemary, though her birthday is just a week away from mine, because I was the only girl on the street who went to a convent school. Even then it would have been easy to get myself invited over to your pool, if that was what I had wanted. Your father would have loved nothing more than to show off in front of someone from my stepfather's family. Just think of it; I could have lain there in the sun with the other neighbourhood girls, adjusting our swimsuits every five minutes, watching you males throw each other into the water and waiting in jellylike expectation to be thrown in ourselves. But I never went. After all, I reassured myself, you were too young to marry!

Instead, I read a lot, curled up in corners. I painted a whole series of watercolours on the theme of Schéhérazade. Locked in my room, lying on silk scarves and an old Kirman rug, I made secret drawings of my naked reflection, discovering a splendid resemblance to the bovine young creature in the lower-right corner of Le Bain Turc. I hid them in the back of a drawer where my mother no doubt found them. (Perhaps she still has them—she never wastes other people's secrets—though if I ask her she'll be astounded, then sarcastic: "*Regarde, chérie,* you think I had time to bother about things like that?") I had long, argumentative phone conversations with my few friends, the only girls in the convent who were English-speaking. I insisted on being called Helen—not Hélène—and talked French only as a matter of obligation to my mother. I tried to do all that was asked of me, and more. I wanted to please, even to the point of putting half my allowance in a savings account to impress my stepfather. I changed the grades on my report card because I thought that would please him, too. In my brown uniform—remember, David, I still wore it, but with a different style, that first year we were lovers?—I walked down and up the steep, slippery, slushy Westmount hills through the interminable winters. I did everything our daughter Ann now does, that I don't even recall. I waited to be happy.

It was by accident that I met you one day when I was sixteen and my plans backfired. I was coming out of the public library with an armful of books and saw you standing, nonchalantly unaware of me, in a phone booth. In a panic I turned and hurried off in the opposite direction, but stumbled over the curb and spilled the books on the sidewalk. Could I leave them there? As I knelt trying to gather them together, I saw your legs beside me. They had to be your legs, I would have known them anywhere, though I didn't dare look up. I hoped my hair would hide me.

"Need any help?"

"It's okay." I kept on looking down. The pile fell over again.

"Here, let me." You picked most of them up. "Do you want a ride?"

"It's okay," I said again.

You dumped the books behind the seat of your car and opened the door for me.

I babbled. All the important things I'd been saving to tell you slipped out of my mind like those stupid books. You asked me what I was reading and I told you. Walter Scott? Dumas! I meant to say Sartre and Camus—I really had read *L'Etranger,* after all—and *Ulysses.* As I lay on my bed afterwards I dug my nails into my bare thighs in self-disgust. You had asked me what I was doing for the summer and I had said, "Nothing much!" But you *had* known my name and I stayed awake that night inventing marvellous ways in which you could have found it out.

And then the next day you called and asked my mother if I might come sailing at the cottage that weekend. My mother asked who would be there—your parents? good—and reluctantly agreed that I could go. But just for the day on Sunday, mind, and you would have to be sure I was home by ten. By ten! I was furious with her ridiculous conditions. Didn't she trust me? Everybody else would be there for the whole weekend. Did she want to make me a laughingstock? And you would have to drive back specially to pick me up. I cried and she lost her temper, saying I wouldn't go at all.

In spite of that, the Sunday was a success. We sailed and swam. You took me back into the woods and showed me a beaver dam. At dinner I spoke too much, too haughtily, too intelligently, but your father teased me, which was a good sign, and I didn't blush. And then you had to take me home. Halfway back you stopped, out in the open where there were no mosquitoes, and put your arm around me—yes, David, yes—and talked about my stepfather for an hour and a half.

All your father's friends were afraid of my stepfather, you said. They thought he was dangerous with his high principles, his concern for the welfare of his workers, the way he turned over sixty percent of his income to charities. If his board weren't intimidated by his tedious sermons, they would have kicked him out long ago. "But it's an example we'll all have to follow," you said as I shivered. "Look, if we don't do it ourselves the socialists'll take over and do it for us. The way he handled his plant in Alma when he had to close it down—that was superb. Anybody else would have turned his back and walked away. But he went and ran the whole business from up there for two months. And by the time they closed, there were only—what was it, five? —yeah, five out of nearly four hundred workers that he hadn't found another job for." You knew more about my stepfather than I did myself. "Nobody else in North America would have done that. It's the European attitude, and we're going to have to catch up."

That was the direction you were heading in yourself, you said, after this last year at McGill, then Harvard. Of course, it would be different in an import-export business. "We've always been traders. For three hundred years we've never dealt with people, only merchandise." But still, it had to be done.

Finally, nearly two hours late, you left me unkissed on my doorstep.

How could I expect my mother to believe me?

"But all we did was talk about Molly," I protested as she stood there, stern in her nightdress. (I called my stepfather "Molly" and said *"vous"* to my mother! In a country where nobody says *"vous,"* apart from the more obsequious waiters, I addressed my mother formally, and still do.) "He really admires Molly. He wants to meet him." I began to cry and my mother laughed, which made me cry more.

But I made you interested in me that summer, didn't I, David? My parents trusted you, so we were free to do whatever we wanted. We went out to the cottage a lot, not at the weekends when there would be hordes of friends and relatives, but on our own during the week. And it was there that, for the first time, I made love to you. Yes, *I* made love to *you,* isn't that so? It was I who showed you, guided you, though I didn't know myself. It was I who sensed the right rhythms, the best places to touch.

Actually, "making love" is hardly the right phrase for what we did. Or if that was what it was, it was a very fifties' lovemaking. You never came in me, though once or twice I tried to make you, perched on top, the sun on my back, not letting you withdraw, but in the end you always wrenched yourself free, spilling out in a whimpering climax between my fingers.

Later you told me why, told me about the girl you had been phoning that day outside the library. She was a secretary in your father's office—couldn't you look any further, David?—and you had fucked each other furiously for a couple of months. Nobody ever knew; she was never one of the blonde girls in the M.G. One night the condom must have slipped or burst. Of course, you didn't put it so crudely to me; just, "Something must have gone wrong," and, "These things aren't safe, anyway." What could you do? She was a secretary—no, a typist—and Québécoise. So you paid for the abortion and made hundreds of self-justifying, self-pitying phone calls.

It was the only cruel thing I have known you to do, the only consciously cowardly thing. I think I could hate you now for the way it corrupts those memories. But at the time it made me glad. It spiced our love with danger. During those endless, sticky afternoons of tortured manipulation ("Slower, more slowly, wait"—I held you), it confirmed my mastery. Now I find myself wondering what became of her.

We talked constantly of our love for each other. I don't know what the word means any longer; it has been overlaid with so many deposits of other emotions, so many forms of caring and uncaring. But we knew then we were in love. It was simple: the two of us together was all that mattered. We talked of marriage. We would have to wait, of course, three years at least, till you had finished at Harvard, but we could have waited twice as long. We filled the future with promises.

Within a year we were married. After my last term at the convent—how superior I felt to all those nuns!—and yours at McGill, what point was there in spinning it out any longer? Who cared about an M.B.A. from Harvard? "What he's going to have to do he could manage with grade 8 from Trois Rivières," your father laughed when we asked him. And our parents, who at first had been so doubtful, would have had us running down the aisle in the end. "They'll only get into trouble if it's put off any longer."

The wedding was not what I wanted. My mother arranged everything, so it was very expensive (political principles get shelved for weddings; fresh *foie gras* from Pau and the Périgord) and very formal. The one boy I knew, apart from my stepbrothers, Sam from Point St. Charles, who went to the same art classes and talked to me in coffee-bars afterwards about his alcoholic father and pimp of a brother, hitchhiked all the way up the hill to our house with a portrait of himself he had painted for me. And I stood outside the front door and gave him a bottle of champagne. It took us ten years to get rid of the presents we got from everybody else. But we were married; that was final.

And now, David, thirteen years after, what is left?

Bits and pieces of our lives.

I don't mean that badly. There are many good bits and good pieces. I'm being unrealistic, I know, wanting more. But if love is the force that could have held it all together, there is no love. None.

This is the last love letter I shall think of writing to you, damn it.

I like you, David, and I hate the idea of causing you to hurt. You are the most thoughtful person I know. The little things you do, not the big ones. The fur coats are easy, the little things move me deeply. Two weeks after I got to London for my first show there, I found a letter you had hidden in my case, and I knew that you knew it would take me two weeks to find it. Thank you; I don't thank you enough. I love—yes, love—the concern you show for the kids: how you think about their needs, the small day-to-day problems, which obsess them, that I don't even notice. But there is no passion in your life.

You never touch me without my having touched you first. Do I stink, do I repel you? I want to scream sometimes. But no, you just don't touch people. When we have sex, you say, "We must make love more often." But we don't. You don't like your body; it is to be washed, fed, not caressed or probed. I doubt if you masturbate, even, and I do, David, I do.

You do the things that have to be done: the business, the family, the house, the insurance, the garage, the bills. You're the perfect husband, and there's no time for anything else. You want there to be no time for anything else, because the passions have receded from your life. Your passion for me, your passion for the ideas you bored me with that first night. What has happened to those ideas? At best, you're a closet liberal; you hold society's purse strings.

No, that's not fair. You do care, you care deeply. Injustice offends you and you see it clearly for what it is. But what are you going to do about it, David, you fuckhead?

Our lives have drifted apart and face in different directions. After all this time, you still don't understand how my painting could be anything more than a hobby. And I, for my part, sense how dissatisfied, how unhappy, how desperate you are. Everything in your life has come to a dead end. That is why, at thirty-five, you are old. But there is nothing I can do about it. I can't help you. Yet somehow, somewhere, I am deeply afraid that it's all my fault, that I have not been able to awaken you to a meaning in your life, that I have not been able to make you happy. There's a tiny trigger mechanism I haven't been able to find.

It is my fault, David, my love. I deceive you because I have not been able to make you happy.

As soon as she got home from Claire's, Helen fell asleep on her bed—her own bed—soothed by its cleanness. She didn't dream, but when she wakened, three hours later, she thought it must all have been a dream. She lay, not yet believing, with the early afternoon sunlight falling around her, feeling teased by the absurdity of this fantasy. Where had it come from? Who was playing this trick on her? But little by little, it dawned on her that it all might really have happened. She looked for proof and found the scrapes on her knees from the coarse rugs on Claire's floor. They burned. She glanced at herself in the mirror and put her hand up to her mouth. And then she laughed for a long time.

She looked around the bedroom, a dazzling, airy, formal room made by an earlier self. It was almost all white, and the light poured into it through a Plexiglas dome in the wall. Steel and leather furniture, mirrors, two beautiful bent plants, an intricately patterned antique quilt: cool and controlled, like everything she had tried to do here when they bought this old house in Westmount and spent double its price on having an architect rip it apart. One of her largest, most perfect paintings hung on the wall above the bed. She twisted to look up at it. It was by that earlier self, too. The paint drifted across the canvas, each wave like a veil in front of and behind the previous one, a pulsating surface. It had worked; the light blue against the deeper green had been daring. The critic in *The Star* had talked about "her sensitive, vibrant use of colour," and the critic in *Le Devoir,* who must have been reading Greenberg, approved: *"Dans les traces de l'école de New York, elle mène ses propres recherches aux frontières de l'expérience visuelle."* But it wasn't frontiers that she had been exploring at all.

"Just the margins," she sniffed and got up.

She walked about the house touching things absent-mindedly. The kids wouldn't be home from school for another two hours. Lately, the house had seemed more and more dead to her. But it didn't matter one way or the other anymore.

It was irrelevant now, so she could quite enjoy it again.

Finally, she was ready for the test. She opened the door through to her studio and tried to surprise them—the five new paintings—with her new self. And yes—she felt the adrenaline spurt in her—they were right, this was really what it was all about, she could be sure of it now, she could feel them respond to her. She went over to them and touched them, not minding her fingerprints in the places where the oil was still wet, wiping the paint off elsewhere. They would fall to pieces in fifty years, the wood, the glue, the paper, the acrylic, the oil, all expanding and contracting at different rates. But what would it matter? They were a mess, they were junk. Good, that was what she wanted: collages of worthless material. What, after all, is the intrinsic value of the components of the human body? Less than seven dollars? So she had taken the magazine images of her own time, the violence this house had been designed to keep out, and glued them onto thick board and painted them, layer upon layer, till parts of them were healed by the colour and other parts exaggerated, made into sores. She had gouged into them with a router and started again, image upon image, oil on acrylic, acrylic on oil, and in amongst the images were the words of the revolution she had finally had to recognize, incomplete as the paintings themselves would always be incomplete. Those other paintings, made by that other self, had needed no viewer to complete them; they went on being themselves exactly, even when nobody was around. They would survive the human race. But these paintings needed her, needed an audience to finish the work they could only start—not only someone to see them and say, "Oh, how beautiful," but someone to act upon them.

They were full of conflict, the conflict that was bound to invade her life. She felt weak from the certainty that she and these paintings were one. She should have known that they would predict what had happened last night.

Perhaps they had even demanded it.

I lie in bed on Sunday morning. It is my old life still. David sits by the window talking to Ann and Mark. They are dressed already, waiting for me so we can leave for mass. But I am still in bed, naked under the sheet. I pull the sheet right up over my head, the sunlight filtering through it in a white glow. I can see my breasts and the tuft of pubic hair and my feet sticking up full of awkward bones. How fine it would be to be dead like this.

David pauses and I can feel him watching me. "What d'you think you're doing?" His tone is amused.

"I'm just lying here in my tent."

They laugh.

"Can I come in, too?" Mark asks. He is six.

"Get your own tent, buster," I growl toughly.

I can hear him climbing into David's bed and David and Ann go on talking about tennis. But after five minutes David's patience is strained. "Come on, Helen, let's move, for God's sake!"

I sit up and become a mother.

The dog ran ahead of them. "Querido!" Mark called in his angry man's voice, "Querido!" The dog looked round at him quizzically. He was brown and white, long-haired, a shrewd Pyrénnéen sheep dog, and he didn't bother with adults, unless they deserved it, let alone kids. He turned and darted off into the undergrowth. "Querido, Querido!" Mark shouted and hurled himself in pursuit.

David looked at Helen and laughed, then ran after both of them. Helen watched them sadly. They had spent so many Sunday afternoons just like this: a stroll round Summit Circle above the city. It was the essence of English Montreal's Englishness that at the top of Westmount there should be not a castle or a monument or an illuminated hundred-foot-high cross, but a park full of rabbits and pheasants. Tweed jackets, walking sticks and cashmere scarves; muffins for tea. Helen shook her head and walked on with Ann.

"I'm going to get some weights," Ann said.

"Some what?"

"Weights. Weight-lifting weights."

Helen laughed and knew she shouldn't have. She tried to cover it up. "But why? You're already so . . . well, so well-built." Her daughter was only twelve but she was as tall as Helen, taller, walking with a gawky, muscular determination.

"I want to be stronger. Then you can stop people making you do things you don't want to do."

They came to the lookout and stood between two parked cars with the city spread out beneath them, the river and its bridges beyond. It was the middle of September and already fall was in the air. The tips of the maples and some of the sumac were turning red.

"What people?"

"Boys. Men."

Helen put her arm around her daughter's shoulder. It was tense with muscles. "Not everyone's an enemy," she said.

"I know that," Ann said. "But you have to be ready for the ones who are."

They walked on together.

"What's that?" Ann stopped.

There was a rustling in the bushes and Ann pushed in amongst them. "Oh, my God, it's hurt," Helen heard her exclaim and went in, too. At Ann's feet a small bird thrashed about helplessly.

"I thought it was a snake," Ann said.

Helen bent to the bird. One of its wings seemed to be

damaged. Very carefully, she put her hands around it, enclosing its panic. It fit her hands warmly, perfectly, its heart banging away against her fingers.

"What are you going to do with it?"

"I think the only thing is to move it away from the side of the road, somewhere more sheltered." She walked up the hill till she came to a dead aspen, the base of its trunk completely hollow. She placed the bird on the spongy ground; it squatted still and cheeped. "It's only young. Maybe it fell out of the nest. Its parents will be around. Nature heals itself mostly." She tried to sound as if she were sure.

When they got back onto the road Ann said, "Donnie would have killed it."

"But why?" Helen asked. Donnie, the neighbours' son, was two years older than Ann, with a moustache already.

"There was this chipmunk with a broken leg and he smashed its head in with a rock. He said he was putting it out of its misery."

Ahead, in the middle of the road, David and Mark stood waiting for them. Querido prowled about.

"We found a bird with a bad wing," Ann said to Mark. "Mum looked after it."

"That's nothing. Querido nearly caught a rabbit. He chased it halfway down its hole." Mark fingered the dog's muzzle.

Without thinking what she was doing, Helen put her arm around David and leaned her head on his shoulder. Surely this ought to be enough; she couldn't understand herself.

"Mark wants to go down to the Oratory," he said.

She tugged herself away. "Oh, no," she said, glancing nervously at the great copper dome of the church between the trees.

"But why not? We've got time."

"It's just so much nicer out here."

"All those crummy waxworks," Ann said.

"Well, I don't remember it and I want to go," Mark said stubbornly. "I was just a kid when we went there before."

"Seems to me Mark has a reason," David said rationally.

Reason! Helen had a reason; she hated the place. So much of her early life had been spent there at mass and music lessons and catechism classes. Its corridors and arches encircled her memories like a labyrinth. When she was ten or eleven she had been completely devoted to the cult of Brother André, the tiny insignificant doorkeeper of a boys' school, son of a wheelwright, who had built this gigantic basilica high above Montréal in honour of Saint Joseph, the carpenter.

"We must pray for Brother André, that he will become a saint," the sisters had said.

Helen could no longer believe any of that. She still went through the motions with David, who was a convert, and with the kids. But the services they attended were held in rotation in the houses of the well-to-do faithful, conducted by committed priests in polo-neck sweaters, as far as it was possible to stray from the muttered, threatening rituals of her childhood here at St. Joseph's. Everything was out in the open now, a stainless steel chalice on a teak coffee table. People smiled at each other warmly and discussed the Church's political responsibilities. They took the pill; their children played without guns. But to Helen it was even more unsatisfactory than the old way—too bland, unmysterious. There was still a hidden part of her that yearned for gods. Not one God with a male monopoly of power, but many gods, for different times and places, intensifying the present, whimsical and stern, androgynous, unpredictably caring. But she didn't know how to worship them and her need of them went unfulfilled.

They left Querido outside chained to a railing.

"Why don't I stay with him?" Helen suggested.

"Come on," David said gently. "Don't be a child." He took her hand and added in his awful French: *"Le diable est mort."*

But the devil wasn't dead. Not yet, not here. As soon as they went through the doors, the claustrophobia hit her in the chest. She reeled back. The church had been redecorated, modernized, since her last visit. It was even worse than before, as though the architects had been commissioned to squeeze out every ounce of oppressive horror, all melodramatic and authoritarian. Thorns everywhere, jabbing at her from the altar rails, the stained-glass windows, the walls, the doors. Protestations of God's love abounded; the thorns were its expression.

She tried to force herself to breathe deeply. As a little girl she had stood here, one Christmas midnight mass. All evening she had hovered around the entrance to the confessional, inventing sins in case there were some she might forget, until, freed by the priest's indifference, she had been able to stand here singing carols. But as she sang, the truth of what was happening closed in around her. She focused on the great tortured figure of Christ on the Cross while his tiny minions bustled round the marble altar, an altar not of communion but of sacrifice. She saw herself stretched out on it, naked, the priests' knives in her belly, serpents writhing out. When at last she knelt at the rail she was shaking so much the wafer slipped past her lips. She caught it just in time, looked at the priest in terror and ran to the door, vomiting in the snow outside. Too much candy, they explained.

Helen's legs still shook. She followed Mark to the back. Even the organ looked like a great Aztec bird.

But Mark was unsubdued. "Why don't we come here more often?"

"Why should we?" she asked weakly.

"It's so scary."

"I don't like being scared."

"Does that mean we can't come?"

"Not with me, anyway." She put her hand on his shoulder.

"What a rip-off!" He slipped away.

They went down the escalators to the crypt, with its stacks of crutches thrown away by cripples who had been cured through Brother André's intercession.

"Why can't they be used instead of just lying around there?" Ann asked. "I mean, what if the cripples who left them there weren't really cured after all? Could they come and get their crutches back?"

David laughed. "You can't believe in miracles *and* say, 'But just in case, I'll hold on to my crutch.' "

"I don't know," Ann said. "I would."

Mark insisted on going into the small museum, too, where mementoes of Brother André were laid out on display. Brother André's rosary, Brother André's towels, Brother André's galoshes. Waxworks of Brother André in his office, one hand on the Bible, the other on a bellpush. Brother André on his deathbed, dying of indigestion. All he ate was porridge and potatoes. *These are the actual bedclothes he died in,* read the sign. But there was something here, in spite of herself, that moved Helen; a dedication, however joyless she found it. She had prayed to him often, or rather, to his heart. In the red glow of the shrine where it was kept she had pressed carefully written prayers through the grille. What had she prayed for? She couldn't even remember. But as they stood in front of it again—the brown fistlike muscle in a pickle jar—she did remember. She had prayed that she wouldn't die—of polio, in a train crash, a meteorite falling out of the sky. Well, she had lived, hadn't she? The floor was littered with prayers; she felt tears in the corners of her eyes. But suddenly she remembered André's bomb. André's bomb! The image appalled her. Her fists clenched. David looked at her questioningly, but didn't say anything. If only she could tell him.

"Ugh!" said Ann and turned away.

As they left the crypt, the sun was slipping in the sky. Helen's head ached; she felt exhausted. She looked down the steep slope and remembered the long lines of pilgrims crawling up the steps on their knees. How she hated this place! Then another memory released her. Wintertime. Freezing rain.

She held on to Ann's arm. "Do you know how I got out of violin lessons?"

"I didn't even know you played," David said.

"I don't," Helen smiled. "Not anymore. But I used to come

here for lessons. Once a week. It was awful. I was no good at all, but Bonne Maman made me keep on. She said in the end I'd be grateful. Anyway, one winter evening I came out after my lesson and there had been some freezing rain on top of the snow. Really icy. Some kids were sliding down the hill."

"Jeez," said Mark. "It's steep."

"For sure. Well, they teased me until I did it with them. I was terrified. Halfway down I got turned around and went head first the rest of the way. I was lucky I didn't kill myself. But I was luckier than that, too. I landed on top of my violin case and squashed it flat."

Ann laughed with her. "What did Bonne Maman say?"

"She said I'd have to pay for a new one. But then she forgot." Helen smiled. "After that I could paint."

"I'm hungry," Mark said. "Let's go back to Bonne Maman's."

They started to climb back up the hill to the road, David and Mark in front.

"We've been so long," Helen said. "Poor Querido."

Ann turned and flung her arms around her. "I really love you."

They hugged. "Why, beauty?" Helen asked, taken aback.

"Because you're so good with animals. You know how to handle them. The way you said, 'Oh, the poor thing,' when we found that thrush. Just like you did in the summer when I showed you that red-eyed vireo the car had hit."

Helen kissed her in return. But try as she might, she couldn't remember saying the words at all. And she was quite sure she had never had any idea what a red-eyed vireo was.

"I don't see the point of it," Hélène says. She sits in her thronelike Louis Quinze chair, embroidering. And I sit across from her, this mother I was named after, whose name I have dropped. We are talking about bombs. David is watching a football game on television, the kids are playing Ping-Pong, and I am talking to my mother about bombs. I don't want to be talking about bombs; I would much rather be asking her if she was ever unfaithful to either of her husbands. But she has the ability to involve me constantly in arguments I don't want to have. I don't recall where this one started and I've no idea where it's going, but I find myself supporting, as I always do, a position I don't want to support, for that is another of her abilities—to make me defend the indefensible.

"I don't see how you can defend them," she says.

"I'm not defending them," I say desperately. "But you have to understand why."

The late afternoon light falls on her short steel-grey hair. Behind, below her the city shimmers. She is the model of severe elegance, a tall straight woman with a carved face.

"Pour me another whisky, will you, *chérie?*" she asks. "It's getting very intricate."

I do as I am told. Though I am thirty, she makes me feel as if I were seventeen again.

She concentrates on the pattern she has drawn for herself. "Ah, yes, I see." Then she returns to the attack. "What good do you think will come from blowing up children?"

"None. And they're not trying to blow up kids, anyway. But when people are humiliated and frustrated for centuries, they'll do anything to free themselves from the feeling of impotence." And that's something I know about, I tell myself. It's what I feel now.

She looks up at me over the top of her spectacles. She takes her time. "Do I understand you correctly? Are you equating bombs with freedom?"

"No," I say, my voice rising. "Of course not, it's a momentary release, that's all. They're not political, they're just symptoms."

"Victims?" she asks, leading me.

I shrug.

"The country's full of people who think they have a right to do anything that pleases them because they're victims. But if we're all victims, who's going to be responsible for clearing up the mess when it's all over?"

Her favourite word—responsible. I try not to reply. It's not my argument, I tell myself. I don't want to argue with her, I would much rather talk to her. But I can't. I would never dare to ask her that question about being unfaithful to her husbands. I'm afraid of this woman, my own mother. I respect her, but somehow my respect undermines me. I love her, but my love is thwarted, bouncing back at me like a ball in a squash court.

I find myself staring at her forehead, repeating again and again under my breath: I'm going to leave David, I'm going to leave David, I'm going to leave David. I imagine it so intensely that she has to look up and hear me. The intensity frightens me. I didn't even think of leaving him until this moment and now I'm sure she must have heard me. I'm leaving David. She carries on with the embroidery.

Tension pricks my palms. I try to find something else to say: "I didn't go to see Helena this week. How is she?" I call my grandmother by her first name and say *"vous"* to my mother.

She shakes her head. "I think she's going to be thrown out of this home, too."

My grandmother, who is eighty-six, has been asked to leave seventeen old people's homes in the past six years.

"What's she done this time?"

"She accused the matron—right in the middle of the dining room last Sunday dinner—of stealing her toothbrush. Her toothbrush! In front of the priest!"

I try to suppress my laughter, but then I realize my mother is laughing herself, a deep, full, throaty laugh that draws me to her across the minefields we have planted between us.

"She's got guts," I say softly.

My mother nods. "She's never lacked that." But then she grows solemn. "I pray to God I'll die before I get to that stage."

I close my eyes to shut out the thought. But the mood is broken by Mark who comes rushing in. "Bonne Maman, can I have a chestnut?"

"They're not chestnuts, they're *marrons glacés,* little savage." She pulls his chin. "It's like calling *foie gras* goose liver."

"Can I?"

"If you say it in French."

"S'il te plaît, Bonne Maman," he begs, *"puis-je avoir un marron glacé?"*

"Bien. Fetch me the box." She gives him two.

"I can spin the ball now," he tells me as he runs out again, his cheeks bulging.

"He's getting spoilt," my mother says absentmindedly.

"But it's you who spoil him," I protest.

"Chérie, it's obvious. Everyone can see it." Her voice is light, tolerant. "And while I'm being an interfering old grandmother, don't you think you're a little hard on Ann?"

"No," I reply in surprise. "No, I'm not." What really surprises me is that it's Mark who's always been her favourite. She doesn't even like girls; they bore her. And in any case, I carry on, what makes her think that she knows how to bring up children? Look at what she did to me. "At least I don't have a strap," I say petulantly.

"A *what?"*

"A strap. But no, it wasn't a strap, was it? It was a whip, a real whip, with leather thongs. You used to keep it hanging just inside the door of the pantry. I'll show you the hook." I feel the leather again running between my fingers.

Her jaw clamps tight. "You're making it up."

"I'm not," I say gleefully. "I remember being so scared of it, I used to cut off one of the thongs every day. But when I'd cut half of them off you just went and bought another one. I gave up after that; there was no point."

"Listen, Helen, that's enough. Do you think I don't remember?"

"Do you think *I* don't remember?"

We glare at each other till Ann comes in. She hunts around the room for the box of *marrons glacés,* opens it and starts to take one.

"What do you think you're doing?" my mother shouts.

"Mark got two," Ann whines.

"Mark asked properly. Put it back."

As Ann does so, she makes a face which is intended to be behind her grandmother's back.

"Don't you *dare* do that," my mother screams. "I'll slap you." She half rises to her feet and the embroidery falls on the floor. "Get out of here. Get out."

Ann runs from the room, trying not to cry.

My mother's face is white and trembling. "I tell you, Helen, I can't stand the sight of that girl."

"You can't stand girls, period."

"With reason."

We look at each other as we have looked at each other for more than twenty-six years. She is in the rear seat of the dirty Citroen, her body rigid. There is blood on her white blouse, I don't know whose, hers or the Canadian's. He showed me how the radio works. I run to the car and look at her in alarm. I want to ask her what is happening, where she is going. Her eyes freeze me. As the car jerks round the tight bends, I stand out in the open waving wildly, hoping she will see me.

She has never told me what the Gestapo did to her.

David comes in and sprawls on the sofa. He looks at us curiously, sensing the tension. "Miami has these incredible running backs, Kiick and Csonka," he says. "With names like that who'd want to get in their way? And there's another one called Mercury Morris who's supposed to be even better."

Neither of us looks at him.

He gets up and pours himself a whisky and sits down again. "What were you talking about?"

"We were talking about Helen's Commie friends and their bombs," my mother says. *"Ses amis Cocos"*—she sneers the phrase because she knows it will irritate me.

I sigh heavily.

David looks at me and raises his eyebrows. "I don't think Helen's friends are the bomb-planting variety," he laughs. "They talk too much."

"And fuck." I say it, really say it, but so softly neither of them hears. I try one last time to get things straight: "Please, mother. Just listen, just for a moment. Okay? First, the F.L.Q. are not my friends. Second, they are not Communists. They're not even Marxists; just opportunists with a bit of the rhetoric. Right?"

"But why didn't you—"

"And *third,*" I interrupt, "third: the people you worked with in the Resistance, weren't they mainly *Cocos,* as you call them?"

She embroiders. "Yes, but that was different."

"How?" I push her. "Just because it's history? How?"

"Then we were all part of an alliance. The Communists, the Church . . ."

"Les Cacas?" I mock, trying to get my own back.

She nods. "The Church, the Socialists, the Gaullists. It was a common front. Of course, there were disagreements, but they were resolved. There was unity against the Fascists. The Communists weren't isolated like they are now. When they're isolated, that's when they bite."

"They don't intend to remain isolated."

"What worries me is the effect the F.L.Q. will have on the municipal elections," David tries to change the direction. He's sympathetic to a vaguely left-wing group that's running against Mayor Drapeau for control of the city council. They don't stand a chance, I keep telling him. They're just playing. Drapeau's for real. He's got the whole city in his pocket. David has given my mother a new target and she turns enthusiastically to argue with him, forgetting me for the moment.

I don't listen to them. I hear their voices, see their lips move, but I don't want to listen to what they're saying. Let them have each other. I watch my mother, the movement of her hands, gesturing, pulling the needle through, so definite, so sure, and I respect her for her toughness, the courage which I doubt I have in me. But that courage—though I'm proud of it in her, immensely proud—that courage has no meaning any longer, no focus. It just leaves her more irritably old. It's *her* isolation that makes her bite.

And David? I watch him, too, imagining him as Jean-Claude, my fingers in his fine thinning hair. David's hair is thick and wiry.

I am drifting away.

To keep from falling asleep, I shake myself and go over to stand in the bay window. I hear their voices from a different world, the noise of a table being set in the dining room; the smell of cooking.

Behind me my mother gets up to switch on a light. She glances at me suspiciously; she thinks I'm sulking. She comes and touches me gently on the shoulder. "I'll say one thing for them. *'Les Cocos'* never let us down."

For a moment my hand rests on hers. "The most responsible?" I suggest, and she smiles.

But as she goes to sit down again, a responsibility strikes her. "Helen."

"Yes."

"See your grandmother, won't you?" And then she adds, so that it won't seem like an order: "You're the only one she cares about now, you know."

I look down over the cluttered rooftops. The setting sun bounces on a million windows. The whole city is on fire. As I watch, the Bank of Commerce building curls up at the edges; its glass walls melt and flare.

"It won't work. It's bullshit," Peter Abbott shouted with his usual certainty. "Painting is the art of meditation."

He was drunk. Helen was drunk. They sat in the Rainbow, a good bar to be drunk in at two in the morning. The low-hanging lights cast a warm, deceptive glow. The murals, half landscape, half reclining nude, lurked in the shadows. Everybody was drunk, some sitting in a stupour at the tables, others animated by the sex-market at the bar. The waitresses prowled. Rock music bounced from wall to wall. Nobody could imagine any other world.

Helen struggled to hold on to the point she thought she wanted to make. Her forehead creased. "That's just dumb. And it's the opposite of what you're doing yourself, anyway. Meditation"—she drew her finger through the beer that had sloshed onto the tabletop—"my ass. What you're doing now, it's pure action. That's all it is."

She strained to focus on Peter's eyes, trying to make out if he was listening. With Peter you could never be sure of anything. One moment he would seem to be slumped in a mindless heap, the next he was lucid and cruel. In either state, dogmatism defined him.

Over to their left, a group of men were squabbling about who was, or wasn't, gay. Helen glanced across at them and Peter said, "Ah, but the key word is pure, purity. Not action." By the time she looked back at him his eyes had disappeared.

"What the fuck do you mean by that?"

At forty-four Peter Abbott was at the high point of his career, with controversial shows all over the world. Helen had known him for a long time, since he taught with a mixture of carelessness and insight at the *École des Beaux Arts.* She thought he respected her, but she still couldn't make up her mind about him. He was a little fat man, almost bald on top, with long greasy greying hair and tiny piglike eyes. His clothes seemed always to be rumpled and stained with glue or paint or food. Yet sometimes she thought he was the most compelling man she would ever meet; there was an intense force about him that sucked people in. That was what she didn't trust. He could get away with anything; he recognized no limit. Whenever she met him like this, by accident maybe twice a year, she came away exhilarated, wondering how she managed not to end up making love to him. Most people did, at one time or another, so she heard. But she always steered away and he never pushed. It was what he did to his friends that she didn't like; what they would do for him. She remembered Charles Sinclair. Charles, an amateur gymnast, had stood on his hands for ten minutes on the balcony rail of a sixteenth floor apartment just so that Peter could record his pulse rate, feed it through an oscilloscope and convert it into patterns of light and electronic sound.

Who was more accountable, Charles or Peter? Either way, she wanted none of it.

Peter stirred himself and waved vaguely at the waitress. "Claire says you're leaving your husband."

"Claire shouldn't go around saying that. It's not true."

"But you've got an apartment on Laval."

"It's a ruin. It's just a studio. So I can get away when I'm working." Damn it, why should she have to explain?

The waitress put two more bottles of Brador on the table. Helen fumbled for the money. As the waitress counted out the change, Peter reached across and stroked the long leather money belt that was slung around her waist. "Doesn't that turn you on?" he whispered. The waitress smiled.

Helen watched him angrily. "Shit, Peter, be serious for a moment, can't you?"

He gazed back at her and hummed.

"Jesus Christ, Peter!"

"Okay, but I'm telling you, sweetheart, you're all screwed up. Listen." He pulled his hair into long strands. "Painting is the art of meditation. So is what I do, though it's not, of course, painting. When your archetypal Japanese painter makes a watercolour of bamboo, or whatever, the real creativity goes into the prolonged period of concentration on the idea, the essence of bamboo. Or"—he shrugged—"whatever." He gulped his beer and helped himself to some peanuts from a bag on the next table. "Now, the momentary act of painting, though admittedly orgasmic, is really secondary. It merely transfers the contemplative experience out of which the work is formed to the contemplative experience by which it is perceived." He made a bridging motion with his arms and the table lurched. "Simple, eh?" He applauded himself slowly and fell back in his seat, exhausted.

"Bullshit!" Helen argued angrily. "You know that's not what you're doing. It's not the idea, some Platonic idea, that's central, it's the process. And the process is governed by the world about you, by accident, by conflict."

Peter was paying no attention. He was watching two women cuddling at the bar. One, with long black tangled hair, was so drunk she could hardly stand. The other, slim and small with thick-lensed glasses, was running her fingers up and down the inside of the dark one's thighs.

"Nice," Peter murmured.

Helen blinked to keep the two images she had of him from drifting apart. Why, she began to wonder, did they always end up arguing like this? But no, she couldn't start thinking about that or he would slip away. She had to pin him down. "Take Exchange, or whatever you call it."

Exchange was Peter's most recent experiment. It had begun the previous winter when a group of workers with chain saws hacked out the form of a vagina 440 feet long in the ice of the St. Lawrence River. The vagina, according to the bilingual catalogue, was that of a woman chosen at random from the forty-fourth page of the Montreal phone book. As the shape was being cut out of the ice, Peter hovered overhead in a helicopter giving directions and taking photographs. One of the workers fell into the hole he had just made and nearly drowned. He suffered severe frostbite, it was all on record.

Six months later, in the middle of summer, a forty-four-foot-long penis—Peter's own, he solemnly announced—was carved out of ice and dumped from a barge into the river where the vagina had once been. As it melted more photographs were taken, underwater and from the air. They were shown in New York, Paris and Tokyo—eventually even here in Montreal.

"Sexchange." Peter yawned.

One of the men at the next table was leaning unsteadily on the back of his chair and glaring down at the others. He had a finely pointed chin and curly hair. "You're not a homosexual at all," he sneered. "You're just pretending."

"Right," Peter agreed enthusiastically.

"You can't say the idea *meant* anything," Helen insisted. "It's a banal joke. It's the process by which it intrudes on people that's interesting. The effrontery, the scale, the way it exploits them. And the way accident intrudes on it, I can buy that, too. But don't try to sell me the idea. The idea's just a god-awful, third-rate bore."

She sensed that Peter might be watching her from under his eyelids. "So I'm saved by the worker, eh?" he suggested slyly.

"Exactly."

"Some goddamn idiot falls into the water by mistake and suddenly gives the whole concept a new meaning?"

She nodded, pleased with herself.

Peter held up his glass to the faint light. "Piss on the worker," he said.

"You don't mean that," Helen said, not knowing why she

should be trying to defend him. "You know you don't mean it." Peter had visited the man every day in hospital. "Damn it, why do you have to pretend?"

"He gets more from Workmen's Compensation than he ever made in his life before."

"Okay, that's my point." Was it? "Part of it, anyway. The only possible justification for all the callous things you do, if they can be justified, isn't some dumb abstract idea. It's the way they pinpoint the hypocrisy of the system we live in. They're kind of moral statements in reverse." She paused, not knowing quite what she meant by that. "Okay? They focus the argument."

Peter started to sketch on the back of an envelope. "I can do something with that money belt," he told himself.

She had lost him. Helen couldn't concentrate any longer. She held on. "Peter, listen to me, will you? Please, it's important. I just don't go along with all this crap about art aspiring to the condition of music. I used to. But it's all wrong. You can't separate art from language like that. It has to have a social function, a role in the conflict. That means the condition it should aspire to is theatre, not music. Don't you see? That's what links us. Why don't you face up to it?"

"I'm bisexual," a boy with a heavy Québécois accent was shouting. "The trouble is you're too feminine for me."

"I'm a *hell* of a lot more masculine than you are," screamed the man with the pointed chin.

They started to grapple with each other and the table tipped over onto the floor. The gigantic Indian bouncer came over and disentangled them, then marched the Québécois kid towards the door. As he disappeared, he yelled back into the bar: "You don't even know what an orgasm *is!"*

"He didn't start it," Helen protested weakly.

"What number on Laval?" Peter asked. His head was slumped and the words ran into each other.

"Fuck it!" Helen shouted above the noise. "You know you're not drunk." She knocked a bottle over with her hand.

He looked up at her and made a V-sign. "Freedom, Helen. Freedom lies in the unpredictable. The only principle we can work on is randomness. Watch out, you're getting too tied down. Art is too important to be contaminated with politics."

"No, Peter, it's the other way round exactly," she said vehemently, surer of herself than she had ever been. "Politics is too important to be contaminated with your crumby aesthetics."

David comes to my bed instead of his own.

I am wearing a kimono that he brought back with him from a business trip to Japan. It cost hardly anything, he told me apologetically, but he knew I would love the design of pine boughs and dragonflies in different shades of blue. Its looseness is cool and clean around my skin. I lie in my large white bed in this large white room and see myself in the mirrors that cover the closet doors. I am part of this beautiful décor, a designer's dream.

I don't know why I'm here. Some nights I stay in the shadowy, dirty apartment I have rented for myself on Laval, and some nights I come back home. I still call it home. Nobody here asks me any questions, not even the children; somebody must have told them not to. Mummy is going through a difficult time; she needs to be left alone for a little while. But I don't feel I'm in control of the choices I seem to be making. It's just that sometimes I happen to be here—and then I am as I always have been —and sometimes I'm somewhere else, right out on the edge of myself. I'm happy, I think, with my life like this, but I know, too, that soon I'll have to find the answers to the questions they don't even dare to ask me, though I see them in their eyes—Ann's especially—all the time.

I lie here covered with blue dragonflies, and read. I read so intensely that whenever I look up and see myself in the mirror, I'm surprised I'm here, surprised it's I who am here. The book I read, its pages pulled apart urgently, is Fanon's *The Wretched of the Earth.* Its suffering fills me with energy.

> It was from that moment on that I made my own decision to take back my wife after the war; for it must be said that I've seen peasants drying the tears of their wives after having seen them raped under their very eyes. . . . So I decided to take her back; but I didn't know at all how I'd behave when I saw her. And often, while I was looking at the photo of my daughter, I used to think that she too was dishonored, as if everything that had to do with my wife was rotten. If they'd tortured her or knocked out all her teeth or broken an arm I wouldn't have minded. But that thing—how can you forget a thing like that? And why did she have to tell me about it all?

I read the words and feel their horror; they have to be true. And then I glance up into my own eyes and I can't make the connection. It's not that I feel an incongruity between this elegant, sensual woman in an elegant, formal room and Fanon's images of oppression and violence and revulsion. For there to be a sense of incongruity, after all, there has to be an implied whole—this part doesn't fit with that. But here there is no whole, only separate pieces. One part of me vibrates with horrified life; the other doesn't really exist.

That is how David finds me when he comes in from the bathroom. He is wearing a blue nightshirt I bought for him in New York. His body glows from the shower. I don't look at him but I feel his presence, smell him watching me. I read the same paragraph over and over again, but the words are losing their meanings. I still don't look at him, but he comes over to my side of the room and sits down on the edge of my bed. Suddenly, it is narrow. His hairy calf is near to my left arm, too near. Gently his hand lifts the book up slightly so that he can see its cover. I still go on trying to read the same paragraph.

"What are you reading?" he asks. He has seen the title but he wants me to speak. I don't. *"The Wretched of the Earth,"* he says. "Sounds a bit heavy." He uses the word in its old sense. Nobody around him says, "Yeah, heavy, man!"

I look up at him and smile.

His skin is thick, wide-pored, like armour, and I notice he has just shaved. His chin is very firm. His eyes are grey, flecked with green and brown, and I imagine there's a worried look in them.

"You should read it," I say. "It's about what we do to the people we live off."

He doesn't respond. "Maybe," he says. "But you know how it is. By the time I get round to reading, all I want is a good thriller."

I look back down at the page but he lifts the book out of my hands and puts it on the table. "Helen," he says. "I love you."

I nod.

"You're changing," he says softly. "I don't know who you are anymore."

I touch his arm—muscled, freckled, hairy—and that's my mistake. Just that reflex of caring is enough to give him a reason for what happens next. But God, does that make it my fault? As I touch it, his hand moves over to the other side of me, palm down on the wide sleeve of the kimono between my right arm and my breast. At the same time, his body twists so that he is leaning over me, one knee on the bed, the other leg braced on the floor. His face is right above mine.

"David," I try to protest, but his lips press down on my mouth.

My right arm is caught in the sleeve, but with my left hand I try to push him away. I don't think he notices. I don't panic yet, I'm detached from what's happening, but as he fumbles with my belt I remember quite lucidly how I used to reproach him for not making love to me often enough; that was my only bitterness.

The kimono opens easily and his fingers urge my thighs apart so that he can squeeze a leg between them. His other hand grasps my breast. Later, I will lie in the dark and wonder: Both my arms were loose then, why didn't I pull his head back by the hair, why didn't I jab my nails into his eyes, why didn't I bring my knee up into his balls? But I didn't. I didn't do any of those things, and the thought which will keep me awake, frightening me most, is not just that I didn't, but that I was too cowed even to think of it.

He forces himself against me and his cock is enormous. It hurts me; there's no room inside me for him. "No, David, no," I sob, but he takes it for ecstasy. After all, haven't I sobbed before as I lay beneath him, caressing his neck—Oh, David, I love it when you come into me? And haven't I sat on top with all of him inside me, all his body, and mine expanding infinitely, wide enough for a thousand cocks? Yet now I have no cunt at all, it's sealed, the lips welded together, he has to batter his way in. Surely, he will cut himself on the edges.

I scream in pain and struggle wildly. My heels bang against his buttocks and he pushes faster to their rhythm. I try to squirm out from underneath him but his elbows hold me. All I can see is the reflection of bits of our bodies in the mirror: absurd, detached, my legs wave ineffectually in the air, his balls bang against my thighs. My eyes stare out of the face I see there. I can't breathe, my mouth opens and closes. Beside the mirror is the beautiful Plexiglas dome that during the day is like a goldfish bowl of light. Now it is dark, a great black barrel with just a few twisted shadows in it. Hollow, it closes over my head. I gasp for air and David is gasping, too. His body falls on me, his chin digs into the nape of my neck. I bite his shoulder and he squeals, then murmurs my name into the pillow. But at the end, it's not nothing I feel.

Later, on my own, huddled into a tight little ball like a dead spider, I'll remember a story my mother once told me about a friend of hers who was raped by her interrogators. Was she talking about herself? I don't know. But whoever it was, when they had taken, as they say, their pleasure, she lay on the floor and grasped the leg of a chair which had been overturned in her struggles, and pushed it into her vagina as far as it would go, till she bled, staring at them all the time in disgust. "As if," my mother said, "to show them she felt nothing." Yes, I'll remember that and tell myself, for shame, your cunt should be cut out with a razor. Because I do feel; this is what humiliates me most. I feel my skin beginning to tingle, back as far as my asshole, the lips swelling. I am moist inside, melting like fat. That's what I struggle against in the end, not against David but my own goddamn body. "No," I whimper, "no. No!" And David comes too, gasping my name.

His sweat is mixed with mine between my breasts. He lies beside me panting and takes my hand in his. "It's great we can still make love like that."

His cock stays as hard as wood with its triumph.

In my mind I say, "I hate you, I hate you, I hate you." And though I still can't bring myself to say them aloud, I long for him to hear the words.

Helen stood shivering in the entrance to the Joliette métro station. She rubbed her arms to warm them and looked out of the dirty window to see if there was any sign of Roger. All she could see was the rain pelting down on Hochélaga, collecting in puddles and filling the gutters.

She didn't know where she was. Twenty-three years in Montréal and she had never been here before, had never come as far east as this on the métro system. The street outside gave her nothing to hold on to, no images by which she could define even her alienation from it. Cutting through tight rows of cheap apartment buildings, it was neither city street nor suburban highway, just a long artery stretching from nowhere to nowhere. Funeral parlours, churches, take-out restaurants and little knots of stores were dotted at random on either side of it. The city seemed so much more vast out here, so much more anonymous than it ever was downtown. It went on and on forever.

An old woman in a raincoat went by outside with an umbrella in one hand and a plastic shopping bag in the other. She was tiny, with a pallid, lumpy face. As she came level with Helen, a car moving fast veered in close to the curb and a wave of water flew up over her. She paused and looked round in puzzled anger, muttering to herself, then took off her glasses to wipe them on a tissue and disappeared round the corner.

Helen looked irritably at her watch. Roger was a quarter of an hour late already. She decided she would give him another five minutes.

Two girls came through the door, giggling and flicking water out of their hair. A gust of cold, gritty air blew round Helen and she shivered. Helen was wearing only jeans, sandals, an embroidered cotton shirt. Just that morning the sky had been blue, now the greyness of the city had washed up over it.

Damn! If only she had known where the meeting was to be, she could have driven. Roger wouldn't tell her on the phone. He said it was the line he wasn't sure of, but Helen knew he didn't trust her, either. She turned and stared impatiently at the garish ceramics on the wall, then back out the window at the empty street. Okay, from his point of view, she could see why. She came from the wrong class, had the wrong accent, painting was frivolous, unreliable. Still, he'd had time enough to see she wasn't just playing at this. For six months, she hadn't missed a single meeting, she'd ploughed her way through the dullest texts. She'd do much more if only he would ask.

She was trying not to look at her watch. But finally . . . well, that was that. Twenty-five stupid minutes. Reluctantly, she turned to go back down the escalator, but just as she did so she caught a glimpse of Roger in the subway entrance on the other side of the street. She looked again. She was sure he hadn't been there a couple of minutes before, but now he was pressed against a pillar staring intently away from her. She followed his eyes, seeing a laundry first of all with a delivery truck parked outside, then a light blue police car pulled in behind. Why hadn't she noticed it before? While she watched, a man in a maroon hockey-jacket got out of it and climbed into the cab of the truck and drove away. She looked back towards Roger but he wasn't there anymore. Thirty seconds later he came running up behind her.

"They've gone," he said.

"Who was it?"

"The guy in the truck? A pig. Undercover. I've seen him at demos. He hangs around, pretends to be interested." Roger spoke rapidly, the phrases clipped and thrown away.

"What was he doing?" she asked, a little excited, trying not to show it.

"Coincidence." He shrugged.

"Are you sure?"

He smiled at her seriousness. "No." He seized her by the arm. "Come on, *tabernac,* we're late." As if it were her fault.

They ran across the road against the lights and set off up the hill. The rain had eased to a drizzle, but already she could feel it seeping into her clothes.

Roger walked quickly, getting ahead of her all the time, shuffling sideways for a few paces, till she drew level. He was a small man whose energy made him look bigger. A bushy black beard swung from side to side and tiny dark brown eyes darted everywhere. She couldn't imagine him asleep. She liked him and knew nothing about him, not even his surname. Roger probably wasn't his own name, either. Once when they were talking about the *Mouvement pour la Libération du Taxi,* he mentioned that he'd worked as a taxi driver for a while. Was that all she had to go by? Well, no, she also knew that he was dedicated, stubborn, cautious—abstract qualities that were good to be able to fall back on, but not defining. Not enough.

As if she had spoken, he suddenly said, "I was born just a couple of blocks over from here."

Trotting to keep up, she looked at the two- and three-storey brick apartment buildings that lined the street. All she could respond to was the pattern of outside steps and curving iron railings that led up to the doors, the green and black paint dancing in the rain. She had no idea what it would be like to have to spend the whole of her life in one of them.

"Do you still live here?" she asked.

He looked at her out of the corner of his eye. "Now and again." Personal details were irrelevant. And dangerous. But as they turned down a side street past some garages covered with anti-English slogans, he tried to explain about himself in his own terms. "The people who live here, they don't know what they want. They grow up with politics, with the idea that politics can change things. No, it's true," he insisted, seeing the disbelief in her eyes, "they're very politicized. But it's never thought out. They run after the easy solutions every time. Look, not so long ago, even when I was a kid, this whole area was Fascist. Fascist-Catholic, that kind of thing. Not my father, he was always in the union. But a lot of blackshirts, anti-Semites? Now it's the F.L.Q. The real contradictions—the class struggle, eh?—get lost in the process."

Helen nodded. She knew what he was talking about, but it was still too abstract. She needed to know more. Since experience couldn't provide a base for her politics, the imagination must invent it. "Is your father still alive?" she asked.

Roger looked away, then changed his mind and answered her. "Sort of, I guess. He sits about, watches the hockey. He used to work in the C.P. yards up the top of the street here. One winter I was eight, he slipped on an icy step, fell under the wheels. They cut off both his legs."

She stopped. The details crashed into her mind. Roger stopped, too, five yards further on by an unfilled hole in the side of the street. He looked round, questioning. Helplessly, she put her hand out in his direction. "My God, that's awful."

He shook his head slightly. "Happens every winter."

They turned right up the hill again along a back lane. More garages on either side and yards enclosed with rusty wire fences. Bits of cars lay about with weeds growing through them. Behind each apartment the balconies tilted at odd angles, a web of grey wooden beams littered with flowerpots and broken furniture, kids' toys, beer crates, garbage cans.

Roger opened a gate and a large black dog in the next yard hurled itself at them. The fence bulged, Helen drew back. As they came to the porch, Roger pointed at one of the steps. "Watch that one. It's rotten under the paint."

"Who lives here?" Helen said without thinking, and immediately realized she shouldn't have asked.

Roger's eyes rested on her for a moment. "A friend's mother. She's at work." He unlocked a back door.

They were all there already. What a strange place for a nest of revolutionaries, Helen thought. They sat in a cramped little kitchen on wrought-iron patio chairs around a shaky chrome table. Luminous velvet pictures hung above them on the wall and in the middle of the table a bowl of plastic flowers was set on a vinyl doily.

"You're wet," Monique said disapprovingly.

Helen sensed the glow in her cheeks and the wet shirt sticking to her breasts. "It feels good, the rain," she said.

"Sit here, Helen," Gérard stammered. "I'll m-m-make some more coffee."

"You're late," Monique pursued her.

Helen pulled the strands of hair back from her face and laughed with pleasure. She despised Monique and didn't try any longer to hide it. Monique was a tall, awkward woman with bulging eyes and large drooping breasts. Even on the hottest days she wore so many layers of loose clothing that her body was only a shapeless, slightly rancid presence underneath. She was stupid and bossy, and she hated Helen with an intense pettiness. At first, Helen had been puzzled and hurt, because she didn't know what she had done to offend Monique and wanted, nervously, to correct it. But now she realized that Monique hated her simply for what she was, hated her above all because she was in the process of revolting against what she was, her bourgeois origins, thereby depriving Monique of a rationale for hating her. Realizing that, Helen found it easy to accept. Indeed, at the moments of doubt she had been through in the past six months, it was Monique's hatred that had made her determined to carry on. When the readings were sterile and the discussions childish, it was the thought of Monique being left to boast of how she had been right all along that kept Helen coming.

She climbed past André's sharp feet into the corner where Gérard had been sitting. André was playing with one of the plastic carnations, bending it backwards and forwards between his bony fingers. He didn't even bother to look up at her.

"Hullo, Andy," she said in English to tease him.

"Bonjour," he grunted, turning his head away. He refused to speak English any longer, even though his French still wasn't very good. Actually, he was the only one whose real name Helen could be sure of, because his family, the Goldmans, lived up in Westmount near her mother. Three years ago, when he returned disillusioned from Israel after the Yom Kippur war, he'd disowned them and changed his name from Andrew to André. Now he sat with his long thin arms pulling his long thin legs up into his chest, as if he wanted to make himself as compact as possible. His black hair was cropped close to his skull so that the forehead seemed enormous.

Roger came in from talking on the phone in the other room. *"Merde!* What are you doing now?" he asked Gérard.

"J-just waiting for the coffee."

"Come on. Let's get started."

"It's almost through." Gérard rattled the filtre.

Monique, who looked on herself as Roger's deputy, said: "André still thinks we ought to be joining up with the F.L.Q."

"Tabernac!" Roger swore softly. "We've been through all that before."

"Yeah, but the line we've been taking is out of date." André sniffed the flower noisily. "The situation's changed completely. Can't you even feel it? The volcano's heating up." He giggled. "Shit, if we're not careful, we'll be talking so goddamn much we won't even hear it when it explodes." He stared insistently at each of them, and each in turn looked away.

Roger never let himself get angry. "André, listen," he tried to explain, pressing his fingertips together. "Okay, the situation's changing. There's nothing new about that. It's changing all the time. But that doesn't change the F.L.Q. The F.L.Q. is not a revolutionary party and never will be. They're a bunch of bourgeois adventurists. Bombs in mailboxes, even a few dead pigs, Jesus Christ, that's not going to make a revolution."

André leaned across the table, pointing his finger. "It's not just mailboxes anymore," he shouted.

Roger glanced down at his own fingers. "Objectively, the conditions for a proletarian revolution don't yet exist. We're still in the preparatory stages."

Gérard put a mug of strong black coffee in front of Helen and smiled at her nervously. "I'm not sure about th-that," he said.

Helen looked up at him encouragingly. Gérard didn't often speak at their meetings. He had long wavy hair that always seemed to be bothering him, and his voice, like his body, was soft and hesitant. For a long time he had written endless surrealist poems—*"une poésie infinie"*—full of objects that faded organically into each other. It was published under several different names. Then he met Monique and became her lover. Why, Helen could never understand, because Monique bullied him, as she tried to bully everyone, mercilessly. Now his poetry was harsh and impersonal, full of struggle and contradiction. "Not just the image, the just image," was the slogan he had painted on the wall of his room. Helen had never had a chance to be alone with him, to talk about how his ideas might be linked to what she was doing in her paintings. But a link of some sort was there; she felt close to him in a way she didn't feel with any of the others.

Monique glared at him. "What do you mean, you're not sure?" she asked disdainfully. Then, as he opened his mouth to explain, she interrupted him. "Fuck, can't you sit down like the rest of us?"

"Sorry," Gérard mumbled. He pressed the edge of the table between his fingers, his knuckles were white. "The people of Québec are turned off by the old language. It's a language of passivity." He spoke slowly, struggling to control his words. "The priests tell them: Be patient, endure your suffering, the meek shall inherit the earth; after you're dead, the Kingdom of Heaven awaits you. And the bosses tell them: Be patient, work hard, you'll get a gold watch to make up for the emphysema. And what do we tell them?" He blinked through his thick hexagonal glasses. "We tell them: Be patient, objectively, the conditions for a proletarian revolution don't yet exist. We tell them to be patient?" His face twisted with outrage. "That's an insult, Roger, an insult to their suffering and their anger. They want a language of the present. A language of change, of action now. And if we don't give it to them, the F.L.Q. will."

"That's bullshit," Monique said. The whites of her eyes shone.

Helen smiled and Monique saw her smiling. "This isn't one of your fucking dinner parties," she yelled.

"That's Chairman Mao," Helen said.

"What d'you mean?"

" 'The revolution is not a dinner party.' It's Mao Tse-tung, isn't it? His *Investigation of the Peasant Movement in Hunan?"*

Thwarted, Monique turned her fury back on Gérard. "I don't know how *you* can be so fucking irresponsible. If you change your line all the time, nobody knows where they are."

Roger tried, as he always did, to cool them down. "No, in one sense, Gérard is right." Monique scratched her stomach. "If all we're doing is telling the people to hang around and be patient, then we're no better than the priests. But that's not what we're telling them, Gérard. Hell, you know that. What we're saying is, certain objective changes have got to be brought about, in ourselves and in this society, so that the revolution can become possible. We don't just hurl ourselves into the void; we build it, the revolution, piece by piece." With his hands, he sketched the blocks on the table. "So that it's solid, so that it can't be twisted into some cosy little racist backwater, right? Terrorism is just a gesture of romantic despair."

Gérard nodded and pushed the glasses back on his nose. Maybe he could be talked into silence, but not André. He got up and began to bump into things. Helen felt the room getting smaller. "Talk, talk, talk, talk, talk," he said in a strained, scornful voice. He held the plastic flowers over the hot ring on the stove that Gérard had forgotten to turn off. "Can't you see what's happening, any of you? This is a war, you don't fight wars with words. Québec is full of guilty people, on the left as well as on the right." He looked at them threateningly, as the petals, without his noticing, began to melt. "Now is the time to stamp them out. They're vermin. When the rest see what we're doing, they'll follow. They'll follow."

A leaf fell on the stove and flared. "Look at the mess you're making," Monique screamed and tried to wrestle the flower away from André. But he clung on to it till a piece of burning plastic stuck to his hand. He howled and let go.

"There's no way terrorism can be justified," Monique claimed triumphantly, brandishing the stalk.

"But that's not true," said Helen, and they all looked at her in surprise. "Doesn't anyone remember Trotsky's open letter to

Kautsky?" Nobody did. "We read it in . . . in June." She got out her notebook and they watched as she thumbed through it. "Here it is, 1920: 'The revolution logically does not demand terrorism. But the revolution does require of the revolutionary class that it should attain its end by all methods at its disposal—if necessary, by an armed rising; if required, by terrorism.' " She closed the notebook and looked up at them. "That's clear enough, isn't it? The option is there. We may not want to act on it. But we can."

"We must," André insisted.

The room was absolutely still. They heard the rings on the stove pinging. Then the fridge came on with a noise that startled them. Roger and Monique looked at each other. "Okay," Roger said quietly. "Let's go back over our position and analyze it again."

The argument went on all afternoon and, of course, reached no conclusion, beyond Roger promising to raise their initiative with the organizing committee. Helen took very little part in it, in any case, after her intervention. She was shocked at what she had found herself saying. She had nothing in common with André, he appalled her. She had wanted to make a theoretical point, a matter of factual accuracy, but it had become a fulcrum in the argument. How could she find herself justifying terrorism, even the possibility of terrorism, when the least violence filled her with horror? The image of Roger's father had stunned her: the body like an oozing garbage bag beside the railroad track, the mangled legs of his pants, blood steaming in the snow. But wasn't that the point? Wasn't that terrorism also, the terrorism of the system? And the worker who fell through the ice creating Peter's vagina, wasn't that the terrorism of the system? The faithful who crawled up the great hill to St. Joseph's, their knees bruised and bleeding? The thorns they adored?

When the meeting was over, Roger walked with Helen to the door. "Till next week," he said. The sky was blue again, but the grey paint on the handrail was still wet. "Helen?" She looked round at him, there were white hairs in the black beard, especially at the back of his chin. "You were right to raise the letter to Kautsky." He smiled. "But we have to learn to work together, too, eh?"

"Where next week?"

He told her the address.

I hammer on Claire's door until I hear her fumbling with the latch.

"What the fuck," she says, rubbing her eyes. "It's only half past ten."

"It's incredible," I say. "That brown painting I've been doing, eh—the one you thought was dull? All the images I painted out, they're still there. You can see their outlines coming back up to the surface again."

"Yeah," she says heavily and stumbles through to the kitchen. I go with her and grind some coffee while she clutches herself and groans.

Oh, Claire, forgive me, I'm so full of my own stupid excitement, I don't even see how awful you look. You burp and shake.

"It's as though the whole thing's alive," I say. "When I touch it, it feels like elastic."

You reach out your arms to me in what I take to be pleasure. And then you break down and cry. I look at you in astonishment: Claire, everyone's comforter, everyone's pillow.

"I'm fucking pregnant," you say.

Later, as we sit with the quilt pulled round us, drinking the last of the Scotch, I say, knowing that perhaps I shouldn't, but not being able to prevent these questions: "Do you know who—?"

You laugh bitterly. "Shit, no. Half the men in the world don't have fucking names. The other half don't have any balls."

But later again, you say: "I'm glad you came, Helen, I don't know if I should say this, but I think, well, I don't know, but last night when I couldn't sleep, I was trying to count and I think, oh shit, I'm lousy at math, right? Well, look, I'm sorry. It was Jean-Claude." You look at me questioningly. "Fuck, I've probably got it all wrong; it doesn't matter, does it?" You kiss me deeply on the mouth. "Only one thing we can be sure of: it ain't Akiyo." Drunk, we giggle together.

Chapter Two

Helena

I melt into the past.

For everybody else I might as well be dead. They have lived so long with my death they are surprised, even a little irritated, to find me still alive. It is only I for whom I am not dead.

My daughter says to me: "But listen, Maman, you live too much in the past. It's not healthy. You should take an interest in what's happening around you." She says it, as she says everything to me—with a note of triumph in her voice, as though she were talking to a slightly retarded child. She comes regularly, twice a week, and sits with me for half an hour, never looking at her watch, never staying a moment longer. God knows, I have never given her any reason to love me, and she holds that against me, as she should, because her conscience tells her she ought to love her mother.

"But that's not true," I protest, hearing an edge of senile hysteria cracking my voice. "I read the papers. I follow things very carefully, Hélène. I know what's happening to Princess Ann and the Pope, or . . . or Elizabeth Taylor." I say the first names that come to my mind, pointing at the piles of magazines.

She laughs at me: "Be serious, Maman. That's tittle tattle. It's for bored housewives."

She comes and fixes my hair. So gently.

But it's not true what she says, I insist to myself. I don't live in the past as an escape. It's a way of making sure I'm all right. I wish I could make her understand that. My granddaughter Helen, who loves me more and comes to visit me less often, says: "Mamie, you have the most incredible memory. I wish I could remember one tenth as much as you do." But that's not the point, either. The past is a discipline to me, a test. I go over it again and again—all the details, all the names—because if I can get it right, keep it all in order, I shall know I haven't lost my mind.

There are no winters in my memory until they forced me to come to this godforsaken country. Since then, it is all winter, damp snow and their icy sidewalks they never bother to clear, as if only their wretched cars matter.

In my memory it seems always to be the two months after Lent, spring with the scent of blossom everywhere.

There are other times of the year, too, of course: Christmas and the feast of the Purification of the Virgin; the Nativity of John the Baptist in June and the great public feasts and dances of August. But those are only moments and, after lighting on them, my memory circles again and returns to Easter, the true beginning of the year, such a great joy after the harsh winds of February, the abstinence of Lent.

All day on Easter Sunday my sisters and I prepare for midnight mass, pressing our dresses, looking in mirrors, brushing a deep blue sheen into our hennaed hair. And then at night we ride in two carriages to the church—there are ten of us after all, including my mother and father, my unmarriageable aunt, my four sisters and two brothers. Being his favourite, I ride always on my father's knee.

In the churchyard we stand under a huge tree and hear the gospel read, and when that is finished, there's a great shout from the congregation: "Christ is risen!" Gongs are banged and fire-crackers explode everywhere. I cringe into my father's astrakhan coat and feel his arm around my shoulders. Later, inside the black church, the priest holds up his consecrated candle and calls out, "Come and receive the light." Tapers are lit from his candle and passed back from hand to hand to everyone so that little by little the whole church comes to life. The golden icons blaze; wild shadows dance on the roof.

The carriages have been sent away, so we walk back through the dark streets calling "Christ is risen" to our friends. I hunch over my candle trying to get it home without it blowing out. Then I shall be sure to have good luck for the rest of the year. Once, my younger brother, Sava, when his had gone out because he was running around so much, waved his sleeve above mine and put it out, too. I would have been seven or eight at the time. I cried and my father slapped him and he cried also.

From then on, it is lamb, roast lamb on a spit and lucky red eggs, and in the next month flowers blossoming everywhere. Blue irises and the bright yellow dog iris in the swampy places where the streams flow into the harbour, orchids and prickly pear and wallflowers, the spring asphodel with its branching spikes of white leaping out among the grey olive groves. There's the bleating of sheep and lambs as the shepherds take them back up into the mountains. Golden marigolds fill the fields and gorse bursts out on the hillsides.

When I was older, all the most handsome boys in the town would make wreaths of flowers and hang them on our gates on May Day, trying to outdo each other for our attention, mine most of all. And soon the Judas trees were blossoming, great splashes of magenta stippling the countryside, and the wild thyme filling the air with sweetness—I can smell it still—till my mouth waters.

Clematis climbed the back wall of our house, covering it with gaping white flowers—swallow flowers we used to call them because they appeared just at the time the swallows returned to our eaves.

When I was very small, I knocked down one of their nests with a broom.

"Don't do that, you silly girl," my aunt cries. "You'll get freckles."

September 4. A bad day. Heartburn, and that damned Haitian maid, pitch-black, peering in at me all the time and casting her curses.

I was my father's favourite. He took me everywhere with him, so that I missed school often. "She'll learn more with me," he argued when the schoolmaster dared to criticize him.

In his office, full of heavy oriental furniture and thick carpets, elaborate models of boats in glass cases, he had a special chair for me, covered in brocade, next to his desk. I would sit there, trying to keep as still as possible, a china doll in my arm, while he listened to the reports of his captains. From time to time, he would stop and ask me what I thought he should do. I would reply with some nonsense, and he would roar with laughter. But once, I remember—or rather, I don't remember; I have been told, oh, so many times—he asked me about a ship that was due to call at Haiphong for a cargo of rubber, and I said solemnly: "Please, Papa, you mustn't send it to Haiphong." Why I said it, I have no idea; I had no idea, even, where Haiphong was. He took no notice of me at the time, of course, but two months later, the ship was caught in a typhoon in the South China Sea and smashed against a reef off the Annamese coast. From then on my father didn't laugh at my remarks; I could see him listening carefully, trying to make sense out of them. He would pat my head and crack pistachios for me and call me "my little oracle." How absurd those tough sailors must have found us, but they never dared to show it.

My father, you see, was the largest shipowner in Greece. Like so many Greek seamen he came from Chios, Homer's island, and had started out with a small, rotten caique carrying figs and raisins and olives from Smyrna or Edremit to Athens. But he had chosen his cargoes shrewdly, he had had good fortune, ranging further and further afield till there were freighters with our flag—the sphinx of Chios—in every corner of the world. I played with the pins in the map that marked their positions.

Why was I his favourite? I never even thought to ask, it seemed so natural. I was the youngest of his five daughters, the prettiest, everyone said; certainly the most self-centred. I think I was just a doll, a plaything for him at first, but he was superstitious, and slowly he convinced himself that he needed me. Without me, his luck would slip away.

He was old enough to be my grandfather—sixty-one when I was born—but he never seemed old till after he was eighty; a man full of fire and an enormous glutton. He dressed in the most expensive suits, but never managed to look elegant like the Lebanese spice merchants in the bar at the Cercle Européen. He was too muscular, with large buttocks and a short neck, grey curly hair that blew wild in the wind—the despair of my fashionable mother—and skin that felt and smelled like rope.

He was a figure of importance in the city—third only to the Turkish governor and the Orthodox archbishop. In a sense, he had saved the city. For years the river Gediz—the Hermus of ancient times—had pumped mud into the harbour north of Smyrna and soon nothing more than a fishing boat would have been able to enter it. Traders were beginning to look for other ports; there were speculators who wanted to modernize Ayvalik, even Çesme, stuck right out on its peninsula away from everything. But in 1886, three years after I was born, my father came up with a grandiose scheme to divert the river, making it flow west to the sea at Foca rather than south. It ought to be easy, he said, because that had been the original course of the Hermus—he had old maps to prove it. Well, when it was done, you can imagine how respected he was; if it hadn't been for him, Smyrna would have ended up like Ephesus and all the other stagnant, silted ports along the Anatolian coast.

He could go anywhere, and he did. But he was never at home for long in the clubs where everybody tried to speak French and discussed Verdi and Scribe and each other's latest affairs. Instead, he would take me down to the coffee shop right on the harbour wall in front of his office. Some days he sat there from morning to night, under the awning, and his people would come to him: farmers and traders and leathery fishermen, clerks with papers for him to sign, ships' officers and little hunchbacked porters, white with flour or black with oil from the quays. He would buy each of them coffee, leaning back in his chair with a big straw hat on his head, talking, asking them questions, listening to their stories and their complaints. The waiters were kept running back and forth all day long, bringing him kebabs from a nearby restaurant which he ate wrapped in pita, the grease running into his moustache and down his chin, or great bowls of spiced, stuffed mussels.

To keep me contented, he would send out to Sukran's in the Turkish bazaar for dishes of strawberries and thick clotted cream or to Abdullah's for his lemon sherbet.

Towards evening he began to drink; not the Greek retsina or ouzo, nor the champagne which was becoming more and more fashionable in Smyrna in those days, but Turkish raki. He drank it clear and neat, the anis cauterizing his tongue, with a large pitcher of water to wash it down. He smoked then, too—the nargile, the waterpipe—and he taught me how to roll the tobacco for it properly. "It's only in Smyrna," he told me, as I watched his thick brown thumbs, "that they do this right. In the rest of Greece or Turkey they make it too dry and it's burnt out in a quarter of an hour. It's got to be damp like this, do you see, tight like a tulip bulb, so the charcoal just smoulders on top of it. There, that's the way, my little Helena; that's one more thing you will do perfectly."

I wonder if they still pack the tobacco for the nargiles like that in Smyrna.

As the sun went down over the harbour, with the lighthouse silhouetted against the purple sky, the waiters ran between the tables clicking their tongs and bringing fresh charcoal. There was always a crowd around my father, and I was always next to him. They listened as he began—not drunkenly, though he never did it sober—to recite Homer. He had had no education, other than what he had picked up on his own, and he couldn't read the original, but when he was a child an old man in Pirgi had taught him the words and he had never forgotten them. For me, he would recite passages about Hector and Achilles and Helen. They made me cry and, as his friends laughed and applauded, I would blush. But his own hero was Odysseus and he would have gone on forever with his stories.

When it was night, my aunt would send my younger brother to bring us home. Later, my older brother, Costa, would be sent too, and still we sat there in the darkness with Homer's rhythms live around us, the smell of charcoal and fat lamb, the water lapping against the harbour wall.

I will not go out and sit in the sun in the garden.

The matron came and tried to persuade me. "It will be good for you to get some sun before the winter," she said in her wheedling voice.

And then the nurses came, too. I thought they were going to carry me out, but I was ready to fight them and they saw it.

It isn't the sun that they have here. They don't know what the sun is. There's nothing sharp, nothing pure about it. It's just a warm, wet haze, and the stink of motorcars everywhere.

And besides, the garden is full of old people.

Today, I told my granddaughter Helen about the matron and the nurses.

"Do they want me to be burnt up and shrivelled like an old fig?" I ask her.

She laughs. She's a good girl; like me, beautiful, though not as slim as I was. She eats the wrong things and wears the wrong clothes. She should eat more lemons, they clarify the skin.

"The sun is bad for the skin," I explain to her. "You shouldn't go out in it so much. It gives you cancer."

My aunt used to tie a red ribbon round our wrists to prevent us from getting sunburn.

And Helen's daughter, Ann! I cannot say *my* great-granddaughter; she's too far away from me to be anything of mine. I don't say that unkindly; on the contrary, I like her, she's full of feeling. But she's as black as a peasant from her swimming and tennis and sunbathing up at the cottage, and so strong I think I'm going to be crushed when she hugs me.

She's too big, built like a man. The next time they come—and I hope it's soon—I must remember to tell Helen she should feed Ann less.

My father's name—I forgot to tell you—was Adamantos.

The Turks in Smyrna were our masters, but they were also our slaves.

My father had been brought up with terrible stories of the massacre on Chios the year he was born. The people of Chios had taken very little part in the revolution of 1821, but the Turks, nevertheless, when they reoccupied the island the next year, killed at least 25,000 out of the population of 120,000 and sold another 35,000 citizens as slaves. All the women and children hid in caves and empty cisterns in the mountains, and it was there, near the monastery of Nea Moni, that my father was born on the same day that soldiers broke into the great Byzantine chapel and raped the nuns and cut off the head of the Virgin.

His father, a fisherman, was one of seventeen men under the command of the famous hero, Kanaris, who in revenge attached a fireboat to the flagship of the Turkish admiral while the Turks were celebrating Ramadan. The fire reached the powder stores before anyone noticed, they were all so drunk, and the ship sank without any survivors.

I remember how proudly my grandfather, when he was ancient and I was very tiny, would take us to see the statue of Kanaris in the park in Chios and then to the tomb of the Turkish admiral in the fortress. Somebody had translated the Turkish inscription for him, and he would recite it with great glee in his high-pitched voice:

> "Here lies the Turkish hero, Ali Pasha, commander of the navy, a lion of bravery on the battlefield, who gave his life for his religion and his country. His ships were anchored before Chios when a filthy Greek treacherously blew up his ship and Ali Pasha delivered his spirit to destiny."

My grandfather made us all spit in turn on the grave.

So you would expect my father to hate the Turks, but he did not. Most of them he despised and some he distrusted, but there were a few who were good businessmen, and those he accepted. He would do business, he boasted, with any man who kept his word. I remember him quarrelling with other Greeks over it.

He talked politely to the Turkish governor, Kiazim, when they met on the terrace of the Hotel Nain, and for a brief moment they had closer dealings when the governor fell wildly in love with a Greek boy who happened to be the son of one of my father's cousins. My father tried to speak to him about it—Kiazim Pasha, he said, was normally a reasonable enough man—but in the end he had to smuggle the boy out to Athens on one of his ships. Within a year, the boy was living with an English clergyman, anyway.

Most of the Turks were poor. They came into the city from their stony villages in the mountains and stood about on the corners gawking at the tramcars and the dazzling lights. Their fortunes had turned down as ours had swung up. They didn't understand what was happening to their country, why it was falling apart, why the Greeks whom they had ruled for so long were suddenly so prosperous, so much in control. It made them sullen, unreliable. We allowed them to work for us, but not close at hand, not in our houses or our offices. On the docks, in the factories, on the new railway line—labourers, you understand.

"Dirty Turks!" I used to yell at them when I was a child, and run. I had nightmares about them catching me and throwing me in the harbour.

When they attacked lonely Greek villages they didn't stop at killing the men and raping the women; they ate the children. You laugh, you think I'm a senile old woman, full of gossip. But it was true, I tell you. Everyone knew about it.

So it was impossible to think of having a Turk as a friend. They were Asiatics, uncivilized, heathen. That was why it was so unforgivable when my husband ended up taking their side.

And yet I did have one friend, Safiye.

I don't want to talk about her.

Perhaps she was the closest friend I had, the only woman I ever loved?

Yes, but I have put her out of my mind. It upsets me to think about her.

She was beautiful, not as I was, but strong, determined to take what she wanted. She did nothing against me personally. Yet I hate her, hate her. She stole something from me and I don't even know what it was.

Forget her! She will have no part in my memories.

One day, when I was a girl of fifteen, I was walking on the promenade and I saw a Turkish boy about my own age, sitting on the seawall, fishing with a line. His legs were dangling over the wall and his back was to me. What was it that made me watch him? His body? That makes it sound disgusting, physical. But I hid behind the trunk of a palm tree and followed every move he made for at least an hour, the ripple of light on his shoulders and his back as he threw the line out again and again, catching sardines. He wasn't muscular, but shiny and smooth. And I thought then, though there was nothing I, a woman, could do about it: How sad they should be different from us!

September 14. The worst day, this. Forty-eight years now, and still there is horror. Smyrna in flames, but not a fire, nothing so small as a fire—this is an inferno, the whole city erupting.

The Turks' doing, though they tried to blame the Armenians.

The end of my world. In one day I became what I am now.

The matron has stolen my toothbrush. I have proof.

The story slips away from me. I must hold on to it.

But how? I am too old. I am in the wrong place, this awful house on the Rue Bernard, grey and stinking of rot and antiseptic, surrounded by people who wait for me to die. No love. I am a body, to be taken care of, not cared for, cared about. Why should they want to hear my story, these witches with cold fingers? If I was somewhere else—Athens, Firenza, Cannes—with the sun, the real sun, and a shaded patio full of vines and bougainvillaea. But no, it would be the same thing there. I can't escape them, they would be there, too.

I am crying. They look in and see me and I hear them muttering in the corridor. They shake their heads, senile old woman. But I have a right to weep, don't I? It is not for myself, you must understand, but for all those who are dead, my family, my people, the dead city, that I weep.

My daughter never cries. She is proud of it, she thinks it is her strength, but I know it's her weakness, too, and that I am to blame.

I will tell you what I cry for.

I cry for Smyrna, the city that is dead. A new city stands there now, a Turkish city, Izmir, but it can never be the same. I wouldn't even want to go there. My granddaughter and her husband stopped there for a few hours on a cruise and sent me a postcard. "You would love it here," she wrote. "We think of you and wish you could be with us." It was kind of her to say so, but she was wrong. In the photograph, I can still make out the curve of the bay, but it's lined now with cheap apartment buildings—like Florida or the Costa Brava. I know what they must be like inside: mean rooms and low ceilings, rough white-washed walls and bathroom tiles on the floors, varnished doors and rust running from the window frames six months after they're built.

That is not how it was.

The house we lived in was a hundred yards from the sea, sheltered by plane and palm trees from the northeast wind. The outside was decorated with painted tiles and moulded plaster and the entrance was the finest marble from Lagada. Inside there was coolness and space, ceiling fans turning gently, deep balconies with the shutters closed in the daytime. Vines and climbing roses grew over the terrace and the verandahs, and in the back court-yard there was a small pavillion where we could rest in the afternoon.

Mostly, we preferred the upstairs sitting room which projected out over the street. You could see everything that happened in both directions from up there. My sisters and I would sit or sprawl on cushions, talking, reading the latest novels from France, doing embroidery, and when a street vendor came round selling lokum—Turkish delight—or pistachios, we had a small rattan basket hanging from the window to let down.

Always there was music. We sang Greek folk songs, or arias from Italian operettas, and each of us played the piano. And at night our suitors would play their lutes in the street below while we pretended not to notice, till it got too late and my father chased them.

It was the finest city in the world to live in, there can be no doubt of that. As cosmopolitan as Paris and as prosperous as London, the essence of the Mediterranean but with Asia all around it. Why, we used to sneer at the Athenians as the dullest provincials. The way we lived shocked them.

The promenade along the harbour in the coolness of the evening was different from anything else in Greece. In all the other towns it was staid and demure, so slow you might as well have been at a funeral. And you daren't be caught more than glancing at a boy. But in Smyrna there was always a touch of madness in the air as we strolled back and forth along the edge of the bay, calling openly to each other, teasing and challenging. The harbour brought the whole world into the heart of the city and there were sailors everywhere. The old men sat in their teahouses and coffee shops and watched suspiciously as we all went by. Poor countrywomen in veils and baggy pants squatted with babies in their arms on the harbour wall. Men in the lighted taverns drank and played backgammon and danced. The fires of the food vendors glowed and the organ-grinders churned out their noise. Everyone ate, whether it was freshly-roasted nuts or kebabs or peeled cucumbers. Boys let off firecrackers and played their drums, and men held their girl friends' hands quite freely, regardless of what the neighbours might say. When I was older, we would hire a horse-drawn carriage and have it race up and down through the milling crowd, shouting and laughing and singing. The sky was stained with the last of the sunset above the ring of mountains; the smell of the sea filled the air with possibilities.

I didn't like my mother, though I treated her with more respect than she deserved.

She was Alexandrian, and not as beautiful as she thought she was. She came from a well-to-do family, and my father must have married her, I think, as proof of his success. She had borne him plenty of children, so the marriage was deemed satisfactory, but I never saw the least sign of affection between them. The household was run by my father's sister and the servants, so there was time for her to please herself. In the morning, her music teacher would come to give her singing lessons and the hairdresser to do her hair. In the afternoon she played bridge with her friends or took tea with the gigolos on the terrace at the Sporting Club. And at night? Everyone knew about that, except my father. I don't know how he could not have known, but his life was so much apart from hers, and then perhaps in the end he didn't care.

She had an angry face and long dark brown hair that she was very proud of, brushing it all the time, though it lacked lustre. Her nose was too narrow and pointed with a slight hook in it, and by the time I was old enough to remember what I saw of her, there were lines at the corners of her mouth and vertical wrinkles in her neck that she tried to hide with thick powder. She wore the most expensive dresses she could find, but her body underneath was scrawny, apart from her disproportionately large, firm breasts.

She starved herself to stay thin. My aunt told us she had swallowed tapeworms deliberately, though I don't know if that was true.

She always distrusted me because I was so close to my father and I learned even less from her than my sisters did. The only advice she gave me was: "Never let your husband get all he wants. That way he'll stay interested." It was ruinous, and I despise myself for having listened to her.

There was a silk store in the bazaar I used to go to. It was run by an old Turk from Crete who had lived with Greeks for so long he was hardly Turkish anymore. He was small, with bandy legs and a very deep chest, and as lecherous as a goat. I hated the way his eyes rested on my neck and his fingers that poked into me when he held up a bolt of silk against my body. I wouldn't have gone to him if he hadn't had the most beautiful silk in Smyrna.

He had wives you never saw, but I could always feel them peering at me through the curtains. One afternoon—I must have been seventeen—I went to his store and he wasn't there, though the door was open. I stood and waited and parted the curtains, but there was no sign of anyone. And then, from the loft above, I heard the sound of bumping and grunting. At first, I thought he must be moving a heavy bale, but soon, though I was still a virgin, I realized what it was. There were two noises: his gasps and wheezes, and a woman who made little birdlike noises that grew deeper and louder until at the end she let out a hoarse guttural squawk.

Not wanting to be found there, I ran and sat at a café across the lane. I was shaking and drank some fresh orange juice to calm myself.

Ten minutes later, my fifty-year-old mother emerged from the silk store and hurried off up the street with a package under her arm. Her cheeks were a lovely glowing red that makeup never gave them, and she looked younger than I had ever seen her before.

I hope his wives were watching.

September 19. I remember the excitement when the house of the Virgin Mary, the house in which she was said to have died, was discovered in the mountains above Ephesus, fifty miles from Smyrna.

Without any sense of incongruity, my mother was a devout Roman Catholic, with her holy pictures and her elegant porcelain crucifix. She despised the rest of us for our Orthodox superstitions, but did little to try to convert us, except for Sava, her favourite. Indeed, he was the only one of us she seemed to care for, and she would drag him with her to mass when she fancied going.

I have never been obsessed with religion, unlike the old women around here, who go into a faint and think they're dying whenever the priest is out of their sight. Of course I believe in God, it would be senseless not to. But my religion was always part of my childhood, my family, and when the family fell apart, there were only fragments of my faith left. For the years I lived in France I followed the Catholic faith and didn't seem to suffer any loss, but now in age I return to the Orthodox ways. To be honest, I'm not sure it matters. When you're as old as I am, it's as though you outgrow such needs. The ecstasy is gone, and much of the consolation. Only the fear remains.

Well, I will not be afraid. And if I go to the Orthodox services from time to time, it's not out of fear, but because that's what I was in the beginning.

But oh, that summer, the summer of the Virgin, was a joyful one in Smyrna. Pilgrims came from all over the world, and even the Turkish shops sold Christian souvenirs. Two young girls claimed to have had visions, though these were never confirmed.

One Sunday in July, we all went out there on the new railway to Selchuk. There were crowds everywhere, at the station, in all the carriages. It was desperately hot and within five minutes my nostrils were clogged with dust and smoke and the smell of sweat. But it didn't matter; there was a carnival feeling in the air, with people waving to each other, women gossiping, men conferring, children screaming. Musicians played and shouting vendors pushed along the aisles selling cheap paper parasols and food and rotogravures of the Virgin.

My mother held a vial of rosewater under her nose.

I hung out of the window where the air, despite the soot, was clearer. The fields were all burnt and rows of Moslem women stretched across them, deceptively gay in their many-coloured trousers, scarves wrapped around their heads, ripping weeds out of the stony soil. Three thousand years they had worked these fields, and all they could cultivate was stones. As the train passed, they straightened their backs and stared, but didn't wave.

At Selchuk we hired mules for my parents and my aunt, but the rest of us, fired with enthusiasm, wanted to walk. Halfway up the steep, exposed hillside we were holding on to the bridles, our beautiful taffeta frocks stained with dirt and grease. Our faces were burned by the dust and sweat and glare of the sun, for all our silk parasols and veiled straw hats. But soon the pathway curved in among the pine trees and cypresses, the ground was springy with needles and the air was cool and fragrant.

We came to a clearing full of kneeling pilgrims and my father pushed his way through, pulling me behind him. There was nothing to see. Just a small stone cottage tucked in against the rock, a dirt floor. An altar had been set inside and candles burned, but there was nothing else to show it was a holy place. My mother complained loudly and bitterly and my aunt crossed herself in resignation. But I liked it there. It was so peaceful, in spite of all the people who milled about.

I went and sat beside my older brother, Costa, who was lying with his back against a tree eating grapes. I could talk to him. "Do you really think she lived here?" I asked him.

He shrugged. "The priests say so."

"Yes, but why? She was seventy. Why would she come all the way here, so far from home?"

He handed me some grapes and spat seeds on the ground. "Ephesus was crawling with Christians by that time."

"But up here, Costa. Right up above the city. Why would she cut herself off like that?"

Now that I'm seventeen years older than she was then, I think I understand.

All the way back down the mountain, my mouth sweetened by Costa's grapes, I tried to imagine what Mary's life must have been like. Was it full of grief for her dead son? Or was she caught up in all the hysteria about him? Neither image came to life. All I had was the sense of an old woman who had lived too long, wrapped in shawls against the cold mountain air, huddled over memories she could no longer be sure of.

We came down through the Roman city with its overgrown marble streets, its tangle of fallen pillars and displaced statues, its gigantic theatre that held 24,000 people.

I caught up to Costa and one of his friends peering into a courtyard.

"It was a brothel," the friend whispered, trying not to let me hear. "Three storeys high."

"Bigger than anything in Smyrna," Costa laughed.

The size of the city, its dazzle, depressed me. Later, my husband would explain it to me: "The Romans had no sense of scale, no proportion. They built big so they'd be noticed. And they didn't know how to fit their buildings to the landscape. That's why everything they made is lifeless." He said that when he was excavating the tiny temple of Dionysus at Teos.

Back at the station, suddenly remembering, I tugged my father's arm. "Papa, we haven't seen the temple of Artemis."

He was irritable because my mother was blaming him for the way her mule had farted all the way down the hill. "I'd have thought you'd have seen enough for one day."

"But it was so famous. Please. Even Alexander worshipped there."

Reluctantly, he mopped his brow and went and asked a farmer who pointed back up the dirty street.

"But there's nothing up there. We just came down that road."

The farmer showed us the way.

I didn't want to see the temple out of any reverence for Artemis. On the contrary, she frightened me. She stood for all that I hated, even then. Severe Artemis, goddess of the hunt, who forbade her followers to fall in love, who killed Orion with a scorpion because he dared to touch her. Dark Artemis who murdered Niobe's children and insisted on Agamemnon sacrificing his daughter, Iphigenia, to her. Proud Artemis, who punished Admetus, when he forgot to make offerings to her at his wedding, by filling his bridal chamber with poisonous snakes. Artemis, you make me quake because I know you wish to destroy me.

Imagine my joy, then, to reach her great temple and find nothing there; not even the peace there had been back at the cottage on the mountaintop. Just a few broken columns and a vast rectangular pit in the swampy ground. Mosquitoes, some scraggy chickens and a mangy dog. All you deserve, Artemis, all you'll ever get from me!

"I'm at my wit's end," my daughter says.

She brings a doctor to see me. He tries to be sympathetic, but his eyes keep shifting away.

"Why do you cut up your clothes?" he asks me.

I hug the harsh linen gown around me. "I don't."

"The matron says you tried to cut up all your things with your nail-scissors."

"Not I. It's the black maid. She put a curse on me."

"Why would she do that?" he asks tolerantly.

"The goddess Artemis commanded her."

He looks alarmed—I don't think he knows who Artemis is—and takes my blood pressure to cover up.

"Your heart is strong," he says.

"It has to be."

"Don't you like your clothes?" he asks.

Droll question. "I don't want her wearing them after me."

"Who?"

"The black witch."

My daughter in the doorway is angry with me. She considers it a racist remark.

The branches whip my flesh, but I pass through.

I am exhausted by the chase. Your hounds almost had me that time, Artemis. But I won't submit. I owe you nothing. One son you took from me and I have nothing more you can take. Even if I had a thousand children I would keep them back from you. I spit in your face.

September 26. As I stood this morning hesitating at the entrance to the dining room, Monsieur Prud'homme, the retired pharmacist from Chicoutimi, came up beside me silently.

He is a tall man still, but bent, with soft blue eyes under shaggy brows. He shuffles in bright yellow carpet slippers. For a long moment, he looks at me directly, not a sidelong glance but full in the face. And then, ever so gently, he reaches out and touches my cheek.

"We have missed you," he says.

There are others pushing behind us—they fight like wolves for their food, these old women—so nothing else happens. I go and sit at his table; we don't need to speak. I must tell no one about this.

My back was the finest part of me. I would look at it for hours in the full-length mirror in my room, feeling the softness of a silk scarf around it.

Women worry about their breasts, but they're foolish to bother. It doesn't matter if they're big or small, upturned or heavy like a bag of dough, all a woman has to do is give a man a glimpse of her nipples and she's got him. There's no beauty in that.

I have never seen another back like mine. I don't say that loosely; I mean exactly what I say. I have watched hundreds of women in gowns and bathing suits, I flick through these wretched magazines that are passed on to me, dog-eared, the pages stuck together with marmalade and egg, and none of them, not one, is quite so perfect. It was the way the strength and straightness curved into the soft places of the neck and arms. You think I exaggerate but I could show you still. It hurts me to see how dented it is, how full of holes and yellow folds, but when I hold my head back like this and my shoulders . . . ah!

I could have had any man in Smyrna—Armenians or Greeks or Lebanese, French cavalry officers or English lieutenants. At the balls we went to at the Cercle Européen my card was always filled first. I loved those balls for their elegance and romance, the swirl of silk and men in uniform, the trembling in dark corners of the garden. But I didn't want to get married, to be any one man's.

My sisters all had husbands long before me and it suited them; but I loved the freedom to do as I pleased. My aunt and my mother nagged me endlessly, my aunt most of all, for no man had ever asked her to marry him—which was foolish; ugly and crippled though she was, she would have made a good wife, a far better one than I. It seemed a kind of sacrilege to her that twenty eligible men might beg me to marry them and I should turn them all down. I couldn't explain to her that, while they were lovely to flirt with, living with them would have been a demanding bore.

Besides, my father needed me. Age made no real inroads on him till he was into his eighties, but then, suddenly it hit him. From one day to the next you could see it clutching him more tightly; he became slow, repeated himself, would lapse into silence in the middle of sentences. It was horrible to see in such a man. He wanted me always with him and was furiously jealous. In 1906 he had a stroke which paralyzed him and for the next two years, till he died, I sat beside his bed. When the end came, I felt older than I do now.

But there was another reason for my not marrying. Even now, I don't want to admit it. I think I must have been afraid, I who claim I fear nothing. I was afraid of the dullness of being a wife, of the household things my sisters took to so easily, of childbirth and children. Of living with one of my fine young men and finding we had nothing to say. But more than that, I was afraid of what would be wrenched from me, of my life invaded by somebody else, my body.

Yet when I did marry, perversely I married the strongest man I knew. The bull, they called him, the red bull, some in mockery, others in fear. The only man I've known who was stronger than my father.

I was driven to it. I couldn't go on any longer on my own. At home, my aunt drifted pathetically after her brother; my mother, ugly and ridiculed, shut herself in her room and drank; Costa's wife was filling the house with her brood.

But I married him for love. And I love him still, though he's dead now for twenty years, and for twenty before that, lived—so I hear—with a succession of different women.

It will take some explaining, what passed between us.

He insisted on playing polo. I laugh at it now, but at the time how embarrassing it was. I went to watch him once, but never again. Everyone laughed at him, caught in the middle of all those dashing French and Italian and English officers. He had never been taught to ride; all he had ever ridden before then, he told me, was a pit-pony in the field behind the colliery where he grew up. But now, since the other men in Smyrna played polo, he had to play polo too. He was the wrong shape to start with, short legs and that immense potato of a body, bouncing up and down on the horse's back as if he would fall off at every step. The wrong colour even, all sunburn and curly red hair. He kept on charging up and down, bumping into the other riders, swinging at them with his stick, shouting in his wild accent. I hated the young gentlemen who made a fool of him, and their tittering females even more. Yet he played, a good friend told me, with such determination, spurring his horse till it was covered in lather, that it was because of him his team won. Despite themselves, they were always glad to have him on their side.

I can laugh at the memory now, so many years after, wishing to have him here with me.

But there's a second image, too.

Polo again. I sit in my room with my hair undone. I am happy, exhilarated with my new life. I brush my hair and feel it shifting on my back. And then the door slams open and he stands there filling the doorway. His hair is spiky, his shirt sticks to him with sweat, his riding breeches bulge from his boots and make his body look even broader than it is. He pants. He comes over to me and puts his arms around me, his red palms on my breasts. He won't stop kissing my neck, though I try to pull myself away. He drags me backwards onto the bed and forces my legs apart, ripping open his buttons and grasping my hips like a shepherd boy with a wild ewe. He enjoys my struggling. He doesn't even bother to take off his boots. His spurs.

Chapter Three

Hélène

So Hélène is left to last. That's not how it would always have been. Nor how it should be.

Hélène should be the pivot, the strong centre between myth and motion, the point where history defines itself.

She is at the height of her powers and she finds herself powerless. If she were a man it would be different; that is the most bitter of all her truths. If she were a man she would surely be in control, a director, a minister, president of something between a biscuit company and a country. When you think of the male incompetents who rise so buoyantly to such positions, how much easier it should have been for her. But she was a woman, and to be a woman, in her generation, in her culture, from her class, meant—with a few exceptions and sadly she isn't one of them, though she is exceptional—that you had to learn to act deviously, through others, not directly. You proved your devotion by becoming a nun or a nurse, preferably both; but if you wanted power, you chose a man and moulded him to your own ends.

For a while, it worked well for her, and if we had caught her five years ago, you might have thought her fulfilled. But now she is a widow and once you're a widow, if you've played that game, the game, sweetheart, is over. Count them, all those widows of powerful men, men they have made powerful, sitting in the bar drunk at midday on their cruise ships, squabbling late at night in the corridors over who gets the Filipino cabin boy first. A nightmare; and Hélène has far too much integrity to descend into it. Bad enough to see it happening to friends.

So she sits and watches and tries to tell the truth. Caught between her mother's romance and her daughter's confusion, she tries to protect herself with the truth. Noble task, but the truth without love—and how is she to love?—withers.

"My mother never cries," Helen had said. And Helena, too: "My daughter never cries." Oh, how terrible, this woman who never cries, how cold, how heartless, how bitter she must be. Well, perhaps she is, but tell me this: if you had been brought up by a mother who, as a chic society lady in her forties, pinched you a dozen times a day for no reason other than her own insecurity; if you had had your toenails ripped out one by one by a dedicated boy who peered at you inquisitively through thick-lensed glasses; if you had lived with a man whom you respected and who respected you and had built something together and then one morning woke to find him dead of a heart attack in the bathroom, his head jammed between the toilet bowl and the wall, would you cry because some memory made you sad?

Hélène sits by herself.

The couple near the piano might be possible. She will watch them.

The waiter brings her whisky in a crystal glass, malt, Talisker, with just a touch of Perrier, no ice. She lets it run along her lips and feels its sharpness on her gums.

The man is tall, distinguished, fiftyish. His hair is grey at the temples, gently curling, dark eyes, a ruddy complexion, a thin and scornful mouth. He motions to a waiter for more wine from the ice bucket beside him and swirls it in the long-stemmed glass. The woman, the girl, is much younger, too young for him, Hélène finds herself thinking; his own daughter is older. She is plump, with heavy breasts that shine though the slit in her embroidered dress, short blonde hair and a round face, baby-soft skin and thick lips she never quite closes.

Their lives begin to take shape in Hélène's mind. He must be English; she can see the reddish brogues on his feet without having to crane her neck. He served in the army during the war in North Africa and France and rose to the rank of major. After, he returned to Oxford and finished his degree, then a B. Litt. in history, specializing in the Restoration; it gave some leeway to his suppressed sensuality.

As he says something to the girl, his lips curl, more at one side of his mouth than the other.

He married a conventional Englishwoman and came to Canada to teach at McGill. They had three children, two boys and a daughter, and lived happily in Mount Royal, where they played together in an amateur chamber group. But ten years ago, the marriage ceased to protect him. The female students he taught began to fill his dreams with torment; their easy sexuality touched him with doubt. Rumours went around about him feeling their knees under seminar tables; one claimed to have been pushed into a corner and kissed as she tried to get out of his office; scandals were only just averted by alarmed colleagues. His wife left him and his career was on the verge of collapse until he met this latest girl—Janice, let's call her. Something about her holds him again. She is only twenty, from a firm Methodist middle-class family in Sherbrooke, a virgin when she first went to bed with him. But there's a mixture of piety and passion in her that has freed him from his compulsions; enough tenderness to comfort him for the self-respect he's lost.

But no. Hélène breaks off in anger with herself. She has turned them into stereotypes, sentimental stereotypes. Maurice would never have let her get away with such rubbish.

She tries to start again. It isn't the girl's tenderness that holds the two of them together, their fingers playing on the linen tablecloth. There's a threat in her soft flesh, a mother who has to be obeyed. The man may be much older, but she dominates him completely. See how she interrupts him, a pencilled eyebrow raised, and his face falls. The scorn is in her pouting lips, not his. He's less successful than Hélène took him to be at first. Though he wears his suit well, the cut is cheap; how could she not have noticed? He never recovered from the war in Burma, never adjusted to peacetime, ran through three wretched marriages and dozens of different jobs. Now he works for a driving school in Westmount, his nerves gone and his charms increasingly mechanical as he seduces his female clients. This girl has saved him all right, saved him from the need to be strong. From her rich parents—she will pay for the meal, of course, and will do so openly—she has taken the habit of possession. He will grovel for her afterwards, lick her feet as she stands over his back.

Hélène laughs at herself. What fantasy is this now? The story may be slightly better, but it's still thoroughly predictable, the stereotypes merely reversed. Maurice would never have tolerated it.

But what if the man were a priest?

"Are you ready to order yet, Madame?"

She looks up and sees the waiter hovering over her, trying to catch her eye. The menu is still unopened on the table in front of her. She doesn't need to look at it. "Yes, of course. To start, the *potage Saint Germain*—the caviare doesn't agree with my liver any longer. And then, yes, the kidneys in Armagnac."

He smiles, not too familiarly. He's a pleasant young man with a trace of a Gaspé accent.

"And wine, Madame?"

"Yes . . ."

"I shall send the wine waiter."

So often she sat here with Maurice before he died. Despite his money they ate frugally for the most part. His diet required it after the first attack; some days all they would have for dinner was brown rice and artichokes. But once a week they dined out, always on their own and usually here, the Café de Paris in the Ritz Carlton. Its perfection pleased them both, the waiters who were never obsequious, never forward, the marble and soft mirrors, the cooking of Chef Demers.

She reaches out and takes a large black olive from an ice-filled dish.

And so often, when they came here, they played this game together, making up the most outrageous stories about the people round them. Sometimes she was reduced to whoops of laughter, puzzling the stolid or carefully glamourous couples who happened to be at the next table. Maurice played with such flair, piling incredible details on top of each other, standing back in pleasure as the whole ridiculous structure collapsed. Nobody would have believed it of him. He had the reputation of being so solemn a man of principle that nobody could have understood it was his wit, his esprit, she married him for. At the dullest receptions he would sidle up to her with that familiar mournful expression on his grey, slightly hollow face and only she would see the pursed muscles at the corner of his mouth. He bent towards her and murmured a few words that left her like a giggling schoolgirl. Mayor Drapeau was his favourite target; *"la mère Drapeau,"* he called him. *"La pucelle perpétuelle. C'est pour ça qu'il y a du sang sur les draps de Drapeau?"* Strange bedfellows, mayor and Mafia? There was nothing dazzling in Maurice's humour. Often it was just a schoolboy pun, sometimes simply gross.

It was the contrast, the complete unexpectedness that was wonderful.

Now she tries to play their game on her own. But it's no good. It needs two.

The wine waiter hands her the list. She has known him for fourteen or fifteen years.

"We haven't seen you recently, Madame Grieve." He pronounces her name in two syllables. "I hope you haven't been ill."

"I've been in France. I still have old friends there."

"In what region?"

"This time, mainly in the Languedoc, near Carcassonne."

"Ah, yes, it's like going back into the past, the old city. And then, *le cassoulet.*" He waves his hand loosely up and down. "You don't get *confit d'oie* like that anywhere else."

They smile at each other knowingly. She remembers he once told her he was born in Toulouse.

Well, then, a bordeaux. "The Gruaud Larose '59," she says.

He nods. "A bottle, Madame?"

"Of course." She can't stand half bottles of wine—ugly things. If she's going to drink, she'll drink properly.

Her brother was shot in Carcassonne. When the Germans finally managed to catch him, they tortured him first, learned nothing, then marched him out one drizzly, green morning and stood him against the mediaeval walls and shot him as an example. There's a plaque in the wall there now:

MARC MACLEOD, 1918–43
Fusillé par le Gestapo
le 28 décembre, 1943
Mort pour la France.

Do the tourists who snoop around the old battlements wonder about the resistance hero with the Scots name? Probably they never even notice, though still from time to time a bunch of flowers is left lying on the grass. Cécile says she doesn't know who leaves them: a romantic schoolgirl with a penchant for history, or a nostalgic baker's wife recalling an early love?

Hélène was only just beginning to get to know him, her own brother, in the months before his death.

"You knew him so much better than I did," she said to Cécile this past summer. They sat on the *terrasse* behind the store, shaded from the afternoon sun by a giant fig tree, three middle-aged people who had drunk a little too much. It made Hélène less hard than usual, Cécile more garrulous. Jacques was just as drowsy as he always was on a sunny afternoon.

Cécile didn't mind talking about Marc in front of him, though in the past he was full of jealousy, even after his rival was dead.

"Marc never did a lot of talking, but yes, I knew him." She made patterns on her plate with the spoon. "He was just a boy. I couldn't understand what was wrong with him. Twenty-five, after all, it's not so young, and then . . . well, all the danger, the dying, you'd think, wouldn't you? But no, in bed he was just like a baby." She gurgled at the memory. "You had to do everything for him."

She tried to smooth the apron across her fat thighs. Her arms and breasts and chins bulged and gleamed; her cheeks shone with the wine and the heat. She wore a blue dress with small white spots on it that was too tight for her, and Hélène realized that Cécile had never worn dresses that were anything other than too tight for her, even when she was a young girl. There was a time when she could pedal down the streets of any town in the southwest of France and every eye would follow her.

"It was my mother's fault," Hélène said.

Cécile brushed a strand of implausibly black hair out of her eyes. "He only mentioned her once, but so full of hatred. She gave him a bad time, eh?"

Hélène smiled. "Yes, but not the way you think. She wouldn't let go of him." Helena had taken Marc to bed with her each night her husband was away, which by the time the boy was ten was almost always. She cuddled him as he tried to slip out of her arms and stroked his silky red hair. Hélène remembered the pleading look on Marc's face as the door swung closed between them, her own sense of deprivation standing alone in the dark corridor. Each night she prayed that she could make herself so impossible she'd be sent off to a boarding school.

Jacques suddenly began to snore and Cécile kicked him. He sat up with a start, his teeth half out of his mouth. "Excuse me, Hélène," he mumbled. "We begin early in the morning." He struggled to his feet. "I think I'll take a little nap."

In the war this man was a guide between here and the Spanish frontier, half Basque and headstrong, disappearing for days on end when he was in one of his moods, but always turning up again, as crazy and cunning as ever. Once he talked a German guard into letting him examine the sights on his rifle; then shot him with it.

"The only trouble with bakers is they fall asleep at all the wrong times," Cécile groaned. "Would you like some more tart?" Customers came from all over the region to buy her *tartes aux figues*.

"Enough, Cécile, enough," Hélène laughed, holding her hands out in front of her stomach. "Just some coffee. I'm dropping off, too."

The whole horizon was hazy in the afternoon heat and dust, but in the mornings you could see the blue towers of Carcassonne twenty kilometres away to the east.

"I expect it's ready." Cécile hoisted herself up and waddled into the kitchen. And was this the woman who carried messages and hand grenades from village to village through German roadblocks? Impossible, Hélène thought, and then: Have I changed as much?

"Madame Griève?"

"What—"

"I decanted it for you, Madame." The wine waiter stands with the decanter poised. "There was rather a lot of sediment." He pours some out for her and stands with his grey brush-cut tilted to one side.

She holds the glass up, red and glowing against the light, then sniffs the richness of the grapes mingled with the flinty soil. *"Merci,"* she nods.

Rough fresh yellow wine they were drinking that morning she met Marc in the bar on the square in Carcassonne. It was dangerous for her to be there, so far west; suicidal for him. They touched glasses gently, their eyes searching, and winced at the sourness of the wine. October 1943; a cold raw day with the wind blowing out of the mountains. She clutched the thin coat around her—a patched, man's coat; it helped not to look too fashionable when you bumped into a patrol on a dark night. The old woman who ran the bar was grumbling as she tried to light the sawdust in the stove. Sawdust was all that was left to burn because the Germans had banned any more tree-cutting; they wanted the wood for themselves. Besides, the Maquis were in the forests. *"Sales boches,"* the old woman muttered as a draught blew some of the sawdust up into her eyes.

Marc tilted his shaky rattan chair back on two legs. "So, big sister, you're in the resistance, too."

"That's what you call what you're doing, is it?" she said.

The laughter went out of his face. "Of course."

"Some wouldn't agree."

"Cowards," he said. "They'd rather sit and talk."

She hadn't seen him for five years since he came back from Spain for her wedding, and two before that when he ran away from home. They had never known each other, their mother like a wedge between them, and neither knew how to start. He must hardly recognize her, she thought, with this awful coat, the scarf tied tight round her head, grey threads showing in the hair that did hang loose. Heavy black boots on her feet. The last time she was in a wedding gown, a small bouquet of lily-of-the-valley in her satin fingers, and it was he who was wearing the boots with holes in them. All the way back from the Ebro he'd come to see her get married and before the reception was over he'd quarrelled with her husband and driven her mother to tears.

"I'm sorry," he whispered as he kissed her good-bye on the landing. "I shouldn't have come."

"I'd have been sad if you hadn't," she said. "Are you going back to Spain?"

"No, it's over, *foutu.* They sold us out."

"Who?"

He stood away from her. "Take your pick. Russians, Communists, French, Socialists, the Church, the Trotskyists." He counted them off on his fingers.

She held on to his arm, not wanting him to go. He looked more than ever like their father, who had sent his apologies and a bronze Chinese incense burner, together with a roll of silk for his wife. His red hair stuck out beneath a greasy cloth cap. His jacket was frayed and shapeless.

"Where will you go?"

"Don't worry. I've got friends." He turned and went down two of the wide curving stairs, then stopped. "Hey, big sister. Don't let that new husband of yours turn you into a Fascist." He laughed. "I'd hate to see your head cut off, too." Goatlike, he ran down the rest of the steps three at a time.

"Mère Rosa," he called, banging his glass down on the table, "this isn't wine, it's vinegar. Don't you have anything better?"

She came over from the smoking stove and stood beside him, a little wrinkled woman with her hands on her hips. "What's wrong with it?"

"It's piss. I haven't seen my sister for five years. I can't give her this to drink."

"It's all the Germans left."

"Come on," he winked at her. "Behind one of those loose stones in the cellar . . ."

"Well. For you," she said grudgingly. She went away and came back a couple of minutes later with a dusty bottle of Sauterne. "Is this too sweet for you?"

He put his arm round her. "You know me, Rosa. I've got a sweet tooth."

She pinched his stubbly cheek.

Maybe, Hélène thought; maybe for some he was a hero. But what about the women whose husbands and sons were taken out and shot in reprisal for one of his raids? "A gangster," a Gaullist organizer had called him, not knowing it was her brother. "If the Germans don't get him, we will."

The Sauterne was golden in her glass. It tasted of honey. She leaned towards him, an intense, demanding woman. "Marc, listen to me. What's the point of killing one German if they take ten of our own people in return."

"It depends," he said lightly.

"On what, damn it?" she challenged him.

"On which of ours they get." He faced up to her as he wouldn't have done in the past. "For every one we kill, they kill ten. Right? But for every ten they kill, I get two more who'll fight. Add it up, Hélène. Who wins?"

"Pretty cynical, your arithmetic," she said angrily.

"Do you know how many men I had with me two years ago? Six, maybe seven. And now? Over ninety. In these parts that's as good as an army."

She tapped the table with her finger as she worked it out in her mind. "Four hundred and twenty," she said, nodding.

"Four hundred and twenty what?"

"Four hundred and twenty lives your *private* army cost."

He pushed his chair back and rose. For a moment she thought he was going to leave, but he walked over to the window. A file of schoolchildren passed in their blue smocks. The steel tips on their shoes rang on the cobblestones. The young teacher who was with them glanced in and saw Marc standing there, a short stocky man with bright blue eyes; she looked away hurriedly. He was known everywhere from the Pyrénées to Toulouse; peasants sheltered him while the Germans and the

Milice hunted him down. And yet he came openly into the towns, challenging the enemy, playing with them, disappearing again before they had a chance to corner him. On the other side of the square three men stood gossiping around a farm cart loaded with turnips; beneath the turnips their machine guns were ready.

When he turned back towards Hélène, there was nothing playful in his eyes. He sat down and poured some more wine in both their glasses. He leaned his elbows on the table, his chin on his fists, and looked at her desperately.

"I know the cost, Hélène. These are my people, too; more than they'll ever be yours. We have to do this. We can't just sit around and wait for somebody else. It's a war, damn it. To pretend there's some kind of half-measure, some things we can't do, is . . . well, it's capitulation. I've been fighting for seven years now, remember—since Madrid. It's always the same war and don't think I'm not sick of it. But now we've got the Germans running scared. They can't move about freely any longer. A bunch of farmers and shepherds and they're scared of us, the strongest army in the world. Shit, Hélène, they can't break us now. They can't even catch us."

She held his fist in her hand. The Gaullist had said: "These anarchist groups, they're all the same. They'd rather raid banks or steal tobacco than attack a German outpost."

Hélène shakes her head. The plate of soup has appeared on the table in front of her without her even noticing. Automatically, she takes a spoonful and feels its richness on her tongue; then the crisp crouton.

She peers at the couple by the piano. How boring they seem now, and how contrived it was to try to make them interesting. They drink their coffee and the girl eats a petit four, sliding it in and out between her lips.

Behind Hélène a group of businessmen are enjoying a tax-deductible lunch. She doesn't bother to turn and look, but fragments of their conversation, in a mixture of bad French and bad

English, intrude on her. There must be four, maybe five of them.

"Helmuth wants to go cross-country skiing again this winter."

They all guffaw.

"Son of a bitch, he'll just sink in up to his ass."

"He don't need no skis, just his shoes and some poles, that'd be enough."

"What for? He never got out of the sack last time, not after he made that blonde at the lodge."

"Jesus Christ, what a madman! Did you ever see that shotgun he bought, great big fucking Belgian shotgun, must of weighed a ton and a half? Only Helmuth was big enough to lift the fucker. First time he went out with her he fell over a rock and nearly shot off both his feet: boom, boom: two barrels. Laughed his fucking guts out, goddamn comic."

"I thought Helmuth only used shotguns to jerk off with."

"He tried to tell me it was a German gun, but I said, 'Hell, no, man, look at the stock, it's Belgian,' and he says, 'That's why it's no fucking good.' "

"All German guns have got square barrels."

Hélène shuts out their laughter. That argument she was having with Marc, is it the same one she has now with Helen about the F.L.Q., the bombs, the riots, the plot to kidnap the American consul? But no, the situation's different. Then it was Fascism they were fighting; now . . . what? She no longer knows.

When Cécile came back out onto the *terrasse* with the tray of coffee, Hélène watched her and wondered who it could have been who sold Marc to the Gestapo.

Cécile poured two demitasses and passed one to Hélène. She soaked a lump of sugar in her own coffee and sucked on it. Then, as if she were responding to Hélène's thoughts, she said: "You know, I still wonder who turned him in."

Hélène felt the oily bitterness drawing her gums. "We didn't get coffee like this in the war."

Cécile laughed. "Acorns."

"It could have been anyone," Hélène said.

Cécile nodded.

Yes, it could have been anyone. There was nobody you could be sure of: the Communists, the vengeance of a farmer whose son had been shot, orders from de Gaulle, Jacques, Mère Rosa, even Cécile herself. But no, not Cécile. When Marc was trapped and finally wounded after a gun battle in Mère Rosa's bar on Christmas Eve, he was with Cécile and they had been in bed together just an hour before. The Germans had taken her with them, too. They hadn't tortured her, merely raped her, all five of the interrogators, after they decided she knew nothing. "Whore!" they shouted at her as they flung her into the gutter outside her home.

Less than three months before, when she came into the bar where Marc and Hélène sat arguing, she was just an eighteen-year-old girl who glowed with life. It was cold and damp outside and she wore only a short flowery dress and a darned cardigan, bright yellow rubber boots on her bare feet, but she seemed to bring warmth in with her.

Marc stood up and kissed her. "Cécile, this is my sister, Hélène."

She sat down.

"Would you like some wine?" Hélène asked. She admired Cécile's smooth creamy skin, the black curly hair. Her own beauty was hard and angular.

"No, I'll just have a coffee." But when Mère Rosa brought it to her, she took one sip and her nose wrinkled up. "Acorns," she said. She looked at Hélène more closely. "Nobody would ever guess you were brother and sister."

"Big sister's the right word, eh?" Marc laughed. "When I was a kid I used to think, in two years' time I'll be as big as she is. But I never was. Stand up," he told Hélène. They stood back to back. "You see, she's still six or seven centimetres taller than me, damn it. God knows where she got it from. Our mother's small and Dad's about my height, only even wider, like a barn door. And our uncles are short, aren't they? I guess Maman must have gone to bed with one of the Armenian giants from the circus." His face darkened. "How is the old bitch?"

"Lonely. She misses you."

He stared at the table. "And Dad?" He used the English word. "Has anybody heard from him?"

"There was a message that came through the Red Cross last year. The Japs have got him in a camp in Shanghai."

"Jesus! What is he now? Sixty-five, sixty-six? How'll he stand up to that?" Marc turned to Cécile. "Do you know how many times I've seen my fucking father since I was ten?" He held up four stubby fingers.

Cécile responded the only way she knew. She stroked his thigh.

"Four?" Hélène asked.

"Yeah, four. The last time was in Gibraltar. I was walking up the main street when I saw him coming out of a hotel and climbing into a cab. His back was to me, but you couldn't make a mistake, it couldn't be anybody else: really smart white suit, straw hat, ebony cane. He was with Maman."

"Maman!" Hélène exclaimed.

Marc nodded. "I shouted out to them and he turned around. He was just the same, the same energy, the same—you know—eagerness. He came running down the centre of the road towards me, bumping into people, knocking them over. And she got down from the cab behind him; of course it wasn't her at all. But Hélène, really, just like her; exactly like Maman must have been thirty years ago—small, dark, firm. More eastern even; Dutch Indonesian she turned out to be."

"It's always the same type," Hélène said bitterly.

"I had dinner on the boat with him before it sailed. He gave me a suit," Marc smiled wryly. Their parents had cast a shadow over them.

"Madame."

Hélène looks up.

"Be careful, the plate's extremely hot," the waiter warns.

Steam rises from the rich sauce that smothers the kidneys; she leans over it, sniffing greedily. She smiles: Heavens, I'm getting as bad as those old women in my mother's home, fighting to be the first ones into the dining room. Gingerly she raises a forkful to her lips and blows on it. She tastes the sauce with the tip of her tongue and almost burns herself; the cream and the armagnac blend perfectly. Then, with care, the springy meat.

She has always hated kidneys.

A long time ago—she must have been thirteen—one of her mother's brothers who had come to visit them from Marseilles decided to take Hélène and Marc in hand. "Look at them. No table manners. They're like savages," he complained to Helena.

"They need their father," Helena said.

"I tell you what we'll do then. You'll come to dinner with me, all three of you, next Sunday at La Pyramide. It's the best place in town at the moment. We'll teach these little savages how to behave. Won't we, Hélène?" He stretched across the table and pinched the thin girl's arm. She didn't smile back at him; why should she? He was reputed to be a great gourmet, Uncle Sava, but to her he was just a very fat, greasy little man who stank of perfume. He deceived his wife with every prostitute on the *côte* —or so her mother boasted—and threw a fortune away in the casinos.

Sunday came. The restaurant with its heavily carved chairs and bowing waiters overawed the children. They had too much of their father's boisterousness to be at ease there. The elaborate Egyptian murals made it feel like a tomb. Their uncle ordered everything, discussing the various ingredients with the maître d'hôtel, reminding him to add this, not too much of that. The children had no say, though if they were good, they might be allowed to choose which cake they wanted.

"Merci," Hélène said when there were two large spoonfuls of kidneys on her plate.

"No, no," said Sava, "give her some more." She noticed he

took very little himself, though he tucked the napkin into his jacket and spread it all over his enormous stomach.

By the time she had finished, the kidneys were sticking in her throat.

"Bring some more for *la petite,* she needs to eat," Sava commanded the waiter.

"But I've had enough," Hélène argued.

"It's polite," Helena said.

"But what about Marc? He's had hardly any."

Marc kicked her. "I don't like them."

"Well, neither do I."

"Marc's only eleven," her mother said.

"Well, what about Uncle Sava?"

"He has a bad liver," Helena hissed angrily.

Sava was only satisfied when her plate was piled high again. He watched intently as she chewed each kidney laboriously and swallowed it with a gulp. Mentally, she divided the plate into portions: thirty congealed forkfuls. There, twelve; now for thirteen, her own age, an unlucky time. Her mother laughed in pleasure.

"One has to learn to discipline one's taste," Sava explained.

When she had finished, Hélène was allowed to choose whatever cake she wanted. She pointed to the richest and creamiest. Her stomach heaved.

"I've got to go to the bathroom," she said, getting to her feet.

Helena pulled her back. "Wait till the end of the meal."

Hélène was sick all over the carpet. For the next week her mother slapped her whenever they came within arm's length of each other.

And now Hélène forces herself not only to eat but to enjoy the kidneys out of spite for the memory.

"Maman's still in the same place?" Marc asked. He put his arm round Cécile's shoulders.

Hélène nodded.

"You should see it," Marc explained to Cécile. "She has this enormous apartment right on the Promenade des Anglais. She hates the sea, but she insisted on living just across the street from it. I don't think she even notices it's there. She spends most of her time watching the people go by."

"Is that all she does?"

"There are two German officers billeted with her now," Hélène said.

"How does she like that?"

"She hates them. After all, they were allies of the Turks in the last war, weren't they?"

Marc laughed.

"She got the oldest mattresses out of the cellar as soon as she knew they were coming. Now they complain about their backs all the time."

"She would certainly know how to make their lives a misery," Marc said and for a moment they felt a kind of tenderness for their mother.

"And you, big sister?"

"Me?" She shrugged. "I have a daughter now. She'll be four soon. She's full of joy."

Marc got up and kissed her on the forehead. "What's her name?"

"Hélène too, poor thing. We've got an old farmhouse just outside Saint Jeannet. It's falling down, but it's isolated. That's the important thing."

"What does your Fascist husband think about you working in the resistance?"

"Oh, God, Marc," Hélène put her hand up to her mouth. "I haven't heard from Philippe since May 1940. He was on the Meuse with his tank battalion. The last word I got from him was a letter saying the front was collapsing. The whole of the French command should be court-martialled. They didn't know how to fight a war. They hadn't even committed two-thirds of their tanks; they just gave orders to withdraw all the time, and then it was too late. The letter had been opened, of course. After that there was just a telegram saying he was missing."

She looked round the dingy little bar with its zinc-topped counter, its tarnished mirrors with adverts for Dubonnet and Ricard printed over them. The air was full of woodsmoke that stung her eyes. And still it was cold.

"He wasn't a Fascist," she turned on Marc vehemently. "You got it all wrong. You were just judging him by his family. It wasn't his fault he was a count. Where the hell would you be if you were judged by your stupid family?"

Cécile's eyes flicked between them. Her own people had lived in this region for hundreds of years and never, as far as she knew, been anything more than peasants. For her there was no problem.

Marc was insistent. "Would he have been with you now? Would you even be doing what you're doing if he was alive?"

"Yes," Hélène said strongly and, seeing the doubt in his eyes, added. "I'm sure." Though truly she wasn't. The regular army had been so full of men with a tradition of obedience who feared anarchy more than defeat. How would Philippe, with his useless titles, have adapted to being a rebel? She couldn't really tell. And then, just the fact of being on her own had made her a different person, too.

"Who runs your network?" Marc asked.

"I do."

His eyes narrowed. "How many?" he asked in the gentlest tone.

"Eighteen who're with us all the time. Another hundred and fifty we can draw on. I took it over the last time the Germans broke it up. There was nobody else."

"What kind of work?"

"Escape routes mainly. From Italy and from the north. That's why I'm here. The chain was broken at Montpellier. I've got a dozen airmen hiding out around the Col de Vence just waiting to get to Spain."

"How did you get a permit to come this far?" Cécile asked.

Hélène shrugged. "I don't have one. But I've got a motorbike and a gasoline ration because I work as a district nurse. That lets me move about without too many questions. And one of our aunts—Aliki—is dying of cancer in Marseilles, so that was a good enough cover to come that far. It wasn't till I was in Montpellier that I heard about Marc again. Not by name even, just a description. But it couldn't be anybody else, could it? El Toro Riojo! So I took a chance and came."

Cécile wished she could understand them better, this strange pair who risked their lives to see each other and then squabbled all the time.

Marc took out a half-smoked cigarette and lit it carefully. "Why don't you hold on to your dozen airmen and fight?"

"They're more use back in England. They just get in the way over here. The one thing I do need right now is a good radio operator."

"If we don't build ourselves into fighting units now, when the war's over we'll be back to the same old system. Business as usual," Marc said in English with a mock accent. "All the bankers'll come out of their holes, and the bosses and the landowners."

"But I've told you, Marc, I'm not doing what you're doing. I'm not making a revolution."

He sucked in the last of the tobacco. "Then there's no point in resisting," he said stubbornly. "Without a revolution all your talk about freedom is just a lot of rhetoric. It's not *Liberté, Egalité, Fraternité* you're fighting for. You might as well be on Pétain's side, too: *Travail, Famille, Patrie.*" Work, Family, Motherland—he spat out the slogan the Vichy collaborationist government had painted in place of the old republican words on every town hall in the country.

And what if Marc was right, Hélène wondered as she looked across at Cécile snoozing in a ray of sunlight that pierced between the branches of the fig tree.

"Perhaps Marc was right," she said aloud.

Cécile jumped and looked at Hélène without quite focusing. "I'm sorry. What?"

"That argument I had with Marc in Mère Rosa's bar, remember?"

Cécile shook her head. "I only remember the last night in Mère Rosa's. I wish I didn't. I still dream about it." She squeezed her eyes shut.

"What Marc said was, unless we turned the resistance into a revolution there was no point in fighting. Everything would be the same after the war. And after all these years, it still is, isn't it?"

"Not for Jacques and me," Cécile said, looking around the garden with its climbing flowers, the stuccoed back wall of the house. "We're comfortable now."

"Yes, but for society, Cécile. For women in general, even. Look, who was it who kept the resistance going?"

Cécile stretched and yawned. "You, me, I suppose."

Hélène nodded. "Yes, women, Cécile. It's not our names in the history books, but a lot of men we never saw. In 1940 when the men that were left were sitting on their asses and talking about how the English had let them down, it was the women who had the guts to get things moving again. The million widows of France, the mothers, the sisters. Who fed the Maquis while they were playing at being soldiers? Who carried the messages? Who nursed them and sheltered them and went out and found food for them? You, me, Cécile. Damn it, I cycled seventy kilometres one day because I heard there were some potatoes in Mougins."

Cécile laughed. "Yes, that was the way it was all right."

"And what did we get out of it? Nothing. Nothing's changed."

"Oh, it's not so bad." Cécile pouted and for a moment there was a hint of the eighteen-year-old girl in her face, dimples in her cheeks. "We know how to get what we want, eh."

"But the price," Hélène insisted. "The price we pay for it. . . ."

"Would you like some dessert, Madame?" the waiter asks.

"No, no thank you," she says. "Just coffee. But please tell the chef the kidneys were perfect."

"Thank you, Madame."

She has hardly tasted anything she's eaten. She has sat here at this small table eating mechanically and staring into space. The couple she was watching have gone. And if anybody was watching her, what would they have thought?

"Why, Hélène," says a voice behind her. "All on your own?"

She turns and sees Sally Benson bearing down on her. Bruce stands further off and waves vaguely. He used to be, in a manner of speaking, a friend of Maurice's. The four of them visited each other from time to time—even a weekend at the Bensons' cottage—and Bruce allowed Maurice to bully the semblance of a social conscience into him. But since Maurice's death, Hélène has seen nothing of them.

"I keep on telling Bruce, we must have Hélène over some night." Sally's tired face has been transformed into a carefully lit mask, the wrinkles have been drawn up into her temples, her hair is beautifully styled; only the small, nervous eyes give her away.

"Are you keeping better?" Hélène asks. "I was sorry you were ill."

"Well," Sally laughs, "none of us get any younger, do we?" She brushes an imaginary hair out of her eyes. "How's Helen?"

"She's well, of course," Hélène replies, knowing what's coming next.

"But I heard—I can't remember who—that she and David . . ."

The waiter brings a coffeepot and a plate of petits fours.

"And an *eau-de-vie de framboise,* please," Hélène says.

"Oui, Madame."

"I don't interfere," she says when he has gone.

"But it must be such a worry for you."

"No," says Hélène, "it's not."

Sally looks at her in astonishment. "Well, we really do have to run. But we must, you know, get together . . ."

". . . sometime," says Hélène.

Bruce waves vaguely again from the doorway.

Hélène sips her coffee furiously. For a moment, self-pity drills into the centre of her skull. She knows how dangerous it is for her to give herself over to anger; she knows the danger of becoming dried-up and bitter. But damn, damn, that doesn't make it any easier to bear. This pygmy, Bruce, was Maurice's friend; for a time the closeness of Maurice almost enabled him to grow to normal proportions. But now look at him, soft as a rag doll! Why did one of them have to die and not the other? Why always the best? She presses her fists into the tabletop and every muscle in her neck is rigid. She takes another sip of coffee. Very deliberately, she starts to move the little finger on her right hand; now the other fingers, the thumb, the wrist, the muscles in her forearm; now, the other arm. Relax; it's all a matter of self-control.

"Ah, Cécile," she said, letting her arms dangle in contentment, "if I lived here, I think I could grow old easily."

"It's the air," Cécile said.

"No, my dear, it's your tarts."

Cécile grinned with pleasure. But then: "You wouldn't really be able to settle down here, would you?" Hélène, though she might yearn for peace, would always need disturbance around her.

"No, but I'm not sure I can anywhere else, either. It's not that I'm a discontented person, Cécile. With music, with my plants, I'm happy enough; but it's too passive. I feel I'm wasting myself, and I live in a country, a continent where waste is part of the system." She got up and paced nervously about the *terrasse,* pausing at a large purple azalea—so much energy bursting out of it.

Cécile watched her knowingly. "I'm not sure I could live without a man."

Hélène turned and laughed dryly. "I'll tell you this: It's the only fire that doesn't die down when no fuel is put on it." Cécile's legs were parted and her skirt had ridden up so that Hélène could see a line of white thigh at the top of the dark stockings. She sighed and sat down again.

"But you must meet other men," Cécile said.

"Oh yes, I meet other men all right. All my friends were trying to marry me off again six months after Maurice died. Do you know, I didn't even realize what they were doing at first. I'd be invited to dinner and I'd think, that's nice, they still want to see me for myself. And then I suddenly understood that this empty, nervous apology for a man sitting across from me was meant to be my . . . my date, Cécile!" She snorted. "They were just playing at matchmaking. It was disgusting. You're better off with a banana!"

Cécile laughed raucously at the idea, but Hélène's bitterness upset her. "After your first husband died—what was his name, Philippe?—was it the same thing?"

"No, not at all. I was never even sure he was dead. There was always a chance he'd be in a camp in Germany. Maybe he'd just turn up one day. And then, when that hope ran out, there was the war, and Helen; just surviving was a full-time business. And when I did need someone, well, out of nowhere Maurice appeared."

With a sigh Cécile eased her feet back into her shoes and heaved herself up. She straightened her dress and her hand rested on Hélène's back for a moment. "You must have been praying hard, my dear. For that one to fall on top of you." She chuckled softly and waddled unsteadily towards the kitchen.

Hélène smiled as she stared off into the afternoon haze. She had never once prayed for herself; it was the radio that had brought her Maurice. They had needed a new operator ever since the summer of 1943 when the last one was given away by his girl friend in Antibes. For months they had had to get their messages out through other networks—which was dangerously insecure just as German activity in the area was building up. But then, one morning in January, their call-sign came through on the B.B.C.: *"Périsse l'univers pourvu que je me venge,"* the quotation from Cyrano de Bergerac that an earlier leader, Delvaux, the lawyer, had chosen. "Let the universe perish, provided I have my revenge." Rather melodramatic, Hélène had thought, but poor Delvaux had perished, had thrown himself from a window of the Gestapo headquarters in Nice, and still he hadn't been avenged.

"What do you think it'll be?" old Raphaël, the cobbler, asked as they sat in front of the battered wireless set in the kitchen of Hélène's house. "The machine guns or the radio?"

The adrenaline pumped into them.

"Both," said Michel, whose father had been deported the previous spring.

All afternoon they went from door to door through the narrow streets of the village making sure there would be enough people up on the plateau ready for the drop. "We'll need five for the lights, ten to bury the parachutes, thirty to bring down the canisters; at least fifty," said Hélène. "I'll have the torches, but you make sure there are enough shovels, Pierre; and picks, too, in this weather."

The small, sleepy village was almost empty, except for a few cats and dogs, the babies and the old women, by eight o'clock. As soon as darkness fell—which was later than it used to be because the whole of France was on Berlin time—the alleyways leading out of the village were full of shadows heading for the lower slopes of the Baou. At the bottom of the cliff face they roped themselves together so that no one would get lost, and then they started the difficult climb. Most of them took the slightly easier route through the gulleys to the east, but some of the younger men went up the sheer thousand-foot rock face itself. They knew the footholds and ledges and chimneys as well as they knew their own stone walls. Still, the danger horrified

Hélène, though it was all part of the excitement, the shared exhilaration that at last they were doing something. The climb was as festive as a picnic, the groups shouting to each other, challenging and teasing; the women flirted with the men and hands held on more tightly. Breathless, Hélène paused for a moment and looked down; a few chinks of light shone in the village; dislodged stones rattled on the rocks and voices called out across the darkness. How could they not be noticed? And what if they were? She climbed on quickly.

At the top the wind cut across the plateau like a knife. There was a thin coating of snow on the ground and they huddled together in the hollows for warmth. The whole village seemed to be up there, nearly a hundred people, and Hélène went about trying to get them organized. They had to be told everything. She formed the triangle of lights but they kept moving out of position. She reminded each of them to count the parachutes. "You know what happened in Digne? They forgot to bury one of the parachutes and the Germans found it blowing loose across the fields. Twenty men from the town were shot."

"Marie-France says I should keep one for underwear," giggled Marthe, old Raphaël's widowed daughter.

"Yes, and a farmer in Nîmes used the ropes to tie his sheep's legs in the market. The Germans hanged him."

Pierre, the mason, cursed as his pick bounced on the frozen, stony ground. *"Merde,* I'm glad I'm not a farmer," he said, spitting on his hands.

Hélène cut a chunk from the blood sausage in her rucksack and gave it to him.

As he chewed on it he grumbled. "There are too many people out here, Hélène. They're not serious. They're in the way."

"They'll learn," she said. "We'll need every one of them yet."

They waited and they froze. René and Lucien, two farmers who had fought in the First World War, got drunk and started singing army songs. "It's too late, they won't come now," said Marie-France, pulling a shawl around her shoulders. And then they heard the engines of the Halifax. The lights flashed on; the plane made one pass and disappeared. Then it returned, black mushrooms blossoming behind it.

"Count!" Hélène yelled.

As the canisters thudded to the ground, there was a rush towards them and kids threw themselves on top of the parachutes to deflate them. People milled around as the containers were opened like beanpods.

"Here's a Bren gun," shouted Michel excitedly, his fingers thrilled by its smoothness.

"And a bazooka," said a voice that Hélène didn't even recognize.

In all the confusion, she heard her name being called: "Hélène, Hélène, over here."

"There's a man," young Thierry told her. "He's hurt. He's an American."

She found him propped against a rock, feeling his ankle. A cluster of villagers stood silently around him. She knelt in front of him. "Let me see."

"It's nothing." He recoiled as her fingers prodded the bone.

"I think it's only a sprain." She got out a bandage and wound it tightly round his foot.

"You're very professional," he said. His French accent was almost too correct.

"You don't sound like an American."

"I'm not. I'm Canadian."

"I thought it was the same thing. There, that should hold it."

He stood up awkwardly. He was taller than she was, gangly and, for a young man, already slightly stooped. His face was long and solemn with hair that flopped over it, his voice deep. Formally, he held out his hand: "My name is Maurice Griève."

"Hélène de Mirebeau." Her grip was firm.

"I must find my radio. There's a cross on the canister."

"It's over here," said Thierry. Maurice stumbled through the grass and knelt down beside it.

Hélène watched him as he lifted the radio carefully out of its rubber packing and strapped it onto his back. She liked his seriousness; no girlfriend would betray him.

"One of the boys will take you down," she told him. "You can stay with me for a few days, till you get your papers."

"Can't I wait for you?"

"I have to see everything finished before I leave."

He waited as Hélène inspected the trenches where the parachutes and the canisters were buried. Then the weapons and the crates of grenades and ammunition were lowered halfway down the cliff to the caves where they would be hidden. In the distance, the Mediterranean was a silver streak in the moonlight.

"How peaceful it looks," he said, then laughed softly as a gun barrel rang against an outcrop of rock.

"How's your ankle?" she asked.

"It'll be okay."

"Lean on me."

More than three hours it took for them to get down, stopping every now and again while he rested. He told her about his family, the Québécoise mother, the Scots father, his studies at the École Normale Supérieure in Paris, holidays here on the *côte,* and she told him about the village and the German installations in Nice and Vence. By the time they got to her house his face was white with pain; her own legs felt as if they were made of rubber. And there, inside in the cold kitchen, Cécile had been waiting for five hours, frail and exhausted, with the news of Marc's death in Carcassonne.

Hélène finishes the last of the coffee. One of the petits fours is left on the plate and for a moment she's tempted; but no, no gluttony. She has kept a drop of the *framboise* for the end, a pure bluish white in the tiny glass. She sniffs it, quintessential, more truly raspberry than the real fruit; its strength bites into her tongue. Was the force that drove Marc to seek his own death, she wonders, just the need to escape from his mother's love? Her mouth bends into a sad little smile. Surely, nothing is ever as simple as that. She folds her napkin and pays her bill, thanks the waiters and the maître d'hôtel, and then she stands, straight-backed and proud, in the gritty wind on Sherbrooke Street while the doorman whistles for a cab.

Appendix I

10:30 P.M., October 8

It was the interior of one of those anonymous apartments that Helen's imagination had not managed to penetrate: 10945, Rue des Récollets. Three bedrooms, a bathroom, kitchen, living room. The six people inside had been together for eighty-five hours, since five of them had kidnapped the sixth from his house in Westmount. They wouldn't part for another eight weeks.

In the back bedroom, twelve feet by eight, James Cross, the Senior British Trade Commissioner in Montréal, sat on a mattress on the floor. His arms were handcuffed in front of him and he wore a black cowl on his head to prevent him from seeing his guards. He was allowed to look out from under it in one direction only, towards the television set in the corner. The window was boarded over and the door into the corridor had been removed and was propped against the wall. On a chair in the doorway Yves Langlois sat with an M1 rifle in his lap. The television was tuned to Channel 2, Radio-Canada.

In the living room, Jacques Lanctôt, Marc Carbonneau, Jacques Cosette-Trudel and his wife Louise waited in front of another television set. There was almost no furniture in the room: a couple of kitchen chairs, a table with Lanctôt's typewriter, some books by Vallières and Fanon, three transistor radios and a .22 Beretta on it. A naked light bulb in the ceiling; a box of dynamite in the corner.

They watched television as they always had, but for the first time in their lives they also controlled what they saw. Of all their demands—the ransom, the release of political prisoners in Québec jails—the most important was that their manifesto should be read on the whole Radio-Canada network. Without that, they would just be a bunch of crazy extremists, but with it . . .

The Government knew the danger of publicity. "I don't intend bargaining on television," Prime Minister Pierre Trudeau had announced the day before. But the Government had given in, and at 10:30 the newscaster, Gaétan Montreuil, began to read the complete text of the manifesto in a dull monotone. It lasted for thirteen minutes; a subtitle flashed across Montreuil's chest, *Texte de Manifeste F.L.Q.*

What is one to make of it ten years later? At the time, commentators talked about its Maoist clichés, but I'm afraid I can't discover a single Mao-inspired line. Indeed, most of my friends on the left—Robert and François and Françoise, for example—dismiss it now as a reactionary document. They see the demands of Québec nationalism as a deliberate attempt to deflect the proletariat from its revolutionary course. But haven't all revolutions, I ask, derived much of their impetus from nationalist pressures? In any case, the argument, though time-consuming, is irrelevant. Of course, the manifesto is not a revolutionary statement; as a dialectical analysis of social and economic conditions in Québec it's pathetically inadequate. And of course, it is a revolutionary statement, too. Because, for the first time, the truth was told from the viewpoint of the oppressed and the deprived of this country. Not the truth in a factual sense—there are probably as many falsehoods in it as correct statements—but the truth as it's perceived by those who vaguely sense that again and again history has been used to screw them.

The Front de Libération du Québec is not a messiah, nor a modern-day Robin Hood. It is a group of Québec workers who have decided to do whatever must be done so that the people of Québec will take control of their destiny.

The Front de Libération du Québec wants the total independence of the Québécois, united in a free society, purged forever of the clique of voracious sharks, the patronizing "big bosses" and their henchmen who have made Québec their hunting ground for "cheap labour" and unscrupulous exploitation.

The Front de Libération du Québec is not a movement of aggression but a response to the aggression organized by high finance and by the federal and provincial puppet governments.

The Front de Libération du Québec is self-financed by "voluntary taxes" taken from the same enterprises that exploit the workers (banks, finance companies, etc.).

We once believed that perhaps it would be worthwhile to channel our energy and our impatience into the Parti Québécois, but the Liberal victory showed us clearly that what we call democracy in Québec is nothing but the democracy of the rich. The Liberal Party's victory was nothing but the victory of the election riggers. As a result, the British parliamentary system is finished and the Front de Libération du Québec will never allow itself to be sidetracked by the pseudo-elections which the Anglo-Saxon capitalists toss to the Québec people every four years. A number of Québécois now realize what has happened and will act on it. In the coming year Bourassa will have to face reality: 100,000 revolutionary workers, armed and organized.

Yes, there are reasons for the Liberal victory. Yes, there are reasons for poverty, unemployment, misery, and for the fact that you, Mr. Bergeron of Visitation Street, and you, Mr. Legendre of Laval, who earn $10,000 a year, will not feel free in our country of Québec.

Yes, there are reasons and the guys who work at Lord know them, the fishermen of the Gaspé, the workers of the North Shore, the miners for the Iron Ore Co., Québec Cartier Mining, and Noranda, also know the reasons. And the brave workers of Cabano whom they tried to fuck once again—they know the reasons.

Yes, there are reasons why you, Mr. Tremblay, and you, Mr. Cloutier, who work in the construction industry at Saint-Jérôme, cannot pay for the Vaisseaux d'Or Restaurant, with all that beautiful classy music and all the pizazz as does Drapeau the aristocrat —who is so concerned with slums that he puts coloured billboards in front of them to hide our misery from the tourists.

Yes, there are reasons why you, Mrs. Lemay of Ste. Hyacinthe, can't pay for little trips to Florida like all these dirty judges and members of parliament do with our money.

The brave workers for Vickers and Davie Ship, who were thrown out without any reason being given, they know these reasons. And the Murdochvills guys who were attacked for the sole and simple reason that they wanted to organize a union and who were forced by the dirty judges to pay $2,000,000 because they tried to exercise this basic right—they know justice and they know plenty of reasons.

Yes, there are reasons why you, Mr. Lachance of St. Marguérite Street, must go and drown your sorrows in that dog's beer —Molson's. And you, Lachance's son, with your marijuana cigarettes . . .

Yes, there are reasons why you, the people on welfare, are kept on it from generation to generation. There are lots of reasons and the Domtar workers at Windsor and at East Angus know them well. And the workers at Squibb and Ayers, and the guys at the Provincial Liquor Commission, and the boys from Seven-Up and Victoria Precision, and the blue-collar workers in Laval and Montréal and the Lapalme boys, they all know these reasons well.

And the Montréal policemen, who are the strong arms of the system, they should understand these reasons: they should have been able to see that we live in a terrorized society because, without their strength, without their violence, nothing could work.

We've had our fill of Canadian Federalism which penalizes the Quebec milk producers to satisfy the needs of the Anglo-Saxons of the Commonwealth; the system which keeps the gallant Montréal taxi drivers in a state of semislavery to protect the exclusive monopoly of the nauseating Murray Hill Co. and of its owner-assassin Charles Herschorn and his son Paul.

We've had our fill of a system which exercises a crazy policy of imports while turning the lowly paid textile and shoe manufacturing industry workers out into the street in order to provide profits for a bunch of damned money-makers driving around in Cadillacs.

We've had our fill of a system which rates the Québec nation on the same level as other ethnic minorities in Canada.

We've had our fill, as have more and more Québécois, of a government which does a thousand and one acrobatic tricks to charm American millionaires into investing in Québec, La Belle Province, where thousands of square miles of forests filled with game and lakes filled with fish are the exclusive preserve of these all-powerful twentieth-century lords.

We've had our fill of taxes which the Ottawa representative in Québec wants to give to the English-speaking bosses to "encourage" them, if you please, to speak French, to do business in the French language: "Repeat after me: Cheap Labour; you say it in French as: *main d'oeuvre à bon marché.*"

We've had our fill of promises of jobs and prosperity knowing that we will continue as dutiful servants and bootlickers of the big shots for just as long as places like Westmount, the Town of Mount Royal, Hampstead and Outremont continue to exist: for as long as all the fortresses of high finance on St. James's Street and Wall Street continue to exist, for as long as we Québécois fail to use every means to chase out, yes, even with guns and dynamite if need be, these economic and political big bosses, who are ready to go to any lengths in order to fuck us up.

We live in a society of terrorized slaves, terrorized by the big owners, Steinberg, Clark, Smith, Neaple, Timmins, Geoffrion, J. L. Lévesque, Herschorn, Desmarais, Kierans (in comparison with these big shots, Rémi Popol the girl chaser, Drapeau the dog, Bourassa the sidekick of the Simards, Trudeau the faggot, are just peanuts!).

We live in a society terrorized by the capitalist Roman Catholic Church, even though this seems to be diminishing (who owns the property on which the Stock Exchange stands?); by the payments to reimburse Household Finance; by the advertising of the grand masters of consumer goods like Eaton, Simpson, Morgan, Steinberg and General Motors.

We are terrorized by those closed circles of science and culture, the universities, and by their monkey directors Gaudry and Dorais and by the sub-monkey Robert Shaw.

More and more of us now know and suffer under this terrorist society and the day is coming when all the Westmounts of Québec will disappear from the map.

Production workers, miners, lumberjacks, service workers, teachers, students, unemployed workers, take what belongs to you —your work, your determination and your freedom. And you, the workers at General Electric, you're the ones who make your factories run, only you are capable of production; without you, General Electric is nothing!

Workers of Québec, start today to take back what belongs to you; take for yourselves what is yours. Only you know your factories, your machines, your hotels, your universities, your unions. Don't wait for an organizational miracle!

Make your own revolution in your own districts, in your places of work. And if you don't do it yourselves, other usurpers, technocrats and others, will replace the iron hand of the cigar smokers we now know, and everything will have to be done all over again. You alone are capable of building a free society.

We must fight, not one by one, but uniting, using every means we possess to achieve victory, just as the Patriots of 1837–38 did (those whom our Holy Mother the Church went out of her way to excommunicate, as part of her sellout to British interests).

From the four corners of Québec, those whom they dared to call "lousy French" and "alcoholics" will plunge into the fight against those who bludgeoned liberty and justice. We will put all these professional thugs and crooks out of commission: the bankers, the businessmen, the judges and sellout politicians.

We are the workers of Québec and we will stop at nothing. We want to change this slave society of ours into a free society, functioning by itself and for itself, a society open to the world.

Our struggle can only be victorious. An awakening people cannot long remain in misery and error.

Long live Free Québec!

Long live our comrades who are political prisoners!

Long live the Québec revolution!

Long live the Front de Libération du Québec!

In the shoddy apartment on Des Récollets, five of the six occupants were shouting, *"Vive le Québec Libre";* the shouts were echoed in the Nelson Hotel on Place Jacques Cartier, in the bars on the Rue St. Denis, in Chibougamau, Asbestos and Trois Pistoles. Perhaps James Cross was the only person who listened to the announcer's closing words: "This broadcast has been read for humanitarian reasons, with a view to saving, if possible, the life of James Richard Cross."

Meanwhile, what were viewers watching at exactly the same time on Canada's English-language television network? If they hadn't all switched off, they were listening to a rerun of the Governor-General's Speech from the Throne at the opening of Parliament that afternoon. In his fruity, slightly quavering voice, Roland Michener, the jogger, read the text that had been prepared for him by the Government:

> Notwithstanding its difficulties, Canada continues to enjoy social stability to an exceptional degree. This stability is not simply a matter of luck. Good fortune is a factor, but we should accept gracefully the fact that we are also more amenable to reason and, perhaps, more capable of wise decision than we are normally willing to admit. The burden of our European inheritance and our fascination with our American neighbours tend often to distract us and cause us to be unaware of that reasonableness and that wisdom.
>
> We forget to our disadvantage, for these are traits that have made Canada a land of freedom. Canadians should pause on occasions such as this to reflect that their country is regarded by others with envy. It is a high place of liberty in the world. It is held in esteem because in Canada respect is paid to the individual; privacy and freedom of thought are honoured.

Part II
OCTOBER

Chapter Four

Helena

Everything my husband ever touched grew into an obsession.

All the little things that little men take as hobbies—collecting, playing, travelling—exploded in him like great bursts of energy. His life was filled with wild enthusiasms. They never died down and he took it for granted everyone else would share them just as intensely. They weren't the fashions or crazes that pass in a month or two. They expanded and multiplied: "I've got to get to the bottom of it," he would say. And he had to explain every detail: "Aye, but wait till I tell you this." Diagrams, plans, the latest techniques. Whatever it was—archaeology, polo, the making of a steam turbine—I was dragged in too, kicking and struggling, against my will.

He had the first car in Smyrna, but half of the time it was in pieces. Screws and gaskets in the Sèvres fruit bowl my sister Aliki gave us for a wedding present.

When he took up golf—he'd always regretted not having the chance as a boy—he bought the best set of clubs he could find, then brought them home and dismembered them. The heads were all over the walnut dining table. In the middle of the night I wakened with the noise of him sawing and filing away in his workshop. I went down to him because I couldn't get back to sleep. "What are you doing, Nicol?" I asked angrily. "It's three o'clock. I can't sleep."

He crouched over the bench. "Come here, girl, and I'll show you," he said in his rough way.

He had gouged holes out of the backs of the wooden heads and was filling them with molten lead. "They need more weight in them. Come here, come here," he waved impatiently. "You hold it like this." He stood behind me, his arms around my thin waist in the silk nightgown, pressing a golf club between my fingers. "The wrists are the fulcrum, you see, so the more weight you can get right out at the edge of the arc, out here, the more energy can be transferred from the body—through your arms and your shoulders—out to the ball." His fingers were hard against my bones. "That way you'll get more distance, you understand. Provided the wrists are strong enough to control the pressure, of course." Standing there shivering in the middle of the night, the noise of cicadas rasping outside in the garden, I was given my first lesson in the principles of golf. And I still remember it. After all these years I cherish the details—now I really do understand, Nicol, my love—but at the time I'd have liked to break the club over your skull.

"Oh, come to bed," I yawned and tried to pull him away.

"You go along. I'll be up in a minute."

For months he worked on those stupid golf clubs. Nobody else could play with them, they were so heavy, but every day he'd be fiddling around with them, till finally: "I think I've got it licked now. Maybe a wee bit off the baffie, but the others'll do." He teed the ball up and banged it more than three hundred yards into the gorse behind a green. He looked around proudly to see if anyone was watching. "Och," he laughed easily, "I may not have the finesse yet, but I can beat these English buggers for distance any day of the week."

Yes, that was the kind of man he was.

I remember him now with such warmth. There was so much life about him, and here, surrounded with shadows that eat and dribble and fart, there's so little.

Yet he used to irritate me more than the noise of a pan being scoured with ashes outside the kitchen door. You couldn't share his interests; you had to be caught up in them, driven, dominated by them as he was.

It's not that he was a selfish man. He was full of generosity. If one of his workmen was hurt, he'd be round there the next day himself with a basket of food. And when he stayed out at Sigacik, near Teos, he would buy a lamb and have it roasted for the whole village to eat with him. But I don't think he ever understood the basic fact that other people might be different from him.

Most of his obsessions, like most of his desires, were simple. He could work them out, lick them. But the frightening ones, the ones that drove and, in a way, destroyed him, or at the very least prevented him from achieving any kind of peace, were those he couldn't fulfill.

There were two of them.

The first was his obsession with a man named Abel. I don't even know if Abel was his Christian name or his family name. Just that he was Welsh and, like my husband, an iron founder.

"When did he live, this Abel you keep on about all the time?" I asked him in exasperation.

"I don't know. It doesna matter. Sixty year ago, maybe."

"How do you know he did it then? Perhaps it's just a story."

"Sammy Inglis—the man I served my apprenticeship with —he saw it. He wouldna make up a thing like that."

"I don't believe it. It's not possible."

"Aye, but it is. Abel did it."

What it was that this Abel was supposed to have done was to make a bird cage with a door that opened. Simple, you say. Yes, but all in a single casting? Ah ha! That was the problem I had to put up with in every corner of my life for twenty years. I don't think there was a single day my husband didn't think of it. He would jot notes on the backs of envelopes in the middle of a meal; we would be at a ball at the Club and I'd go and find him out on the verandah staring at some half-finished drawing. Once, he just disappeared for five days to go to Constantinople to talk to an American who was reputed—falsely, it turned out—to have made some new discoveries about the casting techniques in Chinese ritual bronzes. And at any hour of the day or night I'd find him huddled in a corner with Tammy Letham, his pattern-maker, all brown and burned and scarred, a foul little walnut of a man.

"Why don't you get rid of him?" My nose wrinkled. "He's so awful."

"Tammy? You've got to be joking. He's the best pattern-maker in the world. He's been with me more than twelve year."

"But, Nicol, he's so rude."

"Aye, he's the tops at that, too." He spat in the fire and the grate sizzled.

Mother of God, how did I stand it? In Scotland before he came to Smyrna, in Marseilles afterwards, in Hong Kong, I'm sure, when he had finally left me for good, Abel's spell hung over him.

"Why does it matter to you so much?" I asked in frustration.

"Because I don't know how he did it."

"But it's only a bird cage. What use is that?"

He looked at me and laughed raucously. "Aye, it's only a bird cage, lassie. That's all it is."

I almost forgot. The second of his unfulfilled obsessions—his love for me, of course.

Flies.

Sunday, and my room is full of flies. They breed in the radiator. I waken in the night, gasping for breath, afraid my mouth is stuffed with them.

"They bite me. Look at the swellings," I tell my daughter.

"But, Maman, they're houseflies. Houseflies don't bite."

All the same, she gets me a can of insecticide. I push the nozzle into the grille of the radiator and they rise in a great buzzing swarm around my head. I flap them away and spray everywhere in panic. The linoleum floor is covered with little black currants.

Outside in the corridor I hear my daughter talking to the matron.

"There really are a lot of flies," she says. "Can't we do something to get rid of them?"

"It's the weather," says the matron.

No, it's not just that. Haven't you noticed? They're drawn to old flesh. It's the presence of death that attracts them.

October 5. All afternoon the old women cluster around the television set. Some Englishman has been kidnapped.

Monsieur Prud'homme comes up to me in the corridor and wants to talk about it. I brush past him. I have more important things to do.

If I love my husband now, now that he's dead, why could I never find a way to give him my love when he asked for it? My memories may be full of romance, yet how I despised his materialism at the time. He had to see everything so literally, so concretely; he wanted to take the mystery out of everything I believed in. How could I let him become a hero? His fingernails rimmed with dirt!

Perhaps if I had known him better, if we had been childhood sweethearts? No, that wouldn't have made any difference. Maybe it was myself I didn't know? And maybe it was knowing so little about him that attracted me in the first place. That and his strength. Only my father could have been a match for him.

Imagine: five feet six and two hundred pounds. Well, my brother Sava was that, too, I'll admit, but with Sava, half of it at least was fat. With Nicol, every ounce was hard. And how I yearned for a soft hollow in that body!

Where did he come from? I don't even know the answer to the simplest question. Airdrie, it said on his birth certificate, but I don't know where that is and he certainly never wanted to take me back there.

"What about your family?" I asked him when we were getting married.

"I don't have anyone," he said. "All the ones I cared for are dead. The others might as well be."

When he was only twelve he was working in a coal mine, but he escaped from that into an iron foundry, got himself apprenticed, learned the craft, saved money, made money, prospered. The first time he took me to see the factory in Smyrna the size of everything astounded me—the twenty-foot-high flywheel for the air blower on the furnace. "Mind where you're going now. It broke a poor devil's neck last month."

I jumped back. "But how did you ever manage to"—I couldn't find the word and gestured weakly. "Well, all this?"

"Me? The poor wee Scots laddie, you mean? Because I'm no afraid of what I'm doing, like most of the others are."

So he took risks. He could take them because in the end he had no roots; there was nothing he was afraid of losing. I could never understand that. But now that I have no home myself, now that the very word is false and this prison they've shut me up in is called a home, I wish I could have seen things his way. Would I have been able to share his freedom then?

When we were married, what I wanted most of all was to take him to Chios, my father's home. We decided to go there for our honeymoon. As we sat on the harbour wall in front of the old Genoese fort in Cesme, Nicol looked across the strait at the blue mountains shaded against the sky. Some fishermen on the jetty in front of us were mending their nets and loading gourds of fresh water into the boats. Reflected light rippled on the undersides of the hulls.

"Just look at how clear everything is," he said. "I'll tell you this; it's not like that where I come from."

I touched his hand. "But you still must want to go back there sometimes."

"Damn it, no. There's nowhere to go back to. The English drove us off our land a hundred and fifty years ago. That's how we ended up in a hellhole like Airdrie. Slaves."

He hated the English. Whenever he had the chance he charged them double for any work he did. And then despised them all the more for their foolishness.

But he loved that week we spent on Chios. It was May and climbing roses flowered on every stone wall. We strolled along the promenade in the evenings, so sedate compared to Smyrna.

"How can any human manage to walk as slowly as these people do?" he whispered. "It's killing me."

Canaries sang in cages that had been hung from windows in the cool breeze from the sea.

"Look at that," he said in surprise as two young soldiers came towards us walking quite openly hand in hand. "You wouldna catch them doing that in Glasgow." And another soldier with a pink chrysanthemum between his fingers.

And how excited he was when he found out that Glaucis had been born there. I had told him, of course, that Chios was Homer's island, but that didn't seem to matter to him. Except for history, he never read. He liked paintings and especially sculpture; he loved music and singing, but books bored him. Then, one morning, while I was still drowsy, he came bursting into our room from his early walk through the town.

"Why did you not tell me this was where Glaucis was born?" he asked, flinging the shutters wide open.

"Glaucis?" I didn't even know who Glaucis was.

"Why, you ignorant wee girl," he teased. "It was Glaucis who discovered how to weld iron back in the seventh century before Christ. It's in Herodotus."

I suppose I didn't look sufficiently impressed.

"Well, do you not see? That's more important than your Homer. What did Homer do, after all? Told stories. Good ones, I'll give you that, but just stories. But if Glaucis hadn't found out how to stick one piece of metal to another and make it hold, where would we be today, eh?"

He stood with his hands braced on the balcony rail and looked out at the harbour full of bright caiques and screaming gulls.

I forget myself. I make up stories, too.

I hated that man, and I have every right to hate him. The tenderness of the men on Chios may have pleased him, but there was none in him at all. Not an ounce.

All he ever did was hurt me. Not deliberately; he didn't have to do it deliberately. He simply had no idea how to be gentle. I could lie naked on my bed with the sun streaming in the window and its warmth would do more to awaken my body than any time he ever touched me. Yes, the sun, and a silk embroidered cover beneath me, my whole body starting to tingle, my fingers just touching the skin, lightly like this, swallows swooping over the tips of a plane tree's branches.

But with him, all I ever got was his huge thumbprints in my flesh. I can feel them still.

That first night in Chios, with the noise of fishermen eating in the cafés down below, sucking up their spaghetti and mussels,

I thought he was trying to kill my body as he hammered away on top of it. I lay silently. He's my husband now, I told myself, and I would surely have wept if there had been any moisture left in me.

He deceived me with my own sister, Aliki, though she was a coward and denied it. "You're mad," she screamed. "Mother always warned us you were mad."

And with Safiye, our neighbours' daughter, my closest friend, he must have done it, too.

And with every Turkish whore in Smyrna.

That fat ugly sow, Madame Arsenault! She stinks of garbage. The furry carpet slippers her nephew gave her for her birthday are already matted with pus from the eczema on her legs. She thinks she speaks French, but she speaks it as vilely as a Corsican goat.

Since her husband died, she's been angling for Monsieur Prud'homme.

Today in the dining room she suddenly started shouting at me: "I saw you, I saw you under the table, rubbing Monsieur Prud'homme's thigh!" She turned to everyone and shrieked: "I saw her. She was squeezing his balls."

I jumped up and threw my water in her plastered face. "Everyone knows you killed your husband," I spat at her. "You poured acid into his ear."

She clutched at her throat and pretended to faint.

"It's a sign of guilt," I tried to explain. But nobody would listen; they're all so stupid.

And Monsieur Prud'homme, what did he do? Oh, the weakling! He just sat still and stared at his plate with a silly smirk on his face. It pleased him to have women fighting over him. The first time in his miserable life he's been the centre of attention.

I shan't go back. From now on, I shall eat in my room.

October 10. I hear them running up and down outside in panic. Another kidnapping, is it? They scramble into their rooms to hide their trinkets.

With what I lost when we were driven from Smyrna I could have bought them all.

Do they think anybody's going to kidnap a handful of old-age pensioners?

Who would notice if they did?

"What a shame!" my daughter says when I speak to her about the scene in the dining room last Friday. Her mind is made up. She has heard somebody else's side of the story, I can tell.

She is restless and I wait for her to go.

"Your father would never have left me here to be humiliated," I shout after her as she leaves.

She turns round, her eyes raised to the ceiling. "Maman!" she says reproachfully.

But it's the truth. Though he hurt and deceived me, he adored me, too.

When I first met him, he wasn't a sensual man. Physical, certainly, but not sensual. All his energy had been directed into work. And I was the opposite. I lived with the thought of sex. Since I was a child it had filled my dreams with mystery, a teasing gentleness. The weight of his body—the curly hair on his chest scraping my skin—crushed that out of me. I lay frozen beneath him, but the deadness he felt in me electrified him. It drove him all the more frenziedly, clumsily, to try to awaken some response. He had to make me feel. The less I felt, the more he was tormented. Yes, yes, I can explain it to myself now, though I never saw it in time to be able to talk to him about it, not that talking would have helped. The only place he could find me was in someone else.

But for all that he was never cold, never deliberately cruel. He might be puzzled or frustrated, but he always cared for me.

Why, the first thing he did when he was released from the Japanese camp in 1945 was to go and look for some silk and have it sent to me in Nice. And I had seen him only three times, and then briefly, in fifteen years. I remember the parcel arriving just before Christmas. It was a bad time for all of us in France; the excitement of victory had drained away and we were left with the recriminations, the bitterness, the undefined sense of loss. There was nothing to look forward to any longer; only a terrible lassitude. I felt so old.

Until the postman came one morning. "I'm afraid it's been damaged," he apologized. The wrapping had split and water had seeped in; I screamed at him in disappointment. But the silk was still beautiful, black heavy Chinese silk with an inlaid pattern on it. I draped it around my body and danced in the hallway. I knew that Nicol would have imagined me doing just that as he bought it, holding it up against the slim body of the Eurasian shopgirl.

And there were always moments of togetherness. Even in the last years as we drifted away from each other.

After we fled from Smyrna, he bought a large foundry in Marseilles. He did some work for Sava, who had transferred what was left of the business there, and for the Messageries Maritimes, but mainly he concentrated on French navy contracts. That was the kind of work which interested him most; it was more complicated, more demanding than anything he had had the chance to do in Turkey. It brought the challenge of Abel closer.

His work did not come between us, as with most families. Instead, his enthusiasm infected us all.

Sitting at the dinner table with the dishes pushed aside, he held Hélène on his knee. She was ten years old, big for her age —too big. A pencil in his fingers, he's telling her about steam engines. "Aye, Nellie, it's an exciting time for steam. Ten year ago, the boiler would be working with pressures of 200 pound to the square inch; now it's up around 2,000. And the temperatures are up above 800 degrees, too; they'll never manage to push it much beyond that."

Hélène looks at him in dumb admiration.

"Nicol, she's just a girl," I say softly, my fingers trying to smooth down his hair. "What's the use of filling her head with all that nonsense?"

She glares up at me. "It's not nonsense. It interests me. I *want* to hear it," she shouts impertinently.

I scold her.

"Shsh," he hushes both of us. "It'll no do her any harm to learn about it."

"Well, Consuela is waiting to clear the table, anyway."

But when it came to their pouring a heavy casting down at the works I was as thrilled as the children. We all went along to watch. He would get one of the workmen to bring armchairs out of the office for us, a bottle of champagne for me, and we would sit in awe as he gave the order for the huge fifteen-ton ladles to be poured. They had to be canted over gradually with a chain and pulley so that there was a steady stream of fiery molten metal, foaming and spluttering, spitting stars into the night sky. I was with Nicol completely. He controlled everything, watching every move the men made, lending a hand here, checking the flow there, never panicking, though a month's work would be lost if anything went wrong. Afterwards, he would sit with us, exhausted, streaks of dirt and sweat on his face, his collar open, and pull the flask of whisky out of his pocket. He always carried it with him, a silver flask covered in crocodile skin, a silver cup screwed on the top of it, and always the same Scotch, malt, Talisker from the Isle of Skye. He gulped the first two cupfuls and sipped the third, catching his breath as he started to explain to us what had happened.

Yes, I loved him then, the power, the daring. I wouldn't have changed him for any gentle lover.

He was proud of what he did. He envied no other man.

Politicians, businessmen, merchants, he dismissed them all: "They're a tricky bunch of bastards!" He worked with his hands and his brain together, and he did as he pleased.

I had to leave him. He began to live openly with a little Algerian slut on the Cannebière. She had a bastard by him and got him to buy her presents. Everyone knew.

I told him I would go to Nice. He said he understood. He cared for me still, I'm sure, but he wouldn't give her up.

By 1935 he was bored with her and with all the ones who followed her, bored with Marseilles and the work he had to do just to keep the foundry going. With the depression, there was very little heavy casting to be done, so he was reduced to chasing around after all the dull, repetitive jobs he despised.

"If I'm going to have to turn out frying pans and bathtubs like mudpies to make ends meet I might as well do it somewhere a bit more interesting," he said when he came to say good-bye. He made sure we'd have enough money from the sale of the factory and then he went off to Hong Kong with a Chinese girl who claimed to be a princess.

I didn't see him again for more than ten years, till he came back from Shanghai after the war. An old man with pure white bristly hair, but a twinkle still in his eyes. An ebony cane with a gold-mounted handle.

"Oh, Nicol, it must have been terrible." I clutched on to him.

"Just the boredom," he said. "Can you imagine being cooped up with all those bloody Englishmen?"

He was killed four years later in Buenos Aires. A steel girder slipped and crushed him. His ashes are on the chest of drawers in that blue Chinese jar, the colour of his eyes.

October 16. Soldiers everywhere.

I awoke with the noise of their trucks grinding through the streets. Young men sitting in the back, unsmiling, worried, guns in their laps. Later, a detachment went marching past, the metallic noise of all armies, Greeks, Turks, Germans, Italians, French, Americans, the same clatter. A sergeant shouting orders in English.

Where have they come from? What are they doing in this quiet part of Outremont? I don't understand. It's something to do with these kidnappings, of course, but how can soldiers help?

This afternoon there was a screech of sirens. Some police cars pulled up in front of a house across the street. There were soldiers, too; they waited outside while the police went in. A few minutes later a man and two young women came stumbling out. I have seen the man before; he wears a fringed suede jacket and has his hair in a ponytail. I don't like the look of him. But one of the girls used to sit on the steps in the summer playing a guitar and singing in a high thin voice. She tried to go back into the house, not to run away, I think, but just to get something she had forgotten, a cardigan perhaps, or a blanket. A policeman pulled her roughly and she fell. The soldiers covered her with their guns.

"I don't like these uniforms," I say to Monsieur Prud'homme.

"They're here to protect us," he says. His voice is like a sack of flour.

"From what?"

"Well, from the bombs and the kidnappers. From the F.L.Q."

"But I don't like the uniforms. They're not gay." I try to describe the uniforms the officers used to wear at the Cercle Européen in Smyrna, but he doesn't listen to me.

"It's the Liberals' fault," says Monsieur Chabot. "They've let the young people get out of hand. What we need is the Social Credit. They'd restore order." He squeaks. As if he knew anything, the old fool. All he ever did was sell furniture in Saint Léonard.

"Yes, order," says Madame Pipriac who repeats everything Monsieur Chabot says.

"Fascisti," I mutter.

"What's that?" asks Monsieur Prud'homme, cupping his hand to his ear.

"The *Fascisti,*" I say more loudly. "They wanted the trains to run on time. As if it mattered. I hid Madame Beckermann and her children in the maid's room while there were German officers living in the apartment. Would you have done that, *any* of you?"

They don't know why I'm shouting. They look at each other in alarm, then turn back to the television.

Tonight my daughter phones to say she won't be able to come and see me tomorrow because Helen has been arrested.

"Arrested? By the police? But what has she done? She's a good girl, isn't she?"

"She doesn't have to have done anything, Maman." Hélène's voice is strained and she puts the phone down.

"I don't understand," I say into the emptiness.

And what about the children? What will they do without a mother?

October 18. I have prayed all day.

This morning Madame Pipriac was fiddling about with the television set—she can't live without it—to see the wretched church services they broadcast. But instead, there were reporters talking, photographs of an old car caught in spotlights, soldiers surrounding it. Then more photographs of the trunk open, some sacks, oh, my God, no, the naked stomach of a man, his body being lifted out, heavy and sagging.

I didn't say anything to anyone. I got up and put on my coat and went to church. I don't go very often, though it's Orthodox, the Church of the Holy Mother and Saint Nektarios, and the priest tries to be kind. But it's full of shopkeepers and waiters and streetsweepers. I don't mind them being poor—a lot of them are making money hand over fist, actually—but they're as flat as the stodgy pita bread they eat all the time. They take all the life, all the beauty out of the ceremony till it depresses me.

But today I had to go. I don't know this man Laporte. I don't know if he was a good man or not. Nobody will tell the truth about him now, anyway. And anyway, it doesn't matter: no man should die like that.

I pray for him, for his soul. And for his wife. And I pray that Helen, my granddaughter, had nothing to do with this.

I've had enough of their wars, their armies.

They think it's all a game. But it's not. When you've lived as long as I have, you know what it is to lose the best men and see them replaced by the worst. Costa, my older brother, was killed; Sava—sweet, soft Sava, rotten to the core—survived. Marc, my son, was betrayed and shot; nobody could replace him. The waste of it!

Yet I taunted my husband for speaking out against the war. I tried to shame him and called him coward, which he never was; the word shames me.

The war was passing Smyrna by. Turkey might be fighting the British, the French, the Italians, yet it hardly touched our lives. Suddenly we felt as though we were cut off in a backwater. The fleets no longer anchored in the harbour; when the young cavalry officers departed, the standard of polo declined; there was no more Italian opera. We were becoming dull, provincial, middle-aged. So we longed for the war to sweep us all up.

Just a hundred and fifty miles to the north of us Gallipolli was turned into a hell when the British tried to grab the Dardanelles.

"Do you want that to happen here?" Nicol yelled one night

at Costa. "Here in Smyrna. Here in the middle of your own damn dining room?"

We were back at my father's house, Costa's now, or rather, Costa's wife's, for she had filled it with her children, her chandeliers, her expensive furniture from Paris. The table glittered with ridiculous gilt ornaments.

"Not here, no," Costa said, taken aback. "Obviously not. But this is our chance. If we don't take it, it'll be too late."

"Costa, it's not your war, it's not mine. It's not the Turks' even. They were fools to get into it and they'll pay the price to get out."

"But it *is* your war," said Melina bitingly. "It's Britain's war. I don't know why you're not back there."

"No, it's England's. The English, the Germans, the French. And do you know what they're fighting over? They're fighting over Africa—minerals, markets. They wanted the war fought down here in the Balkans, by proxy. But it's sucked the buggers in and it serves them damn well right." He took a great gulp of brandy. "Two hundred thousand Frenchmen massacred in one week. Not by the Germans, Melina my love, by their own generals, their government. What do you think's going to be gained by that?"

"It's our chance against the Turks," Costa tried to argue. "They're weak now, the sick man of Europe, and strung out all over the place, in the Caucasus, in Serbia, in Mesopotamia. If only Constantine would declare war—"

"He won't," I interrupted knowingly. "He's hardly Greek himself. And his wife's German."

"I suppose it makes a difference, your husband being . . . Scottish," Melina sneered. Until now, she had always backed the King.

"What do you want, all of you?" Nicol asked desperately. "What do you want that you haven't got? Tell me, what would a war give you?"

"Smyrna could be Greek again. We'd be free."

"Free. Are you not free now? How many ships do you have now, Costa? The Turks won't take them away from you. They won't take your house and your kiddies away from you, either. The war will."

But none of us would listen to him. I was embarrassed when he said these things at the Club. All the Greeks in Smyrna opposed Constantine's pathetic attempts to remain neutral. We supported his prime minister, Veniselos, the most brilliant man, so it was said, Crete had ever produced. Veniselos who had driven the Turks out of his own island and now was going to free us all. The charming, the persuasive, the brave Veniselos; women swooned over his picture. But Veniselos must hurry. We simmered impatiently; the war would pass us by.

It didn't. It was saving us till last.

My daughter comes to tell me Helen has been released.

"Thank God!" I say, and cross myself. "I knew there must have been a mistake. Did they apologize?"

"No," she sighs heavily. "It wasn't a mistake."

"But it must have been. They've released her. That means she can't have done anything wrong."

"Maman, all it means is David knew the right people to talk to."

The Turks didn't dare to bother us during the war. In the mountain villages perhaps they still tried to lord it over the Greek peasants, but in Smyrna we outnumbered them. They didn't even bother Nicol, though he was British. When a law was announced that enemy nationals were to be interned, he went to see Nour-ed-Din Pasha, the new governor; they got drunk together and talked about archaeology.

Besides, the rich Turks like Safiye's father had become as Greek as we were. He was a merchant and a shipowner. He had done business with my father but he was the opposite in every way: dry, distant, intellectual, an amateur poet who would rather talk about Paul Valéry than drink raki and chew squid with the fishermen in the port. He and his wife travelled constantly and Safiye was left at home with the servants. They had a mansion in the suburb of Bornova and when we moved out there to get away from the heat and the noise of the city, it was by accident that we bought a villa next to them. We saw almost nothing of the rest of the family, but Safiye was restless and attached herself to me.

She was much younger than I was, sixteen when I first met her, but very precocious. I had to struggle to keep up with her in all the arguments we had. For three years, we saw each other every day, walking, playing tennis, eating baklava with fresh pistachios and clotted cream, drinking champagne till we giggled, talking all the time about anything that came into our heads. She was the younger sister I'd never had. She wasn't pretty—her body was dumpy, heavy-breasted, her mouth wide and down-turned—but she was full of energy and feeling. I loved the way she challenged the world we had grown up in: "I'm not going to end up in a harem waiting for the man to come to me," Safiye said. And she didn't, though I doubt if it made her any happier.

She was everything I was not, hard and tough inside the bouncy flesh. Strange, I loved the hardness in Safiye when it repelled me in Nicol.

And Nicol loved her, too. I don't know when they became lovers. I don't truly know that they were, though they must have been: I come into the room and she is lying stretched on her back on the table with Nicol standing over her, and I see the image of another scene so clearly, a bedroom, sunfilled, and him rising, rising slowly out of her, the two of them satisfied. "I'm teaching Saffy the backstroke," he explains, not guiltily at all, and perhaps he is—she's having swimming lessons at the Club—but I know they're lovers, I even hope they are, I love her so much.

Later, the hardness, the anger she felt would take her away from me, make me an enemy, but when she was young she was soft and warm as well. We held each other when the fear became too intense. And when I finally bore a child, a daughter, after eight years of marriage and my sisters rejoicing in my barrenness, it was Safiye who cared for me. She came back from Paris where she had gone to study law, and found me depressed, crying all the time over nothing. I wouldn't even have the baby in my room, she was so ugly. Not mine, not mine.

Safiye sat with her hand on my thigh. "What are you going to call her?"

"I don't care. Why should she have a name?"

"Doesn't she have to be christened, or whatever you call it?"

I shrugged and turned to the wall as she left the room.

But she came back a minute later with the baby in her arms. "I shall give you a name, little dumpling. I shall call you after your mother because she's so beautiful and you will be, too." She held it up to the light that filtered through the blinds. "But a French name because that will make you even more elegant than she is: Hélène, Hélène," she sang. "You do have rather a long nose, don't you? But it's a Greek nose and they're the finest. Not like mine, all hooked and squashed." She came and sat beside me again and kissed the tears out of my eyes.

Oh, Safiye, I can't hate you, can I? It was my life I think you took from me, but yours has been as cruel as mine, from all I hear. Are you dead, or do you still remember me?

The picnics we used to have, the three of us together. Europe might be up to its neck in mud, but we had the most beautiful picnics out on the beach at Teos.

Nicol was obsessed with archaeology by that time. He had bumped into some Germans in Constantinople who had talked about how archaeology was becoming an exact science of the past, and when he came back he read every book he could get his hands on. The area around Smyrna was littered with ruins, of course—Pergamum, Phocaea, Sardis, Ephesus, Miletus, Heracleia—but instead of being attracted to any of them, he chose Teos. Now, who had ever heard of Teos?

"It was the greatest city on the Anatolian coast in the sixth century B.C," he argued. "After Croesus wiped out Smyrna and Ephesus, it was the centre of everything. Did you not know that?"

He spent more and more of his time out there, sometimes whole weeks, digging along with the workmen and living in the stone hut of a Turkish shepherd. How he stank when he bothered to come back home.

"What about the factory?" Costa asked him.

"Och, Tammy Letham knows where to find me if he needs me."

And when we did go out there one Sunday, Safiye and I together, laughing behind the driver, scarves around our hats to keep them from blowing off in the wind—"the closest I'll ever get to wearing a veil," Safiye boasted—yes, when we got there and the dust had settled we agreed he had chosen a fine site—for a picnic, we giggled. But for archaeology? There was nothing to see.

There were two bays, one to the north, swampy and full of mosquitoes, where the dull little village of Sigaçik squats on the marshes, and the other to the south, olive groves running down to a curving white beach, fresh breezes and the smell of seaweed.

Nicol was burnt and peeling in the sun, red as a side of beef. "That's where the city was." He pointed to the peninsula between the two bays.

"The city?"

"Aye." He showed us some bumps and dips in the uneven ground. "That's where the walls were."

"But there's nothing to see," Safiye protested.

"Nothing to see, is it? Then look at this." Roughly he took

our hands and pulled us stumbling over a low wall into the olive groves. He paused in a clearing. "Sit," he commanded as if he were talking to a couple of little dogs. "Sit. There, isn't that something?"

Everywhere there were white marble pillars, most of them sprawled on their fluted sides, yet somehow without confusion, so that you still felt the perfection of the temple which had been here.

"Oh, yes," I said, "yes."

He raised his eyebrows.

"It's not a bit like Ephesus," I said.

He hugged me because I had sensed what kept him here. "No, it's not a bit like Ephesus. God forbid! This fits. Do you see how the temple would have risen against the curve of the hill? But not too proudly—no ostentation. The Ephesians were so unsure of themselves they had to be grandiose; no wonder the poor buggers always ended up on the losing side."

"My father took me to see the temple of the goddess Artemis," I said. "It was just a hole in the ground." I hadn't thought of Artemis for years.

"Well, it wasna even a real temple most of the time. They were bankers, not priests. That's what it was, a bank. They used to lend out the temple money for mortgages."

"They must have been Jews," Safiye giggled.

"Or Scots," he laughed. "This temple here was for Dionysus, and they kept it pure. It was the greatest of his temples in all of Greece. Actors and musicians used to come from all over to play at the festival. But when they started getting high-handed and asking for more money, the Teans threw them out so they wouldna offend the god with their corruption."

"We should have done that to the Italian opera singers," I said.

We went back down to the beach holding hands. A cook from the village lit a fire and cooked lamb and swordfish over it, and a musician played the lute for us and sang. They were both surprised to see a Turkish lady dressed as Safiye was, but she didn't pay any attention to them: "They're not going to keep women hidden away any longer," she said. We bathed and threw a ball to each other, while children lurking at the edge of the trees chattered and pointed. Then we went back to listen to the music again and eat walnuts as Nicol spread out the plans he had made and explained them to us.

The children crept closer as the evening drew around us.

"But what are you hoping to find?" Safiye asked, her voice slurred with the wine.

"What was here," he said.

Helen brings the children to see me. She looks white and drawn. Her eyes are red.

"Oh, my dear, was it awful?" I hug her.

She kisses me. "I was scared, but really it was good to be there. It would have been an insult not to be arrested. All the other women in there, they were the most interesting women I've ever met. I learned a lot from them."

"Were they prostitutes?"

"No," she laughs and kisses me again. "Singers, teachers, artists—just women."

"But why?"

"Why? I don't know why. I'm not even one of them. Or at least, I wasn't. I just know any society which can do this to people doesn't have a chance." Her face goes grim, the lips tighten.

"Did they beat you?"

"Heavens, no, nothing like that." She smiles again. "But do you know, when they arrested me they searched the apartment and took away the phone book. A whole bunch of other stuff as well, but the phone book? I said, 'Look, I don't mark numbers in there, you're wasting your time,' but they still took it—the yellow pages and all. Now they won't give it back to me, they say it's evidence."

"Pigs," says Ann angrily.

Apartment? Before I can ask what she means, Mark interrupts: "Mum, can I have an apple?"

"Ask Mamie."

"Can I?"

"Of course." I polish one for him. He is so like Marc, my Marc, at his age, the year we left Smyrna, only the mirror would dare to tell me I'm not his mother.

"We brought you this blouse," Helen says. "Mother said that . . . well, you didn't have any left."

"I cut them all up," I laugh. I open it, lovely light blue silk, embroidered. I start to cry.

Ann touches my arm. "Don't you like it, Mamie? We can change it."

"I like it so much."

"Then why are you crying?"

"I was wondering who would wear it."

Ann looks at Helen in puzzlement and Helen pats her hand.

"I don't want this stupid apple," says Mark. "It's not made right. It's full of flour." He throws it in the wastebasket.

"How's David?" I ask. "Is he busy?" Such an innocuous question, but I feel the tension leap through the air as they look at each other.

"He's okay," says Ann.

"I'm not living with David anymore," Helen says. "We're friends, and I see the kids a lot"—her voice is tight and small—"but I want to be on my own."

"I'm bored," says Mark. "Can I go outside?"

"But if David wasn't unfaithful to her, why would the poor girl leave him?" I ask Hélène.

"Maman, nowadays adultery isn't the point. Some couples are unfaithful to each other and carry on living together quite happily; others aren't and they still split up." She plays with the fringe on the bedcover as she lectures me. "The world's changing, you know."

"Well, I don't like the sound of it."

She laughs at me and I feel small.

I hated her the day she was born. I couldn't help myself. She was just a baby and I had no right to hate her, but she was so ugly I couldn't stand the sight of her—that long nose sticking up like a sundial. Gnomon, that's what I used to call her. For a while, when she grew up, it was a fine nose, full of character, but now, as she gets old like me, it's becoming too large for her face again.

I used to try to cover it up with the blankets in her cot. "You silly woman, you'll suffocate her," said Doctor Amantos.

"The best thing that could happen to her." No, I didn't really whisper that, did I?

She has been dutiful, which is certainly more than my due.

If only I could say to her: You have no reason to love me, no reason to feel this guilt that gnaws away at you.

But I can't. So the guilt comes between us.

It was when I was depressed after Hélène's birth that I demanded to be taken to Troy. The house was full of books on archaeology and I started to read all that Schliemann had written about his discovery of Troy more than thirty years before. That was what archaeology ought to be, not these tiresome grids and plans: Schliemann seeing the glint at the bottom of the ancient wall, calling to his young wife: "Quickly, send the workmen away. Tell them they can have a holiday because it's your birthday." They tremble with excitement as they dig into the dirt. Careless of the tilting wall that rises above them, they pull Priam's treasure out into the daylight after three thousand years and wrap it in a shawl. I tremble, too. That's the passion with which the past should burst into life.

"But there's nothing left there to see," Nicol protested.

"Helen's jewels."

"Schliemann stole them all. And besides, they weren't Helen's. Schliemann was wrong; he found them at a level a thousand years before Priam."

How his so-called facts grated on me! "When he found the treasure he gave it to his wife to wear: the diadem, the necklace, the earrings, everything. Why don't you ever find anything like that? Lumps of stone and little bits of metal," I sneered.

He looked more angry than I had ever seen him. He should have struck me. "Damn it, woman, Schliemann was just a bloody gold digger. That's all he cared about—gold. He made his fortune in the gold rush in California and the rest of his life he went on searching for more. Like a pig after acorns. The greatest building in Troy was the temple of Athene and do you know what that bugger Schliemann did? He dug a trench right through the middle of it looking for your precious treasure."

He slammed the door. But in the end, to please me, to humour me, he made the arrangements for us to go. There were bandits in the mountains around Edremit, which meant we'd have to find a boat to take us. That was easy enough; Costa was happy to lend us the new sixty-foot yacht he'd bought just before the war and hardly ever sailed. But the British navy controlled the sea and the islands, so we had to get permission through the American consul. And even then, it would be too dangerous for us to go as far as the Dardanelles. Instead, Nicol had to telegraph to Chanak for a guide to come out with horses and guards and meet us down the coast at Besike, where Agamemnon's fleet had landed.

Yes, he arranged it all, and enthusiastically, too. Just to prove to me that Schliemann was wrong.

"You shouldna believe all that Homer says," he warned me gently. "The war wasn't really fought over Helen."

"But in the story—"

"Aye, well, it's embroidery. Very pretty." He patted my knee. "But embroidery. It was more a matter of the Greeks trying to get control of the trade routes through the Bosphorus."

"Don't wars get fought for love?" I asked sadly.

"No, they're fought for greed." He tried to pull me to him, but I twisted away.

Desolation.

Nicol was right. There's nothing left to see. Piles of rubble and toppled pillars on a burnt hill: all that's left from centuries of earthquakes and Schliemann's frenzy.

Nicol talks to the guide and from time to time I feel him looking over his shoulder anxiously at me. I'm too silent.

I sit in a tiny semicircular theatre in the glaring, dusty sun. My skin is so dry. I don't care what they decide to do. But as I wait, a little nerve of life stirs in me. It's really quite a pretty place, this theatre. Just nine or ten rows of seats and a small stage between them: nothing gigantic, a place where people would be aware of each other. Poppies grow out of the earth between the broken stones. What would they watch? Not tragedy, surely, not here; dancing perhaps. Yes, sitting here in the evening coolness, watching the dancers in their light robes, Helen and Paris holding hands. I hug my arms and feel the rhythm return to my body.

Nicol and the guide stand behind me.

"They would have danced here," I tell them.

Nicol looks at the guide inquiringly.

"Yes, and music, too," he says.

"Just imagine them, Nicol, can't you feel them sitting here, Helen and Paris . . . ?"

"Oh, no, not Helen and Paris," says the guide, a nasty little Turk with thick glasses and a straggly moustache. "This is a Roman theatre built on the ruins of the old Troy."

It's too much. I slump down and burst into tears. "There's nothing here. It isn't Troy."

Nicol sits beside me, his arm round my shoulders. "Dinna worry yourself, lassie," he says, "I ken how you feel," and for once the rough Scottish tenderness doesn't irritate me.

I cower into his hardness, hiccupping.

After a while, he persuades me to get up and walk with them in between the sloping limestone walls to the narrow gate.

I touch the stone. "Is this real?"

"Aye, it was here then."

I lean my cheek against it and look up. The tower at the gate is only two storeys high, for heaven's sake. "It's so small," I whisper. "Like a farmyard."

"But imagine a man like Hector here," he says. He stretches out his arms so as to touch the walls on either side, and yes, I see him—Hector, not Paris. Why have I wanted him to be Paris? Hector, it's Hector who cares for Helen more, is it not, when Paris takes fright at what he's done like a panicky schoolboy; Hector, not an awkward potato nor a side of beef, not graceless any longer, but planted here so no army will ever move him.

"It would be a hard place to take," he is saying. "Can you not see it? A great thick barred gate and the defenders along the tops of both walls shooting down their arrows and hurling rocks. I wouldna like to be on the outside trying to get in."

I take his arm and he leads me into the city.

"It's a real city," he tells me excitedly. "It was right from the start in 3000 B.C. Just a wee place then, a hundred yards across, but a city for all that. There were villages in the country round about where the ordinary people lived, but they'd come in here for protection whenever there was danger. The place was destroyed by earthquakes and invaders—do you see the marks of fire on the stones, down here?—but they always built it up again. That's what a city is; a place where people come to defend themselves."

He shows me the ruins of a house; a palace he calls it. I watch as he paces it out. "Sixteen yards," he calls. His shirt sticks to his body, rough with hair.

The smallness of everything still depresses me. "A palace sixteen yards long."

"But it would be a fine, lively place," he tries to cheer me up. "Look at where the pillars were, five along each wall and two in the middle, marble; and a hearth over here in the corner. Can you not imagine the lady sitting in front of it sewing, and the men sprawled around telling stories and boasting?"

His enthusiasm won't let me go. Together we climb some steps to the watchtower on the north side, between hillocks covered with poppies and small oak bushes. We look out from the cliff, down the gulley and across the flat landscape, the plain of Troy. Peasants plough the patterned fields with oxen; minarets rise sharp and gleaming out of the villages. In the distance, the sea seems motionless.

Nicol hands me the binoculars and points, "That's it, the Dardanelles. That's what all the trouble was about. A skipper off one of the boats was telling me the current runs both ways. Two layers; the cool water flowing down from the Black Sea and the warm water from the Aegean going back the other way."

I see forts along the strait, vague hills behind. I remember maps in the newspaper. "Is that Gallipolli?" I ask.

"Where Kemal drove the English into the sea," he laughs. "Aye, that's it. He's a good fighter, that one. But you can see why men do fight over it, can't you. It's not just the sea route they want; it's the bridge between Europe and Asia, too. Xerxes's bridge of boats was up there behind the hills, past Chanak."

From up here the city is high, invulnerable; it controls all the movements of the world. I look down and step back quickly from the crumbling edge. The peasants in the fields, the Turkish villages disappear.

"This is where Priam stood," I say with certainty. "He stood here and watched Achilles dragging Hector's body behind his chariot, and there was nothing he could do."

"Aye," Nicol says. "After seeing that he wouldna care what happened to the city."

I turn to him and see it in his eyes: he believes the story, too.

We rode back down the hill and through the fields. Then along the steep pine-covered slopes to the beach, where the Greeks squabbled and raced their chariots as they waited for the gods to win their war for them.

I was exhausted, yet full of lightness.

All afternoon I lay on a rock in the sea, not caring for once about the sun on my skin. It dazzled me with its reflections in the water, pulled this way and that, bright and glaring on the surface, soft yellow on the rippled sand below. Jellyfish hung suspended and small fish swam in a clear green world. The dazzle entered my brain.

The servants had set up tents because the movement of the boat unsettled me. When the sun went down, they lit a fire; as the sparks from the pine branches leaped up into the darkness, we ate and drank and listened to one of the sailors playing a flute. And then, with the noise of the waves, the scent of seaweed and resin and woodsmoke all around us, we made love in the tent. For the first time there was gentleness between us. I wasn't violated; I didn't pray he would stop or sneer at him when he did.

In the morning, I awoke with the light and the sound of birds singing. Nicol snored. But another noise, too. I opened the flap of the tent and sheep were nosing around it, fifty or sixty of them, baaing and scuffling. A Turkish shepherd boy stood so close I nearly bumped into him. He wasn't there to spy; he was waiting for me. He had dark, heavy eyes and full lips in a thin, almost sallow face. His black hair was long and curling; his skin oh so smooth and brown. He reached out and touched me here on my arm. I pulled away and felt the spot with my fingertips. Then the servants ran out shouting from the other tent and chased him away and threw stones at his sheep.

Chapter Five

Helen

As soon as I hear André's voice on the phone, I want to hang up. The last thing in the world I need is for him to think of me as an ally. He repels me almost as much as he frightens me.

But why? Why do I detest him so violently? After all, he's no worse than most of the people I rub myself against at parties; than many of my so-called friends, even.

Is it because I still see in him so much of the child I used to know? That weird, slightly scary child who cut himself off from the other Westmount kids by the intensity of his will to believe, absolutely, in whatever he did? Of course, all those kids, even those kids, had to believe in something, to some extent. When the boys played hockey, I guess they might actually have been convinced it was Rocket Richard flicking the puck high to the short side, past the falling goalie. For a moment.

And the girls, as we smeared on surreptitious makeup, must have seen—who would it have been—Grace Kelly, Audrey Hepburn in the mirror. We dreamed of dangerous dates with

Rossano Brazzi or James Dean. But we always knew it was make-believe in the end. Those were cool, rich kids, trained not to be taken in, for whom reality was good enough.

Even I. I was brought up in an atmosphere of conviction and that kept me apart from the others, but even I could draw the line between myself and my dreams. Yes, even as I yearned for them to come true.

I was the only one who was ever at all close to Andy Goldman (which may be why I still can't get away from him). Whatever he did possessed him completely. Naturally enough, he was useless at all sports; he was too ungainly and weak. Yet when he played in, say, a baseball game, running for a fly ball, he'd stop at nothing. "Jees, he'll cut right through you," the others would say with mocking awe. Except he couldn't, of course, he was such a drip he'd bounce right off and lie in a heap of catatonic fury. Playing a gentle game of tag one day near the library, Andy ran flat out into a plate glass door. Stone cold for more than twenty minutes and not a mark on him.

"You're a fanatic, Andy," I said to him self-righteously when we were both fifteen and he was moonily in love with blonde Susie Fitzgibbon—I, who spied on David ceaselessly.

And just a couple of weeks ago, Roger reached the same conclusion: *"Tabernac, il est fana, c'gars."*

"Is your line bugged?" is the first thing André says. Subtle question.

"No. Well, I don't know. No."

"Probably is. Okay, just listen. I've got to see you tonight. In the Berri métro, the Bourassa platform, 9.30. Make sure you're not followed. Wait till I turn up. Got that?"

"But why?"

"Just repeat it."

I repeat it. He puts the phone down.

Fuck André. All afternoon I can't work for fuming over his arrogance. What right has he to order me about? Just because once, just once, I took his side against Roger and Monique, that doesn't mean he can drag me into his grotesque games. Of course, I'm not going to meet him. I'm sick of these men who make a pretence of revolution and then assume that gives them the right to push you around like some redneck husband. I shall stay here and paint.

The only trouble is I can't paint. My arms are rigid with anger. I want anger in my paintings, yes, but it must be hard and focused, not this feeble rage that blurs my eyes like Vaseline.

And where, after all that, do I find myself as the clock hanging from the roof flicks to 9.25? Waiting where André told me to be, naturally. I'm even early, damn it, so thorough is my training in self-abasement. I try to make fun of myself. "God, you might as well lie back and enjoy it," I say, then realize I'm speaking aloud. An old woman looks at me in alarm. I laugh, which doesn't help my image, either.

But where the hell is André? One train whines in on its rubber tires, sucks up its passengers and carries them into the tunnel. I am left alone, except for a drunk who wanders around at the other end of the platform, making me catch my breath every time he stumbles towards the edge. I feel conspicuous; André couldn't have chosen a more exposed place to keep me waiting. New passengers trickle onto the platform, older people going home on this side, the younger ones coming downtown for the action on the platform opposite. They stare at each other with bored hostility. Another train. A middle-aged man with sleek black hair and a neat suit, galoshes over immaculate shoes, saunters up and makes kissing noises at me. I turn my back on him. He comes round in front of me again, not quite touching, says something in a language I don't recognize, rubs his thumb and forefinger together, leers.

"Fuck off!" I say and he retreats.

Another train carries him away. The air whistles past me. I feel as if I'm made of paper.

At last, André comes up behind me silently and touches my arm. I jump.

"Let's go," he says brusquely.

Before I have a chance to be angry with him, he dashes back towards the escalators that go down to the Atwater line. He jerks like a spider with a damaged leg. People pull apart to let him through, then look round after him. He takes a wide arc to avoid a pair of cops patrolling the concourse.

"You could have been on time," I complain breathlessly.

"I was," he says. "I was checking you out. In case you were tailed?"

"Jesus," I mutter in disbelief.

In silence we get on a train and off at the next stop, squeezing through the doors as they hiss shut. Out into the drizzle, past the entrances to flophouses and pizzerias to the bedraggled hookers on the sidewalk of Sainte Cathérine.

André pauses on a corner. "In here," he says, as I catch up.

I look at the dimly lit sign above our heads: Yukon Lunch. The window is full of dying plants and ads for cheap breakfasts. Inside, old bums sit in front of empty coffee mugs, one to a table. Everything is green in the harsh neon.

"Here?"

He smiles and goes in. I follow him to the counter: containers of beef stew, ribs, sausages, grease congealing on the surface. "What do you want?"

"Nothing," I say moodily. "A coffee and a donut."

He has the same and waits for me to pay. I put down the exact amount for my own, and, buoyed with my mean victory, look around for a table. All the places against the wall are taken. We have to sit in the middle where everybody can watch us.

I don't believe any of this. "Do you come here often?" I ask.

André has no sense of humour. "Quite often," he says, leaning forward seriously. "It gives you an idea of what life's like. I mean, at the bottom."

"Okay. But why bring me?"

"Nobody'd ever think of looking for you here."

"Thanks," I say sarcastically. "But haven't you ever looked

around this place, André? When was the last time you saw a woman in here? D'you think there's ever been one? Hell, they're watching every move I make as if I was a cop."

He glances about furtively and his lips tighten. I nod. I stand out in here like the flashing light on a patrol car. André, too, in a different way. On the surface, he might look the part: unshaven, sunken cheeks; a worn overcoat, stained on the front and the cuffs. But there's a passion in André, a wildness that makes you want to duck whenever you see him. His eyes are buried deep in his skull, but they burn. Within these green formica walls there is only resignation. No despair, nothing so demanding.

The old man at the next table is thin and very white, his body soft inside a black coat, his hair grey and wispy. He's incapable of anything but patience. He sits with a paper folded open at the racing page, reading it again and again. Every few minutes, he says something to another man who sits near the window. They talk about the horses. They won't bet, nothing as vital as that, but they discuss the odds endlessly, disagreeing politely. I look back at André. I prefer them to him.

"Do you want to go someplace else?" he asks anxiously.

I shake my head. "No need. We might as well stay here now."

But there's still something I don't understand. At the back of the room, there's a different feel to the place. The men are younger, some of them almost stylishly dressed in cheap clothes. They sit two or three to a table and chat. A man comes in wearing cream pants and a matching knitted jacket with a belt hanging loose. He sits down and somebody teases him. Beneath it all, there's a restlessness, a wary attention I can't make out.

A boy in a nylon jacket gets up and goes to the stairs that lead down to the washroom.

André watches him, but I feel him flicking sidelong glances at me, too. "What's happening?" I ask. "The edginess?"

"Don't you even get it?" He waits with a superior smirk on his face. "Shit, they're all gay. Not the bums in the front, though maybe they were, too, once. But all the guys at the back. Every single one of them. You can get sucked off down in the washroom for five bucks, sometimes for free." His voice is harsh but excited. "Sometimes a guy wants it so bad he'll pay you to let him do it."

I tilt my seat back and look at him questioningly. Without intending it, I wink slightly.

"Don't be disgusting," he protests angrily. "It's just . . . well, we've got to know what's going on, right?"

"Right, André." I pat his hand mockingly and he pulls it away.

He sulks. "I'm going in with the F.L.Q."

Silence.

He expects me to show disapproval, I know, but I don't say anything, I don't want to make it that easy for him. He fidgets and starts to tear a paper napkin into narrow, careful shreds. "They're the only real . . ." He pauses, concentrating on his fingers.

"The only real what?"

"The only real revolutionaries." He speaks in a monotone without looking up at me. "They don't just sit around and talk, month after month after month. They're doing something about it."

"About what, André?" I watch him closely. "Are you going to drop out of the group?"

"Not unless you throw me out." His eyes stare through the table. "And you can't. You can't throw me out, even if you want to. Not after that letter you read at the meeting. There's a place for terrorism, a rationale for it." His close-cropped black hair forms a V on his forehead. "So long as it's controlled, disciplined," he adds stubbornly. The sides of his skull look as though they've been crushed in a press.

High up on the wall there are faded prints of fall scenes. The traffic to and from the washroom continues steadily.

"I don't think you know what you're getting into," I suggest gently.

"What do you know about it?" André asks excitedly. "You're just a bunch of amateurs. Bourgeois dilettantes. The F.L.Q. have been fighting for the last ten years."

I lean towards him. My detachment has gone. "Why do you believe in the revolution, André?"

He looks away from me disdainfully. "That's irrelevant."

"It's not. It's important. Motives don't justify actions. But they do explain them. They tell you where you're going."

He lines the strips of paper into a neat little pile. "The revolutionary act is autonomous."

I smile and shake my head. "Bullshit, André. Tell me why."

"Because the whole system's rotten, *pourri,* that's why. And who made it the way it is? My parents, fuck them, and yours too, for all their big ideals. They've been ripping off the people who work for them for generations." His voice is breaking as though he were thirteen again. "They deserve all they've got coming to them."

Three bikers in leather jackets strut in off the street and go over to the counter. They argue with the owner about how many slices of bread they get with their beef stew. The leader, enormously fat with a thick black beard, sits down at the table next to us and the others follow. Apart from André and the two old bums who are buried in their racing papers, everybody in the room watches them with the same momentary fear.

Instinctively, I pull my chair away. I turn back to André. "I know things have got to be changed, just as much as you do," I whisper. "I know that means violence somewhere along the line, because the system sustains itself through violence. But there's a crazy fallacy in assuming that's all the revolution is. That it stops there, eh? Look, I'm a painter, okay, not a bomber or a kidnapper. The revolution for me is in my painting."

"That's not revolution," he sneers. "Painting for the museums. Art galleries in New York."

"That's not what I'm doing any longer, André. But you're missing the point, anyway. What I mean is, the real revolution has to be in yourself. I'm a woman, so the revolution, for me, is to free myself as a woman, as a painter. I don't know who you are, André, I really don't, but I do know you're not going to make yourself a revolutionary by carrying sticks of dynamite around in a shopping bag."

Contempt has crept into my voice, though I didn't want it to, and I expect him to jump up angrily and leave. But he doesn't. He crumples the shredded paper into a ball and throws it on the floor.

"There isn't time for you to use the revolution as an excuse for discovering yourself, Helen. When there's a war in the street you fight. One way or the other, you fight. Then we'll find out which side you're really on."

From down below in the washroom there are shouts and bangs. One of the waiters runs to the top of the stairs and opens the door. As he does so, a small, plump, middle-aged man in a blue raincoat scuttles past him.

"He stole my wallet," the man screams. "Forty bucks. He stole my wallet."

Behind him another man, younger, taller, with curly hair and a dazed expression on his face, staggers out.

"You whore," shouts the older man. "You're a thief, *un bandit.*"

A silly grin flickers on the young man's lips.

"Putain!" The older one rushes at him and punches him weakly. He is pushed away and stumbles past us, trying not to fall. He bumps into the gigantic biker, spilling a forkful of potatoes and gravy all over his jeans. A bearlike paw grabs the man's wrist and holds it. As the man sees what he's done, his face quivers. He belches. "He stole my wallet," he whines.

"I don't give a fuck about your wallet," says the biker,

poking a greasy thumb deep into his paunch. "Don't ever do that again." Another poke. "Understand?" He throws him on the floor against a table leg and goes back to shovelling up his food. The man yelps in fear, then scrambles tearfully out of the door.

I'm ready to leave, too. "Why did you want to see me?" I ask curtly.

"To give you this." André holds out the bag he's been carrying.

I shake my head.

"It's nothing. Just timers."

"No."

"I thought I could depend on you."

"You can, André. But not for that." I get to my feet and pull on my coat.

He rises, too. "Can I talk to you again, Helen?"

Knowing I should say no, I say, "If you want to."

Helen was only half listening as Claire wound herself deeper into a coil of guilt. It was almost a relief to see Akiyo emerge from the shadows on the other side of the bar. He stood for a moment staring impassively up at the girl on the stage. Helen raised her hand and he hurried over to them.

"Hi, Akiyo," Claire said. She seemed almost relieved, too.

"I'm busy," he snapped. "I can't waste time hanging around this dump."

"Relax." Claire caught him playfully by the arm. "Sit down. Have a beer."

"I'll have a Scotch," he said to the topless waitress who stood beside him. He didn't look at her but before she was out of earshot he said, "Shapeless boobs. In a couple of years she'll be sweeping floors with them."

"I think she's nice," said Claire. "Her name's Tanya. She's Ukrainian."

"No wonder. Fucking Ukrainians, they eat dumplings all the time, don't they? She looks like a fucking dumpling."

"Why do you have to be so offensive?" Helen asked angrily. "You don't even know her."

"Well, tell her to keep her tits out of my ear then." They glared at each other. He turned away and sipped the whisky Helen had paid for.

He looked bigger sitting down than standing up. He was very small but he held his body straight in the chair. Helen knew practically nothing about him. He had been born, Claire had told her, in an internment camp for Japanese Canadians during the war, and though he couldn't possibly have remembered anything of those experiences, the anger seethed in him still. He had studied physics at the university and then become a photographer. He was competitive, intolerant, as full of electricity as a neon sign. What else? He called all women slits. Helen didn't think she should like him and didn't want to ask him for a favour.

"What do you want?" Akiyo asked suspiciously.

Claire brushed her hair back from her eyes and looked at him. She began to giggle.

"Very funny. Now what the fuck's the joke?"

"Helen wants to borrow your cock," Claire spluttered.

"My what?"

"Your cock."

He looked at Helen accusingly. "Talk sense," he said. "She's out of her tree."

Helen took a deep breath. This was ridiculous. "I'm doing this collage. It's a new thing I'm working on. Kind of satirical? I want to use some colour Xeroxes of a penis." She raised her eyebrows. "Erect?"

Claire spluttered again.

"Go fuck yourself," Akiyo told her. He turned to Helen. "Why me? What about Jean-Claude? Isn't he good enough for you?"

"I asked him already. He thought it was disgusting." She shrugged. "Claire suggested you."

"For art's sake, darling," Claire purred mockingly and stroked his thigh.

Akiyo jerked away, rocking the table.

"You'll be famous." Claire pursued him.

"Hell, it doesn't matter," Helen said irritably. "Forget it. I'll find—"

"Why?" Akiyo snapped.

"Why the colour Xerox? It's just that it's dead right for what I want. You know, the hardness of the colour, the way it alienates everything."

"Doesn't sound much like you."

"It's more like me than anything else I've done," she said intensely.

He watched her curiously, crunching ice. "Okay. Do I get paid?"

"Akiyo!" Claire groaned.

"Another Scotch?" Helen suggested.

"A bottle. And some of the prints. And a credit in the catalogue: Cocks by courtesy of Akiyo Watanabe. Okay?"

Helen raised her glass in fake friendship. "It's a deal."

"When?"

"We could go after my next number," Claire said eagerly. "I've got a three-hour break then."

"What do we need you for?" Akiyo asked harshly.

"Helen said . . . oh, shit!" Claire shook her head as tears came to her eyes.

Helen didn't know why she bothered to control the anger in her voice. She felt her hands shaking. "The machine's in McGill. Somebody has to stand outside and keep people from barging in. Unless you'd rather do an exhibition."

"Okay, okay." Akiyo waved the explanation away.

Claire went to get ready and they sat in strained silence. In the middle of the afternoon, the bar was quiet—just a few hard-core regulars and some casual passers-by. Away at the other end of the long narrow room, beyond the circular stage, one of the waitresses was dancing on a foot-high box next to a lone business-man. To the noise of the jukebox her pubic hair gyrated a few inches away from his face. From time to time he said something and she bent to listen; as she did so, a group of raucous students leaned over to peer between her legs. She turned and grinned down at them. She looked very young and slim and bored.

The jukebox stopped and a scratchy fanfare came over the PA system: "And now, ladies and gentlemen, *mesdames et messieurs,* we bring you our star of the week, Miss Claire Cully." The fool made it sound like *Cul-lit,* just to get a few laughs, but it was Claire's own name, and when she swirled into the spotlights it was her own skin and her own hair that shone; no makeup, no candy-floss wig. Her blonde hair floated halfway down her back. She wore no elaborate, kinky costume, just a large black lace shawl draped carelessly in front of her. She reached up and touched the low ceiling with a fingertip and started to move slowly. She was much bigger than the average dancer—she made the waitresses look like children—too big, they had told her at first, for the Québec market, which goes for tight little asses and pointed breasts. She had come to Montréal straight from the English farming village she had been born in, far out on the Gaspé coast near Percé, trapped between the mountains and the sea, surrounded by French-speaking fishing ports. Everything in her had rebelled against it. She learned to speak French, got herself pregnant by a Québécois realtor, had a first abortion at nineteen. Now, here she was, twenty-four, a stripper, pregnant again.

As Claire's body began to pick up the rhythms of B.B. King's guitar, Helen watched her anxiously. Every pulse in the music rippled into the muscles of her legs and stomach. The last girl who had danced up there, in thigh-length boots and green makeup, had banged out a single dominant beat, chopped by the strobes into a thousand postures of aggression. But Claire flowed with the music; she let it take her body and explore it openly in front of this wretched audience. She didn't turn them on with fantasies of fake submission; she allowed them to see her as she was, looking in on herself, a nakedness that filled Helen with horror.

All that Helen was learning to believe in was offended by what she saw. This was exploitation. It was unforgivable that somebody as honest as Claire should allow herself to be displayed in this fetid hole. When she touched the curtains they billowed dust. A man in the front row waved a folded dollar bill in the air. But oh, she was so beautiful and Helen loved her for it, for being strong enough to be herself, even here. There were stretch marks across her abdomen, great tufts of blonde curls in her armpits and crotch. She had come to Montréal because she wanted to be an artist; she'd never make it, but her body was more real than any painting Helen knew. Yet how could that be enough for Claire?

"I've got so many things to work out," she had said in desperation as they sat here waiting for Akiyo. "Everything's so fucked up. Christ, Helen, I've really got to understand why I got pregnant. Why I wanted to get pregnant."

"What do you mean, wanted?"

"Well, I must have, mustn't I? Unconsciously, eh? Why would I have let him come in me when I did if I didn't want it? And yet at the same time, shit, I can't be pregnant, not now. Everything's too disorganized. I've got too many things to get together. I can't have a kid around when I'm going through all this crap. Maybe if I can get some bread together . . ."

The guilt that underlay what Claire was saying repelled Helen. "Must everything that happens be willed? Isn't there such a thing as accident?"

"Yes, but that's just an excuse for not facing up to my own

subconscious. If I don't face up to it—and it sure as hell doesn't want me to—it has even more power over me. I get screwed up even more."

"Okay, but once you start you can go on endlessly in that direction." Helen felt herself getting bored. "Look, it's easy, you could end up showing that what you really wanted—subconsciously, okay?—wasn't just to get pregnant but was . . . well, to have an abortion, eh? Was that what was really driving you?"

Claire had turned pale. Helen wished she hadn't said it; it might be too close to the truth.

Now Claire lay on a sheepskin on the stage, her legs apart, hips in the air. The music had deepened to a slow blues that seemed to writhe out of her. She rubbed and pinched her thighs and breasts, her cheeks glowed. Helen felt her own body responding, too. When the tape ended, Claire stood for a last distant moment, lost in the spotlight. The audience whistled and clapped. She would never be one of their favourites—they couldn't despise her—but her presence disturbed and thrilled them.

Akiyo looked at Helen. "Did she come?"

"How should I know? Ask her."

They drank.

"How are your kids taking it?" he asked.

"What?"

"Well, your splitting. It must be hard for them, right?"

It was the last thing Helen had expected Akiyo to ask about and she searched his face for insincerity. She couldn't find any sign of it; he pulled his small straggly beard, his eyes were opaque. "I guess it is, because I don't think they had any sense that something was wrong. I'm not sure I did, for that matter. We didn't fight or throw things or fuck around."

"Yeah," said Akiyo, losing interest.

Claire returned wearing a long flowered dress.

Helen got up and hugged her. "You were great," she said.

"I don't know, it's never so good during the day. At night when there are more people—I don't mean I get off on them, but there's more energy. You know, from having to kind of shut them out? And then, I guess I was nervous about you being here. Isn't that crazy?" She played with Helen's fingers.

"You were great," Helen said again and kissed Claire's lips.

"Did you come?" Akiyo asked.

Claire laughed. "I try not to. The stage collapses." She stroked his hair that sprouted out in all directions.

"Well, for fuck's sake, I haven't got all day. Let's split."

Outside it was a clear fall afternoon, cool in the shade. They drove in Helen's Volvo down Saint Urbain Street and along Sherbrooke to the university. The maples in the great quad were shedding their leaves; students sat reading in patches of sunlight. The severe stone buildings climbed up the hill towards the exploding yellow and red trees on Mount Royal.

Their feet crunched on the pathway.

"It's so peaceful," Claire said, holding her arms wide.

"For the moment," Helen murmured, remembering the McGill Française riots. Demonstrators howled against the Anglophone university, helicopters clattered overhead, their searchlights spilled on top of her.

Akiyo, trotting along between them, remembered, too. "What're they going to do with it when Québec's independent? D'you think they'll just leave it as a ruin, right in the centre of the city?"

"I guess they'll tear it down and build high rises," Claire said sadly.

"In Leningrad after the revolution they turned one of the cathedrals into a museum of atheism," Helen said. She felt light and full of energy.

"You're not an atheist," Claire challenged her.

"No, but places like this make me one."

They laughed.

In the Xerox room Helen adjusted the machine.

Claire patted Akiyo's buttocks. "I'll leave you two alone. Have fun." She kissed him.

He glared after her and unbuckled his jeans. Helen was surprised at how strong his hips and thighs were; his penis nestled between them. He seemed uncertain, vulnerable, and she wanted to tell him how nice his body was, even as she knew how irritated he would be to hear her say it. Neither of them knew what to do.

"Okay, you want to start?" he asked.

"Well, I wanted it . . . well, bigger." She gestured helplessly.

He looked down and fingered his penis. It looked as if it would never grow. "You could blow it," he suggested.

"Who's paying whom?" she smiled.

"Well, you want me to just stand here and jerk off?" he said angrily.

"Look, why don't we start with it like that. It's pretty." She touched him and unbuttoned his shirt gently.

He climbed on top of the machine and straddled it. It clicked; its glow leaked out around his body like a halo. "Hey, is this thing going to make me impotent?"

"No," she humoured him, though she didn't know. "Just relax." It was like holding a baby in a washtub. She stroked the back of his legs absentmindedly. On the prints that came out his penis grew larger. "Claire said you couldn't get it up."

"Dumb bitch." He turned on his back and his cock waved in the air. "I can't make it with fat women like that. She's so fucking gross it really turns me off. With slim chicks I'm okay. I like to feel their bones. You should see her cunt, rolls of fat, Jesus!" He reached out for Helen.

She pushed him over on his stomach again. "It'd give the machine a heart attack." As more prints came out, she went on: "They're beautiful, Akiyo, purple and red and a lovely strange blue."

"Make some for me, eh?" The machine was warm against his skin. "Have you seen my photographs?" he asked.

"Yes," she said hesitantly.

"What did you think of them?"

She ran her finger down between his buttocks. "There was one I really liked. An old man, a bum, I guess, sitting in the sunlight in Place d'Armes, with a shadow from one of the buildings decapitating him completely."

"Fuck, that's the old stuff. Two years ago at least. What about the new ones?"

They were completely different and Helen wasn't sure what to make of them. Images of corners of buildings, steps, billboards, with no people, just once or twice their shadows. While the print was still drying he had crossed the images out with a ball-point pen, scribbled over them, or sometimes incised their outlines till the paper was rutted and torn. The cool mechanical processes of the camera were filled with frenzy.

"I guess I don't really know what to do with photography when it gets away from . . . well, away from people. That's what it does best, isn't it? You know, the way old portraits kind of reverberate?"

"Jesus Christ, that's all I need. You're so out of date. Bored housewives who like photographs so they can feel sorry for the people in them; that really pisses me off."

She felt the rough surface of his scrotum. She had never seen a man like this before.

"That's good," said Akiyo. "Don't stop. You know, I could come like this. With a bit of help. You want to try it?"

"Yes," she said, "let's." The thought excited her.

He raised himself slightly so she could reach between his legs. She squeezed and pressed, feeling the thick stem bulge against her fingers. "Oh, yes, Akiyo," she cried, "yes," as he jumped uncontrollably, spurting into emptiness. "Yes," she rubbed her face against his smooth back.

"Shit, shit, shit!" He hammered the machine with his fist.

That last print was the best, a green veil blossoming from the pink and purple-shaded barrel with the outline of Helen's fingernail etched along it.

When they opened the door into the corridor, Claire blew a mocking kiss to Akiyo. "Was it good for you, my sweet?"

He pushed past her.

Outside it was cold. They shivered. Helen offered to drop them both off, but they said they'd rather walk. She kissed Claire and held out her hand shyly to Akiyo. "Thank you, Akiyo," she said, looking into his eyes.

"Don't forget the Scotch," he told her.

They stood and watched Helen walking away from them along the path. She skipped lightly for a few paces as she crossed a curb.

"She kissed you," Akiyo complained. "She didn't kiss me." He paused. "Fuck, what the hell does it matter? She probably kisses like a steel trap, anyway."

"Actually, her mouth is very soft," said Claire. "She kisses beautifully." And then, taking him by the hand, "You don't have to walk over people just to prove they exist," she told him tenderly.

All through the city, little flecks of panic flutter in the air.

I see it in people's faces in the street. They push along the sidewalks on Sainte Cathérine, they try to catch the last of the sun at lunch hour in the park, they flow out of the office buildings and into the métro in the daily rush to escape, they do all the things they expect themselves to do every day, the things that protect them. And then the faces freeze, not all together but separately one by one at the oddest moments, waiting for the lights to change, bumping into an unknown shoulder, the face freezes, just for a second, the eyes lose their focus, or rather they focus on the layer of vision between the eye and the outside world. These flecks hang there, we try to brush them away like cobwebs, they won't leave us alone. They touch us lightly with the reminder that nothing, nothing at all, is under control. We step off the curb, by the time we've reached the other side we've forgotten.

What could have made this happen to a whole city?

In October, too, of all months the least likely. October, the most responsible time of the year surely, the time when our lives are brought under control. The lovely craziness of spring is past; the relaxation, the indulgence of summer is over and paid for. We have only a few more weeks before the blizzards, the eddies of ice make the city uninhabitable. Another year is almost gone: it's our last chance to get things done, to clear up, to straighten out our lives. And now, instead of doing all that, we find ourselves faced with these meaningless moments of panic. What is happening?

A man has been kidnapped.

A man has been kidnapped? How can that affect us all? A man nobody cares about, an Englishman, a diplomat. Who cares about English diplomats, pure-bred caricatures? Well, this is a man, too, so somebody cares about him. He has a wife and a daughter, they care about him. He has a lot of cocktail party acquaintances, but a few friends as well, let's say ten real friends. And the men and women who kidnapped him, they care about him as passionately as a mother cares for her child on his first day at school; he is their insurance. So, perhaps twenty people in all really care about James Cross. Yet two million people, a whole city, see little sparks of panic, like fireflies, on their retinas.

How does this happen?

Panic takes many forms. Those who have something to

protect—and in this city many of them speak English—call for authority, order. What we need is protection, a show of force, uniforms and sirens, the sound of marching boots. The specks will be frightened away. Those who have nothing to lose—and in this city most of them speak French—rush wildly into the middle of the street. The traffic stops, the foundations of the banks collapse, the songs of the people will be played on the Muzak systems. Our lives will be free, the panic resolved into dancing.

But nobody, damn it, knows what's happening.

Trapped between the two worlds, I know least of all. All my life I've lived as one of those who have something to protect. I had one God who was mine, one man who was mine, a daughter, a son, work in which order was fundamental and luminous. I could stain a canvas and know at which knot exactly the stain would stop. There were accidents, of course, a spot here, a streak, but they served the pattern, reinforcements. Now, without my knowing why, all that has split apart. It's like breaking open the plaster mould around a casting and finding inside a form you never expected, a fist not a head, a spider instead of a dancer. At my own core I find a woman who has nothing to lose; someone who has nothing to lose precisely because she is a woman. All this time I've been misled into believing I was one of the protected, the privileged, and have gone on feeling a vague sense of guilt and a crushing sense of responsibility because of it. But all that time I was one of the victims, screwed in the name of my own fulfilment.

How free I'm made by this new knowledge that I've nothing to lose.

And God, how afraid! Perhaps it's my own weakness but I don't know if I can face the thought of starting everything all over again. I've been conditioned to cling to the appearance of order. I don't want to fling myself triumphantly into chaos. I can't allow myself to believe that nothing has meaning. I want to take my life piece by piece, step by step, and rearrange it.

Slowly, with care. I need time to work it out. I need this to be a normal October in the city. The kid across the street has time to probe his car, his father has time to dig up the cabbage stumps in the backyard, so why can't I find time to work out the new pattern in my life?

The flecks of panic hang in the air. This city I've always loved is falling apart, too. Its fragments get in my way.

Always in the past there was someone I could depend on. A man. My stepfather could be trusted, he was good, responsible, he didn't trespass, didn't exploit people, surely. Then why is my mother so deprived of meaning by his death? And David, too, could be trusted; he didn't interfere, kept his distance, skirted the unspeakable. So why do I feel such joy in his discomfort?

Those men I used to rely on have slipped away. The men I know now are unconvincing masks; they can't conceal their panic. Not just the Andrés and Akiyos, they're caricatures from the start, no good will come of them. But the men I feel something valid for—a residue of affection, desire, even respect—they climb up the rickety, curving steps to my front door and as I watch them through the curtain, I see them trying to pull themselves together. They have to hide what's really happening to them. They brush the specks away from their eyes.

David sits on the floor and looks awkward. Floors aren't meant to be sat on. He pokes the ice in his whisky. "I just wanted to be sure you were all right," he says. Does he think he can cover up his own fear by pretending he can still look after me?

"I guess this is a tough time to be a woman," he says and I want to laugh at his attempt to understand. You can't understand, David. Understand yourself before you try to understand me.

"The children miss you," he says accusingly. Doesn't it humiliate you, David, to use them, too?

And to think I used to imagine that if we ever parted, which of course we wouldn't, we'd still be friends!

He shifts his legs and tries to sit with them straight out in front of him, but it doesn't work. He nearly topples over. I smile and he bursts out angrily (yes, I like this better; let him be himself): "It's those bloody friends of yours. They've turned you right around, haven't they? Can't you see what they're doing, Helen? I know this isn't the best of all possible worlds, but people at least have a chance here, don't they? Look, wherever you are, someone's going to rise to the top, someone else is going to end up doing what he's told to do. It's common sense. The best we can do is keep the relationship as humane as possible." As in matrimony, David?

"What's the use of breaking everything down if you've nothing to put in its place? I know the family unit isn't fair on the woman, I really do, but none of us will get anywhere by just opting out of it unilaterally. Damn it, if there's one thing I reproach you for, it's the way you trust those bastards when you won't even listen to the people who care most for you."

But David, can't you see, I've been brainwashed, for God's sake?

When he's calmed down, he gets up to leave. "I'd like to come and talk to you again." He turns with his hand on the doorknob. "Listen, Helen, I know it's difficult, what you're going though. If there's anything I can do . . ."

I examine the paintbrush I've been fiddling with, holding its bristles between his eyes and mine. He slams the door.

I know it's unfair, cruel. He really is puzzled and hurt. But I can't bear the pretence he's putting up. If only he had the strength to be himself, perhaps we could relate, perhaps we could fight, on equal terms. But no, it's not possible. Don't even think of it. The purpose in David's life is to control; once that's taken away from him, he just fades out.

Jean-Claude lies with me on the mattress.

Once, maybe twice a week if I'm lucky, he gives me the benefit of his attentions. In return, I'm expected to make dinner for him. Jean-Claude hasn't eaten or slept on his own for years.

Sometimes he phones to say he's coming; usually, not even that. What would he do if he arrived and I wasn't here waiting for him?

When I first found out he was fucking so many other people, I thought I'd be bound to hate him. I lost my temper and attacked him. He lied and apologized and finally he cried. I held him. And then I discovered it was still good to be here on the mattress with him, his compliments in my ear, his fingertips touching the nerve ends beneath my skin. I don't think he's a very good lover; I don't have much to go on obviously, but from what Claire tells me, he isn't exactly the gift to women he takes himself to be.

"For somebody who fucks around so much, he's about as versatile as a Baptist missionary's wife," she says. I know what she means; you do what he wants to do and that's that. But still I like to lie here with his body soft and vulnerable beside me, under me, never on top. I like to hold him like this and feel the pulse in his neck against my breast. He can't bear the thought of losing any of his women. They're his security, the charms he clings to; he'll lose them all in the end.

I try to get him to do something about Claire. "If only you'd talk to her. She needs you right now."

"What do you mean, needs *me?*"

"Somebody who'll share what she's going through."

"Why me?"

"Jesus, you know why, Jean-Claude."

"I don't. Claire fucks anything she can get her hands on."

"Well, don't you?"

He pulls away. One isn't supposed to say that; each of his loves is unique. "It just so happens that mine is one of the few names she can remember."

"She's not asking you to marry her, for God's sake. She needs someone to be with, that's all."

"You don't know these small villages she comes from, Helen. I do. My parents were from the Gaspé, too. It's a terrible, claustrophobic little world, always the family nearby, the aunts, the uncles round the next corner. She wants to shock them, but she can't do without them. She doesn't know how to handle being alone; now she'll just have to learn."

How can I allow him to be so callous? How can I make love to him as he says it? But I do, I stroke his balls. I know he's talking about himself, his own horror of ever finding himself in an empty house. I try to get him to face up to it, but of course he won't. He goes on living his own life, worried by his own fears—of dying, of not getting tenure, of being left on his own—and the events in other people's lives that surround him are meaningless.

"Don't you even feel what's happening out there?" I ask. My fingers coax some stiffness into him, such a small cock, so much smaller than David's.

"Out where?" he sighs.

"The excitement, people's eyes in the street."

"They're just playing games, Helen. Don't get sucked in. They're crazy, those sons of bitches in the F.L.Q. It's too dangerous, what they're doing."

"But don't you want things to change?" I bend over him, nuzzling.

"Not that way. I want"—he cradles my head—"well, I guess I want our emotional lives to change, to expand. We're only tapping a tiny part of them. Politics isn't going to help."

My finger jabs into him.

"Ow," he says, writhing.

"Hasn't anyone done that before?"

"Yes, but not so deep."

"Poor Jean-Claude," I whisper.

It can't mean anything. For the moment, it's good to learn I can have and give pleasure with somebody I hardly know, somebody I don't even care for. It frees me from a whole sentimental clutter. My body isn't tied up by all the old tensions that used to bind me. But I know it can't last or lead to anything. "You'll end up hating him just like all the rest of us," Claire tells me, and I know she's right. Jean-Claude will fade away, too.

Which leaves me with Roger standing beside me in the kitchen.

I'm crying.

"Are you okay?"

"Fuck. These onions." I laugh.

"Here, let me do it," he says. He chops them much more efficiently, rocking the knife back and forth on its blade.

"Hey, you're a professional." I wipe my eyes and pour some more white wine into my glass.

"I guess. I worked in a hotel kitchen for a while."

"Which one?" I ask idly.

"The Ritz Carleton."

"Wow."

"Nothing romantic. Chopping vegetables, cleaning pans. A really authoritarian setup."

"You've done everything, haven't you?"

"All the bum jobs, yes," he smiles.

I start to fry the ginger and garlic together. I like the feel of him beside me. I feel sure of him.

"What are you doing now?"

"I put in quite a bit of time at the food co-op. But that's in a real mess, too."

"How come?"

"Well, shit, ten of us, twenty-five Maoists, three workers. That's a great cross-section of the proletariat, isn't it? We've lost a dozen members in the past month. Some guy who wants to buy macaroni doesn't see why he has to look at a gigantic fucking poster of Mao while he's doing it."

I add the onions and watch them sizzle. Then the peppers and tomatoes and turmeric on top.

"I keep telling them, 'If you want the co-op to have a long-term impact, you've got to make sure it's working properly; the political lessons'll follow.' But no, ideology first; without ideology, there's no correct model. So we fight each other all the time. I mean, shit, we'll end up with half a ton of natural rice and two barrels of olives on our hands and no members at all. But ideologically pure. They've already kicked out one guy because he's a De Leonist, whatever *that* is. Perfectly harmless, anyway. It'll be me next, I guess." He opens the fridge to get another beer, and as he passes me I reach out and touch him on the arm.

Momentarily, his whole body stiffens. Jesus, Roger, I want to scream, I'm not going to rape you. What are you afraid of? But no, it's not fear; it's just that he keeps an open space between himself and everyone else. There's communication, but no contact. I like him, I truly respect him; he's the most dedicated man I've ever known, more even than my stepfather. But he never comes out from behind his commitment. It's a mask, too. What is he hiding? I've no idea, no way of getting through to him. I feel ridiculous, hysterical even, to be asking more of him than he offers. He's strong, honest, he treats me as an equal; when we've finished eating, he'll get up and wash the dishes. David or Jean-Claude (Jean-Claude!) would never do anything as simple as that. But I'll never know what he's thinking and if I say, what are you thinking, Roger, he'll look at me in surprise because what he thinks is the gesture that he's making. How terrible to be so much in harmony with your own actions.

I add the scallops to the pan, some wine, a little more turmeric. "Don't you love the way it makes the colours glow?"

"André's disappeared," Roger says. He expects me to be surprised.

"Yes?" I stir the colours together. "He told me he was going in with the F.L.Q."

"*Bordel,* when?"

"A week, ten days ago."

"Shit. Why didn't you tell me?" His voice rises and he clenches his fists. "Shit. What's the bugger think he's doing? It's so fucking reactionary, this whole nationalism trip."

"It wasn't in Cuba." I try to push him further.

"Here it is. It's an adolescent revolt, not a revolution."

"Maybe that's what André wants."

"Jesus Christ, the whole thing's getting out of control." He paces up and down, holding himself in. "They're going to lose it all, Helen. They're playing right into the Government's hands. I just don't understand. What are they going to be able to do with Laporte, now they've got him?"

I watch him from the corner of my eye as I spoon the rice onto the plates. Roger, I want to say, you'll never understand anything anyone does because you're so afraid of getting caught up in them. You understand the results of what they do, you're perfect at that; but never why.

What would he have said in response? What would we have done?

Instead, we sit and eat. Yes, Roger washes the dishes. Then, after more talk but long before he'll feel any obligation to draw close, he gets up to go. He leaves nothing of himself behind.

I paint my anger.

These men are nothing but fragments that get in my way. If only I could weld all three of them into one, if the force of my anger could somehow fuse them, then there might be some chance of wholeness in relating to them. I don't want to have to cut myself off from half the human race. But as it is, their inhumanity cuts them off from me. They're the flecks of panic that dance in front of my eyes.

I don't want this to happen. I'm frightened by what I see all around me. I don't want this world to fall apart. I'm growing to love the city as I never used to—not the one I grew up in, stone houses and grey boulevards, the dullest place on earth, but the mean streets full of small people whose eyes are filled now with anticipation, excitement, a sense of release. Why then do I keep on seeing a coating of doom fluttering down on top of them? I don't want to. But the specks of panic that hang in front of our eyes are not particles of sunlight. They're like the flecks of soot that fall on everything after a great fire. A fire in the future.

The cops finally got around to picking Helen up at six in the morning on Saturday, October 17. She had been waiting for them patiently for a whole day.

At 4 A.M. on Friday morning, the Government, without debate in Parliament, without a vote, had proclaimed the War Measures Act. Two men had been kidnapped, but the Government defined the situation as a state of apprehended insurrection, and suddenly, retroactively, it became a crime, punishable by five years' imprisonment, to have been a member of the F.L.Q. In peacetime, in Canada, the police were given the power to arrest any suspect without a warrant, to search any building, to hold any person for up to three weeks without any charges being laid. It became a crime to communicate any message from the F.L.Q. to the Canadian public, and in the next few weeks this would even be used to ban the film of Henry Miller's *Quiet Days in Clichy* and to take a programme about the Hollywood Ten off the national television network.

Immediately, the Montréal and Québec police started picking up hundreds of suspected F.L.Q. sympathizers—students, housewives, doctors, lawyers, writers, taxi drivers, the unemployed.

David phoned Helen as soon as they had left.

She was asleep, she didn't know what was happening, she dropped the phone on the pillow. "What?" she said blearily.

"The police . . . they've just been here looking for you," he repeated more urgently.

"What?"

"The police. They want to arrest you. They're rounding up everyone they think might be mixed up with the F.L.Q. I told them you weren't living here for the moment. I said I didn't know where you were. They went through the house and took away a lot of your stuff."

Helen looked out of the dream at Jean-Claude's body curled into a ball beside her. She must be awake, because she found herself thinking how nice it would be if the cops came quickly and arrested him, too. Guilt by association. She smiled.

"Helen? Are you there?"

"Yes."

"Listen, if you want to get out of the country for a while, I can fix it up. You could go to France."

"No, David. No. I'll just wait here. Till they catch up with me. It's so dumb to run away. I haven't done anything, after all. But David? Thanks. And thanks for telling them you didn't know where I was."

"They wakened the kids and asked them, too. And searched their rooms. Mark was a bit upset . . ."

"Shit."

" . . . but Ann told them they were Fascists. Not bad, eh? I asked them for a receipt for the stuff they took, but they wouldn't give me one." He sounded too pleased with himself.

"David, thanks." She put the phone down and waited.

It took them twenty-four hours to find her. Of course, they had other things to do. All that day she was caught in an in-between world, apathetic yet full of tension. She couldn't work; she was too nervous but somehow not angry enough. She didn't want to visit any of her friends in case she was followed. She went out to a call box and phoned a number Roger had given her, but there was no reply. The cops were everywhere. Motorcycle squads escorted speeding limousines or hung about in bunches revving their engines. Soldiers stood outside what used to be called public buildings, bayonets fixed. Curious onlookers watched them for hours. Helicopters clattered back and forth overhead. God knows what they were looking for. Helen waited and wished they would hurry up.

But when she wakened with the noise of them coming through the door, she was still afraid. The light flashed on. There were five of them standing over her, enormous all the way up from the floor to their blue faces.

She pulled the sheet around her for protection. Two of them waved machine guns. "What the fuck are you doing?" she croaked. "Can't you even knock."

"Is there anybody else here?" asked the one in the grey suit.

"No."

"Check it out," he said.

They started emptying drawers onto the floor. One man stood on a chair to feel along the top of the curtain rail.

"Get dressed," said the grey suit.

She went to the bathroom and sat on the toilet. Piss poured out of her. The door was slammed open.

"Get out," she screamed.

"Don't close the door."

"Can't I even piss?"

"If you get permission."

"I have to get permission to piss?"

"Yes."

She dressed. One of them went through her jars of cream with his fingers. One emptied cereal in the sink. Another picked up the Xeroxes of Akiyo's cock and showed them to the detective. They shook their heads. "Take them in," said the detective. Shelves of books spilled on the floor. "There's a lot of political stuff here." Green garbage bags were filled with Trotsky and Fanon, Plato's *Republic,* the Montréal phone book, posters of Che, drawings of the bums in the Yukon Lunch. Helen watched helplessly. One of the gunmen leaned with his back against the door.

"Don't you get tired of being hated?" she asked. He went on smiling.

"I'm sorry," said a nervous voice behind her. This one had gotten red paint all over his thumb. "I hope I haven't messed it up."

"That's all right," she smiled. She took the thumb and pulled it gently towards a painting that was dry. She pressed it into the picture. "There." A red thumbprint to finish it off.

"Quit fooling around," said the detective. "Get your coat."

"Why?"

"We're taking you in."

"Can I make a phone call?"

"No."

With her wrists handcuffed in front of her, she stumbled and nearly fell down the curving steps. The lights on the police car flashed, rain glistened on its hood, the radio chattered. Garbage bags were flung in next to her. An old man stood watching on the sidewalk in the wet dawn.

"What am I supposed to have done?" she asked.

There was no reply.

"Do you have to be so fucking hostile?"

"It's been coming to you," said the detective.

"What for?"

"What do you think Madame Laporte's going through right now?"

They howled through the empty streets, squealing on corners, across red lights, to the police headquarters on Parthenais. Outside the concrete building soldiers stood on guard, backed by waves of barbed wire, camouflage on their helmets. What use is that in the city? Helen wondered. Trucks and jeeps and armoured personnel carriers were strewn about as if they had been abandoned; a helicopter crouched on the tarmac. The car plunged down a ramp to the underground garage and skidded to a halt.

"I hope we're in time," Helen said weakly.

Nobody smiled. They hustled her inside, then up in the elevator to the women's floor. Guards in baggy skirts slumped about and yawned, sweat stains under their shirt-sleeves from the clammy heat. They took away her wallet and her beads, the belt on her jeans, and shoved her into a shower room where two of them stared dully as the lukewarm water ran over her wax body. Then they pushed her into another room to have her photograph and her fingerprints taken, and from there along a corridor to an office where a tired young man was waiting behind a desk. He didn't even look up at her. He had a three-page questionnaire to fill in.

The colour of her husband's eyes?

"Well, I guess they're brown, but they change and there are flecks of green and even black in them."

"Brown." Children's birthmarks? Names of her cousins? Father's occupation?

"He was an aristocrat and a soldier," Helen said with a smile, and it was duly recorded. Anything you say will be taken down and forgotten.

"Are you a member of the F.L.Q.?"

"No."

"Do you sympathize with the aims of the F.L.Q.?"

"Hey," Helen jerked herself back into the reality of what was happening. "When you started bringing people in yesterday morning, did you ask them that?"

"Of course. It's on the form."

"Without telling them it had suddenly become a crime while they were asleep? They'd confess to breaking the law without even knowing there was a law. You pricks!"

"Do you sympathize with the aims of the F.L.Q.?"

"No."

"Did you kidnap James Cross?"

"No."

"Did you kidnap Pierre Laporte?"

"No."

"Do you know who did?"

"No."

"Will you sign this, please?"

"No."

She was shut up in a cage. She wanted to draw. "Do you think I could have some paper and a pencil?"

"No."

Sitting cross-legged on the cot, she tried to make her mind

blank. All around her were the sounds of boredom, feet tapping, mumbled telephone calls, aimless banter, one woman telling another, "Well, do something about it, don't just take it lying down," though what "it" was, Helen would never know.

Two hours later a guard came and told her: "Okay, you're going."

"You mean, I can go?"

The guard laughed. "To Tanguay, yes."

"What's Tanguay?"

"The women's prison."

Each of us, locked up with three dozen other women, learned what it was to be somebody else. We learned each other's stories, each other's skills. I learned what it was to be a mother on welfare with a lover who had to take off down the fire escape whenever the social worker came to the door, what it meant to run away from home because your drunken father beat you every night. We talked about our jobs and our husbands and our kids, about abortion and women's rights. I told them about being a painter, and though they had never heard of Morris Louis or Olitsky, they knew what I was rebelling against and why.

It went on all day long. Some of the women cried because they were worried about their families; others were glad to get away from the mess things were in outside. A couple of girls sat on the floor of the corridor and chanted, "Trudeau sucks, Trudeau sucks," for hours on end. But for the most part we sat together in the common room and sewed or read, played dominoes and talked and sang.

Of course, we sang. After all, Pauline Julien, the greatest French singer in the world, was one of the prisoners. She tossed her hair out of her eyes and her body flared with power. She sang the songs that had made her famous, turning sugary love ballads into pained explorations of her identity. And the rest of us sang with her, in and out of tune. Even the guards couldn't keep their lips from moving.

Then we talked again. We argued about politics all day long. Because I said that independence couldn't be an end in itself, I found myself having to tell them about Trotsky. We argued about the unions, and Francine, who worked for the C.S.N., taught us the history of the labour movement in Québec. The government had locked us up as political prisoners, so we learned more about politics in prison than we ever would have done on our own. That was the good side of it.

The bad was the boredom, the hollow anxiety. There are worse places to live in Montréal than Tanguay. It's warm, there's a nutritionist, the windows are made of thick plate glass. "You almost forget it's a prison," Nicole said, half closing her eyes one sunny afternoon. But that was the worst thing you could allow to happen. Suddenly, I saw the barred doors at the end of the hall, I saw the armed guards pacing nervously on top of the walls. The realization kicked me in the face: this isn't a holiday, Helen, it's the way things are going to be for the rest of your life if you don't learn to fight against it.

At night was the worst time. The sliding steel doors on the cell clanged shut. I sat down limply on the hard, clean cot and stared at the shiny walls, the chair, the seatless toilet. They had given me everything I needed: soap, a towel, blankets, a roll of rough toilet paper—everything I didn't need. The panic closed in. I couldn't fall asleep; I couldn't stay awake. I was slapped back and forth between shattered memories. The dreams began, but my eyes were open. The black barrel was inserted through the empty peephole. I cowered into the angle between the wall and the mattress, the sheet tugged up over my head. It couldn't last forever, could it? Couldn't it?

For others it must have been worse. I heard them whimpering all night long. But during the day, together, we were strong. It looked as if that would be just about enough.

When Suzanne came back from the interrogation, she was crying. They'd said her kids would be taken away from her if she didn't tell them what they wanted to know. "I don't even know what they want to know," she sobbed. We held her and then we discussed it together. She said she wouldn't give in.

We worked out answers to all the questions they were asking. "Okay, when he asks you, 'Do you believe it's legitimate to overthrow the government by force?' what you've got to say is: 'I believe the government in Havana is the legitimate government of Cuba.' They can't tie you down on that." We laughed together at the expected triumph.

Still the threats went on. Lise was told she'd be shot if she didn't confess; confess to what? Jeanne was promised she could go home if she reported what the rest of us were saying. When she told us instead, it made us all stronger.

I hated Tanguay and wished I could stay forever.

Helen shakes herself awake. There are voices all around her. Claire is standing in the middle of the cell with her father, Helen's father, the father she never knew, he's just a sepia photograph, a black uniform, but oh, so tall and elegant with that wavy hair, wonderfully gentle eyes. Claire is holding him but he slips out of her arms and folds up on the floor. Helen rushes forward and lifts him, he's light as Styrofoam, her fingers poke right through him. He collapses again and again, he can't stand alone. "Claire, help me," she pleads, but she has to do it on her own. Finally, she manages to prop him against a shelf and turns joyfully to Claire, but it's Claire now who's lying in a heap on the floor. Helen bends to her, Claire is heavy as lead. "Get up," Helen shouts in frustration, "get up, get up."

"Get up," the voice above her was shouting. Sharp fingers dug into Helen's cheeks, shaking her from side to side. Sleepily, she tried to pull away and banged the back of her head against the wall. The light blinded her. Above her stood a woman she had never seen before. She was wearing a uniform the colour of duckshit. Her skull was covered with tight curls.

"Debout," she yelled again and raised her arm.

Helen squirmed sideways off the bed and fell on the floor. She crawled to her knees.

Leaning against the door was a man in his forties in a heavy blue suit. His hair was perfect silver, but his polished pink face sagged with concern.

Helen's gums were dry. "What the fuck do you want?"

"Just to talk to you." He had a loose, doggy mouth that quivered.

"Always in the middle of the night," Helen muttered.

"We've a lot of work to get through." He smiled apologetically.

She shivered and tried to pull a blanket up round her shoulders.

"Put this on," the woman snapped, holding out the regulation nightgown that Helen hadn't bothered with.

Helen felt the man's gaze burrowing into her. She grasped the blanket tightly in front of her and stood up with her back against the wall.

"We've had reports of guns being smuggled in here," he said.

"Bullshit." Helen didn't move. The wall was cold against her thighs.

"You can sit down." He waved her to a chair and held out a pack of Craven A.

"I don't smoke."

"Only pot?"

"What?"

"We found some in your house." He lit his cigarette.

"So, is that what I'm in here for?" Helen tried to laugh but couldn't. The woman was standing right behind her; she could smell the tobacco smoke on the uniform.

"We could charge you for it. If we wanted to."

"Go ahead."

The man's eyes focused above Helen's head and he nodded slightly. "Okay," he murmured.

She felt the violence of the movement behind her and jumped sideways. But it wasn't aimed at her. The woman ripped the clothes from the bed and angrily heaved the mattress on its side. She unzipped the plastic case that covered it.

"There's nothing here," Helen said in amazement.

"We have to be sure." Smoke leaked from his lips and nostrils. Helen watched it spread out. "What I can't understand," he said, "is how you got mixed up in all this in the first place. You're not even a separatist, after all, are you?" He waited with his bushy eyebrows raised for her to reply. She said nothing. "I mean, you've had everything of the best, right? Every opportunity. A good family, a husband, a career, a couple of nice kids." He ticked the points off with a nicotined finger. "I don't understand."

"It's none of your fucking business."

The woman was bent over the mattress like a bulldog at a bone. Her skirt strained against her buttocks.

"What do you know about the death of Monsieur Laporte?" the man asked.

"Nothing."

"Ah, but you knew he was dead," he said, as though he'd trapped her.

"You can't keep the news out of here." Helen's stomach turned over.

The woman held up one of the cotton sheets Helen had drawn on with a ballpoint pen. Portraits of the two girls sitting on the corridor floor, their bodies twisted with fury. Helen had scrawled "Trudeau sucks" all over them.

The man examined the sheet and his mouth tightened. "Rather childish," he said.

"Go fuck yourself."

"Look, Helen." He tried desperately to sound sincere. "I'll be honest. We've got nothing against you personally. People like you and Pauline Julien . . . well, you're artists, you're not terrorists. We know that. We're just trying to weed out the few who are."

Helen smelt the woman standing behind her again. "I thought you were trying to cultivate more," she said bitterly.

The man sighed and stood up.

The woman's hands grasped both sides of Helen's head and dragged her to her feet.

"What are you doing?" Helen gasped.

"She has to search you now." The man's voice was like syrup.

It began with her hair. Cold fingers against her skull, digging into her ears. The man leaned close.

"Where is Andrew Goldman?"

Helen's head swung from side to side. "Andrew who?" she panted.

The blanket slipped from her shoulders and she bent to pick it up. Absentmindedly, the woman hit her with a forearm across the face. Blood seeped between Helen's teeth and she coughed.

"We know you know him."

"I played with him when we were kids."

The woman pulled on rubber gloves and instinctively Helen drew away from the acrid smell. She was gripped tightly. "Lean back against the table." Helen saw the man crouch forward. She struggled to stay upright as her feet were shoved apart. She knocked off the woman's thick-lensed glasses. They fell to the floor. The back of a hand slapped against her throat and another hand forced its way into her vagina.

The man's voice rose. "You've seen him twice in the last month."

"I don't remember." She coughed again.

She was pulled upright by her hair. "Turn round." Her face was smashed down into the wood of the tabletop. Vaseline. A huge fist driving its way into her anus.

Helen screamed.

The man was kneeling beside her. "Once at an apartment on Cuvillier, once in the Yukon restaurant on Sainte Cathérine."

Helen spat in his face with what little saliva she had left. She was flung sideways onto the bedsprings and the metal jabbed into her back. She looked up at the woman standing over her and searched the face for some expression. "Why are you doing this?" she whispered.

Without looking away, the woman peeled off the glove and threw it in the garbage.

Helen begged in desperation. "Really, I want to know." It was the only thing that bothered her.

"C'est mon job," the woman said without interest.

"Oh, no," Helen murmured hopelessly. She fought to keep the tears out of her eyes.

The man unlocked the door and stood looking down at Helen. He didn't bother to smile anymore. "We know where he is, anyway." Then, as the woman pushed past him roughly, he said out of the corner of his mouth, "We don't need to hold you any longer."

Helen lay still, not wanting to believe him. "You mean I can go."

He nodded, his face pale. "In the morning."

The bruises were starting to burn. "Why me?" she asked fearfully.

His eyes filled with anger. "Mrs. Dawson," he sneered, "if I were your husband, I'd get someone to smash your legs and your arms." The door slammed behind him.

As I leave the prison, I walk backwards, watching it get smaller.

The first thing I must do is see Claire, I have so much to tell her. About the songs and the fear and the arguments, this anger that makes me see clearly at last. The day is grey and damp, excitement races through me. I know what I'm up against, there's nothing to protect me any longer.

Claire lies propped up in bed in the stifling room. Her face is the colour of soured milk. The energy drains out of me.

"Oh, no, Claire," I say and touch her. Her body doesn't respond. I sit back and try to look at her, her eyes switch off. "When?" I whisper. "When did you have it done?"

"Last night." She turns her head away from me. "Jesus, I was so fucking fed up. I couldn't carry on, not knowing what I was going to do, eh?" She bangs the pillow with her fist. "Shit, Helen, I really needed you."

I take her hand, she pulls it away.

"I wanted to talk so much," she says. "I stayed here all weekend just talking to Cass." The cat. She tries to laugh.

I get up and walk over to the window. "Didn't you get my message?"

"Yeah, yeah, it must have been lousy."

"No, the rest of it."

"About the kids? Sure, I phoned David. They're fine."

A yard full of grit and weeds. The backs of other buildings

are jammed against each other. Balconies added on at odd angles, windows with plastic nailed over them for the winter. Down to the left a garage tilts. The seat of a broken swing hangs from a single chain.

"Not *my* kids. That wasn't what I asked her to tell you," I say. But when I look round and see Claire's hollowness, I can't go on. It would punch a hole right through her. "Never mind," I murmur. "It doesn't matter now." I go back to the bed.

The silence drags around us. I can't think of anything to say. "Would you like some music? I could bring in the stereo."

She shakes her head. "I'll get up later on."

"How do you feel?"

She swallows. "Empty." Tears gleam in her eyes. "God, I feel awful, Helen."

She lets me hold her hand.

When Mark was born, I wanted David to see how brave I was. I lay between the porcelain sheets and looked at a faded picture of the Virgin high up on the wall. Beside her, a large electric clock ticked off the seconds. The ache in my back was getting worse. I wanted to be free, to turn over on my side, but I couldn't with the drip in my arm. I was trapped between the chrome bars of the bed. I wanted to draw, to comb my hair, anything to relieve the tension. A thick elastic band tied my spine to my navel.

I tried to concentrate on my breathing. This birth was for me, to prove myself. With Ann, the doctor had bullied me into an anaesthetic. "Helen, you're exhausted, it's going on too long, the baby's heart is weakening." The next thing I knew I was being trundled past the nursery with a twangy voice telling me how lucky I was. This time I was going to stay in control. I forced myself to wait.

But later: "Why doesn't the doctor come?" I gasped to a nurse who was filling in one of her charts.

"It's too soon for him." She turned away. "It'll be a long time yet."

"But it's close. I can feel it."

She looked at me from the doorway. "The dilation's only five centimetres."

"What am I meant to do?"

"Do you want me to give you a needle?"

"No." I twisted like a worm. "Just something to drink."

"I can't. You may have to have surgery." She disappeared.

I lay and moaned. A pulse filled my head. This wasn't working out at all. I couldn't handle it on my own, I needed someone to help me. Not to tell me what to do or treat me like a backward child, but to go through it with me. I looked in panic round the empty room, it burst in my eyes.

"How's it going?" David asked cheerfully from the doorway.

I couldn't even speak. I cried, and already the crying relieved me.

"Helen, Helen." He wiped my face.

"She said it's not close and it is, I know it is, what does she know about it? The pressure's changing." I grasped his arm as my whole body was driven downwards. My pelvis was going to split apart. I howled, then started to whimper.

David stroked my abdomen and little by little the muscles relaxed. I watched his face, then it came again, he held me tighter.

"Where's the bloody doctor?" I groaned.

"Do you want me to get him?"

"No, don't leave me." I clung to him, he stroked me gently.

"You mustn't do that," the nurse snapped as she came in. "It disturbs the monitor."

"Please," I begged. "It makes it so much better."

"We can't read baby's heartbeat," she said accusingly, pointing to the blips on the screen.

"I'll see if I can find McGee," David whispered.

"Don't go."

"I'll be back." He kissed me.

When the doctor came in, he bustled round, taking charge, glaring at the nurse. It's not her fault, I wanted to tell him, she's only doing what you told her. "Now, Helen," he coaxed, "I think I ought to give you a little injection."

"No. Why?"

"It'll ease the pain."

"But it's not painful right now," I lied. What I needed was David's fingers, not a hypodermic.

"It will be," he insisted.

"No, I don't want it." He made me sound like a spoilt child.

"Later, then."

"No."

They pushed my bed out of the door and across the corridor. The IV burrowed into my arm, a pain I could control. I leaned my weight against it. David stood in the hallway, and as I was wheeled past, he touched my moist hand for a moment. I tried to hold on to him.

The lights in the delivery room dazzled me. All I could see was eyes I didn't know. Precise fingers strapped me into the stirrups and washed me with antiseptic the colour of urine. It was cold, I began to shiver uncontrollably. But then I saw David's eyes, too, brown, with green and black flecks in them, full of anxiety above the white mask. I reached out to him, he took my hands.

I struggled against the stirrups. "I can't do it like this," I whined. "I want to push down."

David glanced at the doctor.

The doctor nodded. "Get some pillows," he ordered a nurse.

David pressed them in behind my back. I reached up and touched him, a grey cashmere sweater beneath the open gown. So soft in the middle of all this hardness; my body tingled.

"Oh," I gasped.

"Come on, push," urged the nurse.

"No," I whispered. "Let it come on its own." As a little girl, with a mother who told me nothing of sex, I'd never understood how a baby could come out of me without ripping me in half. I held a mirror between my legs and gawked in terror. But with David's strength in my hands, the nurses just a reflection in the bright lamps, I didn't even need to force myself to push.

"Push," they yelled.

My whole body expanded, my vagina, my asshole, it came out on its own with just a small tearing, a good pain, not twisting inside me, but clean, on the outside, the end.

Two grey patches on the mask beneath David's eyes.

They gave me the baby to hold. I wanted to lick it clean. It lay on my breast and as it squealed I felt a surge roll through me, the placenta slid away.

I hold Claire's hand.

"Akiyo was great," she says.

"Akiyo!"

"Incredible, eh? He came with me to the doctor's, and then to the clinic, too. They thought he was the father." She tries to smile. "He insulted everyone. But he didn't let them push me around. He stayed with me all last night."

"That's good."

"Yeah."

An empty silence. All I wanted to tell her is irrelevant now.

"Helen, what's the matter? Do you think it was wrong?"

"Wrong? Of course not." I run my fingers over her knuckles. "How could I?"

"Well, you're a Catholic."

"A Catholic atheist? Maybe I am, I don't know. It's not important." I can't even think about it clearly. "There's not much time for it right now." I rumple her hair.

"But when we were talking about it, do you remember, you

said maybe what I wanted wasn't so much to be pregnant but to have an abortion."

"That was dumb. It didn't mean anything."

"You must have meant something," she insists.

"No," I lie. "It was the argument we were having. The words become abstract; they lose their connection."

"Sure?"

I nod.

She sighs. "I'm just so tired of myself, Helen." A pause. "And Jesus Christ, so fucking angry."

"That's better."

We start to laugh.

"Will you stay with me?"

"Yes."

"No, I mean stay. Like, for a while?"

"A few days. Yes."

I wait for her to fall asleep. The message I asked the guard to give her was that I'd help her with the baby. If she decided to have it, we could look after it together. My eyes blur; I watch her swollen face as she starts to snore. Over and over again I remind myself I must never—even in a moment of weakness when I want to show her how good I am—tell Claire that.

All evening long little flares of anger spurted in Helen. Everything she saw, everything she heard, fueled them.

"I hate your fucking party," she yelled at Peter Abbott when she bumped into him in the crowded kitchen.

He smiled and chewed a strand of grey hair. "Why?" he asked mildly.

"Why?" She shook herself with anger. "Why should I know why?"

He laughed and turned to a knot of guests.

"You're such a fucking mess," she shouted and heads glanced round in momentary surprise.

Everything was a mess. "What a ridiculous mess," was the first thing she said to Claire as they came up the drive. It was an old farmhouse in the rolling country to the southeast of Montréal, down towards the Vermont border—stockbroker country, tax-shelter country. All the lights in the house blazed, the noise of a live jazz band crashed into the sleepy darkness. Porsches, Fiats, Saabs, Corvettes were marooned on the neat lawn, their wheels leaving deep ruts in the damp ground. "Somebody cuts that damn grass," Helen said as she stopped on a patch of gravel.

"Not Peter, I bet," said Claire.

A pink Bentley slumped up to its axle in a rose bed.

"Trust him to buy a place out here."

"Must have cost a quarter of a million."

"More. What's he want with a farm, anyway?"

Inside, it was just as bad. Over a hundred people, drunk and stoned, milled through the elegant rooms with their high, moulded ceilings. Once a family, parents and children, had lived together here; now there was just a crowd of Peter's ever-changing hangers-on. Men, and women too, had worked this land; now Peter had his bright, random ideas and transmitted them to the world on his own telex. Everything she saw was turned into junk: an old pine table with a greasy hibachi on top of it, a Corbusier chair piled high with sleeveless records and empty jars of acrylic, a can of clams in the arms of a Tibetan bronze. Everything reduced to junk in the name of art. And at the centre of the mess was Peter, balder than ever, his thin hair long and dirty, a matted sweater and torn jeans, shuffling about and smiling at everyone with his dark, cold eyes. "Enjoy, enjoy," he commanded. "What do you want to eat? Caviare or hot dogs?"

Helen slammed through it all night long. She knew most of

the people who were here, and individually there were a good many of them she could like or respect. But together they turned into pathetic, cruel cutouts.

George Molnar, the Hungarian critic, passed her a joint. "Who's that chick over there?"

Helen looked. "That's Liz. Don't you know her? Liz Novak." She liked George. "Do you want me to introduce you?"

"Does she fuck?"

Helen was stunned. "How should I know?" He was a staid, middle-aged man in a neatly pressed suit. "She's Czech," she added irrelevantly.

"Fucking Czechs. All they did was throw flowers at the Russian tanks." He sauntered off.

"God!" She whirled, looking for someone to hit. Claire was standing on her own, very pale and thin. "That son of a bitch," Helen spluttered.

"Who?"

"George."

"Oh, he's all right."

"He's a fucking son of a bitch."

"Yeah." Claire swayed and put out her hand to keep herself from falling. "But he's all right, too."

"Are you okay?" Helen tried to see into her eyes. "Do you want to lie down somewhere?"

"No. I'm going."

"I'll take you."

"No. I'll get a ride." Claire pulled away.

"Let me take you."

"No, Helen, it's okay. Really. Look, Steve's taking me. It's okay." She wandered vaguely towards the door.

Anxiously, Helen watched her go from the porch. She felt deserted.

"What's the matter with Claire?" Peter asked, coming out behind her.

"Well, wouldn't you feel weak if you'd had to go through all that?" she asked irritably.

"Sure, sure." He ran his finger over the carving on the door; stylized, phallic vases. "But I didn't mean weak. Underneath, it's the opposite; she's gone all hard inside somehow. You know, withdrawn into a hard little shell. Okay," he shushed Helen, "I know there's a reason, but it's only going to make it worse for her in the end."

"Peter, what the fuck are you talking about? You don't have an inkling of how her body's changing right now. The whole hormonal balance is swinging about all over the place. Christ, it happens to us all the time, every month."

With one hand he touched her arm very lightly. "I guess men can never be as conscious of their own bodies as women, eh?"

He said it almost regretfully and she felt herself warming to him. But before she could follow it up, he disappeared into the house again. "Enjoy, enjoy!" She drank a lot of Scotch but it only made her anger more unbearable. She felt the aimless cruelty swarming all over her.

Weissmann and Boucher, the art dealers, were talking about Claire's hopes of getting an exhibition. Boucher turned to his Swiss boyfriend. "I'm afraid I'll be accused of being a chauvinist pig, but poor Claire isn't really much of an artist, is she?"

Weissmann smiled. "My dear fellow, you don't have to start from a chauvinist set of assumptions to arrive at that conclusion."

"Do you really think so? That makes me feel a little better then."

When the laughter had died down the Swiss boyfriend said, "An artiste rather than an artist perhaps," showing off his command of the language, and they laughed again.

Was it only to torment herself that she stayed here? Helen drank some more, then stumbled over Akiyo, sprawled tiny and morose in a dark corner.

"I hate this fucking party," she said, lying down beside him.

"You want to dance?" He didn't make any move to get up.

"God, no!"

"Good."

"What makes everybody such bastards, Akiyo? I mean, look, I know these people. George Molnar, he's a nice guy, gentle, he cares, why does he have to pretend to be such a prick? There's a whole tangle of intense, destructive emotions around us—people fucking, dying, never connecting. The only thing that joins us is an aimless callousness."

Akiyo spluttered. "Aimless callousness! Don't be such a god-awful bore, Helen."

"Well, fuck you, too," she laughed and bit him lightly on the ear. He tried to kiss her mouth. "Oh, stop it, Akiyo, stop it." She flapped her hands. "I'm putting on weight, can't you see? You won't be able to get it up."

"Cunt," he said and stopped.

"Akiyo, what are you trying to prove? It was good what you did for Claire. Why hide it?"

"Silly cow, she's too dumb to look after herself."

"There you go again."

"You want to know what I think, Helen?"

"What?"

"I think you're a repressed dike. I think you really want to make it with Claire."

"Claire!"

"Big juicy Claire." He smacked his lips.

Helen thought about it. The idea hadn't even occurred to her. And if it hadn't, well . . . "I don't think so," she said slowly. "I mean, it's never crossed my mind. I like Claire, I love her warmth—"

"Her warmth. Come on, admit it."

"No." The image grew in her mind; she pushed it away. "No."

"You're so fucking slow, Helen. You don't know what you want. I'll bet you don't even know who's in love with you here."

She blew him a mocking kiss.

"Not me, for God's sake. Peter."

"Peter?"

He nodded.

"Peter Abbott? You've got to be joking."

"He told me. Well, Thérèse actually, she told me. He was worried you wouldn't turn up."

"Bullshit."

"Okay, have it your own way." He got up. "He's a good artist, though. I'm going to look for some more whisky."

Somebody was being sick in what was left of the ratatouille. Boucher and his boyfriend were having a fight about who was going to drive. The jazz band were snorting coke in the kitchen. In the dining room a couple were trying to jive to a Mozart symphony.

Helen closed her eyes.

"Can I sit down?" said Peter. He looked exhausted.

She was tired, too. "I'm just going," she said.

"Stay," he said, holding her arm. "Why don't you stay the night?"

The membrane that held her anger burst. "I'm not one of your fucking groupies, Peter."

He looked at her in surprise. "Who said you were?"

"Can't you see what you're doing to yourself, for fuck's sake? You've surrounded yourself with sycophants—all these people you just prey on. You're really screwing up their lives, you know that? And they hate you. I guess you don't give a fuck, eh? But you're screwing yourself up, too."

He fingered the string of blue Venetian glass beads around his neck. "What's all this about, Helen?"

She pierced him like a laser. "Just don't ask me to watch it, that's all. Those fucking beads. How old are you, Peter? Forty-four? Okay, a couple of years ago they were a nice little touch. Now they're just a tired pose. Can't you see what you're doing?"

He blew out his cheeks. "I like them; is that so bad?"

"Fuck it, Peter, don't pretend to be so simple." She swung herself onto her knees. "You need to get out of this place. The way you live, there's something really corrupt at the core of it." She dashed out to the bathroom and when she got back, hoping he wouldn't have gone, Akiyo was squatting beside Peter with a glass of Scotch for her.

"What are you putting in it to make her so fucking aggressive?" Peter asked nervously.

"You know what's wrong with the way you live? Both of you; you, too, Akiyo," she said. "There's no social meaning in it. No commitment." She gulped the whisky and coughed.

"Fuck off! You're so predictable. It's *boring,*" Akiyo yelled at her. "Boring. Go back to prison. Bore them."

She held him by the shoulders fiercely. "Listen, Akiyo, the law I was imprisoned under, do you know what it was?"

"Sure. The War Measures Act."

"When was the last time it was used?"

He shrugged. "Who cares?"

"To intern Japanese-Canadians during the war."

They looked at each other warily.

Peter rubbed his heavily lined forehead. "What I'm doing does have a social focus, damn it, Helen. It's not just aesthetic, you can't say that. Maybe it doesn't preach, but it has a point. It works through irony, that's all."

"Oh, Peter, Peter." She hammered his arm desperately. "I admire what you do. It's so clever. But it's fake; it's just meant to grab people. It's all on the surface, like the way you live."

"Irony works on two different levels at the same time," he said stubbornly. "You don't need slogans."

She gave up. How tired of him she suddenly was. "You're so fucking trite."

Liz came in peering shortsightedly into the shadows. "I thought you were lost, Peter," she said in her soft, accented voice. He stared at her without seeing, without responding, and finally she drifted away.

He breathed deeply. "I'm going to bed." He knelt and took Helen's hand in his. "I like you, Helen. I don't know what we're fighting about."

She glared at him.

He went on holding her hand. "Will you come?" he whispered.

"Me *and* Liz?" she shouted. "How many of us do you want? Two at a time?"

He shook his head, still looking at her questioningly.

"I'm better off with Akiyo," she said harshly.

So Peter went away and through the half-open door she saw him kissing Liz in a puddle of light at the bottom of the stairs. Helen turned to Akiyo, shaking uncontrollably. But five minutes later Peter was back standing over them. "I brought you this, my children." He spread an old patchwork quilt on top of them. "There are rooms upstairs."

"You know what I can't stand about you?" Helen shouted. "The way you buy up a fine old farm like this and turn it upside down. It's a fucking insult to the people who built it."

He looked down at her for a long while, biting his lip. "I didn't buy it. It was my parents'. I was born here, Helen." He went away.

"Oh, Akiyo, hold me, please."

Absentmindedly Akiyo hugged her. "Let's find a place upstairs," he suggested. "I can't function here."

But upstairs all the rooms with beds were occupied already. So were the sofas, the cushions, the armchairs. Along the corridor they dragged their quilt until they found a small room, completely empty, with green linoleum on the floor.

"This'll do," said Helen.

They spread the quilt on the floor and lay on top of it, but the early morning air was cold and they had to get underneath. The floor was even colder. They kissed. Without passion, their cold fingers dug into each other.

"Akiyo, I'm sorry, this is no good," Helen said.

"I know," he groaned.

"I'm sorry."

"My hip's disintegrating." He stood up. "I'm going home."

She couldn't move. "I'll stay here."

He nodded dully.

She wasn't even conscious of his going. Now she was able to wrap herself greedily in the whole of the quilt. Fitfully she slept. She woke with Peter standing above her, the curtainless window grey behind him. He had a Mexican blanket draped over his shoulder. "I came to see if you were okay. Where's Akiyo?"

She looked around. "He left."

Peter gave her his hand and pulled her up. She stood hanging on to him. "Oh, Peter, it's gone on so long. I don't know what's happening."

"That makes two of us." He put the end of the blanket round her. "Come and lie down."

"Where's Liz?"

"She left ages ago."

"Ages?"

He smiled. "Come on, you can sleep."

Next to him in the creaking oak bed, she was surprised by the firmness of his body. She stroked it. "I thought you'd be such a mess, too," she murmured.

She began to play with his foreskin but he lifted her hand away. "Shsh, sleep."

"Don't you want me?"

"I want you to sleep."

She dozed off, then wakened with what seemed like a jolt of enlightenment. "Are you gay?" she whispered.

"Not with you, shweetheart." He massaged her neck. "Sleep."

She slept.

When she wakened again she felt as though she had been sleeping for days, but it wasn't even eight o'clock. The night chill had vanished from the room and bright sunlight poured through the window. The end of a big red barn filled half of it. Cows mooed.

Peter's eyes were open. "Peter?" Peter! She shook her head. "Did you sleep?"

"No, I watched you."

"Thank you." She kissed his collarbone.

"And the dawn." He rolled onto his stomach and looked along the pillow at her.

She touched his ass. "I'm going to rub your back," she said.

He pulled his head into his shoulders till his hair brushed the skin. "It feels okay."

"I want to rub it."

She sat over his thighs, kneading the muscles. "You bugger, Peter," she said, "why didn't you want to fuck me?"

"I was scared."

"Of me?"

"Well, you're a pretty scary lady. But no, not that really. Of myself. Of what you said about me." He reached round to her and she pushed his arm away. "Am I still a bird of prey?" he asked.

"No, your back's really quite nice."

"How about the front?" He twisted right round and reached up to her breasts.

She looked into his wrinkled eyes. She felt hot and suddenly breathless. "David, let's go outside."

"I'm Peter—remember me?" He plucked her chin. "It's freezing out there."

"But it's stifling." All the heat in the house seemed to have been sucked into this one room. She traced the outline of his mouth, feeling the rough skin.

"Okay," he said wearily. "You know what my problem is? I do what everyone else wants." He heaved himself up, then reeled back onto the bed. "Jesus Christ!"

She took his arm. He walked hunched over like an old man.

Everywhere, among the ruins of the party, bodies were stirring. Thérèse was in the bath. Somewhere someone was trying to play a Chopin Prélude. Akiyo was slumped over the kitchen table with a cup of lukewarm coffee in his hands. "I don't even have a hangover," he said in amazement. "At least, not so long as I don't stand up."

"I thought you were going home."

"I didn't make it that far."

"I'll get us some breakfast," Peter said, switching on the stove. He made a big flask of cocoa and added half a pint of Armagnac. "Fortification," he said, shaking it all together. Then he cut some not quite stale French bread and buttered it carefully.

She watched him. "I don't understand you at all."

"I don't think one ever understands anything," he said, looking for a bag. "Understanding's a form of possession. It's like saying: 'There, I understand you, you're a part of me now.' " He wrapped some cold ham in foil and smoothed down the edges carefully. "All you can ever do is recognize a person and be happy or, I don't know, sad maybe in the recognition. Just as you recognize a colour. Yellow, green. . . . Ready?"

"Yes." She smiled. But outside the cold wind tore the door handle out of her grasp and slammed the door. She cringed back into the rough stone wall of the house.

"It's not too bad." Peter waited for her. "Over there, just inside the edge of the wood, there's a clearing by the stream. It'll be sheltered there."

They crossed a field, climbed over a broken cedar fence, then another field. Helen glanced at him from time to time; he walked stolidly into the wind, looking around him, his eyes catching every detail, a new molehill, the flight of a lone merganser. "Silly bugger, you're going north," he shouted. He stopped by a dead elm and peeled off a piece of bark. He seemed completely absorbed in it; she wasn't even sure he wanted her to be with him any longer.

"Did you hear what Boucher said about you last night?"

"Look at how it's been eaten away. Like veins. Boucher's an idiot."

"He said you were the kind of artist who gave charlatans a bad name."

He laughed easily. "I told you he was an idiot. He'd sell his granny for a bon mot."

"But you are a bit of a charlatan at times, aren't you?"

"No," he said pensively. "No, I'm a bullshitter. There are only two kinds of artists, bullshitters and pedants. Take your pick. I'm a bullshitter, thank God. Maybe you're turning into one, too." He pinched her ass.

She caught his arm. "But I can't make the different parts of you fit together, Peter. They keep on contradicting each other."

He scratched his chin. "Well, dear girl," he said in a geriatric croak, "if you can't ride two horses at once you shouldn't be in the goddamn circus."

She hugged him tightly, ramming her tongue into his throat.

"Peter. I do like you, you know. Not what you do, but I like who you are."

He bowed with mock courtesy.

By the stream it was still cold and the sky was clouding over. She shivered. "I'm sorry. This is ridiculous."

"You've got to get right down into the ground." He pulled the blankets around them.

She swallowed some of the cocoa and tore hungrily at a slice of bread. Just beyond them the stream flowed into a small swampy lake with dead trees along its edges. For once she didn't feel threatened by the stumps. Two plump grey and white jays perched on the branches of a Scotch pine not six feet away, and looked down at them with cocked heads.

"Do you think they're spies?" Helen asked.

"Tame spies. The R.C.M.P. plants tiny transmitters in their assholes," Peter said. "Buy them off." He held out a piece of bread, coaxing, cooing, till one of the birds swooped and picked it out of his fingers.

"Lie down on your back," he said. "Now close your eyes."

She trembled as he laid a crust on her lips.

"Lie still. Here it comes."

A sharp claw pricked her chin and then the bread was gone. She opened her eyes and blinked at the sky. Clouds rushed across it beyond the pattern of branches. A chipmunk ran among them, chattering frantically.

"Hurry," she said, pulling the blanket right up over their heads. She wrenched at his belt.

"It's like being inside a tent."

"A collapsed tent," she said, putting her thighs around his waist.

She was camouflaged, part of the ground. The orgasm bit her wildly. The animals ignored her cries.

Gasping, she stuck her head out. It had grown colder still. Drops of rain fell on her shoulders and the wind cut through the blankets. They clung to each other, their thighs sticking.

"Does this mean the war's over?" he panted.

"I don't know." She stroked his face.

"A truce then?"

"I won't hurt you," she said.

They sat up cuddling, her legs still around his waist.

"Why don't we stay out here all winter?" She nibbled his pale skin. "Nobody would ever find us."

"Just the grey jays in the spring."

"Where did they go?" She pulled away to look about her. As she did so her cold foot touched his balls and he yelped. "Oh, Peter," she laughed, "I'm sorry. That must have been terrible." She bent down and kissed him.

Sleepless, I sit in the window. It will be a cold, damp day. The sky is heavy, gunmetal, dark as the unreflecting water, with just a slight thinning of the cloud above the horizon. The Canada geese that landed last night are tiny black dents in the ruffled lake. They have been drifting from the middle in towards the shore. I am the only point of life here, only just alive.

When I was still with David, these nights of insomnia wracked me from time to time. I twisted beside him, my pulse racing. But now, when it happens, I can draw into myself, a hibernating animal.

The kids will sleep for hours yet, I can be on my own. I have come up to the cottage with them for the weekend. It used to be one of the family rituals, closing things up, jollity, raking leaves, bonfires, Monopoly at night. Now there is no ritual in what we do, nothing to protect us from each other. Or ourselves.

I think about how I'm going to live. I shan't see Jean-Claude again; no good will come of it. And Peter? I don't know. When I left him I said good-bye.

"When shall I see you again?"

"I don't know. I don't want a permanent relationship. And I won't have a casual one." I kissed him. "This wasn't casual."

I'll have to wait and see. I will be responsible for what I do. I will learn to live through my own vulnerability. I will not live without love like my mother, even if it's the only way to be safe.

There, I smile at myself, you've solved all your problems.

The gap in the clouds just above the horizon has widened. It fills with red wires.

Stumbling, Ann bangs into the room behind me.

"Why, hon, what wakened you?"

She rubs her swollen cheeks and yawns. "I had a dream."

"What was it about?"

"Pretty gruesome." She wrinkles her nose and bumps her way through to the kitchen. "That little punk, I'll kill him," I hear her shout.

"What's the matter?"

"Mark's ripped off all the Honeycombs."

"Have some granola. It's better, anyway."

"Yuck."

She comes and sprawls at my feet like a big, awkward dog.

"How's Mark taking things?"

"He's okay. He's really tough, you know. Yesterday I was playing hide-and-seek with him and he found this place in the basement, in the crawl space really, a kind of root cellar I guess it was. I never knew it was there. Anyway, he hid for it must have been half an hour. I was worried sick, eh? I thought he must have gotten trapped or fallen into something. I was looking all over the place for him. For his corpse? And he just waited in there in the darkness. Pitch darkness. I could never do that."

The undersides of the clouds are turning pink and purple. Ann leans her chin on my knees.

"Do you believe in heaven?"

I stroke her hair. "I don't think so. Not anymore. I used to."

"Neither do I," she says vehemently. "But I think there's an afterlife. Only, it's exactly the same as this one. Kind of parallel? We carry on there as the same people we are here, except we don't know the same people or have the same relatives anymore. Like, you're there and I'm there, eh, but we don't know each other. Pretty weird!" She nods in approval and drinks some more milk. "You don't think we just die, do you?"

"No, I don't think the energy is wasted. It goes into something else. I guess it's up to us to use it well while we have it."

"I think we carry on forever, as ourselves. When we die in that afterlife, we come back here."

"Doesn't that mean we'd all be getting older and older?"

She frowns. "I've got to work on it some more yet."

Her hair is short and thick between my fingers.

As we watch, the sun bursts blindingly into the gap between the clouds and the lake. Its light flashes on the fallen, frost-covered leaves, turning them for five minutes into mirrors. Then the clouds eat up everything again. It becomes a cold, damp day.

"I saw a snowy owl last night," I tell her. "When you were playing with Mark."

"Wow. They're rare. Are you sure it was a *snowy* owl? There's lots of other kinds."

"I checked it in the book."

"God, I wish I'd seen that. I wish that more than anything else in the whole world. Almost."

I hold her tight against me. For so long I've tried to possess her, to make her mine. I don't want to do that any longer, yet desperately I still want to protect her.

She pulls away from me. "You know what really scares me? More than death?" Excitement muffles her voice.

"What?"

She whispers the word so that I have to bend to her. "Birth. Giving birth."

"Why?"

"It hurts so much."

"No." I hold her face in my hands. "No." The skin is so smooth. Soon she will have spots. I have to get this right, or it will be too late. "Sure, it hurts, it hurts a lot, but listen, hon, the hurt stops, I promise, it changes into something else, a different kind of feeling. Look"—I squeeze her in desperation—"there was a woman, an anthropologist . . ."

"What's that?"

"Someone who studies different societies, cultures. Well, she went to this really primitive tribe in Africa, and the women gave birth very quietly, matter of factly, squatting on the ground with just one other woman to help them. No fuss. But the men, who were never allowed to see it, would act out what happened during childbirth in a kind of pantomime. And they writhed about all over the place and screamed in agony."

As I talk, we hear the geese calling more urgently to each

other. I stop, Ann isn't listening to me. With a great flapping and splashing and barking they hoist themselves, hundreds of them like black flies, into the air. Forming into a V, they turn towards the south, breaking through the space between the clouds and the water.

"Holy shit!" Ann says in awe, her hand tight around mine.

Chapter Six

Hélène

Hélène waits. It seems to her she will spend much of the rest of her life waiting. She waits and the crowd swirls around her. The eyes are drawn to her; some of them she recognizes, more recognize her. She smiles firmly, distantly. Still, at fifty-four, she is a very beautiful woman. She stands straight and tall in a white Ricci suit, not slim, not willowy. It's not the kind of beauty that's fashionable right now, not cheeky in a fake feminist way, certainly not cute. Fashion, when it needs strength again, will catch up with her.

A fat little man looking for his wife backs into her. She doesn't even rock. He looks round, up. *"'Scusez,"* he mumbles.

She nods disdainfully.

Usually, at the beginning of the concert season there's a feeling of anticipation in the air. But not tonight. The city is under siege, and these people are the ones most threatened. You can sense it in the way they walk, a tension as they come to a corner not knowing what lies around it. Outside in the cold square soldiers patrol beneath the banked lights. The situation is under control, but you can't feel secure when you have to be so obviously protected. It makes you scurry and hunch your head in like a turtle. Not Hélène. She is one of these people but she wants nothing to do with them. She knows too much about them —time-servers, cautious bankers, corrupt officials—to believe that they have any right to survive. And yet she *is* one of them, all the same, by background, by training. By her own choice. "The bourgeoisie," she will say to Helen, "is the source of all that's best, all that's strongest in Western culture." Well, that's not strictly true, but for Hélène it's the centre of her social creed, a creed that's challenged by everything she knows of these people swirling past her.

And that's why there's so much tension in Hélène, too: not the tension of fear, but the tension of someone who has to strain constantly to reconcile belief and conscience. If Maurice were here it would be different.

He had little taste in music. He liked folk songs and old music-hall numbers. " 'Tea for two and two for tea,' " he used to sing lugubriously to tease her. But he came here with her. The symphony concerts were just one of the things they did together regularly.

Would Helen never understand?

"There are things you do with another person not because you want to do them, but because *they* do, because there's something bigger involved that's made stronger by doing them together."

"That sounds fair enough," Helen said, "if it wasn't always the woman doing something to please the man."

"But it's not," Hélène insisted. "That's not the way it was with Maurice. You know that."

"Oh, you and Molly, that was different." Helen patted her mother's hand as if she were some sort of prehistoric remnant. "I just don't think that people can live by that kind of contract any longer."

Yet her parents had. It wasn't always easy, but it made each of them immeasurably stronger. Maurice had given Hélène the focus she seemed to have lost now. With him she could have stood here in the Place des Arts and together they would have recognized what all this moral confusion round them meant. On her own, she felt it swamping her. She didn't know what line to take. She was reactionary yet instinctively rebellious; she wanted everything to change, but she wanted it to fit into the old structures. It wouldn't work like that, she knew it wouldn't, and the knowledge was making her all the more . . . well, difficult.

With Maurice— Oh, she was making it sound so one-sided and that's not how it was at all. She had depended on Maurice's clarity, but he relied on her determination just as much. More at times. When she had come to Canada to marry him in 1948, that was when he needed her most of all. His life was in danger of losing its sense of purpose entirely. . . .

"Madame, the doors will be closing in just a couple of minutes," says one of the young ushers in his trim fawn suit.

Where can Helen be? It's not like her to be late. Even the opposite: she always makes a point of being early. Hélène looks around anxiously at the lines of stragglers still coming in, women trotting in tight gowns as their husbands stride ahead. Then she sees Helen running, loose-limbed and breathless, through the long foyer. She is wearing a wide batik dress, sandals; one of the sandals slips off and she stops to pick it up, takes the other one off, too, and runs on barefoot. Her breasts bounce. She looks so much better, so much more relaxed than when Hélène saw her a week ago, the day she got out of prison. Hélène smiles. Helen comes on eagerly, her cheeks flushed, and it looks for a moment as if they'll crash into each other, but a yard from her mother she stops, straightens her dress and flicks back her hair. They embrace without emotion.

"I'm sorry I'm so late," Helen pants. "Ouf, I've been running."

"My dear, I can see. I'd almost given you up. I thought you might have forgotten."

"Mother! Of course, I didn't. But I was with this friend, Claire? And she started to tell me about, about . . . well, I couldn't leave straight away, you know how it is."

"Yes, *chérie,*" Hélène says without listening. "But let's hurry now. No, not the escalators, I can't stand them, stupid things to put in a concert hall, as if it were the métro."

Halfway up the stairs she stops and lays a hand on her daughter's shoulder. "It's good to see you looking so much better. You've even put on some weight."

"Tons."

"It suits you. And you've got some colour back in your cheeks as well."

"Fresh air. I've been out in the country for a couple of days."

"At the cottage?"

"No, I'm going there next weekend with the kids. A friend's farm."

A shrewd sidelong glance. "Something serious?"

"Who knows?"

Hélène turns away irritably. "Well, I'm not going to pry. Now come on or we'll miss the first movement." She strides up the stairs and Helen has to run to catch up with her.

The red and grey concert hall is already almost full. The musicians are beginning to tune their instruments. The audience waits and waves and chatters. "Excuse me," Hélène says as she squeezes towards the seat she always books in the front row of the balcony. A plump woman in a fussy satin dress pretends to ignore her. "Excuse me!" Reluctantly, the woman gets to her feet, her bracelets tinkling. Ridiculous things to wear to a concert; she'd better keep them quiet once it begins.

They settle into their seats and Hélène looks around her. What a dull group of people, so stolid and respectable and full of fear. The last people in the world to appreciate Mozart's refined passion. But that's the point of coming here, too, because there will always be the moment when the energy flows across, when the coughers and the shufflers are caught up and transformed. She feels it in her spine; the excitement is touching her already.

"Do I know your . . . farmer?" she whispers to Helen.

"No." A pause. "But you've heard of him." Helen relents. "Peter Abbott."

"Ahha," Hélène nods knowingly, suddenly relaxed. "Are you going to be his next happening?"

"Mother." The little girl in Helen giggles and leans her head for a moment on her mother's shoulder.

Hélène strokes her arm. "Your grandmother thought you looked so ill. She was worried about you. I told her not to be silly."

"I didn't feel so good there for a while. I guess it was the strain. Too many different things." Helen runs her tongue nervously along her lips. The air is too dry. "She's in good shape herself, anyway."

"But, *chérie,* if only you knew the trouble she gets into. Why, sometimes I have to deal with that stupid matron on the phone two or three times a day. It's only greed that keeps them from throwing her out."

"What's the problem this time?" Helen asks quietly, waiting for the outburst.

"Oh, the same old thing. She just can't live with other people, that's what it comes down to. She never could. Look at how she fell out with everyone she was ever close to. Her mother, her sisters, her husband, her friends." Hélène tries to control the shrillness in her voice; she knows what Helen's thinking. "She's so immature. If she's not constantly the centre of attention, she turns against everyone around her."

"I don't know, it's just that she's so full of energy. She's so alive."

"Perhaps," Hélène agrees grudgingly. "But if you can't live

with other people what good does it do you in this life? Last week she suddenly started accusing all the other patients of being Fascists. You can't do that sort of thing." She snorts, then gets a grip on herself. "Even if it's true. Most of them are."

"She's superb," Helen murmurs. "Politics at eighty-six."

Hélène can't stand such sentimentality. "You wouldn't have said that if you'd known her at the beginning of the war."

A young man comes on to the platform carrying a violin; the leader of the orchestra. The audience applauds perfunctorily.

"Nice was occupied by the Italians to start off with," Hélène hisses. "Your grandmother thought they were just wonderful. All those naval officers in their white uniforms smothered in gold braid. She was bowled over by them. The flower of Italian manhood." A tight, sarcastic smile. "It was the Germans she could never stand. They weren't elegant enough for her."

"But those stories she used to tell me about the Jews she hid in the maid's room. What was that woman's name again?"

"You know how she exaggerates all the time. She doesn't know what the truth is. It wasn't till after your Uncle Marc was killed that she began to take things seriously. And even then it had nothing to do with politics. It was just a matter of vengeance, pure and simple; nothing rational."

The audience roars in appreciation as von Karajan emerges from behind the curtain. He bows; a real man, craggy-featured, full of power. Hélène applauds. He raises his baton.

"Madame Beckermann, that was her name," Helen whispers.

"You should ask her about Admiral Cavalieri. Shsh."

The energy of the G Minor Symphony floods out over the audience. All day Hélène has been listening to the record of the Berlin Philharmonic playing it, and still it takes her by surprise. The sound comes at her in drifts, carrying everything before it. All of the passionate hurry of Mozart's life has gone into it, at thirty-two with still so much left to be done and only three more years before he'll die. And not just the urgency of one life; a whole century, a whole civilization rushing headlong into the unknown, the French revolution only twelve months away. Von Karajan drives the orchestra forward; Hélène has to breathe deeply to free herself from the pressure on her chest. But then the woodwinds find a gap and flow into it with a melody that's full of wistfulness, the memory of something lost and lonely. She looks from a train window and sees a boy and girl standing hand in hand beside a stream. The train howls into a tunnel. She tries to hold the image, if only in her memory, to project it out onto the pulsing black walls. But the train sweeps it up and smashes it forward.

Those immaculate Italian officers, they even used to hold musical evenings in her mother's apartment. It was Viennese music, too, but as far from Mozart as you could get, waltzes full of false and sticky emotions. Hélène went only once and that was enough to make her sick. The Italians danced with poor little shopgirls and seamstresses dressed up as ladies. The men drank looted champagne, the women eyed each other with hatred. The musicians poured syrup over everything. Two Germans stood in a corner, stiff and embarrassed. Helena watched over it all, her eyes twinkling, her body swaying to an imaginary wind. She flirted shamelessly with the admiral. Yes, that was the only word for it. At her age, she flirted, her head held back at a grotesque angle to smooth out the wrinkles in her neck. How humiliating!

Hélène went out onto the balcony. The black Mediterranean shushed away; the palm trees bent over the deserted promenade. One of the Germans came out behind her. She felt him watching her.

He coughed. *"Madame la comtesse."*

She didn't look round; she said nothing. Her muscles stiffened as he came closer.

"Will you come in and dance with me?"

She shook her head. "Thank you, no." The light breeze blew the perfume of hibiscus to her.

He placed his hand on the rail close to hers. She took hers

away. "Dancing will relieve your sadness," he said awkwardly.

"I'm not in the mood for dancing." She turned to look straight at him. "And I'm not sad."

His lower lip was thicker than the upper one. Thicker and somehow longer too, so that it sagged in the middle, quivering slightly as he talked. "You live in Saint Jeannet."

She glanced back towards the room. The sounds of laughter were stifled by the thick curtains.

"It's a dangerous place to live, Madame."

"You mean the cliff? There hasn't been a rock slide in years."

"I think you know what I mean."

She began to move over to the door but he touched her arm. "Half the people in those villages up on the plateau are in the resistance."

"No, monsieur, not half. Now please, I don't want to catch a chill."

"We have friends there. You could help us, too."

She turned her head away. "There's nothing I could do to help you." She was trembling as she went back into the room. She looked around her in disgust, at the debris, the drunkenness, the couples openly caressing.

One of the Italians staggered to his feet. "Let us drink a toast." He spilled champagne on the front of his uniform. "Il Duce."

Admiral Cavalieri, tightly corseted, his face glistening, had to propose another toast to Hitler and Hélène couldn't escape. The Germans were watching her; she felt the panic rising like feathers in her lungs.

Her mother swayed into the middle of the floor and called for yet another toast. Hélène clung on to the edge of the table. Helena raised her glass, staring mockingly at the Germans. "My friends, *à l'amour. L'amore.*"

Her friends roared their approval.

"Maman, it's disgusting," Hélène said the next day. "Don't

you see how humiliating it is? Those pathetic little girls don't know what they're doing, but you do. How can you?"

"Cavalieri's a personal friend, my dear. He'd do anything for me." Helena played with the lace around the collar of her dressing gown. There were brown spots on her shoulders.

"What do you have to give him in return?" Hélène asked angrily.

"I don't know what you're talking about." Helena poured herself another cup of coffee and sipped it luxuriously. "It makes such a difference to have the real thing, doesn't it?" She put the porcelain cup down carefully in its delicate saucer and looked up from under her eyelashes. "He'll tell me anything I ask. I could get anything you wanted to know out of him."

And indeed, from then on, she did. Little by little, with a sly skill, in têtes-à-têtes at teatime or drunken confessionals late at night, Helena got the information they needed. The admiral was cajoled into afternoon expeditions along the coast in his staff car, until finally they had pieced together every defensive position from Nice to the Italian frontier.

Why did she do it? Not for any political reason, nor for love of a country that wasn't hers, anyway. She liked the admiral. He was her friend; he flattered her. But she loved to deceive him, to play with him without his knowing. The love of deception, then? The idea revolted Hélène.

Later, though, when the Germans took over in the south of France, when they executed Marc, it was a different story. The story of the old woman who comes on a dying enemy in the street. The enemy calls for water. Cackling, she gathers up her skirts and pisses in his mouth.

Hélène shakes the memory out of her head. The slow movement promises relief as the tension begins to relax with the shift to the major key. Here, after all the swirling currents, is a pool of tranquillity, the woodwinds dappling it with little points of light. She feels it cool on her fingers; there is still the chance of peace, an ordered pastoral. She sees the countryside outside of

Vienna, a house with a garden. But something slow and ominous grows here, too, something more threatening than all the hurtling passions of the outside world. Mozart likes the little house in the Währingergasse. Its simplicity pleases him; he can work with its noises in his ears. Yet just beneath the surface despair is lurking. He writes abject letters to his friend Puchberg begging for money. He's the greatest composer in Europe—everyone knows it by now—and still he has to beg. What use is it to keep on working for an art that glorifies incompetent princes? His plump, sloe-eyed wife can't understand him. He fears she'll be as unfaithful to him as he is to her. His baby daughter, Theresia, with the beautiful curls, has just died. But it's his own death he feels rising inside him. There are no thunderclouds here, only a heavy greyness fogging everything. The little pointed notes begin to clump and drag. They nag away; echoing horns slur downwards in the distance; the sound collapses. This music squeezes out from a terrible lethargy. Hélène's fingers jab into the arms of her seat, for this is the hardest mood of all to fight against.

Yes, shameful though it was, the Germans did have friends in Saint Jeannet. One by one, tit for tat, they were eliminated.

The first, the easiest to do away with, was Larouche, the pharmacist. Though he kept to himself and was never known to have done anything harmful to anyone, he was disliked by the whole village. How had it started? Nobody knew. But generations of children, as they grew up, remembered chanting rude songs in the narrow street outside his neat little store. *"Larouche, tu couches avec ton dada; Larouche, ta bouche est pleine de caca."* They ran off giggling down the cobblestoned alleyways as soon as he came out. He waved gloomily after them. He lived with his mother; his mother died; he lived on his own.

When the war came and the resistance groups began to organize, there was an implicit understanding that Larouche must be told nothing. On his own, he wasn't to be trusted, but beyond that, he had suspicious friends. He was seen sitting in backstreet bars in Cannes with a man who was linked to the Corsican gang bosses along the coast. Nothing obvious; maybe it was just a small matter of drugs, but already the gangs were beginning to realize they could make more money working with the Gestapo. Their thugs filled the ranks of the Milice, the French auxiliary police, tracking down Jews, blackmailing, bribing, beating. So keep an eye on Larouche, *les gars,* till we know what he's up to.

Soon they began to get reports of people, strangers, arriving at his store.

"Watch him more closely."

One evening a car pulled up in front of his door and a dark-haired woman in a fur coat got out. She hurried inside. The driver carried in three heavy leather suitcases and a hatbox, then drove off quickly. She didn't come out.

"Are you sure she's still in there?" Delvaux asked.

"There's no other entrance."

"Are you sure?" Delvaux, the sceptical lawyer.

"We've been watching."

"Maybe she's just a mistress. Maybe that's what he was seeing the guy in Cannes about."

"But why is he hiding her away?" Hélène asked.

"With Larouche, everything's a secret."

They waited and went on watching. Three days later a doddery old man with gold-rimmed spectacles went into the store and didn't come out, either.

Hélène and Delvaux went there the next day.

"Why, madame, this is an honour," said Larouche, rubbing his hands together. He was a tall, stooping man in his fifties. He had a long nose, a strong cleft chin and a mouth that seemed to be cut right back into the centre of his skull. "And Monsieur Delvaux?" He looked around anxiously.

Delvaux jerked down the blind.

The store was full of the smell of antiseptic. The mahogany cupboards with their rows of tiny drawers were brightly polished. Bottles glowed with different coloured liquids. Larouche's long fingers were pure white.

"Sit down." Delvaux pulled out a gun.

Hélène opened the door that led into the house and Larouche rose to stop her. Delvaux threw him back into the chair. Upstairs she found three fur coats in one of the closets. In the kitchen, the old man's suitcases: I. S. Vidal engraved on them. Downstairs in the basement, his body. It was a hot day but the furnace was going full blast. The body was intact except for its head, which lay in a sink, its penis, its testicles and its left foot. The body of the woman, much younger, had not yet been dismembered, though one breast was lightly slit with a knife. It was turning brown and beginning to smell.

Hélène choked and forced herself to look.

In Larouche's meticulous files they found the papers of twenty-seven Jews whose trips to South America he had been arranging. Each of them had paid a quarter of a million francs, a trifling amount for one's freedom. Most of the money had gone to Larouche's connections in the underworld or to the hairdresser and the milliner who made contact with the victims. His own profit margin, considering the risk, wasn't all that big.

The three bodies and the charred bones were buried that night in an olive grove.

Yes, Larouche was easy to get rid of. But not Beaubien, one of the most popular men in the district, a little, laughing farmer who turned in his neighbour to the Milice when they fell out over the ownership of a field. Or Léonardo, the alcoholic tilemaker, or Giselle, whose lover, the radio operator, was playing around with another girl. Or Blériot who betrayed Delvaux later in '43, or Solange, or Saint-Amant.

The minuet, with its lovely, peaceful trio, slips by and Hélène doesn't even notice. Damn, damn, she's missed it. Perhaps that was the crucial moment, perhaps it would have explained everything. A couple behind and to her left are whispering something to each other. Raising her chin, she turns her head about fifteen degrees towards them, and they stop. She must listen.

Listen. Over in one of the boxes to her right a dark, square-jawed young man leans across and strokes a woman's cheek. Hélène watches them.

Listen. The finale sweeps through the audience with overwhelming vigour, but she finds herself resisting it. She's not ready for what's happening. She wants to stand back and see what Mozart's doing, but she can't. The man beside her leans forward, his chin on his fists. There's as much energy here as there was in the opening movement, and yet it's different. It doesn't smash into the objects in its way; the sonata form controls it. Something happened back there in the minuet and Larouche, damn him, made her miss it. She concentrates. Listen. What is Mozart doing? The flutes, off on their own and poignant, repeat the second subject and something beautiful is happening; there's room now for the individual instrument within this great torrent of sound. For all its vulnerability, it can't be wiped out. But how can Mozart manage it? That's what she doesn't understand. After all that terrible apathy and depression, how can he bring about this muscular balance of forces? The great discords blare out and then the individual players have their chance again. How, she insists, how can this be possible? Is it only the wonderful complexity of Mozart's imagination that's able to bring about this reconciliation? In that case, then surely only the genius can make sense of it. For the rest of them, sitting here so earnestly, it must be a lie. But no, that's not how it is; there's no elitism, no romantic exclusiveness. There's room here for every contradiction, every contribution. No simple statement, no single person can be enough. The revolution that will destroy everything in Mozart's world may be only a year away, but harmony is still—just—possible. She listens in wonder. There can't be any greater triumph than this.

The audience leaps to its feet and applauds. Hélène sits stunned, not even clapping. Most of them, she thinks sourly, are just trying to get out more quickly to the bar. The others are only standing because they can't see. "Bravo," shouts a man behind her. Von Karajan bows and gestures to the orchestra. She applauds limply.

Without speaking, she and Helen file out into the lobby. There is nothing to say.

"Shall I get you a drink?" Helen asks.

"Just a Scotch. And a little Perrier."

Hélène wanders about between the groups of people. How can they yammer away at each other so aimlessly? The trouble is she doesn't believe in what Mozart has just done. He's done it, but she doesn't believe it's possible. She's afraid he might have tricked her.

"Basically, it's a matter of technique," says a woman behind her.

"Why don't you admit it?" says the man she's with. "What it all comes down to is professionalism."

God knows what they think they're talking about. Hélène looks up at the elaborate lights in the ceiling: inverted, crystal armadilloes. She walks over to a railing and glances down at the crowd milling about on the floor below. She sees a large, beautifully subtle abstract painting hanging on the wall and smiles in pleasure.

Helen hands her a glass. "I got you a double."

"Look down there." Hélène points.

Helen looks and smiles, too. She made the painting five or six years ago. It was the best canvas in the show and brought her a lot of attention for the first time. "I'd completely forgotten they had it here," she says.

"Doesn't it make you feel wonderful?" Hélène asks eagerly. "Seeing it here? Knowing it's yours and that so many people are seeing it, too? I think that kind of knowledge would just . . . well, explode in me. I'd want to stand up here and shout, 'It's mine. Look at it. I painted it.' "

Helen laughs.

"You know, my dear, back there in the last movement, it

was so wonderful what Mozart was doing, but so complex. In a way, it excludes ordinary people, ordinary mortals. The artist can find solutions that the rest of us can only catch a glimpse of." Hélène grasps her daughter's hand. "You're lucky, do you realize that?"

"I don't know," Helen says, suspicious of this sudden enthusiasm. "They hang that painting down there, but who ever really sees it? All anybody's thinking about is beating the next guy to the bar. It's just décor. It costs a lot, which makes people feel sophisticated, and it doesn't mean a goddamn thing."

"But it's not a question of numbers," Hélène argues. "If just one person really sees it, sees the purity of what you're doing . . ."

"Purity? Oh, to hell with purity, mother. I'm tired of purity. Art approaching the condition of music. It's a bourgeois concept, purity. Only the bourgeoisie can afford it."

"I don't know why you should say that, *chérie.* The bourgeoisie is the source of all that's best in Western culture," Hélène asserts pompously. "All that's strongest."

"God, that's crap. It's the source of all the hypocritical compromises, that's all. There's something I just read this morning down at Peter's. One sentence, but it says it all: 'There's no document of civilization which is not at the same time a document of barbarism.' Now *that* explodes inside me, if you like. It scares the shit out of me. I haven't worked out where I stand yet, but somehow the only way is to struggle constantly against one's art, against the whole idea of purity. I don't know if Mozart did that, but Christ, he must have. In any case, his solutions don't work any longer. Art doesn't reconcile anything anymore."

"Well, if I was a painter I'd be happy to see one of my pictures in here," Hélène says huffily, not listening to what her daughter's trying to say.

"Yoohoo!" A voice blares above the hubbub.

"Oh God, it's Mrs. McLaren."

The woman who bears down on them is in her sixties, grey

hair, a flushed, veined face, a tweed suit, an aura of alcohol.

"All these people! You can't get near the bar. Luckily, I had the foresight to slip a flask into my purse as I was coming out. In case I needed a wee drop, eh? The prices they charge in here are terrible, too." She takes out the silver flask, a plastic glass and a can of Canada Dry. "Would you like a nip, Helen?"

"No, no thank you." Helen smiles. Is this slurred woman the same person as the arrogant matron who awed her so much as a child? Mrs. McLaren's father had commanded a Highland regiment in the First World War and she never allowed anyone in Montreal to forget it. She even tried to keep the Prime Minister's mother out of her golf club because she spoke French. She lost that battle—as, indeed, she had lost every battle—but it didn't shake her confidence. "Poor wee creature, the Lord knows why she wanted in in the first place. Nobody speaks to her. Most of the time she's tight as a tick."

Now Mrs. McLaren is tight as a tick. All of the time. She fingers the clan brooch on her lapel. "What d'you think of these Frenchies now, eh? We've got them where they belong. Locked up, that's where they should all be." She laughs hoarsely.

"Madge," Hélène says reprovingly.

"All right, all right, I know that's where you come from, too, Hélène, but you're not French, and even if you were, you'd have nothing in common with this lot over here. They can't even speak their own language."

"How do you know?" Helen asks aggressively. Mrs. McLaren once told her she would never go into a store or a café —caffy—where there was a danger that someone might try to speak French to her.

Mrs. McLaren ignores the question. "Och, you don't think they could rule themselves, do you, Helen? That Rennie Lavick, what does he know about the price of tea in China?" She looks around the bar, blinking in puzzlement, as if she's not sure where she is. "He can't even get into a car gracefully. For all he's such a midget."

"Were you over in Scotland again this summer, Madge?" Hélène asks, trying to change the subject. She knows Mrs. McLaren makes the pilgrimage every year: St. Andrews, Skye, Prince's Street, Culloden: safe ground, surely.

"No, I'll not go back there again. Not without Harry. We always did it together, eh? It would be too painful." She examines the engraved flask in her hand. "Harry gave me this, you know. Not that I'm much of a drinker, mind." She puts it back in her purse and starts to turn away, then stops with her hand on Helen's arm. "The leaves fall one by one, Helen. You mark my word. I told you." Her lips tremble. Then she stumbles off towards the doors into the concert hall.

Hélène shrugs. "That poor woman." She puts her arm round her daughter's waist. "Come on, we'd better be getting back in there, too." But her legs are weak. Suddenly, she wishes she were at home in bed. Mrs. McLaren fills her with the fear that she'll end up like that herself. "There's nothing worse than losing your self-respect," she whispers.

Did she actually say it aloud? She must have, because Helen stretches up and kisses her gently on the cheek. "That's the last thing that'll happen to you."

No, Hélène won't let go of her self-respect; there's no danger of that. What really frightens her is the thought that that's all she'll be left with. Like one of those walnuts that rot away invisibly on the inside; a hard shell of ego protecting the emptiness. She shudders. She knows why Madge misses Harry so badly. He danced attendance on her, ran himself into the ground trying to please her. God knows why, she treated him like a waiter. That's not how it was with Maurice; no dependence, a constant sharing. Right from the time they first became lovers in those weeks after they escaped from the Gestapo, they lived on an equal basis. They respected each other; that's the only way there can be self-respect, damn it. You don't need to be called Ms. for that, Hélène thinks petulantly.

Without even noticing she bangs into the legs of the woman

who didn't stand up when they tried to get to their seats before. The woman looks up in surprise and sees Hélène glaring down at her. "Can't you be careful?" she mutters. Hélène brushes past her and sits down heavily.

There was only the one time she lost her respect for Maurice and she almost left him then. When he came back to Canada after the war, he had to get a divorce from his first wife. She was living with a lawyer who had managed to keep out of the army, but still the process was full of bitterness; old sores reopened. What with that and all the moral apathy of those postwar years, he almost went to pieces. When Hélène finally came over from France she was shocked at what she found. He was well on his way to becoming a middle-aged roué: drinking too much, hanging about with the callous, cynical businessmen for whom a dirty joke was the finest form of self-expression. And she had saved him, or so Maurice used to say. She told him she couldn't stay with him if all he was going to do was destroy himself. She'd rather go back to Europe and build a life there on her own. He insisted she must stay; he needed her, needed her help. So she helped him, tenderly if possible, harshly when that was the only way. She made him see that power is not a licence to exploit. That business can only be justified if it goes hand in hand with social responsibility. That the Church is not a meaningless ritual but a passionate, living commitment to one's fellow man. "They go about like they were the fucking conscience of the city," was what a friend told her old Sam Bronfman had said about them in one of his frequent rages.

"Well," she replied proudly, "if that's so, we'll just have to learn to live up to it."

Yet here she is now, worried she'll end up like Madge McLaren!

"Why did he call it 'The Jupiter,' anyway?" Helen asks, looking up from her programme.

"Mozart didn't," Hélène says automatically as she watches von Karajan stride back onto the stage. "I don't know where the name came from, even. All the critics claim it's meaningless." The conductor raises his arms; her body tenses. "But they're wrong," she whispers quickly.

The first great blasts of Mozart's last symphony ring out. It takes over exactly where the fortieth left off, full of triumphant assurance, the rejection of doubt. Two weeks at the beginning of August 1788 was all it took him to write it, two languid holiday weeks with nothing of importance happening in Vienna, apart from the scandal that filtered back from the gaming tables in Baden. Yet this first movement is a great public statement of vitality and order. The reconciliation Hélène was suspicious of before turns out to have been no mere aesthetic trick. Somehow —and still she doesn't understand how, but it doesn't matter any longer—that balance has become firm and permanent. It spreads out from the confines of art to the whole world of nature and man. Harmony is no longer just a musical possibility; it's the natural order of things. There's room in it for every kind of mood. The loneliness, the gnawing presence of death, have been left behind. Power and feeling can exist together; they don't cancel each other out. Sadness and joy, laughter and dignity; the opposites no longer clash. They don't crowd in on top of one another, struggling for survival. There's space between them, respect—yes, respect—for the other point of view.

Listen—she almost laughs aloud—to how Mozart takes a comic little aria—"You are a trifle dense, Pompeo; go and study the ways of the world"—and uses it here to develop his most ceremonial work. That's why the name Jupiter is right. Jupiter, Jove, not just the solemnity of the god, but the humour, too—joviality. Just for a moment, as the strings are left on their own, there's a glimpse of desolation through the trees, but a beam of light chases it away. Plenitude can't be denied. This is the great refinement Mozart spent his whole life seeking, a refinement full of playfulness. How was he able to hold on to it with all of Europe preparing itself for chaos?

And how had they dared to play his music, Mozart of all

people, this most humane of musicians, in the Gestapo headquarters in Nice? Hélène fills with a sudden anger. Did they think they could take Mozart away from her? For years afterwards she couldn't bear to listen to him. He was too corrupt, sweet—cheap Austrian chocolate. But she fought them. Little by little she forced herself to listen to a few bars at a time, till she won him back; the final victory of her war.

The Gestapo had taken over a rambling old villa on the hillside behind Nice. The walled garden was filled with giant yews and hundreds of flowering shrubs. The perfume drifted everywhere. Even in the cells, even on the third day, she could smell it.

The Citroen crunched on the neat gravel driveway. In the evening light, the bluish green of the grass and the warm stucco façade of the house seemed unreal to her. Surely, this couldn't be happening. She would awake from this moment of suspension. She did. As the car rounded a curve, Maurice slumped against her and groaned. More blood on her blouse. The man sitting next to her leaned over and pushed Maurice upright, then slapped his face. He said something in German and the others laughed.

They stopped in front of a flight of steps. A small fountain played. She waited for a footman to come running out. An apéritif first; then down to a restaurant in the old port for bouillabaisse; lights rippling on the black water. Her arm was grabbed and she was dragged out of the rear seat. She stumbled, kicked her ankle, almost fell. She caught hold of the headlight and steadied herself.

"You must try not to fall down," someone had told her a long time ago. "If you do, they kick you in the kidneys and the back of the head, and shout at you to get up. When you can't, they keep on kicking you."

Who had said that, Delvaux? She looked up at the lines of shuttered windows on the floors above, and the reality of what was about to happen to her clutched at her throat. From which of those windows had Delvaux thrown himself when death was the only hope left? Pots of flowers dotted the balustrade. She searched the worn flagstones for a sign, a stain.

"If they ever catch you, don't tell them anything at all," Delvaux had warned her when she first joined the group. "Don't try to be clever. People think they can trick them, but they can't. The Milice maybe, but not the Gestapo. They're trained interrogators. They can break any story down. Bit by bit they'll turn it against you until you end up giving them what they want. The only thing to do is to start out saying, *Je ne sais rien,* and keep on repeating it, whatever they ask, however they bribe you or torture you. Just that, not another word, Hélène, remember, *Je ne sais rien.*"

Had those been Delvaux's last words as he flung himself down: I know nothing?

"I know nothing," she muttered in English to Maurice as they bumped into each other in the doorway. A gun barrel jabbed her in the back.

The hall was cool and high-ceilinged, with marble pillars and an elaborate pattern of black and white tiles on the floor. They stopped at a desk with a sergeant seated behind it. Through a half-open door she saw a group of men in civilian clothes sprawled in armchairs and a sofa. They were drinking; crystal glasses. Dance music whined from a gramophone. A woman came and sat down on the arm of one of the chairs. She was pretty, dark, heavily made up. She bent to whisper something in a man's ear. As she did so, she glanced towards the door and saw Hélène watching her. She smiled, then said something else to the man. Both of them looked at Hélène and laughed.

She was pushed towards a staircase that descended into the cellars. Maurice, who was in front of her, tripped and slumped against the wall. She tried to reach out to him but her hands were knocked away. She must steel herself, she realized. She knew already what she was going to see down here; everyone in the resistance had to live with it. She heard the noise; not shrieks, but the endless, semiconscious moans of patients as they come out of the anaesthetic, mumbling, discovering their agony. Dull sounds in an old house. As she knew it would be, one of the cell doors was open. She tried not to look but they held her and forced her. A man lying face down in the corner, his neck twisted at an odd angle. He was naked, except for one sock. His back was covered with scars and black welts. His testicles seemed swollen underneath him. There was blood between his legs and deep brown holes on the sole of his bare foot. No sound came out of him; just an odour of shit and sweat.

A door was unlocked and Maurice was thrown towards it. As he bumped into the frame, the soldier who was behind him lashed at his wounded shoulder with a gun barrel. He yelled. "*Mais non!*" Hélène shouted and pushed at the guard. He turned and smashed the butt into the centre of her face. She reeled away with blood spurting out of her broken nose. Two minutes she had been down here. How long could she last?

In the middle of the night, when she had finally dozed off on the damp stone floor, she was jerked awake again. She didn't know where she was. She was pulled to her feet by her hair and dragged out into the corridor. She had never screamed in her life before. That was when she heard the Mozart. Upstairs.

In his exquisite office on the second floor, Colonel Franz von Stadler was listening to the clarinet concerto. Inside the heavy baize-covered doors the noises from the cellar didn't distract him. The corporal held Hélène by the hair, pulling her head back so that her throat was exposed. The liquid sound flowed round her. The corporal started to say something, but von Stadler put a finger to his lips. With his other hand he gestured to a chair. Hélène sat down.

The room was dark; just one floor lamp in the corner behind her and a reading light over the polished, intricately inlaid desk. There were heavy velvet curtains across the windows, an Aubusson tapestry of Diana on one wall, a carpet from Shiraz on the floor. Neat piles of folders lay on the desk, and a map of southeast France covered with coloured pins and little pieces of paper was fixed to an easel. Von Stadler was reading through a file; a stubby finger kept time to the music.

Hélène sat and waited and tried not to listen. She had heard of von Stadler before, knew his reputation. He was a tall, fat man with a flat face and heavy jowls; a thin mouth that curved up into his plump cheeks in an expression of beatitude. His eyes were a very pale grey; his sparse reddish-blond hair was brushed across his skull and a ginger fuzz sprouted profusely on the backs of his freckled hands. As the music came to an end he motioned to the corporal to take the record off the gramophone. He rubbed his eyes with the palms of his hands; Colonel von Stadler was tired.

"Well, Madame," he said, getting to his feet, "how do you like our Mozart?"

She didn't reply.

His voice was soft, surprisingly light from such a heavy frame. His French was hesitant, almost shy. "Of all his compositions I think I like the clarinet concerto best. It's full of such . . . pathos."

She picked at the congealed blood on her face.

"He wrote it when he was dying. Did you know that? Yes, such beauty. And afterwards he asked them to take his canary out of the room. He couldn't bear its singing any longer."

He lifted a cigarette box and stroked it appreciatively with his fingers. He opened it and held it out to her; it was full of fat Turkish cigarettes. This was her first moment of weakness; she took one. He lit it with a silver lighter. The heat of the flame made her wince. She drew the smoke deep into her lungs.

"You know, Madame, we are very civilized. You didn't expect that. But to be civilized, one also has to be strong. One has to protect one's civilization, don't you think? Now you—it's so obvious—you should be on our side. You can't have anything in common with these agitators, these Communists. Really, it's your duty to help us."

"Je ne sais rien," she muttered dully.

"Perhaps you don't realize all that's involved in our investigations. We don't want to hurt anyone, you understand. We're not barbarians, Madame. But to protect one's values, what one believes in, one has to be a little . . . ah, barbaric at times."

She said nothing.

"I'm sure you'll see my point eventually and tell us what we want to know."

"Je ne sais rien."

He stared into her eyes, a look of sad sincerity in his own. Then he went back behind the desk and straightened his papers.

The smoke was stinging her nostrils. She was happy to stub the cigarette out in an ashtray. She tried to swallow, tasting blood in the back of her throat.

"How do you contact Guérin when you want to see him?" Guérin was the leader of the Francs Tireurs Partisans, the Communist resistance group in the southeast.

"Je ne sais rien."

"But you must. You met him last Tuesday in Cagnes. We have witnesses."

It was true. She had met Guérin in a bar behind the station. They were coordinating an attack on a German troop train. She knew nothing.

Von Stadler watched her and shook his head. His eyes narrowed; his voice became legalistic. "You make it very difficult for yourself. You've got to understand that from now on you're the one who's responsible for what happens to you. Now, please"—he made one last effort, holding out his hands to her—"how do you contact him?"

"Je ne sais rien."

"Madame, I repeat, it's your responsibility." He signalled to the corporal and returned to his files with a sigh.

In the morning she was turned over to Lieutenant Hofer on the third floor. Hofer was completely dedicated. He was a tall, thin boy of twenty-two or three, pale and bony, with startled brown eyes behind the thick lenses of his glasses. One of his legs had been smashed by a shell in North Africa.

"Take off your clothes," he shouted.

There were three men in the room. Hélène hadn't even undressed in front of her husband.

"Take off your clothes." He limped towards her and slammed the handle of his walking stick into her nose.

She didn't give him the pleasure of seeing her embarrassed. She didn't try to cover herself, didn't even look down at the stream of blood between her breasts. He walked around her, a collector in a museum, then reached out and slashed at one of her nipples. She stumbled but managed to plant her feet firmly again.

"How do you contact Guérin?" His French was no better than it needed to be.

She shook her head.

He struck her on the abdomen. "Whore." Again. "Communist whore." Next her thighs, the small of her back.

In the corner was an old bathtub filled to the top with brownish water. Lumps of ice floated in it. If only she didn't know what was going to happen. Hofer's two helpers shoved her towards it, bending her arms up high behind her back. The surface came closer; she heaved and struggled. Her head was plunged in. She gasped with the coldness, as her mouth and nose filled with water. Hofer rammed the stick into her buttocks. "Whore." She came up spluttering. "Guérin."

"*Je ne sais rien.*"

She was thrust down again. *Je ne sais rien.* Again. She blacked out; they slapped her. Again. Again. *Rien, rien, rien.*

In her cell she dragged herself back to consciousness, twisting, gulping, slipping down in panic, vomiting, shuddering. She didn't hate Hofer any more than she would have hated a bee that stung her. He wasn't interested in finding out what she knew; all he wanted to do was destroy her. He would let her die like an animal. She preferred that to von Stadler with his stench of Mozart.

The beginning of the slow movement of the *Jupiter* symphony is full of perfect serenity. The muted strings slide easily through a long pastoral evening. The air stirs gently. Nothing is questioned because the answers to all the possible questions have been discovered already. Hélène shrugs it off irritably; she can't trust Mozart any longer. The past has brushed too close to her. She waits impatiently and suddenly the stillness is slit wide open to reveal a deep pulsing void. It's not the personal despair that filled the G Minor Symphony. There's nothing personal in this, and nothing sad; emotions don't come into it. What she sees here is a slowly revolving emptiness that stretches to infinity, turning over and over in slow motion, with no vertical, nothing to hold on to. You thought you knew everything, and all of a sudden a new world opens up that makes all knowledge meaningless. There's nothing threatening, nothing violent about it. If you feel threatened, Hélène tells herself, it's because you cling too desperately to what you thought would last forever. The pastoral closes over again for a moment, softly, softly, but she knows what lies behind it now, and for all this ease and gentleness, she aches for another glimpse into that shining darkness. And listen, here it comes again and again, caught now by the flute, light bouncing away from its wand in all directions.

She feels her hands shaking uncontrollably.

When at last the reconciliation comes, as of course it must for Mozart, she knows that underneath its intricate surface there's a cold void that will snuff her out without even noticing.

She clasps her fingers around her knees. Her daughter is glancing at her anxiously. Hélène does not fidget like this. She pulls herself together.

On the morning of the third day she was taken to another room. Von Stadler was there as well as Hofer. He examined her with concern. "I wish you would listen to me," he insisted. "It's very simple. You could help us so easily." He seemed disappointed in her.

Hofer gave an order and Hélène heard some footsteps behind her. She didn't look. Hofer twisted her head round. "Do you know this woman?" he asked.

"C'est Madame, la comtesse," said a child's voice. It was Marie-Laure, the daughter of the baker in Saint Jeannet. *"Bonjour, Madame."* She curtseyed, her eyes fixed in horror on Hélène's face. A twelve-year-old girl, small for her age, dark and sallow, asthmatic. They said the flour didn't agree with her. Why had the Germans brought her in, of all people? She had done nothing; just taken a few simple messages, kept watch once or twice. For God's sake, nothing!

They strapped Marie-Laure into a large wooden armchair in the middle of the room. She began to cry. "What are they doing?" she sobbed. "It hurts."

"Let her go," Hélène shouted. "She can't tell you anything."

"You can," said von Stadler. He nodded to Hofer.

Hofer stretched out the child's tiny forefinger on the arm of the chair. She looked up at him nervously. He smashed the finger with a steel rod. She howled.

"Let her go," Hélène screamed.

"You can stop it any time," von Stadler reminded her. "Just be reasonable."

They broke another finger.

"Stop," Hélène begged.

Von Stadler told Hofer to stop. He waited till the howls subsided. "Now, how do you contact Guérin?"

"Je ne sais rien," Hélène croaked.

"Whatever happens to her is your responsibility."

They broke Marie-Laure's wrist.

"Don't make us do this," von Stadler pleaded.

An ankle.

"Don't you like little girls?" he shouted at Hélène in anger.

The noise died down once Marie-Laure was unconscious. Just Hélène's gasping sobs. *"Je ne sais rien."* Von Stadler turned away from her in disgust.

Finally, they shot the child through the head and dragged Hélène away.

On the fourth day, Hofer pulled out her toenails, carefully, one by one.

On the fifth, they raped her. Not Hofer or von Stadler; five or six of the guards. She lost count. Why they had waited so long she could never understand. There must have been a reason. Von Stadler would have a reason. When they began she was like a corpse, but by the time they had finished she was strong enough to hate them again.

On the sixth day, the electrodes.

On the seventh . . . oh, if only this damnable music would stop. She can't stand it any longer. Stop, she wants to scream. This smiling, gentle, loving minuet, stop. She will bury herself in silence.

On the seventh day, Guérin with nearly a hundred men from his Maquis forces in the mountains blew his way into the villa and released them: Hélène, the other mangled prisoners, Maurice whose jaw was broken. His upper gum hung down into the middle of his mouth like a second tongue. As she looked across at him in the back of the truck, Hélène realized she hadn't even thought about him once.

She forces herself to listen. There is no pleasure now, only an obligation not to give in. One never gives in. The final movement is Mozart at the height of his brilliance, she tells herself. She listens attentively to the elaborate, polyphonic interlacing of the five themes, each of them so simple on its own, yet intricately, endlessly combined. Nothing clashes. How can any imagination concentrate so many different moods and still retain its lucidity? Reason. Ah yes, reason triumphs for the last time in Europe. She watches, she listens, she admires. She hears nothing at all. At the end she applauds.

Helen is full of enthusiasm. "My God, that's really incredible," she says and claps faster, a rhythmic foot-stomping beat.

Von Karajan holds out his arms. Hélène smiles wearily. *"N'est-ce pas?"* she murmurs.

They squeeze out through the swarming, excited crowd. Friends call to each other. They've forgotten what's waiting for them in the street outside. Hélène is the only one who remembers. She stops in the middle of the foyer and people bump into her without apologizing.

"Before Mozart died," she says to no one in particular, though Helen happens to hear and thinks it's meant for her, "before he died, he asked them to take his canary, which he loved, out of the room. He couldn't stand its singing any longer."

Helen looks anxiously at her mother. She's really getting older. Has the concert been too much for her? She takes her arm protectively. "Would you like to go for a coffee?"

"Chez toi?"

"Well, no, it's a bit of a mess with all the canvases lying around. But there's a nice coffee house just off Saint Denis. It's not too noisy."

They decide to walk for the fresh air. It hits them like ice. In the bright lights a group of sullen teen-agers stares at the soldiers. Hélène doesn't notice the sidewalk under her feet. They pass the hookers on the corner of Sainte Cathérine and Saint Laurent; they're wearing their fake fur coats already. Two bums huddle in a doorway drinking wine out of a paper bag. One of them lets it dribble down the front of his coat and the other shouts at him.

A family man in a new Impala pulls in beside them and leans out to make sucking noises. *"Tu me suces, chérie?"* It's not clear whether he wants the daughter or the mother. Perhaps both.

Helen slams the roof with her fist and the car spurts away. What in God's name is happening to this city, Hélène wonders. Surely, cities were formed when men drew together to protect themselves against barbarism. Is this one simply collapsing in on itself? She doesn't know. Is she so out of touch she can't even see for herself any longer? She doesn't care. Damn it, she doesn't care.

"It's in here," Helen says, taking her by the arm again.

Warmth immediately surrounds them. The coffee house is full of young people with beards and long hair arguing against a background of Indian music. They look at Hélène curiously for a moment and then return to the serious business of disagreeing. Though they're as alien to her as creatures from another planet, she's grateful at least for their neutrality. If only she had more energy, she might even like them. She orders mint tea.

"Did you enjoy it?" Helen asks and there's still a note of concern in her voice. "Are you feeling okay?"

"Of course. Yes, of course. Just a little tired, that's all." That's enough, she tells herself. Don't be such a boring old woman. Get a grip on yourself. "How's Ann?" she asks, trying to sound interested.

"Fine," says Helen cautiously.

"She's growing up."

"She's fine." Helen nods.

The aroma of the mint rises through Hélène's nostrils. She begins to feel better. "Puberty comes so quickly. Have you told her about the facts of life?"

"Well, of course," Helen says defensively.

"These days, you can't tell them soon enough, you know, *chérie.* It's hard for parents to realize. They want to hold on to their children. What about birth control? Have you had her see the doctor yet?"

Helen can't stand her mother's intrusions and Hélène knows it. "Listen, mother, when I had my first period, I didn't even know what was happening to me. You hadn't even told me." She gulps the steaming espresso.

"Oh, *chérie,*" Hélène says and her voice becomes musical. "Don't be so paranoid. Of course, I told you."

"You didn't. God, I was so afraid. I really thought I was dying. And I was so ashamed, too. I didn't know a damn thing about it."

"Of course I did, darling. You just forgot. Now, that's enough."

Hélène looks at her daughter with hatred. Don't you like little girls? von Stadler had shouted. How could she, how could she?

Tight-lipped, Helen shakes her head. They drink in silence, except for the twanging of an Indian raga in the distance.

Appendix II

Final Report of the Autopsy on Monsieur Pierre Laporte

Sunday, October 18, 1970, in the hours between 3h00 A.M. and 7h00 A.M. at the Institute of Legal Medicine in the City of Montreal, we, the undersigned, conducted a legal medical verification on the corpse of an individual identified as being that of Mr. Pierre LAPORTE. This at the express request of the authorities of the Criminal Investigation Department of Quebec (telephone of M. L. DESCENT, assistant general director of the Criminal Investigation Department of Quebec for Dr. VALCOURT), about 2h00 A.M., October 18, 1970. Present At The Autopsy: 1. Members of the Criminal Investigation Department of Quebec: Cpl. R. MARCHAND, Constable Jean-Claude BOISLARD, Captain R. BELLEMARE and Constable Leopold BOUGIE as his assistant. 2. Members of the Legal Medical Institute: Chemists Bernard PECLET, Jacques DANSEREAU and Pierre BOU-

LANGER. Fingerprints and photographs of the corpse were taken in our presence by Police Officer Leopold BOUGIE of the Service of Legal Identification Department of the Criminal Investigation Department of Quebec. Technician-prosecutor of the autopsy: Mr. Rene LARICHELIERE.

EXTERNAL EXAMINATION

The subject of the examination is that of a well-preserved corpse, male Caucasian, about fifty in appearance, well constituted, measuring 5′ 8 1/2″ and weighing 178 pounds.

Clothing

—Long-sleeved woolen "charcoal" sweater. Note, at the time of our examination, the sweater was raised to the upper chest.

—Trousers olive green with yellow stripes. Brown leather belt with a gold buckle, fastened at the fourth distal hole.

—Undershorts in tissue paper partially torn at the right thigh.

—Shoes brown polished leather of alligator with buckles on the side.

—Socks green.

Details of the Clothes Noted in the Autopsy

1. Sweater: Presence of a little dried blood on the upper chest on the inner right side.

Presence of dried blood on the inside wrist of the left sleeve.

Presence of some small holes in the front of the sweater not corresponding with the chest injury.

2. Trousers: Pockets turned right side out and empty at the time of our examination.

The zipper opened one third.

Presence of spots of dried blood all over the trousers.

3. Socks: Some bloodstains on the inside of the right foot and on the soles of the feet.

4. Shoes: Presence of a little earth on the soles without evidence of blood.

5. Undershorts: Slight staining of red-brown corresponding with a little patch of dried skin on the scrotum.

All the clothes were handed over to Mr. Pierre BOULANGER, pathologist, October 20, 1970, for expert evaluation.

Personal objects: Only a gold scapular neck chain.

EXTERNAL CHARACTERISTICS

Scalp: At the rear of the crown of the head, in a transverse area more or less rectangular, 3″ × 2″, where there were some one hundred forty-eight (148) purplish stitches, symmetrically placed, indicating a nonrecent capillary treatment.

Mouth: Partial dental plate in the lower bilateral area; natural teeth in the upper area. No traumatic evidence at this level.

Beard: Presence of a beard of 5 to 6 mm in length corresponding to a week's growth.

Fingernails: The nails were long, unbroken with evidence of dark black and red dirt in the ungual area. A specimen from under the nails was taken and given to Mr. Pierre BOULANGER, pathologist.

Right Armpit: Presence of small fragments of blue paint on the skin and in the hair of the axillary area.

Likewise, other particles of the same nature in appearance, in the passage of the right side and in the hair. (A sample was taken and given to Mr. Pierre BOULANGER, pathologist.)

STATE OF PRESERVATION

1. Colour: A purplish-blue covered the posterior trunk, especially on the left side.

2. Rigor Mortis: At the time of our examination at 3h00 A.M., rigor mortis was established in four (4) limbs and in the neck.

During the course of the autopsy it became more pronounced: the corpse was much stiffer at the end of the autopsy than at the beginning.

STATE OF NUTRITION

Well muscled without evidence of dehydration.

Fatty tissues evenly dispersed, not exceeding 1″ in the thickness of the abdomen.

TRAUMATIC EXTERNAL MARKINGS

Head: Cyanosis of the neck and head with well-diffused, fine stitches of haemorrhagic cutaneous.

1. Mouth: Bloodstained serosity forming a line at the corner of the lips on the right side of the mouth. This line takes the form of a V. It begins at the corner of the lips, descending towards the bottom of the cheek and then proceeds up some little distance towards the supramaxilla angle where it stops.

There is another line of the same nature at the corner of the left lips, going towards the lobule of the ear.

There is bloodstained serosity at the nostrils advancing to a slight extent towards the inner left cheek.

2. Ears: —left: line of blood from the left meatus auricular, advancing in the external ear towards the rear of the head.

—right: presence of blood, likewise coming

from the meatus, stagnant in the external ear.
3. Eyes: Infiltration of blood at the conjunction of the ocular and palpebra, noticeably marked at the external canthus.
A small, recent ecchymosis, 10 × 15 mm at the upper left outside eyelid.
Neck (*LINE OF STRANGULATION*): This dried line encircled practically all of the neck in a transverse manner, crossing at the front under the thyroid cartilage. The average width was about 4 mm and the depth varied from 2 to 3 mm.
The indentations were very evident in the line, the two (2) sides, particularly to the right, corresponded with the links of the chain.
At the back of the medial line of the neck, to the left, the line intersects, but with a distance of 3 cm. The line coming from the left forms the upper part with a slight direction towards the base of the neck.
The upper portion of the left line moves in two directions (like the sliding of the chain) where the cutaneous indentations were very evident. The pallor of the skin on the underside of the line contrasts with the cyanosis of the head and neck.
Trunk:
The upper right chest: in the area of the junction of the sternum and the right clavicle, the presence of an open wound, transverse, 3 cm in length by 1 cm in width.
The upper lip of the wound, evenly edged, creates a small central tongue.
The left corner is rather rectangular and is of some 3 to 4 mm in width.
The right corner is, on the whole, in the shape of

a V, forming an angle that is somewhat rounded. A sharp object penetrated on a tangent towards the upper right shoulder to a depth of 4 cm.
The subcutaneous tissues surrounding the wound showed a trickling of blood indicating a vital source. Only the superficial muscles of this area were affected.
The microscopic examination of the tissues of the wound showed the beginning of an inflammatory reaction: edema—white corpuscles—congestion. It was this that allowed us to conclude that the wound was made at least two (2) hours before the time of death.
In the center of the chest and at the top of the abdomen, the presence of dried blood.
At the back of the right shoulder, the presence of a superficial scrape.
UPPER MEMBERS:
Left Wrist: On the back side, the presence of an open wound, transverse, oblique, from bottom to top and from left to right, measuring 5 cm in length by 2 1/2 cm in width.
The edges of the wound were irregularly cut, most particularly in the area of the upper lip.
The upper lip was thinner and torn.
The corners of the wound were rectangular with a width of from 4 to 5 mm.
The depth was irregular with a maximum of 1/2″ at the inside median. A sharp object had severed the skin, the superficial veins, the two (2) flexor tendons of the hand (small and large palmars) and the major flexor.
A cubital vein as well as the adjacent artery were both especially lacerated.
It was noted as well, that the sharp object would

have had a direction from bottom to top, forming an angle of 45° with the axis of the limb.

Strips of cloth were wrapped around the wound: the bandaging covering the skin consisted of twenty-one (21) turns of blue material, black striped, with a width of 3 1/4″.

This bandage had been recovered with three other wrappings of torn cloth and tied at the inside face of the wrist.

The bandages facing the wound were soaked with blood.

Right Hand: At the inside face of the base of the thumb to the top of the principal joint, a tangential gash affecting the thumb muscles of this area. The wound is 4 cm in length and shows a tangential penetration of 1 1/4″. The upper lip of the wound consists of a very thin layer of flesh.

The corners have almost the same characteristics as the preceding ones, i.e., rectangular, especially in the upper outside area. An infiltration of blood in the surrounding flesh indicates the activity of the wound.

This wound was also covered with wrappings of strips of material; on the skin, a first wrapping of two (2) turns; a second of five (5) turns, and the last of two (2) turns of blue and white cloth strips fastened with two (2) knots. All of this cloth was soaked with blood in the thumb region.

Right Thumb: At the face of the outside palmar, near the fingernail, a very superficial cut, linear, axial, of 1.5 cm in length.

Right Annular: The right annular, palmar face, at the top of the fingernail, another superficial cut, linear, axial, of 2 cm in length.

LOWER LIMBS:

Right Leg: At the back of the leg, under the knee, a superficial scrape, linear, axial, of 8.5 cm in length indicating a rubbing from bottom to top. The characteristics of the scrape do not allow us to establish the cause.

Feet: —right: presence of dried blood stains on the plantar face and on the inside face near the sole of the foot.

—left: presence of dried blood stains on the toes and on the plantar face.

No other external marks of violence.

INTERNAL EXAMINATION

Head:

Scalp: Under the scalp, the presence of pits or light dots of hemosialemesis, without hematoma. No evidence of contusion.

Skull: No fracture.

Brain: It weighs 1,620 gm and there was only congestion there. No haemorrhagic process.

Neck: Presence of blood infiltrations in the area of the line of strangulation. These infiltrations were situated in the casing of the carotid and jugular on two (2) sides, both at the level of the line and below it. The inner tunic of the right carotid exhibited a slight fissure at this level.

No fracture of the hyoid bone or the thyroid and cricoid cartilage. Intense congestion of the mucus of the larynx and of the glottis.

Note the papillae at the base of the tongue were very turgescent and congested.

Thorax:

Cavities: Without particularity.

Sides: No fracture or evidence of contusion.
Lungs: The right weighs 600 gm and the left 500 gm.
Parenchyma moderately congested with zones of atelectasis.
Petechiae subpleural, especially marked in the interlobulated fissures.
The edges of the lobes exhibited a fine emphysematous edging.
Trachea and Bronchia: Free.
Heart: The weight was 400 gm and there was a slight thickening of the mitral valve.
Neck: Some arethome of the coronal and of the aorta.
The myocardia without particularity.
No evidence of thrombosis or of infarct.
Abdomen:
Cavity: Without particularity.
Liver: Weight: 1,750 gm.
Parenchyma rather congested without other particularities.
Vesicle: Presence of three (3) calculus.
Kidney, spleen, adrenal, pancreas: Without particularities other than congestion.
Bladder: Empty.
Stomach: The stomach contained only 25 cc of greenish, bilious liquid.
No alteration of the mucus.
Intestines: The small intestine contained only a little greenish liquid, bilious in appearance, along its length.
The large intestine contained a similar substance and liquid in the first portion.
The last portion of the large intestine contained greenish contents more or less thick, especially in the area of the rectal ampoule.

Genital organs: No evidence of trauma.
The subhepatic temperature was taken about 5h20 and indicated 24° C or 77° F.

SAMPLES
(1) Samples for histological examinations.
(2) Blood and gastric contents for toxicological studies.
(Compare: report of the chemist.)
(3) Blood for study of group type — a cutting of the nails — hair and particles of paint from the right armpit. (Compare: report of Mr. Pierre BOULANGER, chemist.)
(4) Clothing, bandages and neck chain, handed over to Mr. Pierre BOULANGER, chemist. (Compare: report.)

SUMMARY
—According to the findings of the autopsy, it was apparent that death was due to the process of acute asphyxia by line strangulation.
—The line was the scapular chain.
—The wounds on the right thumb, the left wrist and the chest were probably caused by one or more sharp objects such as pieces of glass or similar objects.
—These wounds were most certainly inflicted before death, at least two (2) hours previously.
—The time of death can be approximately established according to the state and the rigidity of the corpse, at a maximum of fifteen (15) hours and a minimum of four (4) to six (6) hours before our examination.
—Taking into account the rigidity of the corpse and the internal temperature of the body at the time of

the autopsy, it would be reasonable to believe that death occurred October 17, 1970, between 15h00 and 21h00.

JEAN HOULD, M.D.
Legal Medical Pathologist

JEAN-PAUL VALCOURT, M.D.
Legal Medical Pathologist

MONTREAL, November 6, 1970.

Part III

NOVEMBER

Chapter Seven

Helena

"But you must get up," the matron insists.

"Why?"

"Well, you can't just lie here."

"Why not?" I pull the sheet around my neck.

"You've been lying here for two days." Her voice is getting strained. "You've got to keep yourself active."

"There's nothing for me to do."

"That's just silly. Look at the other patients. They watch TV, they talk to each other, they go out for little walks."

"They're fools, every single one of them."

"There's no reason for you to stay in bed." She's beginning to shout now. She really is an ugly woman with her sandpaper skin. "There's nothing the matter with you."

"I'll stay in bed if I want to."

"I'll tell the maid not to bring you any more meals," she threatens.

"I shall scream." Of course, I don't mean it. I don't think I could and, besides, it would be bad for my blood pressure. But I open my mouth wide, then clutch at my heart.

"You're a spoilt old woman," she says from the doorway. She's on the verge of tears and her forehead is covered in red blotches. Only a blind man would ever want anything to do with her.

"Send me my lunch," I gasp.

"I'm phoning your daughter." She bangs the door behind her.

I lie and hug myself. I've won. Ten minutes later, the Portuguese maid, a cowed and awkward creature, comes in with my tray. It's some stinking tuna casserole, full of soggy macaroni.

"Ugh! Take it away," I shout. "Tell them I want lamb."

She scurries off. I laugh. I feel better than I have for days.

But lamb, oh, yes, a young lamb, fed on spring grass and thyme; how wonderful that would be.

It was the taste of victory that drove us mad.

We had waited for it for centuries, the chance to rub the Turks' faces in their own filth. In Smyrna, we had sat out the war, watching and waiting, but in 1918, when it was all over, we wanted blood. The Ottoman Empire lay in ruins. They had lost Macedonia and most of Thrace, their holy places in Arabia and Palestine, the whole of Syria and Mesopotamia. And now we, the Greeks of Smyrna, would rise up, too, and rip the Anatolian coast from their grasp.

Can you imagine a whole city going mad? We were a city of merchants and musicians, and suddenly we wanted to be warriors. The harbour was full of Allied ships, their flags fluttering in the breeze. Their boats raced each other to the quay with coxswains calling out the stroke above the grunts of the oars and the glistening oarsmen. Officers strutted about in dazzling white uniforms, French and Italian and British, and right up there beside them now our own Greek navy. Turks, as soon as they were outside the bazaar, slunk from doorway to doorway. Disarmed and demoralized, their soldiers couldn't help them. Greek villages in the mountains took vengeance for centuries of suffering on their defenceless neighbours. We drank and sang and danced, I as much as anyone. How can I describe it? You feel young again. You thought you were growing old in a stagnant backwater and suddenly the current catches you up. Yes, we were in the forefront of civilization. We would drive the infidels back to their caves and their deserts and the whole world would cheer us on.

Only Nicol and Safiye didn't join in.

One day when she was coming out of a jeweller's near the market, Safiye's dress was spat on by a Greek boy. She turned to slap him but his mother stepped between them and scratched Safiye's face with her fingernails. Nothing like that had ever happened to her before. She was still trembling with the shock when she reached our house.

"My dear!" I held out my hands to her. Her fists were clenched. I tried to take her in my arms. She didn't weep as I would have done, but her whole body was knotted. I wanted to comfort her—I loved her still—but I could hardly hide how delighted I was all the same. I examined the beautiful red grooves in her cheek. She didn't cry out as I dabbed antiseptic on them, just drew her lips down even further into her jaw.

Nicol puffed his pipe. "You should steer clear of the market, Safiye."

"But it's *our* city!" she shouted imperiously. "Why should I hide myself away?"

"You must admit, it's a touch of your own medicine," I said lightheartedly. "That's the kind of thing we've always had to put up with."

"Well, I shan't. This is Turkey." She stormed out of the door.

"It'll be Greece soon," I called after her mockingly.

"Be quiet, woman," Nicol muttered.

Safiye and I made up the next day—she looked so sad with those rough brown ruts carved into her skin—but the argument kept bursting out somewhere else. And Nicol began to side with her.

"You cannie just take a whole country and give it a different name," he told me reproachfully.

"But it's always been ours," I argued. "From Assos right round to Sidé. The Greeks were here long before the Turks."

"Aye, ports, traders, maybe. But they didna really settle. If you're a merchant, you never do. It's a dangerous coast. Pirates in Sidé. Earthquakes. D'you not see, damn it? It's a fault line." He rubbed his two fists against each other. "The divide between two worlds. Those who push too far fall in."

I didn't listen.

I was at my brother Costa's house the day the Greek army finally began to land in Smyrna. My nephew came banging excitedly in the door. We didn't know what he was talking about at first. "They're here," he shrilled. "They're coming off the boats. Thousands of them."

I looked at my sister-in-law, Melina, whom I detested, and we hugged each other in amazement. We could hear the shouting outside, a rhythmic chanting, *"Zito Veniselos,* long live Veniselos, *zito Veniselos."* The middle of the street was full of people running down to the port. We ran with them. I tore the hem of my dress.

The Archbishop, Chrysostomos, was already there at the quay standing on a platform, blessing the troops as they came down the gangways. He was an old man, headstrong and tyrannical, with a great black beard, which he dyed, and a deep voice. "It is God's work that you do," he shouted, and the crowd howled.

Most of the soldiers looked rather dazed at first. They were young peasants, and after all they hadn't done anything yet to be treated like heroes. Some of them had just come back from being driven out of the Crimea by the Bolsheviks. But quickly they became as crazy as the crowd. The women kissed them and gave them flowers and fruit. I saw one boy with a face like a sheep, whose mouth and chin were dripping with crushed strawberries.

"In God's name, free us from the heathen," Chrysostomos boomed.

We tore down the Turkish flags and danced on them, back and forth, arm in arm, merchants and shepherds, soldiers and dainty ladies. I broke one of my shoes and threw them both away. Bottles of ouzo and retsina passed from hand to hand; we overflowed with happiness. But as the day wore on, the mood turned ugly. A company of Turkish soldiers had barricaded themselves inside the Governor's palace, but when they heard there were three Greek divisions they fell over themselves to surrender and came out waving white cloths tied to sticks. They were marched down to the waterfront through the packed streets. Some were beaten with clubs and all of them had their fezes torn off and trampled. One colonel who refused to let go of his was shot in the head by a drunken Greek officer.

Then came the Governor, Nour-ed-Din Pasha, his hands tied and a bayonet jabbed into his back. How we cheered, even though he had never done us any real harm. Chrysostomos stood in front of him in his rich canonical robes, a jewelled cross above his head.

"Shoot him," he screamed, "shoot him." But before there was time, a group of British sailors formed around Nour-ed-Din and whisked him off to one of their ships. We hissed and threw rocks after them.

They couldn't protect all the Turks, though. The crowds ran through the streets, breaking into Turkish stores, looting and defiling. Turkish women had their veils ripped off and were raped in the gutter. And on the quay, we lit bonfires and went on dancing. Every now and again the men would slip away and go over to the terrified prisoners who were huddled against a warehouse. All of them were beaten; some were bound and hurled onto the fires; many were shot and dumped in the harbour.

I danced. In my bare feet, with my bodice torn open and streaks of dirt and oil on my dress, I danced through it all. Till I saw a bunch of young boys who had cornered an old man in an alleyway. He was a Greek from Aydin, a little hunchbacked farmer. I bought figs from him once or twice in the market, but stopped when he tried to cheat me. Like a lot of the old Greeks in the region he still wore a fez. He didn't know what was going on. "It's my hat," he shouted as they pushed him from one to another. One of them pulled it off his head by the tassel. They were joking, but he knocked the boy to the ground and the others kicked him to death.

"He's not a Turk," I screamed.

Early in the morning, with the stink of smoke in my hair, I crawled back home like a sick cat.

A Turkish officer lies on the ground. He is badly wounded. I think his neck is broken. Blood seeps out of his forehead. His eyes stare. "Water," he croaks, "water."

A Greek woman who is dancing goes over to him. She is not a poor woman, not a peasant. Her clothes are respectable. Until today she was a typical Smyrna housewife, in her forties, her face already fixed in middle age. You see hundreds like her every time you walk through the city in the morning. Her cheeks and her breasts are flushed with wine. "Are you thirsty?" she asks him coyly.

"Water," he begs.

She spits saliva on her finger and flicks it onto his lips. She goes back, giggling, to her friends. Five minutes later she does the same thing. And again. The laughter grows more raucous. Six or seven women stand around the Turk, shouting, poking him with their toes. One of them upends an empty wine bottle above his head; the last drops fall out of reach of his tongue. A circle of men gathers, watching in amusement.

Then the first woman bends down beside him. "Do you want more water?" She brushes away a fly.

His eyes are fixed on her, but he can't speak anymore.

"Do you want some wine?"

He tries to nod.

"I'll give you some Turkish wine." She pulls up her skirts and crouches over him. In the light from the fires I can see the thick black pelt between the white linen legs of her drawers. She grunts and a stream of urine gushes into his face. Her friends cheer and dance around them. Somebody bangs on her shoulder and she falls over backwards, squirting into the air and laughing.

The Turk lies still.

"Look, I've drowned him," she cries proudly.

A few days later, to get away from the filth in the city, we went out sailing on Costa's yacht. I had a row with Nicol to get him to come; he sat in the stern in a deep silence. We were riding gently in a light breeze when there was a bump at the front of the boat.

"Maman," one of the children screamed, "it's a body."

Melina and I ran to the rail. "It's a Turk," she said, holding her nose. I caught a glimpse of a bloated paleness bobbing away behind us.

Nicol jumped to his feet. "Heave to," he told Costa.

Costa pretended not to hear. He stood at the wheel in his fine English blazer.

"Put about, damn it, man," Nicol shouted.

"It's a Turk," Melina said in disgust.

"We won't find him back there, anyway," Costa argued anxiously.

"We damn well will. If it takes us all day." Nicol grabbed

Costa by the shoulders and I thought for a moment he was going to fling him into the sea, but instead he banged him down on the deck and seized the wheel. He spun it and the sails luffed and flapped. He threw the small dinghy in the water and jumped in. He almost swamped it. He rowed strongly in a zigzag pattern, pausing every now and then to look around. We waited impatiently. Finally, he stopped. I watched through Costa's binoculars as Nicol bent to a grey shadow in the turquoise water. His lips were moving. Then he tied a loop in the anchor rope and slipped it over the side. The shadow disappeared, bubbles spluttering to the surface.

I apologized to Costa for Nicol's rudeness.

Helen leans over and takes my hand. "Mother says you've stopped eating."

I frown. They all talk to each other about me behind my back. I don't like it.

"You've got to eat, you know."

"I don't like you talking about me behind my back."

"But we're worried about you." She smiles. "Not worried, but a bit concerned?"

"Well, then, tell your mother to find somewhere else for me."

"It's not easy. She's tried, she really has. But, well," she giggles, "I guess they all know you already. What don't you like about the food?"

"It's not food. It's garbage."

She shakes her head. She doesn't believe me.

"You don't believe me, do you?" I say angrily. "But it's true. The meat they use comes from condemned cows. Madame Arsenault's son-in-law told her. It's dog food, that's all it is." I catch a look on her face, a pursing of the lips, just like her mother's. I don't want to talk about all this. What does it matter whether I eat or not? I want to ask her how *she* is. It must be hard for her living on her own. "All right, don't believe me if you don't want to. What does it matter to you if they're trying to poison me."

"Poison you? Nobody's trying to poison you. It's just that they don't cook things very imaginatively, that's all. It's boring. All institutional food is."

"No, it's poison." My voice is too loud. I don't want to talk about this at all. "It's that black maid from Haiti. She's got the rat poison in the kitchen. She's killing me inch by inch." I begin to sob. "She sprinkles it on the food."

Helen tries to hug me but I struggle free. I don't want sympathy. "She's put a curse on me."

"Come on, now, why would she do that?"

"It's Artemis. It's her doing."

"Artemis?" she says incredulously. "The goddess?" She tries to change the subject quickly. "Look, I've got an idea. There's a little Greek restaurant just round the corner. On Park? What do you say? If you got your clothes on, we could slip out and go round there." She tries to make it sound exciting. "It's only five minutes walk, you could manage that. We could have some shish kebab. You'd like that, wouldn't you?"

"They probably make it with beef," I say sulkily.

"We could try."

"Not today." She looks disappointed. It's my turn to console her. She wants to help, but what's the point? "Another day, though. When you come again?"

She gets up sadly and goes over to the window. There's nothing out there in the garden now. Dead leaves and mud and bones. "Okay," she says. "But I'm going away for a while. Not for long. Just to . . . well, you know, get away, get things together. Up at the cottage."

Why would she go up to the cottage at this time of the year?

"She doesn't let go, Helen," I tell her. "Artemis. She never lets go of her prey. Remember that. It was her hounds that killed my brother, Costa. And Marc, too. To punish me."

She looks back at me. There are tears in her eyes. She thinks I'm losing my mind. "Why would she want to punish you, Mamie? You of all people?"

"Because I wasn't afraid of her. I believed in love."

She stands behind me and strokes my hair. When she says good-bye, we both cry. She's a good girl. I shan't see her again.

It's a breathless climb, up over the burning rocks in the harsh sunlight. I mustn't stop. I hear them baying down below me. I tricked them back there where the river flows into the salt marsh, but now they've caught my scent again. I jump from rock to rock and the sweat runs down and stings my eyes. The stone burns my bare feet and the sharp grasses slash my skin. I don't feel anything, though the red footprints stretch out behind me. I don't feel anything except the pelting urgency of my flight. Yes, my flight upwards, up away from the villages, up here where even a goat or a monk wouldn't climb. I cut across to the other side of a gully, sure-footed, full of excitement. I hear them scrabbling behind me. I don't look back. I don't look down. I'm not afraid. What is there to fear? I shall stay ahead of them till I reach the top, I'm sure of it now. And I do, I do. I stand on the summit and look up into the sun. The light fills me, reflecting back into the sky. I look at the sea far below, green over sand and trimmed with white around the rocks. I feel its tang, seawood and salt, the taste of blood, pulse through me. How can it matter what happens to me now?

November 12. I let them think I was going to church. I put on my most devout expression, dredged up from childhood, and clasped my hands together in my best suede gloves. "I'm just going for a little walk, Manuela." Her eyes popped to see me opening the door. They never expected me to get up again, did they? I walked down the steps with great dignity, holding in my glee. But oh, the wind was so cold I thought I'd have to turn back. Never. I thrust my stick into the sidewalk and strode on. Along the street to the traffic lights, then across and down Park Avenue, a nondescript street that's been taken over by waves of immigrants with their cheap clothes and elaborate furniture.

Well, I'm an immigrant, too.

I found it easily, a pink neon sign flashing out the name in broad daylight: Parnassus. Everything inside was false—an American vinyl snack-bar with a few Greek plaster ornaments and posters of Athens and Mykonos. But it was warm and the aromas from the food were right: lamb and olive oil, garlic, goat's cheese and lemon. I sat down and read the menu. Dear God, hamburgers, club sandwiches, milk shakes; but then on the next page I found what I was looking for.

"Are you ready to order?" the waiter asked in English. He was a fat boy with a round, smiling face and greasy hair.

I answered him in Greek. It was like speaking a foreign tongue. "I shall have shish kebab, and a salad. But I'd like something to start with—stuffed aubergines or dolmades."

"Well, we've got the vine leaves, but they're canned, eh," he said, still speaking English. "My mom made a spinach pie. Would you like a slice of that?"

"Are you Greek?" I asked. He nodded. "Well, then, young man, speak Greek to me."

"Would you like some spinach pie?"

Oh, what an awful Cypriot accent, but never mind, never mind. "Yes, I'll have some of that."

"What would you like to drink?"

"Just some water. No, wait." Why should I drink water simply because I'm old? "I'll have a glass of wine."

"And do you want French fries or rice with the shish kebab?"

"French fries?" I laughed at the joke. Who ever heard of French fries in a Greek restaurant? "I'll have rice. And make sure there are pine nuts in it," I called after him.

His mother, a middle-aged woman, came over to talk to me. She was as fat as he was, with a white dress stretched to bursting around the buttonholes, frizzy hair and false teeth that clacked like castanets when she spoke. But friendly, that's the main thing. She told me how they had left their village in the Troodos mountains six years ago to come here; how she had worked in a shoe factory and her husband as a janitor to get the down payment for the restaurant; how they're going to take over the building next door to expand.

"You'll do well," I told her. "You make good pastry. Almost as good as my aunt's."

She thanked me. And then her husband came over, too, when he'd finished grilling the shish kebab, not really to talk, because he was a taciturn mountain man, but to listen and to ask if I wanted some bouzouki music instead of the noise from the FM station.

"I might get up and dance with you," I warned him.

The lamb was rather tough and stringy, not really lamb at all, but it was crisp on the outside and pink inside, the way it should be. With lemon juice and pepper it tasted fine.

"Yes, I shall have another shish kebab," I told them. "And another glass of wine."

They looked at me in astonishment. At three in the afternoon!

"And some baklava, and coffee. Sweet."

"Your coffee beans are too dry," I told them as I paid the bill. "But it was all very good. Especially the spinach pie."

"You must come again," said Mrs. Pappas. "On Saturdays I make the dolmades myself."

Yes, I shall certainly go there again. Already I have indigestion, but what does it matter? I can walk up and down back here in my prison cell and belch and break wind, and what difference will it make? Well, at least they'll know I'm alive. I hope she puts fresh dill and spices in her vine leaves.

In the three years after the Greeks took Smyrna, Safiye couldn't bear to live there any longer. She spent most of her time in Paris, and whenever she did come back, she was sad and angry. Nothing pleased her, though the city was prosperous. In spite of the war in the mountains, the dances at the clubs were better than ever. She talked to Nicol more than she did to me, seriously, secretly, stopping whenever I came into the room. He believed what she told him, but I wasn't even allowed to know what it was. She played with the children, drooling over Marc. "He's just like Nicol, except he doesn't smell of tobacco," she laughed. But with me, she was distant, as I was with her.

Everything came between us.

One morning she peered at me shortsightedly. "You look tired, Helena," she said, trying to be friendly.

"Just wait till you have children," I snapped. "Marc kept me awake all night with his nightmares."

"Poor thing." She cuddled him. "What were they about?"

"Tigers."

"Ow, tigers." She waved her hands in front of her face in mock terror and he giggled up at her. He adored her.

It was I who had knelt for hours beside his bed, dozing off on the hard floor. "He's crumpling your dress," I said.

"That doesn't matter." She nibbled his ear. "When I was your age, I used to have a dream where I was turning into a dog."

"Don't give him more things to be afraid of, for God's sake," I said angrily. "It's bad enough as it is."

"I don't have it anymore," she whispered.

"Now, Marc, it's time for your lunch. Run along." He clung to her till I called a servant.

"He's lovely," she said wistfully as he was carried away kicking.

"Don't you want to have one of your own?"

"I suppose."

A cicada was drilling its way into my brain. "You're not getting any younger." I sounded like my aunt.

"I know, I know." She stretched. "The only trouble is you need a man for it," she sighed, and for a moment we laughed together as we would have done in the past. "But I don't know any Turkish men I could do that with. None I respect."

I peeled another fig. "There are Frenchmen or Italians, if Greeks aren't good enough for you."

"No, I couldn't marry a foreigner, Helena, not now. Not with the trouble my country's in."

"That's an abstraction. It shouldn't get in the way of your own happiness."

I meant it kindly but it only made her angry. "It's not an abstraction," she fumed. "Right this minute your army's outside Angora. When are they going to stop? When you've conquered the whole country?"

"When did you ever stop in the past?" I sucked the seeds out of my teeth. I wished she wouldn't be so tiresome.

"Kemal will drive your army right back to Athens."

"Then marry him, my dear," I said mockingly. "For all I care. Mind you, I heard Costa say he only likes foreign women."

She was so dark and intense when she was angry. She sat in the shade next to a bed of violet delphiniums. I ached to be her friend again.

That would have been July of 1921, the month before the Greek army was defeated on the river Sakarya, fifty miles from its objective, Angora.

In Smyrna we were told it was a great victory. The church bells rang and Te Deums of thanksgiving were sung in the cathedral. A gang of young men broke into one of the mosques and slaughtered a pig to celebrate the triumph of Christianity. We didn't approve of that, of course; yet we laughed over it. Constantine, the king so many of us had distrusted a few years before, was our new hero. He proclaimed himself Supreme Commander of the Army and established his headquarters in Smyrna, the first Christian king to set foot on the soil of Asia since the Crusades. He would be our Alexander the Great, our Richard Coeur de Lion, all in one. Blue and white flags were draped from every building in the city, and as Constantine strode into the Governor's palace, Manos the banker, my brother-in-law, who had always been a supporter, unfurled a Turkish flag for him to walk over.

Some of his pride rubbed off on Costa, his namesake. Of all the family—after my father, of course—Costa was the one I was always closest to. As a young girl I was able to rely on him; I expected him to be strong. He was never especially bright or charming, but in his quiet way he knew what he believed in and tried to act by it. Middle age, though, had grown over him like a vine. His snobbish wife had filled him with her own dull pretensions. And so the war was his last chance to go back to what he might have been. In 1920, at the age of forty, the head of the largest shipping line in Greece, he volunteered, just as if he were some shepherd boy from the mountains. Melina had hysterics; what did he think he was doing, a man of his standing, leaving his children without a father? But his mind was made up. I felt proud of him again.

Nicol, as contrary as always, tried to persuade him not to go.

"Leave Costa alone," I warned him. "Mind your own business."

But no, he wouldn't. "You're not a soldier, Costa. What d'you think they're doing up there, for heaven's sake, shooting pheasants?"

Costa, in his new uniform, faced up to him for the first time in years. "I'm not going to sit around and wait for the rest of my life. Everybody in Smyrna's making money out of the war. Well, I've got to give more of myself than that, Nicol. Maybe I'm not a soldier, but there must be something I can do to help. Surely, they need men who have a sense of order."

"Order!" Nicol shook his head. But he was touched, too, I could see, because it was something he could never do himself.

At the beginning, the letters and cards I got from Costa were all you'd expect from a businessman turned soldier: stilted, full of pieties, requests that I look after his wife. He didn't need to worry about Melina. For the first few weeks she boasted about him unbearably, then found a young French lieutenant to console her as the winter nights grew longer.

One day, nearly a year later, a peasant woman came to our door and argued her way past the servants. Her brother, who had been wounded, had given her a letter for me. It was written in Costa's neat, cramped hand on paper that was torn and stained.

My dearest sister, it said, I am writing because you are the only one I can tell this to. Melina would only be upset, so you must say nothing of it to her. But I shall need your help, and Nicol's, too, if he is willing, so please bear with me.

The truth is, Helena, the war goes badly for us.

We should never have come here. This is not our land. We cannot fight for it as the Turks can. Our men are lost when they're out of sight of the sea, and now we're three hundred miles away from it. Everything falls apart in the space between. The men have fought bravely enough, but we have failed them. I blame myself. I have managed to do nothing. I don't want to live after this is over.

No, I should not say that, even though it is true. It's not what I want to tell you. There is no order here, no organization. The royalist officers fight the Veniselists rather than the Turks. Each group gives contradictory commands. Half the officers are illiterate and can't read their instructions, anyway. There is no food, no winter clothing, no medical supplies. I requisitioned five hundred pairs of boots and received fifty belts three months later. We have no spare parts for our lorries that break down all the time. We keep on running out of ammunition.

And yet we were winning, Helena; we won great victories. We drove the Turks out of their holy city, Bursa. We drove them out of Afyon and Eskishehir. We fought our way up through the valleys, though there was no communication between one of our divisions in one valley and another in the next. We should have been wiped out like that, but we struggled on because the Turks were even more disorganized than we were.

We won until we came to the plateau. In the valleys we were still in our own kind of country. But after Eskishehir, there was just the plateau stretching forever and ever with nothing on it but dust and sand and rock. Nothing grows there. There is no water. Our horses died because there was nothing for them to drink. We ate them, and went on with mules and bullocks. The mules and bullocks died and we ate them, and God knows, we ate sand and dirt constantly.

But still we won. We won on the Sakarya. We drove the Turks back from the river and bathed in it. We drove them from one ridge to the next. We fought without stopping for twenty-two days, and all that we had to eat was whatever we found when we overran a Turkish position. The fighting was so close that once, when I came to a stream and stopped to drink at it, I looked up and saw a Turk drinking on the other side. We drank our fill, then backed away in opposite directions.

We gained ten or twelve miles of rocks. We could have taken the village of Haymana, and behind that the road was clear all the way to Angora. But the Turks would not give up. They used their own dead for cover and their women fought with them. Through my field glasses I saw a line of Turkish women climbing a hillside with their babies strapped to their backs and a mortar shell on each shoulder.

We reached the outskirts of Haymana and then we collapsed. We weren't beaten, Helena. We broke. Like a piece of elastic that's perished, we couldn't stretch any further.

And then the only thing to do was to run. I ran. I ran for hours till my lungs were bursting and my mouth tasted like the barrel of a gun, and when I turned the Turks were still coming on steadily behind me.

We have dug in now along the railway line between Afyon and Eskishehir, but I know that when they decide to attack we shall break again.

I want you to show this letter to Nicol. We have not been much in agreement, but I know he will understand what needs to be done. He should start to dispose of his property in Smyrna, quietly and slowly, but surely, because when the end comes it will be sudden. And if he would, I should like him to tell Sava to transfer our own assets to the offices in Athens and Marseilles. He doesn't need to go into a lot of details. Sava is afraid of Nicol and will do as he is told.

We have made a terrible mistake.

There, that is all I have to say. I am very tired. I don't hope to survive, but if I do, things will be different.

Burn this letter. If it is found, I shall be shot.

Take care, I pray you, of Melina and the children. Pray for us all.

Your respectful brother, Constantine.

I didn't burn the letter. How could I? I hid it in the satin lining of my jewel box. I have it here still in front of me, though the paper has fallen apart at the folds. The pencil marks have faded and I am the only one left who can make them out.

Mrs. Pappas sits opposite me.

Some lamb has caught in my teeth. "I have my own teeth still," I tell her.

"Where was your husband from?" she asks me.

"I had two," I mumble. "One red, one black."

"Which was the first?" she asks idly.

"I had them both at the same time." There, the lamb has gone.

She looks at me nervously, fingering the lapel of her dress.

"The red one was good, but I drove him away. And the black one—he was the one I loved, but I lost him."

All through the winter of 1922 we waited. The people of Smyrna grew impatient for the final victory which they knew was bound to come. Nicol and I waited for the Turkish attack that would drive us all into the sea. Our secret drew us close together for a short, unreal spell.

Quietly, Nicol went around to the foreign consuls—the British, the French, the Italian, the American even—asking them to intercede and arrange a peace. But though they had urged the Greeks into the war, they would do nothing now. And even if the worse came to the worst, well, Smyrna would always survive. It always had, had it not?

We waited, and when the end came, though we expected it to come quickly, its suddenness stunned us. In August 1921, when the Greeks crossed the Sakarya, they fought for twenty-two days without relief. In August 1922, the Turks broke through the Greek lines at Afyon in three hours. The Greek army retreated down the long valley to the sea, burning everything in its path.

In Smyrna all was hope and prosperity. The harvest was over and the warehouses were full of raisins and nuts, olives, grain and figs. In the glare from oil-lights workmen sewed them in bales or hammered crates together. Freighters from all over the world stood by in the port, waiting for their cargoes.

The Greek army was a rabble. When they reached a Turkish village they pushed all the inhabitants and all the animals into the mosque and burned the whole place down. When they came to a Greek village they herded all the people out in front of them and burned everything also. Two-thousand-year-old towns were turned into ash heaps, black scars on the mountainside. Of the eighteen thousand buildings in Manisa, only five hundred were left standing, and that was by carelessness. Men and women came down the railway line clinging to the roofs of the trains. They came on ox carts and mules piled high with furniture and bundles of clothing. Soldiers who had thrown away their guns mingled with refugees who had picked them up and now fired at everything in sight.

Suddenly, Smyrna was full of them. They raped and looted, not only Turks now, but each other as well.

When I saw Costa again, I hardly recognized him. His face was sunken, his eyes bloodshot and glittering. He babbled about a plan to dig in and hold the enemy advance at Manisa and Aydin.

"There's no chance, man," Nicol told him kindly.

"Why not?" Costa demanded. "We can still fight. We've got all the supplies we need down here on the plain. It's Kemal's lines that are stretched now."

"But you cannie turn this rabble back into an army."

Costa went on as if he hadn't heard. "If we can hold them, we can negotiate. Not a Greek province; we won't get that now. But an international settlement, like they have in China. The League of Nations could meet here. It'd be ideal. I've thought it all out." He was going to talk to the Greek Commander-in-Chief, Hajianestis, who was directing the retreat from his yacht in the harbour. "He'll understand."

Nicol shook his head again.

That night Costa banged wildly on our door. He collapsed in a chair. "He's mad," he sobbed.

Nicol brought him a cognac. "Aye, I knew," he murmured.

"But he's insane. He's in command of the whole army and he doesn't even know what's going on. He gives orders and nobody knows what they mean. He doesn't get out of bed because he thinks his legs are made of glass and if he stands on them, they'll break. One of his aides told me that he lay absolutely still for two days last week after the battle of Afyon. Nobody could speak to him. For two days not a single decision was made. Finally, when he was conscious again, he told them he'd been dead."

Nicol put his arm round Costa's shoulders, but there was no comforting him.

And still we wouldn't admit what was happening.

In the clubs the social life whirled round as if nothing had changed. Guitarists played in the cafés; an Italian opera troupe performed *La Traviata* to packed audiences at Le Cercle Sportif. But the tensions erupted to the surface at the slightest excuse. Friends shouted at each other; staid merchants burst into tears. Nobody knew what to do, so we did nothing. Should we leave before the Turks arrived? But no, we had lived under them before; why couldn't we again? Would there be reprisals? Surely the Allied warships would protect us. What kind of man was Mustafa Kemal? He wasn't the traditional Turkish leader. He drank in public, made love to Western women; he wanted to set up a modern republic, freed from Islam. Maybe things wouldn't be so bad. If the situation settled down again quickly, prices would rise. There was always money to be made on the Anatolian coast. Better to stay.

Nicol watched in amazement. "They're out of their minds. The war's not over yet and already they've forgotten it."

"But there'll be peace, won't there?"

"Some wars lead to peace. Not this one."

"But why?"

"Did you want peace two years ago? Will the Turks want it now? This war's been going on for three thousand years."

"But we can just go back to the way we were before."

"Business as usual?" He laughed. "No, there are some things even business willna heal."

I looked at him curiously. I had lived with this man for twelve years, been loved and almost certainly betrayed by him, and still I didn't know who he was. His face was creased and there were streaks of grey in his moustache, but he still smiled easily. Whatever happened to him, he enjoyed. Perhaps that, it suddenly occurred to me, was why things hadn't worked out between us.

He tapped his pipe in the ashtray, got to his feet and lumbered over to me. He put his arms around me, but his presence was stifling. I pushed against his chest to keep a space between us.

"We'll be all right," he said softly. "Dinna fret."

"Where will we go?"

"Where the wind blows," he said teasingly.

I punched him irritably.

He became serious. "Tomorrow we'll start moving our stuff on board the *Pirgi.* It'll no last much longer here."

Outside, on the waterfront, the refugees waited. The soldiers had been taken off in transports, but the villagers who were still pouring in from the mountains squatted listlessly on the marble promenade and gazed out to sea. Their belongings were piled around them, their children squabbled in the gutters, mothers held babies to their breasts. They were black with dirt and ragged, sometimes bleeding. At night fires flared and voices rose in drunken songs or anger.

Offshore, covered in flags, the Allied fleets waited, too, and looked at the shore through binoculars. Bugles echoed across the water as ensigns were raised and lowered. I remember their names still: *Iron Duke* and *George V* and *Ajax;* the cruisers *Cardiff* and *Jean Bart;* the *Waldeck-Rousseau, Edgar Quinet* and *Ernest Renan;* the most elegant of all, the Italian flagship *Venezia;* the little American destroyers, *Simpson, Litchfield, Edsel* and *Lawrence.* On their decks bored officers drank pink gin and waited for something to happen.

They snap at my heels.

The old cat rolls on her back, claws in the air.

If I've learned one thing in my life, it's how to defend myself. How dare the black bitch play her tricks on me. She'll remember me by her scars.

I sneak into her room, squalid, with yellow sheets, water-stained walls. On the shelf above her bed, among the photos of rickety children and slumped grandparents, I find what I'm looking for. A tiny doll, not bloated and pockmarked as she is, but with creamy skin, long shining hair. As I was once. What right has she to a doll like that? She uses it for her spells.

Well, not anymore! I hide it in the wide sleeves of my robe. She accuses me of stealing it. I laugh at her; then, when the matron comes, I protest in outrage. The witch cries, not real tears, just pretending to be sad. I know true grief when I see it.

"It's got to be here somewhere. Madame Arsenault saw her running down the stairs."

They search my room, everywhere, but they won't find it. I can hide anything. Didn't Madame Beckermann live behind the false wall in my attic for five months? The German officers in the room below never suspected she was there. And they'll never find my doll inside this old hot water bottle. She's mine now, and oh, how lovely she is. See how her hair shines; the smoothness of her skin. Touch it, touch it here, feel how it glows.

Who would have thought Mustafa Kemal, our conqueror, would be so young and handsome? With his blue eyes and his fair hair, he was hardly a Turk at all.

I only saw him twice. The most dangerous man I ever set eyes on.

I didn't see him the morning he drove into Smyrna in an open car decorated with olive branches. Nor when he entered the Governor's palace and a Turkish merchant spread a Greek flag on the steps for him to walk over, just as Manos had for Constantine two years before. Kemal walked around it. "That's the symbol of a country's pride," he was supposed to have said.

Nobody I knew saw anything of that. The Greeks were keeping out of sight as the streets filled with Turks who had been in hiding. But we talked about it endlessly on the telephone, till the details were vivid and precise. The olive branches, the flag —they were good signs, surely.

"Perhaps we should wait and see what happens," I suggested to Nicol.

The house was full of workmen wrapping crystal and china. Nicol looked up from a wooden packing case. "We can always come back, if things settle down."

"Aliki says it's silly to run away. She thinks you're afraid."

"Aye, well, she may be right." He smoothed some cardboard round the corner of an inlaid side table. "But I'm no afraid of what Aliki thinks, anyway."

That night we went to the Nain Hotel to say good-bye to our friends. On the terrace, everybody was full of hope. We drank champagne and talked of the future. Smyrna would rise again. We'd be back soon. It was just a holiday that we were going on. Business knew no boundaries. We took no notice of the group of Turkish officers who came and sat at a table near us, until Haniotis, the jeweller, whispered that he thought one of them looked rather like Kemal.

"That's absurd. He wouldn't come here."

"They say before he left Angora he made a vow that the next drink he had would be in Smyrna."

"Which one do you mean?"

"In the centre. The youngest."

"But he doesn't even have any badges on his uniform."

When he realized we were staring at him, he raised his glass of milk-coloured raki towards us. A slight smile played on his lips, but his eyes, like his body, were hard. They didn't seem to move, yet you felt they saw everything that went on. Everyone knew who he was.

We raised our glasses hesitantly in return.

"Did King Constantine ever come here to drink a glass of raki when he was in Smyrna?" he called.

"No," Haniotis stammered. He hadn't spoken Turkish for a long time. "No, he never came here."

"Why would he bother to try and take Smyrna from us, then?" Kemal asked. All the officers who were with him roared with laughter and most of the Greeks giggled politely, too. But we left quickly. Just the tone of his voice was a warning.

Nobody saw him the next day when Nour-ed-Din summoned Archbishop Chrysostomos before him and condemned him to be hanged. The mob gouged out the old man's eyes before the soldiers could get the rope around his neck. Nobody saw Kemal there. He couldn't be blamed. But he must have known it would happen. He was the only one who could have stopped it. He must have wanted it to happen.

It wasn't till two days later that I saw him again. The last time. We were ready to leave the house. I was wretched, not because I loved the place—my father's house was the only real home I've ever had—but because I didn't know what would happen to me next. Order had broken down completely in the city. Gangs roamed the streets, looting and killing, and the Greeks were letting go of any pretence that life would soon return to normal. Only Nicol went about freely, making sure the men who had worked for him would be all right, finding places on the *Pirgi* for the Greeks who wanted to leave, giving little mementoes to the Turks. He spent more time with them than with me.

He was flushed and a little drunk when he came chuckling in the door. I smelt the aniseed on his breath and snapped at him angrily: "I've been waiting for you for hours."

"Have you seen our new neighbour?" he asked.

I didn't bother to answer. What could it matter?

"Come out into the garden." He dragged me by the hand. There was nobody about. "Och, they must have gone inside."

"Who is it?" I asked, curiosity getting the better of my irritation.

"Kemal. The man himself. Mustafa Kemal."

"You're joking."

"No. I was talking to him just a minute ago. I went over there to say good-bye to Saffy. He's moved in."

"But how? How could he?"

Nicol couldn't hold in his laughter. "She went right up to his headquarters and demanded to see him. That wee bit of a girl, eh? And then she asked him to come and stay with her. Just like that. She said he'd be better out here; he'd be able to rest; she'd look after him. Well, I suppose she talked about Turkey, too—the new reforms, the emancipation of the women, that kind of thing—but that wasna what interested him, I'll bet. Or her, either!"

"But why would he? She's not even pretty any longer. She's as fat as a pudding."

Nicol wagged his head with a mixture of pride and amusement. "I don't expect she gave him a chance to resist." As he went in through the French windows, he added: "She's had a picture of him in that locket round her neck for the past couple of years."

"How do you know?"

"She showed it to me." His eyes twinkled. He was so happy for her, I hated him.

I stood alone in the garden, waiting. Jackdaws squawked in the trees above my head. I peered through the shrubbery till they strolled back into the open. Sunlight glittered on his boots. She clung to his arm and laughed up into his face. She was full of triumph. I hated her—how can I explain it? I hated her more than I ever would have if I had found her in bed with my husband. In truth, she could have had him; and surely did. But now I had lost her. That was the most anguished knowledge of all. She was lost to me forever. As a wall hid them from me for the last time, I prayed with all my might that she would never be happy again.

Was that my only prayer that was ever answered?

In the confusion, Costa disappeared. He'd been trying to organize a militia group to maintain some sort of order among the Greeks, but his men kept drifting away. Then he vanished, too.

Nicol left the boat to look for him. He came back covered in dirt.

"He's dead," I began to whimper as soon as I saw the expression on his face.

"Aye," he nodded. "Dinna tell Melina yet."

"She doesn't care what happens to him now, anyway."

"Maybe not, maybe not." His head slumped as he lay on the bunk in the small, airless cabin.

"How did he die?" I sobbed.

"Dinna ask. You'd not want to know."

"Tell me, Nicol."

"He was in the river."

"Drowned?"

"Maybe." He held his eyes tightly closed. "Partly."

"But tell me."

"God, woman, why d'you want to know?" he snapped.

A silence, with just the throbbing of the ship.

"He was nailed, naked, to a door. Crucified. And cut. Bits cut off him. And burned." He belched violently. "Give me my pipe, will you?" I filled it for him carefully. "Who'd do a thing like that?"

"Where did you put him?"

"I buried him."

"You buried him? On your own?"

"Aye. All the priests have run away. I buried him in the Jewish cemetery."

"The Jewish cemetery?"

"Jesus God, d'you have to repeat everything I say? Yes, damn it, yes, it was the closest by. Who's going to care anymore?" He rolled away from me till he was pressed against the bulkhead.

I didn't even cry. I was so afraid for myself, I didn't have time to cry.

This is the night my city burns.

Nobody knows who starts the fire. Some blame the Armenians, who want vengeance on everyone. And some the Greeks, because our army destroyed so many towns and villages in its retreat. But, surely, no Greek—not even the most vicious—would ever burn Smyrna, the last Greek city in Asia. Without Smyrna we shall never return.

No, it has to be the Turks. To kill off all our hopes. Kemal must know. And Safiye, too.

We watch from the bridge of the *Pirgi,* the proud new freighter built on the Clyde and named after my father's birthplace on Chios. The captain hands me his binoculars. At first, it's just another fire, far away in the Armenian slums on the northern outskirts. I watch it with pleasure, a fireworks display, not wanting it to finish. This'll give the Turks something to think about. Let's see how they handle it without the Greeks to tell them what to do.

But then I realize nobody's trying to put it out. Looters are spreading it, and the Turkish mob are paying off old scores. As each new building catches fire, the oohs and aahs from the other ships in the harbour die down. We watch in helpless silence.

The wind changes direction, blowing strongly from the mountains down towards the sea. The flames lick higher and a great pall of billowing smoke is spread like a blanket between the city and the sky. The moon and the stars are hidden. Soot falls on my dress; black smudges on my arms. I brush them into streaks and try to rub them away with a lace handkerchief, but soon I'm black as a slave.

On the waterfront the confusion spreads as more and more people run to the quay—as they always do when they're afraid. The hospitals are evacuating their patients on stretchers and ox carts. Old people huddle together in their nightgowns, with nothing to warm them but the approaching fire. Above the shouts of anger and fear, I hear the flames crackling. Nicol orders the captain to send the life boats ashore for the patients from the hospital.

"But Mr. Sava told me only to take on passengers who can pay the fare."

Nicol moves towards him threateningly.

"They'll swamp the boats, sir. There's too many of them."

"Then I'll go myself. Get me some guns and truncheons."

Explosions whoosh into the air as oil stores catch alight, and heavier thuds boom out when the fire uncovers hidden supplies of ammunition. The sky is a swirling purple and the boats which cut towards the shore leave a deep red gash behind them.

I watch Nicol standing on a jetty helping the seamen to carry stretchers down to the boats. Two men try to fight their way past him. He picks them up, one in each hand, and flings them backwards. A moment later their sharp cries bounce off the water to me. At the same time, the sound of music comes from behind me. I turn. The band on *H.M.S. Iron Duke* is starting to play medleys from the latest Palladium shows.

As the fire comes closer, its noise rises to a roar, but I can still hear the screams of panic from the crowd. People are running up and down, banging into each other, cursing and falling. They surge towards one end of the quay but are driven back by a Turkish machine-gun unit. They turn and rush the other way, trampling those who were following them. Mothers with their children, old men and women are crushed wailing beneath their feet.

Nicol pushes off with the last boat loaded down to the rim.

Behind the outlined rooftops, the fire glows like a luminous curtain. Writhing flames squirm up along a church tower. The dome of a mosque turns from turquoise to orange. Suddenly, with a great blast of power, the fire reaches the waterfront itself, spurting out of the ornate windows of the consulates and hotels, a wall of flame two miles long. The sea glows like sunlit copper. The crowd hurls itself back towards the harbour and those who are near the edge tumble in screaming.

The heat burns my face. Patches of oil on the water are set alight. Sparks and cinders blow around us, flickering and weaving through the smoke. The enormous bundles of clothes the refugees carry on their shoulders burst into flames. A blazing man flings himself into the sea.

Waves of fire more than a hundred feet high lash upwards, and in the middle of them twenty or thirty separate volcanoes roar and hurl incandescent balloons one after another into the choking darkness.

That night will never end. But when dawn comes as a dull stain, all that's left of my city is a flickering skeleton, the stench of burning oil and flesh, and hundreds of bodies bobbing about like toys on the surface of the black water.

I don't feel the pain anymore.

There's nothing to fear.

When finally they come, there's nothing to fear.

All night I lie awake in the darkness, feeling their rough tongues run over me.

Ah, all over.

I fell.

I lie with the sheets pulled up to my eyes and pretend not to hear them whispering on the other side of the screen.

"It's a simple enough operation. But at her age, well . . ."

My daughter's voice shakes. "I just don't know how she managed to get out without somebody seeing her."

Mrs. Pappas said: "But you shouldn't be out in this weather. It's a blizzard."

"I had to come. You were making *loukumades.*"

"Let me get you a taxi, at least."

"I like the wind," I said.

"Her heart's as strong as a young girl's."

They don't come when I ring. I wet the bed. This place stinks of age.

A nurse says, "She keeps on trying to get up."

"Then strap her down."

From another room a voice rises, chanting over and over again like the priest in the Church of the Holy Mother and Saint Nektarios, an old woman moaning, "Let me go, sweet Jesus, I wanna die, let me go, sweet Jesus, I wanna die, let me go, sweet Jesus."

Damn them, I want to get out of here. They don't come when I ring.

A month till Christmas, if I can wait that long. On Christmas Eve we burn incense all through the house. My aunt bakes hot cross buns in the oven. We call them Christ's loaves. When we have eaten, we set the table again with the best linen and china, so that Christ will come and dine with us during the night. Before he goes to bed my father leaves an old shoe to burn on the fire.

To ward off wandering *Kallikanzari,* the long-eared spirits of evil.

Ripe tangerines on the snow.
They don't come.
I shall get up.

Chapter Eight

Hélène

She has grown accustomed to her solitude.

Initially, once her grief over Maurice's death was numbed, it was the hardest fact of all for her to get used to. Till then, she had always lived on the public surface of events, first of all in France, then here at Maurice's side in Canada. Decisions, responsibilities absorbed her. There was never enough time for a private life where the buried roots of her experience could be traced and carefully nourished. They existed; she didn't deny them, but the important thing, she always insisted, was to act in the interests of a wider, less selfish necessity.

She still believes that to be true. Even now, when everything has changed.

She checks the thermostat to make sure the temperature is right. It mustn't fall below 10° Celsius or the delicate roots of the bonsai will be damaged. And if it rises above 18° they'll start to waken from their winter dormancy. Hmm, perfect. It just feels colder because of the snow swirling outside in the blustery wind.

More sleet than snow, it sticks to the glass and blots out even the shapes of the city below her. Surrounded by whiteness, she pulls up the lapels of the tweed jacket and settles into the canvas chair. Every day she sits here for an hour or more, watching the tiny trees as they sleep.

She wears an old trilby hat on her head.

Yes, a long time ago, Helen attacked her for committing herself to society rather than to . . . what? A life of passion? Hélène smiles. What would her daughter have to say about that now? she wonders. Of course, their images of society are very different, but all the same, all the same . . . She nods her head.

It was their first adult row, their first as equals. It started over some trivial arrangement for the wedding. Helen wanted a simple, private, romantic celebration, and Hélène pointed out, perhaps too firmly, that that just wasn't possible. There were expectations, responsibilities: a marriage, in their milieu, was a public and a social event. Why, more than five hundred people would be sending presents. "And besides, *chérie,* when you're my age, you'll be happy you went through with it. It's not such an ordeal, you'll see, when you're looking back on it."

Helen cried, as she always did in those days when she didn't get her own way. But then she choked back her tears and turned on her mother with a kind of astonishment.

"You just don't know what it is to feel, do you? That's the whole problem. It's not your fault. You don't trust your feelings and you can't understand people who do."

It wasn't the voice of an impudent child—Hélène could have handled that—it was that of an adult who had just discovered a crucial item of information which, she realized now, should have been obvious all along.

"It's not a question of feelings," Hélène retorted. "Of course, I have feelings. Everyone does. The point is, you can't let yourself be ruled by them. They're important and valuable, but they're no good as a basis for judgement."

Helen didn't shout. Her voice quivered, because she was a

little afraid, but for all that, she was sure of what she said. "No, no. You've sacrificed them for something else. Your stupid ideals or something, I don't know. You've let that whole part of you shrivel up and die. It's so sad." She frowned. "Well, do what you want to do. I really don't care anymore."

It was a harsh thing to have said and Helen would regret it later on, though she'd never say so to her mother. But somehow, Hélène didn't feel she had been hurt. At the time, she responded self-protectively and made doubly sure she took the chance to get her own way—after all, she was in the right. But the accusation stayed with her, planted in her mind as something that would have to be dug up again and examined when she had the time.

She spoke about it later that summer to Maurice. Yes, it was here in the conservatory that they talked, though it was a very different, simpler place then, before the extension she built to keep herself occupied the year after his death.

He sucked his pipe. He didn't draw on it deeply as her father had, puffing out dense clouds of smoke like a steam engine. Maurice sipped at it almost nervously. He'd been trying to cut down on his smoking since the doctor's warning. "Does the smoke bother them, d'you think?" he asked.

"No," she smiled over at him. "Not with the windows open, anyway." The bamboo blinds were down to keep the direct sunlight from burning the moss-covered roots. But the windows were open behind them. From the garden, she could hear warblers playing in the honeysuckle. And kingbirds, too.

"Helen looks radiant," he said. Sip, sip; a thin trickle of smoke. It was the first visit they'd had since David and Helen returned from Paris.

Hélène went on trimming the azalea, clipping the dark green leaves so that only the smaller, brighter leaves were left. There—she bent her head—that was better; she could see the gnarled trunk again.

"Don't you think?" Maurice asked.

"I suppose she does." And then she told him about the row

the two of them had had, not exaggerating it, but posing Helen's accusation as a problem that ought to be examined, since it affected both of them.

"You shouldn't let it upset you," he said.

"No, that's just the point. It doesn't. But perhaps that's Helen's point, too."

"What do you mean?"

"Well, perhaps it *ought* to upset me." She smiled. "If I was capable of feeling anything."

"That's ridiculous." They laughed together.

"Yes, but not to Helen." She turned the bowl so that she could see the tree from a different angle. "It's just that the really urgent things we've had to do have always been so clearly a matter of common sense, of reason. They don't preclude feeling. I feel"—she chopped at the air with her free hand—"strongly about them. But it never seemed necessary to explore the feelings for what they were in themselves."

Buds were starting to form and two were already half open on the lower branches. She would keep these two, but some of the others would have to go. She didn't want it to be covered in blossom so that it ended up looking like any ordinary house plant wrapped in tinsel in a florist's window. It wasn't a flower; it was a fifty-year-old tree, twenty inches high. Its branches slanted away from the trunk, blown by a wind they would never be allowed to feel. That was where the blossoms would form—on the side sheltered from the imagined wind. She snipped the buds on the opposite side.

"Am I wrong?" she asked, concentrating on the points of the scissors.

"Damn thing, it's gone out again," Maurice said, laying his pipe on the table. "No, of course you're not. We grew up when the choices which had to be made were social ones. Our passions were social passions. There wasn't much time for us to think about ourselves. What had to be done was clear enough, even when we disagreed about the means."

"With Guérin? Yes, that's it exactly. But Helen can't understand any of that."

"Why should she? By comparison, she's grown up in a vacuum. This whole society's scared to death of facing up to its responsibilities. Why should she be any different? It's not her fault."

Hélène smiled. "That's what she said about me."

"There you are. What else do you expect but incomprehension?" He held up his hands in mock despair. "Now, matches, matches." He searched under the newspapers and the cushions. For a man who was the head of a large corporation, he managed to lose almost everything he needed.

"Odile's got some hidden in the kitchen."

"But where do they all go? It's humiliating. I think she steals them as soon as I'm not looking. Just so I'll be dependent on her."

Anxiously, tenderly, she watched him go. He was only forty-seven; he had ten more careful years to live, but already he moved like a very old man, as if the floor was ready to rise up and hit him.

His death has left her imprisoned in herself. She almost regrets having overcome her grief. At least, while it tortured her, it proved she could still feel something. Oh, feelings, feelings. She shivers, but only with the damp cold. The sleet on the windows runs down in ribbons of coagulating water.

She has privacy now, but nothing useful to fill it with. There was a time when she travelled everywhere with Maurice, to conferences in Tokyo, Frankfurt or Rome. They discussed each issue at night in their hotel room. There was the summer they spent in India when he was advising the Nehru government on the reorganization of the state steel corporation. He turned over his fee to an agricultural commune in Bihar. *Time* ran a story on him, cynical and hostile by turns. "That's a good sign," he said. Now, very few people know if Hélène's alive or dead, and the number of those who care is diminishing.

She leans sideways to examine a juniper. It rises an inch and a half from its tiny celadon container, then spills over the edge in the style that Japanese gardeners call *kengai,* cascade. For four years now, she's been training it, bending it further and further till it grows like a tree clinging to a mountainside in a storm. One of its branches has slipped out of shape. She winds the copper wire that holds it back into position. Its bark is rough and peeling with age; she touches it gently.

"Do I feel nothing?" she murmurs.

No, that's not the problem. The problem is that she doesn't like the feelings she does have; she doesn't like being constantly forced to concentrate on them. If one could feel love, if one could feel pity, if one could feel a faint glow of compassion now and again, it would be all right. Let the emotions flourish. But most of the time it's nothing more than a nagging bitterness or contempt.

"I'm growing sour," she says to the juniper and runs her fingers over the fluffy moss around the base of its trunk. And then she grins. An old woman in a trilby hat talking to a juniper tree. "What would they say if they saw me?" she asks it.

But who will be here to see?

When Maurice returned triumphantly with the box of matches he'd found where he'd left it in the bathroom cabinet, he stood above her stroking the back of her neck. "Don't worry," he said.

"I'm not," she replied, glancing up and seeing the loose folds of skin around his throat. She blinked. The azalea was finished. She brushed the clippings away. "How does it look?"

He twisted his head over at an angle. "Very fine," he said in a solemn voice. "Very proud of itself."

Her upper lip trembled slightly and he kissed her. He held her body against his, but carefully, so as not to put too much pressure on her scarred left side.

"Do you know what Helen said to me after lunch?"

Hélène shook her head.

"Well, I told her how well marriage seemed to be agreeing with her and leered in a stepfatherly sort of way. And she said, 'Yes, but I don't want to go on doing this for the rest of my life.' "

"What did she mean by that?"

Maurice made a long face. "Perhaps mother and daughter have got more in common than they think."

"And what do *you* mean by *that?*"

He winked. "She'll be all right. The fifties can't go on forever, thank God. Something's got to break. She'll find the old battles still have to be fought."

"Yes, but with what weapons?"

"Whatever they can lay their hands on, I expect. As we did." He opened the outside door and went down the brick steps to the lawn. "Let's have tea outside. I've had enough of your dwarves for today."

She watched him zigzag across the slope to the shade of a linden.

Yes, indeed they had fought with whatever they could lay their hands on—bazookas and scythes, old muzzle loaders and captured German machine guns—back in the summer of 1944. Up on the plateau behind Nice and Cannes, Guérin, the Communist leader, had gathered a secret army of nearly two thousand men. In units of thirty—*des trentaines,* he called them—they were spread over an area shaped like a neolithic arrowhead, fifty miles long and at its widest point twenty miles across, from the estuary of the Var in the east to the small market town of Castellane in the west. It was a perfect setting for guerrilla warfare. The plateau itself was arid and barren, but it was cut into by winding, tree-lined gorges more than a thousand feet deep. Caves and mines wormed through the limestone; roads were forced to hug the cliffside, diving into tunnels or perched on flimsy wooden bridges. The Germans couldn't hope to control what went on there. Guérin could.

When he rescued Maurice and Hélène, he didn't ask them

where they wanted to go. They were so stunned they couldn't have told him, but in any case, he wouldn't have bothered to ask. He knew where he wanted them. And why.

Together with the other wounded they were unloaded at a stone barn not far from the old village of Coursegoules. The barn had been converted into a primitive hospital: there were no beds, but there were nurses and a doctor. Hélène collapsed on a straw-filled mattress and tried to press herself into the ice-cold wall.

The next afternoon, she limped to the door. Somebody said something to her. She didn't reply. Outside, the sun bit into her flesh. She hobbled away from the barn for twenty paces and slumped on a rock. She looked back at the barn, seeing it from miles away. It was very beautiful, built into a slight depression in the surface of the plateau. Its glowing walls were a yard thick with no window in them; its long roof of faded tiles sloped gently. Behind it an olive tree twisted arthritic branches. Somebody came to the door and called to her. She didn't reply. She stared at the bloodstained bandages on what seemed to be her feet.

The second day, she went a few steps more and looked in the other direction. The burnt plateau stretched for miles to a ring of blue mountains.

The third day, Maurice went with her. The doctor had wired up his jaw so that he couldn't open his mouth. Painfully, he tried to talk to her. She didn't listen. A truck with a steaming charcoal burner strapped to its back crept over the bumpy ground to an abandoned mine. "I wonder what it's doing up here," Maurice mumbled. "It doesn't look as though the mine's working, does it?"

Gingerly, Hélène lifted some of the dressing from her nose. There was a smell of wild thyme on the air.

Each day they walked a little further. They hardly spoke at all, but they began to notice things together. Flowers, a rabbit, hawks circling high above them, a glimpse of a boar crashing from one clump of bushes to another. Maurice picked a large purple thistle and held it out to her. "It's superb," she said, curtseying. One of its spines jabbed pain into her wrist. She laughed.

At the end of a week, Guérin came to visit them. He was a small man with muscular arms bulging self-consciously through a tight pullover. His hair was grey but his thick moustache was jet black. He had been a trade union organizer in the thirties and when the Vichy Government banned the unions in 1940 he gathered a handful of his friends around him and took to the Maquis. The Party was still officially neutral and pacifist, but it was the only way to avoid being deported to the labour camps in Germany. He had always known just how much he could get out of people. He looked from Maurice to Hélène and saw the lassitude beneath the healthy sunburn. They would have to be handled firmly.

Maurice thanked him for what he had done for them.

"Eh bien"—he turned the palms of his hands upwards—"it had to be done."

"Why?" Hélène examined him suspiciously. "There were none of your people in Nice."

"The Gestapo know there's no point in interrogating them," he said boastfully.

"Why, then?" she insisted.

The deep grooves in his weather-beaten face tightened. He looked right past her. "You were too dangerous. You knew too much."

"Ah," she nodded, relaxing.

"If we hadn't been able to get you out of there, well . . ." He shrugged.

"You'd have had to kill us," Hélène suggested.

Guérin's teeth were broken and stained with nicotine when he smiled.

"Well, thank you," Maurice muttered. His hand tightened round Hélène's.

Politely, Guérin held open the door of the truck for them

to get in. Then he climbed on the back to stoke the charcoal-burning furnace. The engine chugged and spluttered as they lurched along the rough track.

"We've got some petrol-driven trucks as well," he explained apologetically. "We stole them from the Milice depot in Toulon and brought them all the way back here. We only use them when we really have to. We're saving the gas. It's the hardest thing of all to get our hands on."

All day he drove them round his territory and they didn't see a single German patrol. He showed them everything he wanted them to see: his headquarters behind a rockfall in the mine, the radio transmitter and the printing press, another hospital in a cave above Entrevaux, unit after unit of well-drilled, hidden men. They glanced at each other in astonishment. Even they had had no idea it would be like this.

Guérin intended them to be impressed. He didn't need to talk, but as he drove back up the Gorges du Loup with the tops of the cliffs on the other side of the foaming river stained orange in the sunset, he leaned forward to shout across Maurice to Hélène: "You must have been worried about your daughter."

She shook her head.

Maurice glanced sideways at her, feeling the tension.

"She's all right," Guérin went on. "We hid her with a farmer's wife near Grasse. We were afraid the Gestapo might try something with her."

The tires squealed on a tight downhill bend and Maurice clutched at the dashboard. The truck plunged into a tunnel.

"You must have missed her," Guérin insisted.

"No," Hélène whispered. "No. Just as long as she's all right." She stared out away from them at the rock face.

When Guérin let them out again, he stood with one foot posed on the running board. "What do you think?" he asked.

"It's a liberated area already," Maurice said.

"Yes, if the Boches don't attack in force." For a moment, Guérin's eyes followed a flight of birds returning to their nests.

"They will. They know they've got to clear us out of here. We're too much of a threat to their route north through Digne. When they know they're going to retreat, they'll try to wipe us out first."

The plateau grew silent except for the buzz of insects. Then they heard a noise of motors from the mine and trucks began to emerge from what had looked like a ruined outbuilding. One, two, three—Hélène watched in amazement—fourteen of them, all in the markings of the Milice. Slowly, without lights, they rumbled away between the rocks.

"It's an attack on the German supply depot in Vence," Guérin replied to her questioning look. "There's a new shipment of food just come in. We've been having a bit of trouble with the local farmers because we're asking too much from them. So we'll clean the Boches out down there. It ought to last us a month."

"What about the roadblock below the Col?" Hélène asked.

"Who's going to bother to stop a convoy of armed Milice?"

"But on the way back. Once they've heard the shooting."

"There'll be no shooting. They won't have any idea what's happened. One of the watchmen works for us. He'll let our men in. They'll take the guards by surprise. There won't be a sound. The next shift doesn't come on till six in the morning. By then our bellies will be full, for the first time this year."

Maurice whistled appreciatively.

"Now," Guérin clapped his hands together like a schoolteacher. "From what you've seen, what are our main weaknesses?"

"Well," Maurice smiled, "I was going to say supplies, food."

"And?"

"Weapons," Hélène said firmly. "That's where you're weakest. I'd say only about a third of your men are armed."

"You're wrong. It's only one in six. We've been asking for a drop for months. But nothing ever comes. Every single gun we have we got for ourselves. It's not worth listening to the radio any longer. They're playing politics with us."

"Because you're Communists?" Maurice asked.

"Sure. De Gaulle's scared stiff of letting us get too strong. He's worrying about what'll happen after the war. He wouldn't mind at all if we got wiped out."

"Come on," Hélène said impatiently. "That's not true."

"Merde, it is," Guérin's voice rose angrily. "You heard what happened in Corsica last September. When the people rose up and drove out the Germans, how much help did they get from De Gaulle? Nothing. And why? Because they were Communists. They were waiting for weeks for support from the American air force in Palermo. Not a chance. Do you know when the first U.S. bombs fell on Bastia? October 4, twelve hours after the last Germans on the island were captured." He banged the hood of the truck with his fist. "That's why we need your help," he said intensely to Hélène. "You've got more weapons than we have and there are only fifty or sixty people with you."

"Three times that," she said coldly.

"Fifty or sixty you can count on. The rest'll go along for the fun. Fifty or sixty, at the most."

He was right. "I'll have to go down and talk to the others about it," Hélène said slowly.

"You can't. It's too dangerous. The Boches are looking for you everywhere."

"At night."

"No."

He would hold on to her, she knew, till she gave in. "I'll think about it." She walked away.

Guérin slammed the door of the cab behind him. "I can't wait long," he called as he drove off. "There'll be a landing soon up in the north. Then all hell will break loose down here."

All that night, Maurice struggled to overcome Hélène's doubts. They lay out on the plateau looking up at the stars, a blanket pulled around them against the mountain air. "Let's face it. You don't have any choice," he told her.

"But we're prisoners here. It's as bad as the Gestapo," she hissed angrily. "I'm not going to be bullied by him."

At midnight they watched the trucks return. There were twenty of them now and the men inside were singing.

She talked about all the disputes there had been with the Communists in the past. Maurice's fingers linked with hers. Anyway, her network's function was to help Jews and Allied airmen escape. That, and collecting information.

"Then why do you need all the guns you've got?" Maurice pressed her.

She couldn't forgive the Communists for the German reprisals they'd provoked.

"It's the only way now," Maurice said. He kissed the side of her chin and felt her body shake. She tried to kiss him back, just managing to feel his tongue between his closed lips. "He's right. You know he is," he insisted. As the peaks of the Alps to the east of them were touched with pink in the distant dawn, they began to make love to each other. She felt nothing.

How easy it would be to sentimentalize these memories, turning the pain and deprivation into passion and sharing. But no, Hélène won't allow herself to fall into that trap. If you do, she reminds herself, you end up living in the past because it's so much more sure than the present. All around her she sees people who've tried to escape like that. Old women, young men. If she's learned one thing, it's that there's no escape in running away.

Like it or not, the resistance has made her what she is today. Resistance is her way of life. Yet what is it that she resists?

Too often her energy is deflected in seemingly trivial directions. But to her they are not trivial; she won't let go of them. In a society predicated on waste, she wastes nothing. She remembers the constant ache in her stomach, Guérin rationing out his supplies like a miser. So she throws no scraps away. She has a woman who cleans and cooks for her, but nothing—she checks —is thrown away.

"No raccoons'll come round your garbage can," Sally Benson once teased her.

"What are you talking about?" Hélène asked, turning from the coffeepot.

"Well, this cup of cooked rice you're hoarding in the fridge. What's it for? A rainy day?" Sally's laugh was light and musical in those days.

"It can go into something," Hélène protested.

"But what? It's all dried up."

"There are too many people in the world who don't have enough to eat."

"Be sensible, Hélène. If you hold on to a cup of stale rice, it's not going to help somebody who's starving to death in—God, I don't know. Where do they starve? India?"

"If I threw it out it would be an insult to them." Hélène knew she was right.

Wherever she eats, nothing goes back to the kitchen. It's a matter of principle. At the Ritz Carlton or, heaven forbid, a drive-in. Why, just last summer, when she was up at the cottage with David and Helen and the children, on the way back Mark insisted on stopping for fried chicken, *Le Roi du Poulet.* Ugh, how can chicken be soggy and dried-up simultaneously? When they had nearly finished, she felt the others staring at her. She looked up at them questioningly and they burst into laughter.

"You don't have to gnaw every single bone, Bonne Maman," Ann said. "It's not that"—she searched for the word —"succulent."

Hélène laughed, too, and smiles again at the memory. She doesn't escape into the past; it entwines her. Is it turning her into a caricature of her old self, a bitter, obsessive, mean old woman? Well, if that's what they think, let them.

She has better things to think about. Trees to plant.

She gets up and goes over to her work table. She has been

working on these seven tiny lodgepole pines for the last two years, making sense out of their twisted shapes, pruning back their roots to control their growth. They sit waiting for her in fibre pots. Now, finally, she will bring them together, all seven of them in a shallow ceramic bowl, turning them from stunted saplings into a miniature forest. She has chosen an oval bowl already, two feet long with a dark blue glaze slightly streaked with green. She holds it up against their feathery needles. Its smoothness sets them off superbly. She lines it with gravel, then a layer of earth mixed with peat and lots of sand. They need dryness. One by one she takes the trees out of their pots and washes away the loose dirt in a bucket of water laced with vitamins. She prunes their roots again, cutting back the taproots still further till only the fine new feeders are left. She works gently, carefully, trying to do as little damage as possible.

Was it only a year ago that Helen watched her working on these pines? One whole afternoon, as fascination turned to horror. "God, Mother, I never realized this was what bonsai involved. I thought it was . . . well, civilized."

Hélène turned with the clippers in her hand. "That's exactly what it is."

"But it's so cruel."

"Chérie!"

"Okay, unnatural, then. It's the most artificial thing I've ever seen."

"Isn't all art?" Hélène scraped some soil away with a chopstick. "Is your painting natural?"

Helen walked over to the window. Sunlight shimmered on the crusted surface of the snow in the garden. Chickadees pecked at the junipers.

"I wish it was. If only you knew how sick I am of the stuff I'm doing now. It's so silent, so meditative. I'm not a meditative person, mother! I don't want to be a nun. If only I could find more struggle in it. More of the struggle to survive."

"Like these trees, then," Hélène suggested slyly.

A smile flickered on her daughter's lips. "All right, all right. Yes, I suppose, like them in one sense. But without the presence of the artist as somebody in control all the time. So, unlike them completely. They do what you force them to do. You're on top of them all the time, wiring, pruning, playing God. I'm tired of playing God in my paintings. I'm tired of turning out boring, aesthetic objects. I've got to find a way of doing something more relevant."

"*Chérie.* You're not going to start painting downtrodden peasants, are you?"

"No, I don't mean relevant in that sense at all. That's just a way of making their suffering acceptable. Oh, shit, I don't know what I want. But I know there has to be a way of defining this conflict I feel inside me as part of something much less self-centered and aesthetic. More—oh damn it, more political."

Hélène was beginning to enjoy the energy of the argument. If only they could talk to each other like this more often. She put down her tools.

"I can see all that, I think. But you're not really being consistent, are you? You say you want something more natural. All right. And then you say you want something more political, more social? But society isn't natural. It's full of restraints that we can't avoid. To live in it we have to be trained. As these trees are trained," she added triumphantly.

Helen turned back into the conservatory and for a moment there was a look of furious hatred on her face. "I'm tired of people hacking away at me, mother. That's what I'm most tired of." A shutter clanged down in front of her eyes. Hélène had lost her.

Will she ever find her again?

She takes the tallest of the lodgepole pines—it's about two feet high—and plants it in the bowl. Not in the centre; a third of the way across. Next the smallest—about six inches high—in close against the largest, sheltered. She sprinkles earth around their roots, using a chopstick to pack it tight so that no pockets of air remain. Rot breeds in them. There. Now the others. She fits them together till the patterns of their branches interlock; a slight clearing in the centre to draw the eye in. A garden stone she's been saving; it becomes a rock. She bends down to look at them at their own level and shifts one of the trunks slightly. Yes —the excitement pulses through her—this is just how she's planned it: a forest extends into a foreshortened distance. She spreads more earth around, forming humps and depressions, leaving a few of the thicker roots exposed. Then she tamps powdered moss into the surface with a small trowel.

She sits down in the canvas chair with a sigh, her heart beating faster. A few of the branches will have to be cut back. Seven trees don't grow together as one would on its own. They constrict and strengthen each other. But the group is formed now; they will stay like this forever. How can this be cruelty?

"Have I been too hard on Helen, do you think?" she asked Maurice that day in the garden under the linden tree.

The creases deepened around his eyes. "An absolute tyrant!"

Hélène wasn't sure if he was joking. "Really?"

"I don't know how she survived."

"No, but really." She punched him lightly on the arm. "Tell me. Have I been too hard on her?"

He sucked at the pipe. "Maybe you didn't let her get away with as much as you might have done with . . . with somebody else's kids."

She watched a robin scuffling through the shadows at the base of one of the honeysuckles. "I was harder on her than I was on the boys, wasn't I?"

Maurice's two sons used to stay with them for weekends. To try to compensate for her instant dislike of them—they were almost as frivolous and selfish as their mother—she paid them far more attention than she ever gave to her own daughter. As they grew older, she'd been able to see less and less of them with a reasonably clear conscience. One, a supercilious law student, still occasionally had strained conversations over lunch with his father; the other had gone off to Harvard to study business.

"The pressures were different," Maurice said.

"But I was, wasn't I?" She wouldn't let go of this dilemma. It was too rich a seam of guilt. "Why?"

"Perhaps not to destroy each other totally is the most one can hope for," he said, "in the best families." The pipe was working properly now. "And then your mother wasn't exactly the perfect model of the maternal instinct." Maurice disliked Helena's constant melodrama—*'Tite Médée,* he called her—though he always tried to treat her with respect.

"But that's terrible," she said, putting her hand up to her mouth.

"What is?" He reached along the back of the wooden bench to brush away some dried-up bird droppings.

"Well, that I should treat Helen badly just because that was how my mother treated me. It's so deterministic."

"Not badly. That's not true. Strictly sometimes, perhaps; but not unjustly. That's the difference."

"Still. Maybe I simply had more self-control."

Maurice drew in his gums. "In a family with a long tradition of hysteria that's by no means a negligible advance."

Hélène threw a cushion at him and in trying to protect himself he let go of his stupid pipe. The ashes sprayed all over his flannel trousers, burning a couple of small holes. Odile, the maid, came out with a tray of tea at the same moment and couldn't understand why they would want to laugh so much over a thing like that. She looked on disapprovingly.

"Don't worry, Odile," Maurice said as he skipped past her. "Madame is practicing the art of self-defence." He went off to change, pausing on the steps to call: "Though she doesn't need to practice."

Hélène waved airily.

In the months of June and July 1944, the war exploded all around them. The Allies had landed on the beaches of Normandy, but in the rest of France, the German armies moved into a desperate offensive. They no longer had to pretend to be an orderly occupying force; increasingly violent repression was the only option left open to them. The resistance fighters, for their part, couldn't sit back and wait to be liberated; this was their last chance to wipe away the stains of a humiliating defeat. The clashes now were face to face and full of viciousness.

Hélène was caught up in it as much as anyone. The only time she even thought about her daughter in all those weeks was the day when she learned Helen had been killed.

The day the Germans burned the wrong village and everyone in it by mistake.

There were two villages in fact, Lagourin and Lagourin-les-Roses, but why would a German officer bother about the difference? Lagourin was the village Hélène and Maurice moved to as soon as they were released from the hospital. It was only ten miles to the southwest of Guérin's headquarters on the map, but a lot further than that along the twisting, rocky roads, with the Gorges du Loup cutting between them.

"The further the better," said Maurice. "I'm very grateful and all that, but he does get a bit overpowering, comrade Guérin."

"Maybe he just wants us out of the way, too," said Hélène, but when she got there she realized how difficult the job he had given them was.

The village had been falling down since the 1930s when the water ran out and the last of the villagers finally abandoned it. Up there on the edge of the plateau, with steep terraced fields that lost a little more of their soil every spring, it was surprising they had stayed so long. For hundreds of years, perched on the edge of its cliff, the village had controlled the lowlands below it. The Saracens were the first to build a fortress there in the tenth century. Five hundred years later the Tuscans erected an elaborate castle on the site with intricate Moorish ceilings and a chapel decorated by Bréa, the Fra Angelico of Provence as he was optimistically called. But all that was gone now; the ceilings had caved in and Bréa's murals were damaged by rain and pigeons. The old men, the women and the children had moved to Lagourin-les-Roses in the valley, a somnolent village with a sickening aura of scent hanging over it.

In 1944 Guérin gave Hélène the task of turning Lagourin into a fortress again.

He had ten units—three hundred men—in the area, but they'd been badly mauled in a number of skirmishes. The commander had been betrayed and publicly executed in the square in Grasse. They were demoralized, drifting back to their homes, turning into bands of armed marauders.

"The southern flank, *merde,*" said Guérin. "It's where we need to be strongest now with the German buildup down there. There's going to be a landing soon. God knows when. Somewhere between Hyères and Saint-Tropez from the way the destroyers are sniffing around the coast. From what I hear they're still squabbling about it in London. They say Churchill wants the whole thing moved to Greece. Greece!" He laughed harshly. "*Salauds!* They won't tell us about it, anyway; they don't trust us. But it's got to be soon because they're asking us for help. Shit, if they're asking us for help, that means it's really soon. They want the Luftwaffe base at Fayence knocked out. I guess they can deal with the airfields near the coast from the sea; it's the ones inland they need us for." He cursed again.

"But Fayence is way beyond Lagourin," said Hélène. "That's right outside our area."

Guérin nodded. "Anyway, while you're working on it, you'll have a chance to see your daughter at least. She's down in the valley in Lagourin-les-Roses." He was still irritated by Hélène's lack of interest in the child. It was unmotherly. "That'll be a consolation," he suggested.

She looked at him unflinchingly. The last thing she needed was Guérin's sympathy.

From the beginning, the whole situation in Lagourin was a

mess. The men didn't trust Maurice because he was a foreigner. And because she was a woman, they trusted Hélène even less. In the daytime they sat about in the shade of the ancient chestnut trees and got drunk and grumbled. At night they disappeared. They were waiting for the war to end and they wanted nothing to do with this pointless mission. So it was the British and Americans who were asking for help now, was it? Well, fuck the British and Americans! They'd kept France waiting long enough.

Hélène tried everything she knew—guile, authority, example—and from time to time somebody would be impressed. But the weight of apathy was greater. There was only one group she could rely on, an unlikely mixture of old Marcellin, a wily, alcoholic peasant, his sons and nephews from the surrounding villages, and a bunch of young steelworkers from Clermont-Ferrand. Somehow or other, they held together, and Hélène found herself trying to plan the attack on the airbase around them.

Still, when the order came they weren't anywhere near ready. She tried to talk Guérin out of it and earned his disapproval. She was a woman, and worse, a bourgeoise; he shouldn't have put her in charge. "It's got to be done," he insisted. "It'll strengthen our hand when the war's over. If you can't do it . . ."

So she told him the plan, skipping over the weak points.

"You're not going yourself, are you?" he interrupted in surprise.

"I can't let them go without me," she said sullenly.

They nearly got lost on the way. A pity they didn't. In fog that swirled around the mountains, with a hundred of the least doubtful men in five of Guérin's Milice trucks, they fumbled their way along the precipitous roads. Drunkenly, Marcellin guided them through, past the village of Mons and down around the outskirts of the little town of Fayence to the airfield in the valley below.

Could the Germans have known they were coming? As they

cut their way through the wire, the machine guns opened up. They lost a dozen men straight away, but they kept on. They found cover behind some empty hangars and began to return the fire. They had detailed plans of the base and Marcellin's son, Christophe, who'd been in the artillery in 1940, got the mortar range on the fuel storage tanks after his first few shots. The whole place went up and the Germans were at a disadvantage again, silhouetted against the flames and trapped in the billowing smoke. Meanwhile, Maurice led a small group round to the south and opened fire with bazookas on the parked Messerschmitts.

Fifteen minutes were all they needed and then they disengaged, leaving confusion, and some of their own dead, behind them. As they climbed into the trucks the mood had changed, whoops of laughter mingling with the explosions and the gunfire. Hélène was anxious; the Germans had seemed to be expecting them. She wanted to talk to Maurice, but he wasn't there.

"Wait," she shouted as Christophe started the engine.

"We can't." He let out the clutch and the truck jerked forward.

She stood on the running board looking back. "Where's Maurice?" she called wildly.

"He's behind. In the last truck."

She held on to the loose door, trying to concentrate. She'd have to decide on her own. "We can't go back the way we came. It'll take too long. They'll be looking for us up there. And the planes will catch us in the open."

"What planes?" Marcellin hiccupped.

"Christophe, listen. It's only a quarter of an hour back along the highway to the turnoff that goes up through Cabris, isn't it?"

"A mile past the Pont de Siagne? Sure. But they'll be watching the highway, too."

"It's that or the way we came. In the fog."

So they took a chance on the highway, but this time the Germans really were waiting for them. As the trucks swung down the hill towards the bridge that curves across the Siagne, the guns on the other side of the valley opened up. *"Merde,* a tank," shouted Christophe and swerved into the ditch. The first shots destroyed the two trucks behind them. The others screeched to a halt. In panic the men tumbled out, running for cover, anywhere, up the hill or rolling down the steep slope to the river below.

Hélène found Maurice lying in a culvert beside her.

"The hillside. Up through the forest," Marcellin was shouting, sober now as shells smashed into the trees above his head. They ran up among the pines that covered the sides of the gorge, stumbling and falling, bumping into branches, turning to shoot at shadows and sometimes at each other. They crossed the suspension bridge below the village of Saint Cézaire, but they didn't have time to blow it up before German motorcyclists appeared on the road above. They fought their way through, twenty-five of them now, and up towards the plateau. But the dawn was opening wide around them as they came to the caves in the hillside.

Marcellin gasped for breath. "We can take cover in here." He stooped between the rocks.

"Is there another way in?" Hélène asked.

Marcellin shook his head, grinning. "It's the only entrance."

Maurice tried to hold them back. "Once we're bottled up in there we'll never get out."

"The Boches'll never get in, either."

Machine guns rattled on the hillside behind them. They plunged down into the darkness.

"Christophe, Denis, and you, Matthieu, stay at the entrance," Marcellin ordered. "Behind the rocks."

With Hélène's powerful flashlight, the rest of them worked their way deeper into the cave. Soon it opened out into a high, echoing chamber. Marcellin hooted like an owl. Casting grotesque shadows, he pranced over to a long stalactite and struck it with the barrel of his gun; it rang like a tuning fork. For a few minutes they lost themselves in the magic rocks—mushrooms and flowers, a rabbit's head and a dancing goat, all bright red from the iron oxide in the stone. They began to chatter like a party of schoolchildren, nervous and a little afraid of the silence which was broken only by the dripping of water. They went deeper till Hélène pulled back with a gasp. There was nothing in front of her feet. She turned the beam into the emptiness and it was lost. A waterfall roared in the depths.

"Is this as far as we can go?"

Marcellin shrugged, then cackled.

"So we're stuck," Maurice said.

"Well, that depends. There's supposed to be a chimney that goes up from the corner over there. But it's dangerous. Even for a climber. It comes out near the Col, so I've heard."

Suddenly, from the entrance there was a shout and an explosion. They ran back towards the light, banging into rocks and cursing.

"Grenades," said Denis. "They're throwing them down the hill behind us."

"The cover's pretty good under the overhang," Christophe said. As he spoke, a grenade bounced at his feet. With a roar he picked it up and hurled it down towards a group of Germans who were setting up a machine gun behind a pile of rocks. It burst; the howls drifted back to them and they laughed.

As the day wore on, the Germans tried everything to prise them out. They rolled bundles of explosive down into the entrance of the cave, but each time the defenders picked them up and threw them down the hill. It was like a game. Then another bundle rolled into view, on a cord this time. As Denis grabbed at it, it was snapped back above his head. He flung himself headlong behind a rock just as it exploded. The others staggered into the cave, their faces burnt and blackened, with tiny chips of stone buried in their skin.

Marcellin wiggled his finger in his ear. "I feel as if I've been blown out. Like a candle."

"I'm not staying here," Maurice said. "We've got to get through to Guérin. I'm going to try the chimney. Has anybody done any climbing?"

"A little," Matthieu replied. "In the Dordogne." He was an apprentice from Clermont-Ferrand, with a face full of spots.

Hélène followed them back. As she kissed Maurice beside the abyss, she said: "I didn't know you could climb."

"I can't," he muttered. "But I promise you, I'm going to learn."

She gave them her flashlight and watched as they edged their way across to the narrow cleft in the rock wall. Then they vanished, with the light flickering behind them. She heard them calling to each other. Their voices faded. A slight glimmer of light still. Or was it her eyes playing tricks? She heard a scream and the light vanished.

"Maurice," she shouted. "Maurice."

In the darkness far below the waterfall roared. She slumped down on the dank rock.

When Maurice came out of the house in a clean pair of slacks, he paused in the middle of the lawn, looking around him and blinking in the sunlight. She held out a cup of tea to him. He sipped it absentmindedly. "It's lukewarm." He spilled it on the grass.

"You shouldn't have taken so long," she said in her Mother Superior's voice.

He looked up at her from under his bushy eyebrows.

"Here," she smiled. "Let me pour you out a fresh one."

"I was thinking. You never blame your father, do you?"

She handed the cup to him again. "Why should I?"

"Well, he treated you as badly as your mother, didn't he? In a different way. A more charming way." He picked up the pipe from the table and tapped it out.

"No, not the pipe, anything but the pipe." She held up her hands in mock terror.

He laughed. "All right. But really, just as irresponsible, eh?"

"I suppose so," she sighed. "But I feel at ease with him. Felt. I never shall with her."

No, I never shall with her. Hélène tastes the words in her mouth again. Not even now, with Helena lying in a coma, hearing nothing, a slight bulge beneath the hospital blankets. Above the bed a cheap, faded print of the Annunciation keeps watch. How does it manage to get so faded in that room where the sun never shines? she wonders.

She allows herself one last searching look at her forest of lodgepole pines. Yes, they will need a few adjustments, but she must take her time. No more work this afternoon. To fix the ideal of them in her mind will take days of concentration. Till then, the most she can do is to make sure they're well protected. She starts to adjust the elaborate water system, thin rubber hoses with a valve in each nozzle that shuts the flow off automatically when the soil's in danger of becoming too wet.

Though Helena has been lying in hospital for nearly two days, it wasn't till this morning that Hélène could bring herself to phone her daughter at the cottage. The line crackled.

"Chérie, I'm sorry. It's your grandmother."

A hissing intake of breath.

"I think you should come. She's unconscious. It won't be long now." Hélène explained how last night she had asked the doctor to take Helena off the support systems. The silence at the other end of the line seemed to have grown harder. "You wouldn't leave her like that. All those tubes stuck in her. The doctor said even if she did survive, she'd be a vegetable. She'd have wanted to die with dignity, wouldn't she?"

A pause. "Yes, mother." Helen's voice was tiny. She started to sob. "I'll be down there this afternoon."

Hélène looks at her watch. She will have to leave in twenty

minutes. Oh, if only her skull would shatter! What she can't accept, damn it, is the fact that she feels no grief. Nothing at all. She believes in conscience—in guilt, even—as a driving force in life, a creative, self-defining force, and the fact that she feels nothing for her mother—no love, and now at last, for that shallow hump of bedclothes, no hatred, either—is the deepest source of guilt of all. Yet she wishes, with all the intensity she can muster, that somehow there could be more than this. Must you feel even emptier when an emptiness deep inside you is about to be cut out?

"You don't even cry," Helena had said once in scorn. "You *can't* cry, can you? You're not a woman."

And Maurice that afternoon in the garden, as she poured out a final cup of tea, reminded her: "She cares for you in her own way, you know. It's just that it's not a very maternal instinct. It's not warm, it's more . . . more agonized?"

"I've never seen much evidence of it."

"No, it comes out in odd ways. Last year—after your operation?—when we were leaving the hospital she was almost hysterical. I wasn't quite sure what to do. You know, a hysterical mother-in-law! You can't slap her, can you? She was weeping, and flinging herself about in the lobby. Dozens of virtuous citizens looking at me as though I'd beaten her up. So I took her in my arms and after a bit she quieted down. I said: 'Hélène's going to be all right. She's as strong as a horse,' and lots of other eloquent stuff. And she tugged herself away from me and said: 'But she's only half a woman now.' And then she made me promise, a solemn oath, that I'd never let on how it repelled me."

"My God!" Hélène gasped in horror, instinctively clutching the padded left side of her chest. She shivered.

Maurice took her clenched hand and pulled it over onto his knee, looking searchingly into her face. "You're cold. Let's move into the sun."

"The old bitch!" Hélène said. "The awful old bitch! What an act!"

"Yes, but it was real, too. She meant it. Every word."

Hélène digs her nails deep into a pile of earth.

For the rest of the day and the night and the whole of the next day, they held out in the cave. Two of them were killed by ricocheting bullets and five slightly wounded. They had nothing to eat, but plenty of cold, hard water to lick from the trickles that ran down the walls. "It'll do you the world of good," she teased old Marcellin. There was no time for grief. She insisted on taking her turn behind the rocks at the entrance, firing in desperation at anything that moved.

"You'd make a good poacher, Madame," Marcellin joked as a winged pheasant fluttered from a clump of bushes she had aimed at.

"I'm not shooting them for the Boches to eat," she said, and then added, without thinking: "I'm a better shot than my husband."

"Your husband, Madame?"

Her eyes narrowed. Maurice had ceased to exist. "We've got to get out tonight," she said without taking her eyes away from the cover where a German was crouching. She could smell the lavender growing on the hillside. "If we stay any longer, they'll pick us off one by one."

"Wait till the moon goes down then," Marcellin whispered. His hands shook so much from lack of brandy he couldn't hold his rifle steady.

Guérin, though, didn't wait that long. As the moon began to sink towards the Montagne de Malay, there was a burst of firing off to their right. Instinctively, they ducked back into the cave, but then they realized it was aimed at the Germans. Mortars opened up from the other side of the river, thudding into the German positions, and within half an hour they were pulling back down the valley in disorder. How could Guérin have known where to come? In a shower of pebbles, Maurice slithered awkwardly down the rocks behind the cave.

He winced as Hélène pressed herself against him in the

back of the truck. "I think the rib got broken. When I fell."

"But I thought you . . . About an hour after you left. There was a scream. The light went out."

"Matthieu," he said softly. "I couldn't get back to the cave without him. So I . . . well, I went on."

"In the dark?" She couldn't even imagine it.

"After a while there was a chink of light."

"How awful." She stroked his back.

"The worst thing was not knowing if I'd make it in time. I didn't get to the mine till just before dawn this morning. Then we had to wait all day."

"What did you tell Guérin?"

"He's a fool. No, I didn't tell him that. Almost. He blames you for losing his stupid trucks. *'Cette femme,'*" he said in Guérin's broad accent, "'she don't know what I had to go through to get those trucks.'"

Hélène smiled gently. "But he came."

"With a little persuasion." As the truck lurched over some ruts, Maurice rose to his feet in pain. The air ripped past them.

"He didn't want to come?"

"'They're useless, all those bastards in Lagourin, *complètement pourris.*'"

"How did you make him change his mind?"

"Oh, various suggestions. I threatened bombing at one point."

"Maurice!" She hugged him and he cried out. "Oh, I'm sorry." She kissed him longingly and Marcellin, who was drunk already, cheered. *"Allez-y, Madame!"*

But the Germans couldn't be expected to take the defeat lying down. One of their informants must have told them the terrorists came from Lagourin. Lagourin, Lagourin-les-Roses. They're all the same, these little French villages, charming, rotten to the core. And perhaps some officer didn't want to risk his creaking busloads of S.S. on the steep road that wound its way up to the abandoned village on the cliff. The bridges would certainly be mined. And anyway—the most telling argument—what's the point of burning down a village that nobody lives in anymore? Where's the justice in that?

So, at ten the next morning the dirty buses ground to a halt in the small square of Lagourin-les-Roses. Some women were doing their washing by the fountain. There were only women in the village. And a handful of very old men playing checkers and gossiping in the Bar de la Paix. And many children. Nothing had ever happened in Lagourin-les-Roses. It had no history. Napoléon had passed nearby on the march northward after his return from Elba, but he hadn't stopped. Roses grew wild in the small fields on the hillside because the perfume factories in Grasse had closed down. But the jasmine crop was still picked and carefully dried.

The S.S. men began to herd the villagers into the church. They protested. Pathetically, they tried to hide. The widow Jollivet hid behind a wall with her daughter's three children. Their dog Toutou started to bark, then ran towards the trees. Lucien ran after him. He was brought down with a single shot in the back and writhed for thirty seconds like a rabbit before he lay still. The rest of the family were shoved towards the church.

It was a dull church, with no architectural distinction. Just the fine fifteenth-century wood carving of the Virgin which had been brought down from the old village when it was abandoned. As soon as all the people were locked inside, the flamethrowers were turned on. Those who broke the windows and tried to jump out were shot. When the screaming was over, every house in the village was burnt down, and all the surrounding farms and the flowers in the fields.

Not till that evening did Hélène learn that her daughter hadn't also died in the flames. The poor child, she had cried at being left behind, so Madame Cheiron took her along when she went off to visit her mother-in-law in Mougins. Her own mother and all her children were dead when they returned.

Hélène rubs the sockets of her eyes with her fists. She has

too much history. It weighs so heavily on her, she wishes sometimes it would just quietly slip away. But no, that's weakness; there's no time for that. "She's all ego," Sally Benson once said of her, and perhaps it's true. A paradox, surely, in one who's always sought to sacrifice herself to her beliefs. But perhaps it's true. All ego, but no self-indulgence.

She pushes herself slowly to her feet and goes over to the window. The sleet has stopped and the sun is trying to burst through the pewter clouds. The muddled outlines of the city are visible again. A shaft of light flashes on a pane of glass. She turns her back on it. "If one cannot have joy," she said once to somebody quite unimportant at a cocktail party after an abysmal performance of *The Magic Flute,* "one should at least try for order."

The bonsai pines catch her eye and instantaneously she sees what needs to be done. It's obvious: the largest shows no sign of age. Quickly, she gets a knife from the work table and carefully strips all the foliage and the bark from the two highest branches. There. The tree was hit—long, long ago, so that it hardly remembers, by lightning in a storm, leaving these dead tips, *jin,* the Japanese gardeners call them. She rubs lime sulphur into the wood to make it turn grey more rapidly.

As she straightens up, the elastic on her bra rubs under her right breast. This morning she found a tiny hardness there, rolling like a ball beneath her fingers. It will have to be seen to; fought against. She has won before, and will again. But not today. Today, there is no more fighting. She puts it out of her mind and goes into the house. She must change into something suitable before she goes down to the hospital, to meet her daughter and watch her mother die.

Chapter Nine

Helen

Already the wound is healing over. Conscience converted into amnesia.

For a couple of weeks the face of the city was hacked open. Energy spurted out. I saw it in every pair of eyes that caught mine in the street: their fear, their excitement. But now the pupils grow dull again. They want to forget. Who was Pierre Laporte? Somebody a few schools will be named after. James Cross still has not been found. Who cares? Even his wife and daughter have gone back to Europe. James Cross no longer exists.

The city falls into tiny, incompatible pieces. We live together out of convenience, not from necessity.

I won't allow this to happen. For a few days I saw things as they really are. Those days in prison showed me something else is possible. I don't yet know how to live that knowledge, but I can paint it.

Yes, this is my freedom. I can paint it. I paint on thick wooden boards now, ripping the surface apart with a chisel. If

I want to paint on canvas, I stick it on top; or discloths or galvanized steel. The images multiply, out from the centre of the painting, up from its surface. I paint the stories of the women I was with in Tanguay, I wipe them out and start again. Then dig down deep to the ones I've buried. I paint helicopters and grey suits, mangled legs by a railroad track. When I need more space I nail more boards to the first.

What I'm doing frightens me. When I used to paint I could stand back from the canvas and see it as something apart from me. It might take me two months to gauge exactly where I had to place a single sharp brushstroke, but when I did, I knew it would be right. I knew that if I mixed just the right amount of white with acrylic blue, then thinned them with water and floated them across the surface, when they washed in there would be a minute separation of the colours. Like the foam at the sea's edge. I knew that, I could do it, I never missed.

Now, I'm not sure what I'm doing half the time. I follow the impulses that come to me. Not inspiration, some holy madness, but the impulses that are jabbed into me by the world out there. The world that mustn't be allowed to forget. I read something in the newspapers and it becomes a part of what I'm painting. Guy Bresson, who worked in a left-wing printshop, has been charged with trafficking. Bullshit. I paint my disbelief. I paint the nerves in Solange's face when she talked of the father who beat her.

When I stop I realize that, for other people, my life is still a mess. But I know that, given time, these paintings will be so solid at their core, everything else will find its place.

But where was André Goldman?

For four weeks, Helen had seen nothing of him. André had gone underground? Well, let him stay there, for all she cared, it was where he belonged. Sewers, crypts, the subway on a sunny day. She laughed. She slept more easily, not knowing where he was.

He was right behind her.

There were no more sunny days. It was a Thursday night when everyone in Montréal was doing the shopping. A blustery November night with Christmas decorations already plastered over all the stores. Outside, the drizzle that hung in the air was only a couple of degrees away from snow. Inside, in the stale warmth of Waldman's fish market, Helen felt his hand on her shoulder.

"André!" She was buying oysters, because Peter Abbott had asked her to go out to the farm for the weekend. She'd told him, defensively, she might not be able to make it, but she was buying oysters and Peter drooled over oyster stew, so she assumed quite comfortably that she might be intending to go.

"André!" she exclaimed. A tiny Portuguese woman, somewhere between thirty and seventy, squeezed past her to get at the piles of clams. "What are you doing here?"

"I want to speak to you."

"You mean, you've been waiting here for me?"

He looked around cautiously. "No."

In Waldman's on a Thursday night there are a couple of hundred people and several million fish. She pulled André into a corner beside the lobster tanks. His arm was like steel wire.

"How are you, Helen?" His voice was low and intense.

"Good, André. Really good," she said boisterously. "I'm getting a lot of work done."

"Work?" he said disdainfully. "You mean painting."

So that was how it still was. "Yes," she said. "And I'm pleased with it. So back off, eh?"

His expression grew gloomier. You could never really define André's expressions, but his colour seemed to become slightly greyer.

"Painting isn't work," he intoned. "That's a typical bourgeois fallacy. A painter may happen to be a member of the proletariat because of some other work he happens to do, but it's false to argue that a painter is, per se, a worker."

"Just a hobby, huh?" She poked him in the bony chest and he grunted. "You ambush me in Waldman's to tell me that?"

He fiddled with the plastic bag he was carrying. An Eaton's bag. Her muscles tensed.

"They didn't pick you up on the sixteenth," she said. It was more a challenge than a question.

"No," he sneered. "I knew all about it even before it started."

She looked at him unbelievingly. "How could you? Nobody knew before that morning. The decision wasn't even made till then."

"I knew. Long before."

"How?" she challenged. They still talked to each other like children.

He shrugged. Then: "I wouldn't let them take me alive, anyway."

She turned away in boredom. "Look, André, I just came in to get these oysters, so . . ." She pointed down at the rusted wire basket full of chipped grey stones.

His fingers were digging into her. "Did they beat you up?"

"Who? No. But, hey, how did you know I was in prison?" He stared her down. "Okay, okay, I know." She waved her hand dismissively. "Listen, I've really got to move."

"Were you followed when you came here?"

"No." She hesitated. "Not that I know of."

"You wouldn't notice, anyway."

"Why not?"

"I've been following you for two days and you haven't seen me."

He had broken through to her. She was angry now. "Fuck it, André, why do you have to play these stupid bloody games? I don't think I've been followed. But I don't climb in windows and run out back doors and . . . and jump off buses just to make sure all the time. Frankly, if somebody is following me, I don't give a shit, anyway. I think it's dumb, and the dumbness scares me a little because dumb people are inclined to do dumb things. But I'm not hiding anything, and I'm not going to for you or anyone else, because once you start to hide it's a tiny victory for all the assholes who want to stop you from—oh, shit!" She ran out of breath.

"It's easy for you," André said. "They can't touch you."

"Listen. The Goldman millions, huh." She rubbed her thumb and forefinger together—vulgarly, her mother would have said. "Don't talk to me about the untouchables. What about when Katie stole that crate of Coke?"

She went off and picked up two more oysters, but André stood by the tanks and she had to go back to him to carry on the attack. "You're a fanatic, André, do you know that? Roger says so, too: *un fana.*"

"Roger's sold out."

"Oh, fuck off! You're full of shit with all your conspiracies." Without rolling up her shirt-sleeve she plunged her arm into the tank of cold brine and pulled out a lobster. "Look, is this lobster bugged?" She laughed and waved it under his nose. "Come on, examine it." Unfortunately, its claws were tied.

He jerked away and banged his head against a metal shelf. He rubbed the short, bristly hair on his scalp. "I'm serious, Helen," he said, and he looked so sincere she began to feel sorry for him again.

"What do you want, André?"

"I've got to find some place to hide."

"But why? Why now? The whole thing is dying down. Even if they do take you in, it'll only be for a few days." She touched his rough cheek. "It's not so bad, André. You can tell your grandchildren about it."

He smacked her hand away. "I'm not joking. I've got to hide." His voice rose. "If they find me, well . . . you don't think they'd let me get as far as a courtroom, do you? After—"

A Haitian woman pushed between them, trying to get to the trays of kingfish.

"After what, André?" Helen asked softly.

He glanced about in panic. "I can't tell you what happened. Not here."

"So you can't tell me, but I have to help. That's it, eh?" She shook her head.

"It's about Laporte."

His voice was so loud that Helen found herself looking anxiously over her shoulder now, too. A man in rubber boots carrying a crate of dried salt cod bumped along the crowded aisle. An old black woman was washing her hands at a basin in the centre of the store, carefully scraping scales off her fingertips. Helen turned to André. She didn't want to get mixed up in his silly melodrama. What gave him the right to drag her into it? If only she could begin to understand what went on in his crushed head. If only she could like him just a little. Was pity a good enough reason for getting involved?

No, it wasn't. "Okay, listen." She made up her mind. "You can stay out at our cottage on the lake for a week or two. There's a place in the basement nobody would ever find. I'll draw you a map."

"You've got to come too," he whined.

"Come on, André. I can't go away right now. I've got a million and one things to do."

"The cops are checking out all the cottages and farms. If they see any activity, they're bound to come snooping around."

"Oh, shit!" She swung away.

He grabbed her arm again. "Please, Helen."

"No." She shoved him away. "No."

"You're the only person I can trust."

She looked at him hopelessly. He meant it. She sighed. "I guess I could take something to work on. My work, eh?" She tried to smile. "But not past the end of the month, at the latest? After that"—she cut the air with her hands—"after that, you'll have to make other arrangements. That's it. That's final."

"Can we leave right now?"

"You've got to be joking." She laughed harshly. "I'm going away for the weekend." She hadn't known for sure until that moment, and she realized guiltily she was only doing it to prove her strength—now that she had given in. "There's a whole lot of stuff I've got to clear up before I leave."

"Tomorrow, then," he muttered sulkily.

"Fuck off, André! Who do you think you are, for God's sake? I said I'm going away for the weekend. I'm going away for the weekend."

"Put it off."

"No. Besides," she lied, "they'd think it was strange if I cancelled it now." There, that was an argument devious enough for André to understand. "Next Tuesday. Next Tuesday night."

"Not at night. I want to see where you're taking me."

"Jesus!"

"Wednesday morning. Seven o'clock. In your car." He turned and started to push his way down the aisle with the carrier-bag cradled in front of him.

"André," she called. "Come here."

Obediently, he came back. "What?"

"No guns," she said. "I mean that. I'll check. And no bombs."

"I don't have any. Not anymore. I left them behind."

She pointed at the plastic bag. He opened it and she looked inside. An old windbreaker and a cardboard box. Gingerly, she turned it over, and then began to laugh. "Oh, Andy, Andy."

Weakly, she leaned on the counter. Frozen fish sticks! Here! In Waldman's. He didn't even understand why she was laughing. How could she think of living in the same house with this madman. Alone, on the edge of nowhere. "Andy." She reached up on tiptoe and kissed him almost tenderly on the lips.

The city lies in fragments around me. I walk through it restlessly, unable to sleep.

The square is suddenly smaller now that the trees have lost their leaves. There's a light on in Claire's window and I'd love to go in and talk to her, smoke some dope, feel her warmth surround me. But I can't, because I know she'll try to persuade me not to go away with André. Damn it, Claire, it's not as if I want to go, I know I'm a fool, yet somehow I have to. Why? I'm not sure why. But when you're all that somebody has left to cling to, you don't tear yourself away, surely. Even if they pull you down with them? Yes, even then, Claire, even then. And that, I know, makes me a dangerous fool as well.

So I stand under the bare trees and watch the light in the window, the hanging plants and a shadow moving across the moulded ceiling. I remember that ceiling, Jean-Claude sprawled beside me, taking up all the sofa. My body aches to be touched.

Why, then, do I cut myself off from the people who think they want to love me?

I walk along the edge of the worn grass past an old bum sleeping on one of the benches. Newspapers poke out from the legs of his frayed pants. On the ground beside him is a brown paper bag with the neck of a bottle sticking out of it. The night is mild, he won't freeze yet.

On the corner of Saint Denis a man walks unsteadily across the street. I move away from him, but he steers himself towards me. He says something in an accent so stilted I don't understand. I tilt my head to one side.

"You got a light?" he repeats gutturally.

I search through my purse and hand him a book of matches. He scrapes one and throws it on the ground, then two more. *"Pas bon, pas bon,"* he splutters, and then says something else in a language I don't recognize.

"Here, let me." I take the matches from him and light his cigarette. He catches me by the wrist. He's not an old man, about forty, and not bad looking, with thick curly hair falling over his forehead. "Let go," I say, trying to keep the fear out of my voice.

He lets go. "I am Greek," he says, looking sad.

"Yes," I say. For once I don't tell him about my grandmother. I start to move away and he touches my shoulder hesitantly. I turn.

"You come with me?" he asks. "My wife"—he breathes smoke and the smell of booze all over me—"my wife go away."

"Fuck off!" I may be a fool, but even my charity, I notice with some relief, doesn't stretch this far.

"Yes." He nods enthusiastically. "Fucky fuck." He rubs his thumb between his fingers.

"Jesus, no!"

He pulls out his wallet and shows me a twenty dollar bill. "I pay. You nice girl." The bottom part of his face seems to have swelled like a dried fig in water. It bulges, too big for his forehead, too heavy.

I'm not really worried yet, not really afraid. Nothing can happen, surely, out here in the middle of the wide street. But what scares me is that I'm not nearly angry enough, I can't find the hatred in me, I don't want to have to kick and scratch and scream. God, am I conditioned to be so passive that I call submission pity?

I walk away from him down the street. He follows me and

I stop. *"Look,* go away," I shout. "Go home. You're drunk. You'll get into trouble. Trouble." He peers at me like a little boy, younger even than Mark, rolling the forbidding word around in his mind. He reaches out to feel my breast, but just as his fingers touch me, he turns and runs with astonishing agility back through the park. I watch him in numb surprise: is it some kind of trick, am I radioactive? Then, only then, I see the police car waiting at a red light up the street. The light changes to green and it cruises towards me, slows to walking pace for a second—don't stop, please don't stop—the heads glance over at me, laugh—all teeth—at a joke, accelerating off down the hill.

Trembling, I follow in the same direction. I should go home, perhaps drop in at Claire's, we could talk about this all night. But the city draws me into itself. What would I have done if the cops hadn't shown up? Now that it's over, I toy with the fantasy of going with the Greek, talking to him about his loneliness, helping him, and then . . . You fool, Helen, you dumb fool.

I walk down the hill towards the lighted student cafés at the lower end of the street. A singer with long blond hair and no teeth sits on the wall outside the National Library. As he picks away at an electric guitar, his small portable amplifier crackles and blares. The half dozen people on the sidewalk in front of him pass round a bottle of wine. It's Tuesday night, Wednesday morning, and the cafés are only half full. But here, still, some of the seriousness survives behind the laughing, arguing faces that lean across the tables towards each other. Each of them knows at least someone who was picked up in the middle of the night, interrogated, beaten, imprisoned. All of them have been stopped in the street, pushed against a wall and searched. They may have hidden their copies of *White Niggers of America,* but they won't need books now to make them remember.

A woman and a man come out of a doorway and walk ahead of me along the sidewalk. She's eighteen or nineteen, small and slight and full of energy, wrapped in a black shawl. She makes me feel younger, less alone. Every few steps they pause to kiss or nuzzle. She carries a rose, twirling it between her fingers, lifting it delicately to her nostrils. As they come up to an old Volkswagen, painted with pink and green flames over the rust spots, she points to a parking ticket on the windshield. She leans over to clamp her rose under the wiper blade. They laugh and turn off down a side street.

On the corner of Sainte Cathérine I pause, not knowing what to do. Shall I go home? But no, I don't want to sleep, I don't want to be on my own, I don't want to be with somebody else I know. I am saying good-bye.

I walk along Sainte Cathérine to Saint Laurent, where the hookers teeter from doorway to doorway, their middle-aged customers tracing every move. I even recognize one of the girls —a girl with a slack, vacant, country face. I smile at her and she scowls back at me suspiciously. I go into a crowded snack bar and order some French fries and a Pepsi. The neon lights flicker and glare. Four guys in the first ten minutes try to pick me up, but they scuttle away again when I don't even bother to reply. An enormously fat, fortyish woman in a tight, low-cut black dress sits down beside a bald man in a three-piece suit. She whispers something to him and he shakes his head. She takes his limp hand and places it on her crotch. He shakes his head more vigorously. She sighs and heaves herself up. As she passes next to me, I see the shadow of a beard underneath the makeup on her chin.

I sit for more than an hour, warmed by the smell of grease and vinegar. Two drag queens at the next table gossip tipsily. One of them is so drunk he keels over and falls on the floor. The girl who scowled at me on the street comes running across from the counter and lifts him up. She brushes down his pink satin dress. "It's split along the seam at the back," she says.

"Oh, fuck," he says and starts to cry.

She smooths his hair. "I'll sew it up for you tomorrow," she whispers.

Outside, the wind whips at me. The street is almost empty, but further back at the intersection the roof light on a blue police ambulance flashes and bounces off the shop windows. What am I doing here? Where shall I go?

I wander haphazardly into the empty centre of the city. Skyscrapers and vacant parking lots. Overpasses, underpasses, métro stations, buried shopping malls. This is the city Mayor Drapeau has made his own—desolate, abandoned by the past. The Mayor Drapeau who built gigantic hoardings in front of the slums to hide them from the tourists who came to visit Expo. The Mayor Drapeau who cut out his city's heart to make it more mechanical. It survives despite him, each limb throbbing to its own pulse.

I walk up another hill, tired now but unable to stop, and come to the old business section, granite insurance buildings and new steel banks, a city—no, a country—built with Scottish thrift and cunning. A quarter of me has roots somewhere far back, beyond even my grandfather, in those solid masculine virtues of the manse and croft. The rest of me—a muddle of French and Greek—rebels against their cautious greed.

I cut across Place d'Armes to the nondescript façade of Notre Dame. We hardly ever came here when I was a child. Just once or twice for Mass. Yet I remember the intricately carved and painted interior, a dazzling melodrama of blue and gold. Years, years ago. Was it too self-indulgent for my mother's tastes? But how lovely it seemed after the cruelty of Brother André's bloated Oratory. And down near the front to the right of the altar, does the toy aeroplane still fly? Hanging from a thread and made of silvered tin, it soars over the banks of candles glittering below it. The sign says: Pray to Mary and let your soul take off. Oh, I'd love to see it again. I rattle the handle, but of course the door is locked.

I am almost running now as I plunge into the maze of cobbled alleyways of Old Montréal, the warehouses and sailmakers and ship's chandlers of another age. I like the men who used to live here more than the bankers and the prim insurance brokers. These men were traders and craftsmen, they knew certain facts precisely, before the deadly abstractions of wealth. But they were just as callous in the end; their objects meant more than the lives of the people who trapped or dug or sweated for them. They're long gone now, wiped out by the moneymen, replaced by entrepreneurs with swinging boutiques and baroque restaurants. All one can say is that it may be slightly better than Mayor Drapeau's wasteland. But lifeless, too; full of deception.

I find nothing to touch that doesn't melt away.

I come out into Place Jacques Cartier and look around in exhaustion. It is empty. The bars closed hours ago, the hordes of kids who played folk music in the doorways or squatted on crates of beer in the middle of the square have all gone home. Littered with their debris, the flagstones stretch up the hill to the alien statue of Nelson and, farther off, the balcony from which De Gaulle shouted to a swaying throng: *"Vive le Québec, Vive le Québec Libre."* The crowd roared. My mother's hero once, but not anymore. "The ignorant old ass," she said contemptuously. "He doesn't know what he's doing."

My stepfather, sick and soon to die but still full of mockery, laughed: "They say he can't even see where he's going any longer. He's too vain to wear glasses, you know. When he's in public he tells them: *'Dirigez-moi vers la foule.'* That should be his epitaph. 'Point me towards the crowd.' "

The crowd has gone into hiding. I sink onto a bench, pulling my coat around me. I look down towards the towering elevators and warehouses that line the riverfront, then back up the square again. If only I could paint what I've seen tonight, all in a single picture. A pigeon flies from the Iroquois Hotel to the Nelson Tavern, and as I watch it disappear, I realize the sky behind it has grown lighter. I get to my feet and walk heavily up the hill, hoping to find a taxi soon.

André will be waiting for me.

André slept in a small visitor's room at the back. They kept the curtains drawn and he never switched on the light. From there, if he needed to, he'd be able to get straight down into the cellar without being seen.

In the mornings, once André had done his exercises, he made omelettes for them both. He was proud of his omelettes, light and fluffy and full of onions, peppers, herbs and garlic. "We had this maid who showed me," he explained, as he lifted the firm edge to allow some of the liquid yolk to run down onto the skillet.

"Madame Langlois in the village store will be wondering how I manage to eat so many eggs," Helen laughed.

André whirled round in alarm, knocking a bowl to the floor. "Is she getting suspicious?" he asked.

"No," Helen shushed him. "She wouldn't notice anything. She's drunk by ten in the morning." She knelt to pick up the shards.

"Why did you say she would, then?"

"I was joking."

"Your omelette's ready and you haven't even heated the plates," he said angrily.

Over breakfast they listened to the radio and then settled down for the long day together, she by the window, he in the shadows. Sometimes they talked, but usually they worked in silence. Helen found it surprisingly easy to live with him. He was meticulous and obsessively neat, but on the whole that pleased her. He didn't get in her way. And yet by the end of the day, by the time he went reluctantly to bed, her whole body was rigid with tension. It was nothing he said, nothing he did, it was simply who he was.

She told herself she was silly, and masturbated to try to escape.

"Fuck," she said, scraping away a layer of cerulean she'd mixed with horsehair. "It's not working." With the palette knife she gouged angrily into the layers of paint beneath, so that just a few traces of the blue clung along the edges of the grooves. There, that was better. New depths began to appear. In the lower left-hand corner the shadow of a police riot squad shone through. Rapidly, she etched in the reflected outlines of a group of strikers and pickets, their heads overlapping the helmets of the police. The picture was a lake in which the violence of the past few weeks vibrated. She knelt back on her haunches, then threw herself into it once more: lake and city, cops and workers, conflict on conflict.

André didn't approve of her painting. It was formalist, he said, a symptom of bourgeois avant-gardism.

"What do you want?" she asked. "Socialist realism again? Smiling women tractor drivers and Red Army soldiers picking peaches? You know what, André? I think you're a closet Stalinist."

"Perhaps," he said. "I'm very disillusioned with Trotsky."

The outline of a picket sign coincided exactly with a riot squad shield. That was what she wanted: an ambiguity that would contain contradiction, but leave no doubt as to its ultimate point. "Why?" she asked, absorbed in the movement of her fingers.

She didn't really listen to his attempt to answer. "Discipline," he mumbled. "Trotsky lacked discipline. He couldn't impose it on his followers. Or even on himself. Look at him: he always got sick at the crucial moment." André's fists clenched. "He was afraid to move till it was too late. He saw clearly enough what had to be done. But it was always too late and the only way out was to make himself sick. He played right into Stalin's hands. There was a fundamental breakdown of the will."

"And will is all that matters?" Helen got to her feet, looking down at the painting. It was almost finished. Flapping her arms about to try to relax them, she wandered over to André's corner and stood behind him. He didn't like that, she knew. He spent precisely two hours a day rearranging the stamp collection he'd kept since he was a child, three reading an ancient edition of the Encyclopaedia Britannica, and another two poring over David's *Sunday Times Atlas.* Afterwards, she'd have to test him. What are the key towns on Mindanao, (a) on the coast, (b) in the interior? What's the distance from Phnom Penh to Aranya Prathet? What's the main border crossing point between Pakistan and Iran?

"How do you know *you* won't get sick at the crucial moment?" she asked. "Supposing you're even able to recognize it?"

André didn't look round at her. He knew he wouldn't get sick. He was fanatical about his health, gargling three times a day, guzzling masses of multivitamins, a hundred pushups morning and evening. Carefully, he fitted a hinge to the back of a stamp, lining it up perfectly with one on the other side of the page. Cyprus, 1947, mint, fifteen piastres.

"Why do you collect such dull stamps?" she asked. "Easter Seals are more alive."

That, at least, made him react. He glared up at her. "I don't think they're dull."

"All these Commonwealth stamps you've got. Don't you ever look at them? Bland, self-satisfied colonial exploitation, that's all I can see. They're all the fucking same. The same pastel colours, the same portrait of the king, the same incompetent engravings of forts and churches."

A puzzled frown drifted across his opaque eyes. "I don't think they're dull," he repeated. "And they're certainly not all the same, you know. There are thousands of variations, watermarks, perforations, overprints, anniversary issues."

He looked so hurt she was sorry she'd attacked him. "I guess you never come to an end of it," she suggested gently.

"That's right. That's why it's not dull," he insisted eagerly. "There's no end to it, no matter how you try."

She went back to where she had been, as far away from him

as possible. How he frightened her. She kneaded the muscles in the back of her neck. The painting, she could see now, was still too simple. She washed a thin veil of watered-down acrylic over part of the picket line.

"Yes," she murmured, and her brain unclenched. She leaned against the window, pressing the side of her head against the glass. From here, she could see down to the clump of bushes, bigger now and leafless, where she and David first made a sort of love. The light was fading and she could hardly see André in the shadows when she turned back into the room.

André is furious when I tell him I'm bringing the kids up here for the weekend.

"You're so *fucking* irresponsible," he yells. "Why didn't you ask me first? Can't you see how stupid it is?"

Blue veins stand out in his shining temples. I try not to back away from him. "No. I can't," I shout.

"They'll tell David I'm here."

"So what?"

He pauses, then kicks the table leg. "He'll think we're lovers."

I laugh raucously. "Of course, he won't. And even if he does, what does it matter?"

"He'll go to the cops."

"Don't be absurd. You're so paranoid, it's unbelievable."

"I'll have to stay in the cellar while you go to fetch them."

"Poor André!" I mock him.

"Can't you put it off? Please, Helen."

"No, fuck it, I can't. They need to see me."

And oh, how I need them!

By the time we get to the cottage, six inches of snow have fallen—the first real snow of the winter. It makes this a private world, cut off from the ill feeling of the Friday evening city. The car slithers from side to side on the steep bends of the driveway, then catches the flat cardboard house in its headlights. The lake is a black space beyond. As soon as he jumps out, Mark flings himself down in a bank of snow. Whooping with joy, he makes the shape of a frantic angel with his arms.

André takes to him immediately. Within half an hour I lose my son as André shows him the stamps, explaining everything in solemn detail. Yet he hates Ann. Yes, hates. How can you hate a child you've never seen before? Somehow or other, he persuades Mark to tell him about Ann's secret crush on a boy called Scott Chambers; then at dinner he teases her mercilessly about it. I see the pained incomprehension in her eyes.

"Shut up, André," I say.

He winks at Mark and they giggle.

Afterwards, in the kitchen, Ann whispers to me, "Are you and André like . . . having a relationship?"

"God, no," I laugh and hand her another plate to dry. "He just needs somewhere to stay."

"That's all? Promise?"

I slit my throat.

"Good," she says and hugs me. "I think he stinks."

On Saturday morning, we see the fox. Not so much a fox as a red streak of astonishing warmth hurtling across the dazzling snow. After it's gone, Ann stands with her mouth open.

"Oh, wow!" She shakes her head violently. "Wow! I've never seen anything as beautiful as that."

The sky is bright blue.

In parkas we go out to look at the tracks. Some chickadees are playing in the cedars down by the boathouse, shaking snow from the branches.

"Look at the position of its feet," Ann says. "It wasn't even going flat out. If it had of been, its rear paws would be right out in front. It was just . . . loping."

She tries to make a cast of the tracks, but the snow melts as she pours in the plaster of Paris.

"Try mixing it with vinegar," I suggest.

It still melts.

"Oh, damn it, it doesn't matter," she says, standing up. "I don't need a lousy cast to remember something like that." She looks around her at the shining rocks and the sharp black trees. "You know what I'd really like to do? I'd like to live up in the Yukon. Where there's nobody else at all." She kicks up a shower of powder. "Nobody. I think the city's really crappy, don't you?"

"What'd you do?"

"I'd write."

"Write!" I wince with embarrassment as I realize I'd always thought of her being a doctor. Or a lawyer. Though a radical one, of course!

"Yeah, I'm writing science fiction now. About two kids who get sucked up into space."

Absentmindedly I try to make a snowball; the dry flakes squeeze between my leather fingers. "You can't just opt out," I say.

Her face is a perfect oval. She looks sideways at me from under long pale eyelashes. "That's what you're doing."

"No," I say. "It's not. It mustn't be. I'm coming back. I know what I'm going to do."

We go inside.

Later, Ann and Mark go off tobogganing. André tells them to be careful. When they get back, it's already dark, they're soaked and frozen and their cheeks gleam.

"Where have you been?" André challenges them angrily. "We were worried."

"André!" I protest. "I wasn't."

"I was."

"There were lots of kids from the village." Mark blows on the hot chocolate.

I hear André's fingers drumming. "Who?" I ask.

"Oh, Mike and Régis and Gilles."

"And Sarah."

"Yeah, and Sarah. And Hank Kochitsky. He went right through a barbed wire fence."

They snicker.

"You should of heard him swear," Mark says.

"Shsh," says Ann.

"What did he say?" I ask.

She looks at André. "I've forgotten."

"No, come on," I laugh. "What did he say? I really want to know."

"He said: 'You cocksuckin', motherfuckin' son of a bitch.' "

Mark hiccups with laughter.

"Who was he talking to?"

Ann smiles. "The fence, I guess."

At night we lie on my bed, the two of us, little mother, big daughter, chattering like birds. Mark and André are playing cards. The TV flickers, but the sound is off. We nibble from a bowl of pistachios between us.

"I like these," Ann says. "Except they really mess up your fingernails." Two years ago she gnawed her nails till they bled. She's changing so quickly I can't help wanting to hold on to her. No, no, I insist to myself, not to hold on, but to help her slow down the rush. Which is what she must want, too, surely.

"Try opening them with a shell," I say.

The bed is big and rumpled and covered with pillows.

"What did you mean when you said you know what you're going to do?"

I look at her questioningly.

"You know." She punches my arm. "What you said this morning, about coming back to the city?"

The horizontal hold on the TV has slipped, I don't bother

to adjust it. "I guess I meant I've got my priorities sorted out now. For the past six months I've been bouncing around like a ball in a pinball machine. Kadunk, kadunk, kadunk, banging into whatever got in my way." She laughs, and nods for me to go on. "I've got it worked out pretty well now. What matters to me? You." I touch her thigh. "You matter to me. I want to be with you more. And my painting. And . . . politics. The rest, well, it's just confusion. But those three things are clear. I'm going to get a new place, not a house, I don't want a house, but a big old apartment with lots of rooms. You know, do it up so you can be with me. If you want to."

She sits up and crosses her legs, looking at me critically. "And Mark," she says at last. "Don't forget about him."

"I wasn't," I say guiltily.

"You do kind of forget him sometimes, though," she says. "Not neglect, just forget. Because he's a kid, eh? And a boy. But he's really neat. We were staying at Bonne Maman's when David was away for a couple of days, and she started to give Mark a hard time because he never folded his clothes. Real trivial, eh? She was, like, shouting at him: 'Does your mother do everything for you?' And he said: 'Yes, she does. And I would do everything for her if she wanted me to.' "

My eyes water. I adjust the TV.

"She was really crabby," Ann goes on, as I scramble back beside her. "I guess it's her age. She told me I was a spoilt brat." She imitates my mother's haughty voice perfectly. " 'What gives you the right to be so difficult?' And I said"—her voice filled with sweetness—" 'Sure, I'm being difficult. I'm an adolescent. Almost. I'm meant to be difficult, Bonne Maman. They told us at school, it's a difficult time. And you're just making it worse.' "

"Heavens. She'd have beaten me half to death for that."

"I made sure I was near the door."

We go on eating nuts.

"Don't be too hard on her," I say, feeling dishonest for encouraging Ann. "Her own childhood was awful. Mamie—

well, you know how sweet she seems, but she was a real bitch as a mother. Really," I insist. "And Bonne Maman, it's not that she doesn't care, she does, desperately, but she can't allow herself to show it." I'm on the edge of sentimental weepiness and Ann pats my hand. "That's why I want a place to be with you. Both of you. I don't want to end up like that, too, because of the way she treated me and the way Mamie treated her. And the way her mother treated her, too, probably. Oh, forever. We've got to break out of that pattern. Do you understand?"

In the darkness, Mark cries out. I stroke his face, my fingers gliding over his skin. He mutters and heaves in his sleep. I can't make out what he's trying to say.

Then: "The tiger," he croaks, "the tiger."

I hold his small, muscular shoulders.

His voice is suddenly loud and clear. "The tiger is so kind," he shouts.

His knotted body relaxes. I look at his face and a wide smile spreads across it. Then it tightens again and the nerves twang in and out. But still I don't waken him. I don't dare to waken him, for fear that what I wake him to will somehow be more painful even than what he's going through.

André heard the tires on the driveway; it was as if he was waiting for them. Helen looked round in surprise as he bolted across the room, banging open the door at the top of the basement stairs. Then she too heard the crunching snow. "Get the stamps," André called. He slipped and fell down the last few steps, letting out a muffled scream.

Helen didn't have time to clear away the albums. She picked up the chair and arranged the books and the loose-leaf pages of stamps into what she hoped would look like a tidy, unused pile. A fist banged on the door; she was out of breath as she opened it.

"Mrs."—the inspector looked down at the clipboard in his hand—"Dawson? Mind if I come in a moment?" He was a big man, about fifty, with short greying hair and a square, heavily lined face. Deep-set, soft eyes. His uniform was neatly pressed, pulled tight across a slack belly.

"I'm working," she said.

"I don't want to disturb you," he said. "It's too cold to keep you standing outside talking." His voice was kind; she let him in.

He kicked off his galoshes. "We're just checking on all the empty cottages, eh? Didn't even know you were here."

"I came up for a few days to get some work finished," she explained nervously, irritated by her nervousness.

He walked about casually, missing nothing. They had been careful, washing up the telltale dishes as soon as they were used, one tube of toothpaste on the bathroom shelf. "You collect stamps, then?" he asked, flicking through the books. The cellar door was swinging slightly.

"My kids," she explained, though the material was much too detailed for children. She felt her cheeks must be blushing. "They were here at the weekend."

He nodded. "That's right. I saw them on Ryan's hill." So he did know she was here. He stood over the painting, reading the slogan that was half-buried under banks of paint: 'Not just the image, the just image.' And beneath that, the open trunk of the car in which Pierre Laporte's body had been found. "Beyond me, I'm afraid." He shook his head, but not rudely, almost in self-deprecation. "The wife paints, though. That paint by numbers stuff she started with, but she's on to her own ideas now. We got paintings all over the house. Closets full of the darn things."

Helen was sure he was listening. "Well . . ." she said, fiddling impatiently.

"You'll let me know if you see anything strange, won't you, Mrs. Dawson?"

"There's a man down in the trees by the boathouse," she said, getting a grip on herself. "Would you say that was strange?"

"No," he smiled. "Just Charlie looking around. We've had this report, eh? One of those guys who killed Monsieur Laporte may be in the area somewhere. Likely as not, it's false. But you got to check it out."

"Why would he be up here?"

"He'll be wherever there's someone to hide him, won't he? I'll tell my people to keep an eye open for you whenever they're passing."

After he left, she squinted through a gap in the curtains at the car. There was another car half-hidden back up the driveway. For half an hour she kept watch on the emptiness, then let André out. She told him what had happened.

"André," she said, trying not to see the contortions of his face, "what do they want you for?"

Claire walked on one side of the path, I on the other. The weather had turned mild, melting most of the snow, then frozen again. The ruts in the path were full of ice and we had to walk carefully, our arms flung out for balance. Once, Claire in her high leather boots started to slide and couldn't stop. "Help," she cried. I stretched out to catch her hand, but couldn't quite reach.

Her fingers just missed mine and I almost fell, too.

"Oh!" she gasped. She sat with the air blown out of her, moaning and laughing.

I pulled her up and we stumbled on, trying to keep to the clumps of frozen grass along the edges.

"Was André mad when you told him I was coming?"

"André!" I said.

"He hates me."

"Not you especially. Everyone."

"Yes, but he wants you all to himself. And then he tried to lay me, too. Said he wanted to educate me politically. Little prick. Have you fucked him yet?"

"Ugh." I shook my head violently.

"Take my word for it. It's wee-urd. Like being raped by ectoplasm. Jesus! You know, in your armpits, your ears, your . . . navel? I guess it could be great if it was tender, but no way." She shivered. "I got him in the end, though, son of a bitch."

"How?"

"Just as he was about to impregnate me—politically speaking, eh?—I sort of contracted." She clasped her palms together. "Squeezed him out like a blackhead." Her voice plunged into a deep, throaty laugh.

I looked across at her. "Oh, Claire."

"Pop," she said, letting the sound resonate on her lips. "Pop. Poor little André. Pop. Squeezed out like a blackhead."

I didn't ask her why she went to bed with him in the first place.

We came to a field sloping down to the lake, dotted with spots of frozen cow dung. Claire prised one up and tried to throw it down the hill like a Frisbee.

"I'm glad you came," I said, taking her hand.

"I'm glad I came."

"Why did you come?"

"I was worried about you. All alone in the fucking tundra with that evil little blackhead."

"Who told you he was here?"

"We have our sources, darling," she said in a bass, theatrical voice.

We saw a fallen elm and sat down on the trunk with our backs to the cold yellow sun. Our fur coats touched.

"Are you okay, Claire?"

"I think so. Just about." She took my hand and traced the seams on the backs of my gloves. "Physically, I'm getting over it. Psychologically, I guess, too. I don't waken up screaming anymore, anyway." Strands of blonde hair hung down from her woolen hat. Her face became preoccupied and the bloom went off her cheeks. "I don't want to live like this any longer, Helen. I don't even know who I am, for fuck's sake. You know, I'm acting all the time and, shit, it's about time I found out what I'm running away from. I go into a room and I know people will concentrate on me and I get a real hit from knowing it. But lookit, I'm just using that to get away from what I really am, aren't I?"

In silence I looked down towards the bottom of the field. Snow was still piled in drifts around the roots of the bullrushes along the shore. These moments of solemn self-pity in Claire grated on me.

"It's so fucking hard. This has got to be the hardest time of all, eh? To be a woman? I mean, everything's changing. Everything. All this talk about freedom. Sure, down in the Gaspé, that sounded easy. I was so fucking naive you wouldn't believe it, Helen. Like, the first guy I went with, he asked me if I was a virgin and I didn't even know what he meant." She shook her head wryly. "Now, Jesus Christ, I'm free from something I don't even know I want to be free from and I'm scared shitless I'm never going to be free from something else in me that, oh"—she rubbed her knuckles into her eyes—"hell, I only know it's there because it's crushing me."

I took her hand.

"I'm not going to work anymore, Helen. I'm tired of all those nasty little mannikins who daren't even look me in the eye.

Their cowardice destroys me." She waved her arms dramatically and her nose started to run. "Have you got a Kleenex?"

As I searched through my pockets, I made up my mind. Maybe she was melodramatic and, now and again, a little dumb. Still, she was so much more palpably real than anyone else I knew. She threw herself about in a self-destructive dance, yet she never let it wipe her out completely. "I've been thinking, Claire. Why don't we find a place"—I hesitated—"a house, or something, we could share together?"

She blew her nose like a foghorn. "My God," she said. The laugh started in her belly and rippled out into the rest of her body.

"What's wrong?" I asked, offended.

With a splutter she controlled herself. "Well, it's incredible. That's why I came up here. Mainly, anyway. To ask *you* that. Liz has found a place in Outremont—a house on Champagneur—and we wanted you to come in on it, too."

"Liz?" I said doubtfully.

"She's all right. Once you know her. Oh, listen, Helen, it'd really be great."

"I guess." I paused. "But three people? I don't know. Look, I need at least four rooms to myself, for me and the kids and a place to work on my own." Suddenly, the idea frightened me. What was I getting into? "I need to be on my own a lot."

I stared out across the black lake. Ice was spreading over the patches of dead water near the shore.

"Helen." It was Claire's turn to console me, though the loneliness I felt had nothing really to do with what we were talking about. "We all need our own space. Liz likes you. The house is gigantic; it's full of space. Right now it's three big apartments, high ceilings, pine floors, the works. Liz's idea is we could each have a floor to ourselves, and be together, too. Listen." With her free hand she turned my chin towards her, her blue eyes looking into mine. "Say yes."

I nodded and kissed her cheek. Her mouth slid across to

mine, her lips warm and gentle, I gasped for breath. Our tongues touched, not forcing, touching, I didn't struggle away. When we did draw apart a little, I darted back in and kissed her more violently, probingly.

An image clogged my mind. "Why did you let André?" My voice was still soft, but the idea of them together horrified me. I pulled away from her. "You're very . . . promiscuous."

"I used to tell myself you could never really know what someone was like till you'd fucked him." She smiled and went into her deep voice. "A rather simpleminded fallacy, I'm afraid."

"Yes," I said. With my teeth I pulled off my right glove and let my hand snake its way beneath her coat. Shaking, my fingers worked through the layers of clothing to the warmth of the flesh around her waist.

"Oh," she murmured, and then she opened her eyes. "This is better than the back seat of a '59 Chev with smelly old Claude Desbiens."

I jerked away and stood up. "What am I doing?" I shook myself like a dog coming out of the water.

She touched the lower part of my back. "It's okay."

I sat down and we leaned against each other. My black hair faded into hers.

"I've got lots of messages for you."

"Who from?"

"Well, Akiyo. He sends his love."

I winced.

"He was the one who found out you were up here with André."

"How?"

"He knows lots of people." She shrugged. "He was worried." She paused as if she were about to tell me more, then went on: "We've sort of been together quite a bit. He's okay, actually. I mean, he's a bastard, but you don't expect anything from him, so it's really good when he's nice." She glanced sideways to see if I would disapprove. "And then he seems to have overcome some of his initial revulsion to all my flesh."

Even as a joke, I hated her for saying that. "Who else?" I asked distantly.

"Oh, well, God's gift himself—Jean-Claude?—he's been phoning constantly. I guess he just can't bear to let go of anyone, can't bear to be dropped. Men do the dropping, women are the droppees, eh? God, how he clings!"

"He's phoned a lot?" I asked, secretly pleased at the thought.

"Yeah, little jerk. 'Claire,' " she mimicked his tremulous voice. " 'I'm really concerned about Helen, eh. She's going through a difficult time. I want to help her.' "

I smiled sadly. There was ice in my eyelashes. "My first lover and it had to be Jean-Claude. What a choice! He makes you feel you're really unique. But now I see what's wrong with him. He fucks because he's empty. He fucks out of hatred." I stood up and started to swing my arms about like a windmill. "God, it's freezing. Those memories don't do much to keep you warm, do they?"

Claire stayed sitting down. "And Peter, too."

"Oh?" I looked away from her.

"Remember him?" she asked.

"Yes." I didn't want to talk about this.

"He's pretty pissed off with you."

"I guess he has the right to be." Our shadows stretched almost as far as the margins of the lake. "Come on, Claire, let's go."

She didn't move. "I've never really gotten through to him," she probed. "He's very distant on the phone."

"He can be. Look, I can't talk about Peter, Claire. I'm not hiding anything. But I just don't know how I feel about him. I like him. I like him a lot. He's a good person . . . I think. I could see myself having a really solid thing with him. In another century perhaps. But I'm not sure I can handle that right now. It would take all my time and energy to make it work. I'm scared of getting too close to him—he sucks you in, and then. . . . Well, I can't stand all the zombies who're around him all the time. Shit, I don't know." The more I tried to be honest, the more unclear my feelings became. "Maybe if he's very, very patient." I stamped my feet in irritation. "Men aren't programmed for patience."

I held out my hand to Claire and she got to her feet. Bumping and slipping, we walked diagonally across the field.

"Fucking men," she said as we reached the gate. "They're like daffodils, eh? With their floppy egos."

"Yes," I said, though that wasn't what I'd been trying to say at all.

"I mean, objectively, women are just so much better, aren't they? It's obvious, the ideal form of human society is a matriarchy. That's how it all started. What we need is a society where men are made to realize that they're completely inessential."

"Mobile sperm banks," I laughed. But again, it wasn't what I meant. I stopped and held on to the worn grey cedar of a snake fence. Clumps of birches grew along the edges of the field. Their twigs were tangled and broken, but the tips glowed red already with next spring's buds. Behind them rose a large oak tree, its leaves still clinging to the black branches—light brown, oily leaves, not dead at all, not giving in. On one sprig snow had nested, wonderful birds with white breasts and rich brown wings.

"I've been thinking," I said. "About my grandmother? Things were so simple for her, and so impossible. She's very physical, sensual, even now. But all she could be, as a woman, was a receptacle. She couldn't have an independent sexuality. I mean, think of the frustration, Claire. It must have killed her. The danger is that when you try to break out of that role, you end up at the opposite extreme. A sort of surrogate male? All the women I know are into it, for Christ's sake, fuck and run, fuck and run, that whole male thing. I mean, look at you, Claire, eh, a cock in every orifice." I touched her face gently. "I know, I like it, too; I like the absurdity of waking up in the morning and beginning to remember the absolutely foul things I did the night before. But I don't want to live like that, Claire. Not as something I end up being. There's got to be more."

She nodded eagerly, with doubt behind it.

"I like you, Claire, I really do. But I don't want to make a fool of myself. Be patient, too?"

We kissed, our bodies touching through layers of fur and wool.

"Come back with me tonight," she whispered urgently. "André's an asshole."

"It's only another ten days. I promised him—the end of the month. Then we'll see."

"Okay," she gave in reluctantly. "But I'm warning you"—she flapped her hands in front of her face in mock panic—"it's like ectoplasm."

When we had stopped giggling, we walked back along the darkening lane together.

Half drunk and morose, André lay on Helen's bed.

The room had been David's parents' once and it was still decorated with their things. Hunting prints on the walls, bulging Chinese vases converted into lamps, comfortable armchairs and old pine chests, a bed that creaked in its carved wood frame. And here was Helen lying on it with another man. A Goldman, a terrorist. Oh, horror, horror! Which was worse? She laughed and reached down to the crate of beer on the floor.

"This is the real Canajun way to watch a hockey game." She flicked the bottle top across the room at one of her mother-in-law's Thai silk lampshades. "A crate of beer under the bed. Don't it make you feel Canajun, eh, boy?"

André didn't reply. His eyes were glazed.

She propped herself on her elbow and looked down at him. "What's the matter, shweeheart?" she asked enthusiastically.

"Nothing."

She turned back to the game. A bunch of players were gathered around, clutching each other's jerseys. "Frankly, I can't think of anything I'd rather do than lie here watching the Leafs play—who is it, the North Stars? With you, André my love."

"Yes." He was green.

"If you're going to be sick, go to the bathroom, okay? You can't drink, can you?"

"No," he said. "Not since I had my gall bladder out."

"I thought only menopausal housewives were supposed to have gall bladders. Do you have a scar?"

"Yes," he nodded.

"Let me see." She began to tug at his belt. "I want to see your goddamn scar."

In his panic he spilled beer on the bedcover.

"Oh, André." She leaned closer to him. "You're a dead loss, aren't you?" She remembered Claire's warning, but in the back of her mind it must have been tickling the edges of her imagination. She didn't want to make love to André—heaven forbid!—but she wanted to tease herself with the possibility. Had she been sober, the idea would have repelled her. But she wasn't sober. She put one leg across his thin thighs and knelt above him. "I'm going to pump some life into you," she said, putting her hands under his rib cage. The top of her bathrobe fell open and her breasts swung free. "Oops," she said. Mesmerized, André reached up to them. She pushed his hands down and pressed heavily on his stomach.

Gulping, he threw her off and ran to the bathroom.

"Oh, God," she said and reached down for another beer. The bed was high off the floor and she almost fell out. She didn't bother to straighten her robe. "André, are you all right?" she called. There was no reply. She balanced the cold bottle on her pubic hair.

"Why did you do that?" he asked when he came back from the bathroom. He slumped down in one of the armchairs. His face was the colour of pastry, dotted with violet spots.

She hummed nonchalantly and bent her legs slightly so that the bottle rose up.

"Stop that, you bitch," he shouted and knocked a lamp on the floor.

The fury in his eyes bit into her. Shakily she pulled the robe tight and knotted the belt.

"I don't want—" he began, then groaned, rolling himself from side to side.

She put the half-empty bottle back in the crate. "I'm sorry, André," she said.

The hockey game continued.

"My mother used to buy me stuff all the time," he said almost inaudibly. Helen listened, he wasn't speaking to her. "Every time something was wrong at home, she'd buy me a present; a toy, a bike, a new suit. When I was seventeen, just after you got married—you were in Europe?—I had a breakdown. The first. I moved up into the attic to get away from the rest of them. I spent more and more of my time up there. 'Andrew needs to be on his own,' my mother said. Then one night I heard someone screaming hysterically, and I saw my mother climbing the stairs and walking towards me and then I felt her slapping somebody in the face. After that, they gave me a car."

Helen watched his body twist, wanting to help him, afraid even to move a finger.

"Pigs," André spat. "They'd never tell me what happened to them during the war. I kept on saying, it's my history, too, but they'd never tell me a goddamn thing. The last time I was up there we had a fight about the F.L.Q. I mean, they're fucking Liberals; Bourassa, even Drapeau, are their friends, for God's sake. I said they were Fascists and my mother broke down and sobbed about having a racist for a son. Then, she told me. But it was too late. She told me about the last days in Dachau. You know, fighting for potato peelings, lying on a bed with ten other people and half of them dead. And about having this vision of her father, who'd been shot, telling her she'd survive. I went crazy that night with a kind of joy. The next morning I phoned her up. I thought, God, it must have been so traumatic for her, letting it all come out like that after so long. And she didn't remember a fucking thing. All she went on about was the fight we'd had, how I'd been so rude to my Dad and would have to apologize. Nothing else. She wouldn't even talk about it."

"André," Helen murmured and went and sat on the rug at his feet. She leaned her head against his knees.

"Cunt," he said. "I can smell them, the stink of them on me. When I was ten I'd wash my hands fifty times a day. Each finger separately ten times, fifty times a day." He stared straight across the room without once looking down at her. "I still do it if I don't watch myself."

"André, I'm sorry for what I did. It wasn't fair." She shivered. How could she have done that after everything she'd said to Claire? I don't want to live like that, she'd protested, and here she was, just a coy little cock-teaser. What a hypocrite she was! She reached up and touched André's long spotless fingers.

"I've got to get rid of them," he muttered. "One by one."

"No," she insisted with all her conviction. "Getting rid of what's ugly doesn't make the world more beautiful." It was, she realized halfheartedly, an aesthetic statement, too. "It only makes it emptier."

The words were irrelevant, he paid no attention. "I couldn't stand the sight of him bleeding," he said.

She pulled her hand away from the current in his body.

"Who?" she asked, though she knew.

"He tried to jump out the fucking window. He heard the siren of a cop car and tried to jump out. The asshole. We pulled him back in. He was cut all over, his wrists, his stomach. He was begging us to take him to a hospital. We couldn't. We bandaged him up but the blood kept on coming through. Like a pig."

Helen shuffled away and sat in a tight knot against the foot of the bed.

"We had to get rid of him."

"Yes," she whispered.

"With the fucking crucifix round his neck." He started to laugh. "Nobody tried to stop it. The cops could have walked in there anytime. They knew where we were. They'd been watching Paul Rose for weeks. And me. They knew I was there. I *know* when I'm being followed," he said. "They could have stopped it anytime. They wanted him dead, too."

How could she believe him?

Though she said nothing, he turned on her in a rage. "Of course, the cops wanted it to happen. Why d'you think they put me on to the Roses in the first place? Shit, half of the communiqués, even, they issued themselves. Who ever heard of the Dieppe cell? There wasn't any fucking Dieppe cell. The cops made it up." His arms were nailed to the side of the chair or he would have hit her. "You dumb bitch, can't you see? Get out of here. They know I'm here."

"No," she said in disbelief. "I'm sure they don't suspect a thing."

"You dumb bitch," he cried in agony. "Of course, they know." André was shaking uncontrollably.

Helen watched him in horror. Knowing it was useless, despite her disgust, she forced herself to crawl over to him.

We stand in line in the plastic chapel.

We have moved to the next stage in the game. My mother is the old crone of the family now. And I, in one stroke, face middle age.

Ann is next to me and on the other side of her, somewhat apart, is her father, a man named David.

My mother wears a black coat and a black hat. David wears a black coat and a black tie. The coat I wear is a rich brown colour, the colour of autumn. I refuse to go into mourning for Helena. I remember her as she must have been, long before I ever knew her. When I was a little girl I walked along a street here in Montréal, my hand in hers, she was already very old. In a doorway some scruffy men were playing music. Accordion, harmonica, spoons, maybe even a guitar, a Québécois jig, their feet clattering out the rhythm on the sidewalk. We stopped. My mother, I remember thinking, would have dragged me straight on by. As we listened, I looked up at Helena, she was lost in the music. Little by little her feet started to dance, her old body swaying with the melody.

Remembering my embarrassment, I start to cry.

But no, I will not allow myself to mourn for her, I shall be strong, like her daughter. Ann sobs loudly and for a moment I'm furious with her, for fear she'll make me break down, too.

When I put the phone back on its hook, I bang my forehead against the kitchen wall. "Fuck, fuck, fuck." I sob.

Even André is alarmed.

Her death fills me with rage.

I stare in anger at the priest. How dare he intrude on this.

"A Roman Catholic priest," I say to my mother in surprise.

"*Oui, chérie,* of course."

"But she was Orthodox."

"She never really knew what she was, *chérie.* She changed with the weather."

The priest is a friend of my mother's. He is very serious, very committed, beautifully eloquent. I shut my ears to his fine theatrical voice. My eyes burn right through him.

"And a cremation," I say in astonishment. "How can you?"

"It's what she would have wanted. You know how the thought of being in a coffin terrified her. She could never bear the sight of cemeteries."

The strains of Mozart's Requiem Mass rise over what I take to be the roar of the flames. "The Requiem. Do you know it?" my mother asks. "It's very beautiful. It was commissioned by a gaunt stranger dressed all in grey, so the story goes, anyway. The one condition he gave was that Mozart should tell no one about it. Mozart knew then that he would die when it was finished. He tried to sing it an hour before his death."

My mother rejoices in the appropriate ritual. But how Helena would have loved the bouzouki. Yes, to dance at her own funeral.

She lies like a shadow on the hospital bed.

I don't know what to do. Should I kneel?

"I'm getting a house where Ann can come and live with me," I say. "And Mark, too."

I imagine her eyelids flicker.

I can see right through her.

"Every time they put the intravenous in her arm she pulled it out. When they tied her down, she pulled it out with her teeth. Such pigheadedness." My mother sighed.

A lavender silk scarf holds her thin white hair. "Your scarf is very pretty," I whisper.

I imagine a smile on her lips.

The city is full of snow.

Steam billows from rooftops, swirling across the glass walls of the office buildings.

Tires whine in the gutters.

Shall we scatter her ashes on the snow? Or wait until spring? My mother will have the answer.

I am not like you, Helena. I will not be like you. Everyone says I am like you, but I'm not.

You were brainwashed. You were brought up to believe in the myth of being a woman. It was a lie. You were destroyed long, long ago by a lie, that's what I should whisper in your porcelain ear, instead of sweet good-byes.

As the coffin slides through the asbestos wall, I refuse to watch any longer. I storm out of the chapel into a waiting room filled with wilting lilies.

"I thought Father Germain spoke very well," David says to my mother. They are both watching me from the corners of their eyes. What will she do next?

I hug Ann. "We'll start moving before Christmas," I murmur. "If that's what you'd like."

She nods, chewing her lips. "Say something to David," she tells me.

"Hullo, David," I say.

"Hullo, Helen." We walk to my car. He opens the door for me.

"You don't need to do that, David."

"Helen," he says, in a white fury, "don't be so fucking self-righteous. Maybe I'm not somebody special like you. I'm just an ordinary guy trying to do things the best way I know"—I nod sarcastically—"but that doesn't mean you've got some God-given right to treat everything I do with contempt."

Hit me, David, I challenge him with my eyes, hit me. He walks away. His Mercedes burps.

The cold wind burns.

My car swings wide on a bend and crunches on gravel. I shout for joy. It doesn't matter what happens to me now.

You have focused my meaning for me, Helena, as no argument ever could. I believe in my revolution, not because it will ever be triumphant (if it is, it will immediately be betrayed), but because it can never be suppressed. That is its pragmatism; it has nothing to do with any candy-pink utopias.

Out of a cloud of snow a car swoops straight towards me, a white car with yellow headlights staring. At the last moment, it swerves away and I'm left on my own.

I hear my mother telling me how irresponsible I am. I hear my stepfather telling me how impractical I am. I hear David telling me how biased I am and Roger how heretical I am. I hear Akiyo telling me how full of shit I am. But I'm right, Helena, thanks to you, I'm right. Whatever kind of oppression triumphs, it will always fall. The defeated can never be beaten. It doesn't matter what happens to me now.

I swing the car from side to side on the icy road till it starts to skid. I brake and it slides out of control. The tail slams into a bank of snow and bounces off again. The soles of my feet are on fire, I drive on into the whiteness.

Helen tried to tell André about the revelation she had had in the car, but he wasn't there. He sat next to her at the kitchen table, huddled into a knot, but everything she said she had to repeat. Even when the words did get through to him, he just nodded listlessly and went on picking away at the food on his plate. She had brought him back smoked meat from Schwarz's, but he didn't notice that, either.

He made her feel as though she were babbling hysterically. She drank some more wine and babbled on. But five minutes later, her mood swung around. "Fuck it, the whole trouble is, it's just a game for everyone here. Just a gross political game. Nothing serious is going to happen here, is it? I mean, in political terms the Third World's way ahead of us, right? That's where it's happening. All we can do is squabble over the price of admission."

Despair closed around her. Fuck André! Why didn't he pay attention? She leaned across and grabbed his wrist. He spilled wine all down the front of his pullover, an almost new one she hadn't seen before.

"Can't you be careful, damn it?" He slapped her away.

"What the fuck's the matter with you, André, anyway?"

He looked at her. His eyes were full of fear. "I'm not interested, Helen. I don't care anymore. I've done what I could, but it's no use." His lips quivered. "I just want to be vulgar and small. It's the only way I can survive. I want to hang on."

She stared at him for a long time. "Fuck!" she said.

"I'm sorry."

She bit her fingernails. "Forget it."

"Why did you come back?"

"I said I would."

"You were away so long. It was awful down there. I thought you weren't coming."

"Three days. I said three days, didn't I, for Christ's sake?"

"You shouldn't have come."

"I know." Was it the one thing she had learned from her

mother? If you don't keep your word, Helen, nobody will ever respect you. "Fuck!" she said again.

"They know I've told you."

"Yeah, yeah."

"Listen, bitch, do you think they'll let you get away?"

His image blurred. "Who?"

"The cops," he yelled. "Can't you understand? I had to tell them you knew."

"Knew what?"

His face twisted with the effort. "That they planted me there. For God's sake." He seemed to be crying.

She lurched to her feet and stood rubbing the coldness out of her arms. "Do you think it makes any difference?" she asked heavily.

"Get out of here," he begged.

"Tomorrow."

"It'll be too late."

She stumbled off to bed.

The numbers next to my head flick to 2.16 as the noise and the light waken me. The light shines brilliantly, announcing something wonderful, around the heavy curtains. A loud-hailer roars in my ears. I can't figure out what's going on in this dream.

I sit up. Where am I? It can't be morning. I jump out of bed and run naked into the corridor. The living room is filled with dazzle, someone is hammering against the outside door. I turn and jar my toe against the leg of a table. I yelp and hop over to the chair to grab my kimono, David's kimono, pine boughs and dragonflies.

When I slam open the door of André's room, he's standing fully clothed in the middle of the floor.

"André," I shout. "The cellar. Get down into the cellar." But he doesn't move. I tug at his arm, then pull him with all my strength, but he kicks and struggles to hold on to the door frame.

"You idiot," I scream, punching him aimlessly. He covers his head with an elbow.

Wood splinters in front of the house. André and Helen are still fighting in the corridor when the cops find them. At the sight of the guns Helen backs away, she bumps into the wall and stops. She tries to close the kimono, but she's lost the belt. "Keep your hands up," snarls the kindly inspector.

André is panting and shaking uncontrollably.

Next to the inspector is a man in a maroon hockey jacket. He holds a sawed-off shotgun. He has a bushy black moustache, a receding forehead. Helen is sure she has seen him before, but no, there are thousands of men just like him in Montréal.

In Montréal? Where in Montréal?

Further back, the tabloid reporters scramble to get a better view.

"Just don't move," warns the inspector. "Everything'll be okay. Just don't move."

Rigid with fear, Helen knows that something is wrong, unreal. It isn't a dream, but something isn't real. She begins to laugh. She remembers the man in the hockey jacket. She saw him that day long ago in the Joliette métro station when she was waiting for Roger. Driving a police car, no, no, a laundry truck. She stops laughing. Something isn't right. Something is jammed, nothing is going to happen next. She catches a glance between the man in the hockey jacket and André, a reassuring glance, a slight gesture of the hand, she's not imagining it, and when she looks down she sees the gun in André's hand. She'd swear he didn't have it when they arrived, and such an old gun at that, rust on the handle, where did he get it?

"André, don't," I scream and snatch at the gun.

He jumps away and crouches. The barrel of the shotgun is pointing at me, not at André, at me. Piss trickles down my legs. The man in the hockey jacket nods and André hurls himself out through the door as the blast burns me.

Epilogue

Ann's Story:

"A Hapening Never to be Known"

Jane and I were walking through the forsaken lands of the Sahara desert. It was extremely hot, the sun was shining brightly on our heads. The glistening light blinded our eyes and burned our faces. Our minds were blank with bordom.

We sat down for a while under a big pink rock. It was like a black cave at the bottom of it, we were scared to go in. We kicked sand and siffed it through our wrinkled hands.

Jane crunched sand between her teath. Let's go, she said, I'm tired of this endless desert. Theres nothing to do.

I told her it wasn't always desert.

It was like an oven even in the shade, but she began to shiver. I thought she might be getting sick with heat stroke. So I put my arm around her back and huged her. What was here before? she asked.

I hear there were farms, I said.

What hapened?

I dont know. Something really disgusting.

Like a bomb?

Yes. Or maybe a man who wanted everything for himself.

Look at that cactus, Jane said.

In the sand in front of us diferant coloured cactie were growing. They were covered with spines and purple flowers.

They are full of milk that gives you hallucinations, I said.

Jane said, We should be going on and finding more things.

We walked lazily, exsausted from the heat. Our paths were wigiling all over the place. I looked up in the sky, wondering what an emense ball of fire the sun must be. I stared at it so long my eyes were burning with pain. Sudenly a flash of light, stronger than I had ever seen before, blinded my eyes. I fell down in a deep hole.

When I woke Jane was crying. Her tears made my hair wet. I told her not to cry, it wasn't helping.

I thought you were dead, she said.

So did I.

I don't think we can make it on our own, she said. Without adults.

We'll manage, I told her. We can help each other.

I stagered to my feet. Everything had changed. All the colours were diferant. The sand dunes were green like grass. Yellow lizards crouched on the rocks. A bright blue vulture hovered in the vermillion sky.

Can you see it to? I asked Jane.

I can if you tell me how, she said.

I can make them any colour I want. I blinked and all the colours changed again. That looks a lot better now, doesn't it, I said.

We walked a lot further on without getting tired any more. We felt like dancing. Then we began to hear music. Not real music, more like the echos of music. We were in a giant cave that was open to the sky and the echos were sucking us up into the air.

Dont be afraid, I told Jane.

Sudenly we were floating over the desert and there were people all around us. We couldn't see them but they were there—all the people we ever knew. We could hear what they said but they couldn't interfear with us. It was like being in a space ship. There were no walls on the space ship but we didn't fall out. And down below we could see our other bodies like shining ants looking up and waving.

We can go where ever we want, I told Jane. Do you want to go somewhere else?

Not just yet, she said. I dont want to get to far away from myself.

I stayed with her, though I would of liked to move on. And at night we went back to the cave to sleep. (We had lots of bird feathers to keep us warm.)

The next day we repeated it all over again. Only it was diferant.

I dont think anyone knew what hapened to us. I dont think we knew ether.